FOR GOD, COUNTRY AND THE CONFEDERACY

Completing the Circle of Acceptance

A Novel

BY

WINSTON A. JONES

FRANKLIN STREET BOOKS

www.franklinstreetbooks.com

ISBN 0-9719414-8-3

Publisher: Franklin Street Books

Printed in the U.S.A.

For Jodi, Elliot and Albert

Some New
Black history
Retold Again
Enjoy the
Read,

Cover Design by
Dane E. Tilghman
Artist
The Gallery at Dane Tilghman Enterprises
610-524-3263
danedta@aol.com

CONTENTS

ACKNOWLEDGEMENTS

For God, Country, and the Confederacy is historical fiction based on historical facts. Many free blacks in the South were enjoying the low hanging economical fruits of the Confederacy when the Civil War began. In New Orleans, free blacks had woven themselves into the economic fabric of the city and state of Louisiana despite the passage of 'anti-black laws'. My interest in writing this book was based on a question I asked myself. Did free blacks support the Confederacy and if so, why? In the book *Bullwhip Days, The Slaves Remember, by James Mellon, Avon Books*, he speaks of slaves helping their masters overcome Union army intrusions and doing their best to help save the plantation. It is evident some slaves had a strong mistrust of the North and anyone or anything associated with it. But I wanted to understand reasons and logic as to why free blacks would live in such an oppressive society. Why would they feel the need to protect this same oppressive society? It would be easy to apply Pavlov's theory of the ringing bell to the slaves; after all, many had been trained not to bite the hand that fed them. But at this period in American history, not all Negroes living in the South were slaves. Why did they stay? Something must have drawn them to the Confederacy.

For me, this has been a ten-year adventure, researching everything I could get my hands on that dealt with free blacks and their supporting role in the Confederacy. My search for actual facts eventually led me to New Orleans. This story is based there because it is where the greatest number of free blacks made their strongest statement in their support of the Confederacy. It is also where free blacks had the strongest hold on a piece of the economic pie in America. There were more free black professionals in New Orleans, at this time in America, than any city north of the Mason-Dixon.

I would like to acknowledge the following for their support and assistance to me in writing this novel.

First, I want to say thank-you to my Savior and Redeemer Jesus Christ, for blessing me everyday with the breath of life. He didn't have to do it but he did and I'm eternally grateful for his grace and mercy.

I would like to say thank-you to my lovely wife Jodi, who put up with me during this period, for her moral support and her undying love. Writing is something you have to do by yourself. I appreciate her patience and understanding when I needed the time. I want to say a hearty thank-you to my sons, Albert and Elliot. They kept me going when I thought I could go no further by repeatedly asking, "Dad, when will your book be done?" To my Mother, Delia B. Jones, thank-you for instilling in me the mental tools I needed to be where I am today. To my sisters Debbie Ford and Donna Brown thank you for your support and love. To my brother, Albert Jr., and father Albert Sr., who have gone home, I miss you both.

I would like to say a special thank-you to my seventh grade English teacher, Mrs. Goldstein, from Upper Merion High School, class of 1965. She read my very first short story and told me I had a gift that I needed to continue developing. To my cousin Nancy Gray-Lee, thanks for the articles you sent supporting my dream.

There is one very special person I want to say thank you to. That special person is my cousin, BJ, Beryl Jackson. She was an invaluable resource as my editor and critic who took the time to help me get my story right, one word at a time and one page at a time.

> Oh, that my words were now written!
> Oh, that they were printed in a book;
> That they were engraved with
> an iron pen and lead, in the rock forever!
> -Job 19:23-24

FOR GOD, COUNTRY AND THE CONFEDERACY

Completing the Circle
of Acceptance

PREFACE

Early in the Civil War, Louisiana's Confederate government sanctioned a militia unit of free black troops, the Louisiana Native Guards. Intended as a response to demands from members of New Orleans's substantial free black population that they be permitted to participate in the defense of their state, the unit was used by Confederate authorities for public display and propaganda purposes. The intention of the Confederacy was to never use the Native Guards for battle. History will later show this to be one of many fatal errors in judgment on the part of the Confederate government.

The free blacks joined the Louisiana militia for varied and complex reasons. One of the primary reasons was economic self-interest. Many members of the Louisiana Native Guards were men of property and intelligence, representatives of a free black community in New Orleans that was both prosperous and well educated. There were many slave owners among its ranks. Not even New York City could boast of having more black doctors, dentist, architects, bricklayers, plasterers, carpenters, or tailors. Furthermore, the 'hommes de couleur libre,' as they were called in New Orleans, enjoyed privileges not afforded blacks elsewhere in the south, allowing them by 1860 to accumulate more than two million dollars worth of property. It was not surprising, therefore, that free blacks were eager to defend their holdings. Another was the issue of self-identity. More than 80 percent of the free black population in New Orleans in 1860 had European blood in their veins. In contrast, fewer than 10 percent of slaves in Louisiana gave evidence of white ancestry. Because skin color and free status were highly correlated, many free blacks identified more closely with southern whites than with the darker Africans.

For God, Country, and the Confederacy is about the St. Claire's, a free black family of the South. The father, Andrew has cast his family's fate to the Confederacy. He joins the Native Guards to fight shoulder to shoulder with his white counterparts in defense of the South. Andrew has concluded free blacks joining the Confederate Army, will have found the final link that they as a people, need to complete the Circle of Acceptance in the white society of the Confederate south. Andy, the oldest son, has three pleasures, driving the slaves by day, gambling and enjoying the attention of Monique, from the French Quarter, at night. The youngest son, Pierre, is an abolitionist. He finds a runaway slave girl in the family barn. He hides her there until he can get her onto the Underground Railroad. Margaret, the youngest of the children, is having a clandestine affair with Jacob, the slave driver of the farm. Jacob's mother, Matilda, works inside the big house as a house servant. Matilda believes her God will one day set her free. Mary St. Claire, mother and wife of the family, struggles to keep her family together with the help of some white powder from their family doctor. Voodoo Man Cato, the slave hougan of the farm, has protected the St. Claire farm from sickness and drought for the last twenty years. Now, he finds he must save the farm from an evil that walks on six legs. He will use all his black magic skills. The oldest slaves, Charlie Boy, used to be a Prince in the Motherland, while Mamma Sarah has never been able to outrun the haunting nightmares from her childhood. This is a story about the trials and tribulations of the St. Claire family, slave and free during the first year of the Civil War.

This story tells how a family shares love for each other, and how quickly family greed and deception eventually leads to a brutal murder. It is a story that shows how African Americans, living in the oppressive society of the Confederate South, were more than just slaves during the bloodiest and stormiest period in American history. It is a history lesson to those who did not know there were Confederate free blacks in the south, willing to fight, if necessary, to maintain the south most inhuman peculiar institution of owning slaves. This story begins on April 16th, 1861, soon after the Civil War began and tragically ends a year later, on April 25th, 1862, on the day New Orleans falls to Union troops.

PROLOGUE

In June 1793 Jean Baptiste St. Claire is part of a revolution in Saint-Domingue. He is one of the many thousands of Haitian liberators in the army of Toussaint L'Ouverture. It is a revolt of the free people of color, and the slaves, freeing themselves from Napoleon's French tyranny. From the burning port city of Cape Francais Jean Baptiste and thousands of his comrades fight their way to freedom, maiming and killing men, women and children, leaving thousands of colonists massacred. For Jean Baptiste St. Claire it is an escape to the Atlantic Gulf seaboard cities of the United States.

And so Jean Baptiste St. Claire, for a brief moment a free man of color, a liberator of Saint-Domingue, suddenly finds himself riding on a keelboat. He is squatting with other free blacks and slaves; all shackled together, floating north, up into the mouth of the mighty Mississippi. He is like a child; his eyes wide open looking about the new land on the shores of this mighty river. The flatness of the terrain, the dense forests, the wide spaces of prairies and the massive areas of marshland surprise him. The next instant everywhere in front of him, wherever he looks there is water. It is almost like being on the open seas again. From atop the flat boat he rides, he sees the streams that seem to lead into the secret places of quiet bayous and mirror smooth lakes.

Patches of farms and plantations line the banks of the Mississippi. He sees the small farmhouses belonging to the small landholders that raise rice and corn and the larger estates that grow what seems to be mile after mile of sugarcane. All of it framed by the black outline of cypress forests in the distance. This is a good place to live as a free man, thinks Jean Baptiste St. Claire; and a free man he will be, concludes Jean Baptiste St. Claire.

"Thar she is," yells the boatman, as the keelboat is drawn into the harbor of New Orleans. It is a slow pull into the harbor from the lazy Mississippi. Jean Baptiste St. Claire bubbling with excitement struggles to get up, pulling his shackled grumpy comrade with him into the upright position. But what he sees does not impress him and instead depresses him. His view is that of little one-story houses, with mud walls and wide projecting roofs. Along the levee he sees lined up, bumped next to each other, the dirty and what appears to be non-sea worthy backwoods flatboats. On these floating vessels there are displays of hams, ears of corn, apples, and whisky barrels' all are scattered about. More food displays are strewn upon tall poles for all prospective buyers to see. There are also keelboats with cotton, furs, whiskey and flour and steamboats, hissing and hooting, while belching columns of black smoke. And there are the smaller merchant boats, the sloops and schooners from Havana, Vera Cruz and others from New York, Baltimore and Europe.

The activity on the levees is loud and confusing. All around the docks merchants and retailers are scampering about, helter-skelter, yelling, pointing, and giving directions, demanding obedience in mixtures of English, French, Spanish, Italian Portuguese, Chinese and Creole. Amongst this confusion, black longshoremen are singing their painful songs in Negro-English dialects as they tote their bales of cotton and roll their barrels of tobacco, molasses and sugar along the levees.

There are the long lines of slaves, chained together in bunches, bent over, dragging what's left of their life, on their ankles. Some look sickly; some look healthy; others cry out to a non-hearing God. Most, if not all, of them are naked. Between the sounds of the chains dragging about the ground, there is the sound of the keeper's whip splitting the air before it finds its mark on some flesh. And so it is for Jean Baptiste St. Claire, a shackled free man in a new land who finds himself standing with other slaves, on a pier in New Orleans. He is lined up with other free blacks and slaves, and then is led off on a long trek across the swamp of the city. He travels along a muddy footpath, and then he and the others are lead along the levee to a market building a few steps from the Palace d'Armes. Jean Baptiste St. Claire is struck by the confusion of tongues, the curious mixture of languages; fishermen speaking Spanish while amongst the rest of the crowd there is an equal mixture of French and English. Soldiers of multiple cultures paraded, marched, or walked about carelessly. Which Army is in charge of New Orleans, wonders Jean Baptiste St. Claire. He recognizes the French and he recognizes the Spanish. He concludes the blond hair blue-eyed fair skin men must be the Americans.

Jean Baptiste St. Claire, staring at the insides of Palace d'Armes, is amazed by what he sees. This great hall is divided into sections for meat and vegetables. Piled high his eyes scour peas, cabbages, beetroots, artichokes, French beans, radishes and a variety of spotted seeds and carawansas. There is more food here than he has ever seen in one place at a time. There are potatoes, sweet and Irish kind; tomatoes, rice, Indian corn, ginger, blackberries, roses, violets, oranges, bananas, apples, fowls tied in threes by the legs, quails, gingerbread, beer in bottles and salt fish. And then Jean Baptiste St. Claire sees something that brings a big smile to his chocolate face, even as he trudges along bound in his chains of misery. Near the pillars of the market hall he sees black women of many shades selling coffee, hot chocolate and fragrant smoking dishes of white rice, along with what he learns later to be gumbo. And the feast for his eyes are not over; for soon he sees other black women circulating the crowds with baskets of delicacies, balanced on their heads, singing the goodness of their contents of gingerbread and rice cakes; and pretty, young quadroons, their hair tied up in colorful tignons, offering bouquets of Spanish jasmine, carnations and violets as boutonnières for the well dressed man.

He is lead back outside and Jean Baptiste St. Claire is once again amazed at the hues of colors in the faces of people that abound in the marketplace. He sees chalk white to jaundice yellow; light brown to coal black; round smooth faces to grizzly unkempt faces; mulatto's, and Indians; long hair, straight hair, curly hair or no hair at all. Jean Baptiste St. Claire is again awe struck by the large bounty of goods that are piled sometimes recklessly on the levee. Mounds of coal, paving stones, and bales of cotton, barrels of tobacco, sugar and molasses, and casks of merchandise unrolling itself as far as the eye could see in both directions along the river.

Jean Baptiste St. Claire, a farmer by trade, a free man in conscience is now himself a slave in this great land of freedom. Standing now in the Maspero Exchange, along with other slaves, Jean
Baptiste St. Claire knows he is not meant to spend the rest of his
life as a slave, a servant to another master. He is better than that.
He will rise above this situation. Through the slave grapevine and
idle conversations he finds out who his strongest competition is.
They are the big black beautiful man slaves from Virginia, with their
chiseled bodies. At all auctions they are the highly prized imports,
the most expensive, and the strongest. It is they who gave Virginia
bragging rights on where the finest Negroes are born and bred. They
are the southern stud farms 'favorite kind of nigger'; and the Virginia women are a different class of slave women, born and bred for
one purpose. They are the young, the fertile, the strong of back,
and like the black soil they work daily, guaranteed to produce an
unlimited number of crops in the form of children.

The others are imported or stolen slaves from Maryland, Georgia and the Carolinas who also ended up at the Exchange because
this is the best market, to get the best price, which can be gotten in
New Orleans. And what a variety of human flesh there is for sale
every day at the Exchange. Kidnapped free blacks are being sold as
slaves, unclaimed runaways, drunkards, vagabonds, and those who
had become street urchins are thrown in with them. African blacks
unable to speak more than a handful of words in English, local blacks,
victims of the financial mishandling of business by their owners, at-
tractive quadroons to be mistresses and lovers to the buyers; cooks,
masons, boatmen, valets, seamstresses, laundresses, the sick, the
crippled, the discarded and the ignored, all appeared daily at the
Maspero Exchange, crying out in chaos and disharmony, crying out
in languages unknown to those around him, crying out in desperation and sorrow, "Buy me, buy me! I will do anything, buy me!"

Jean Baptiste St. Claire knows there are varied and large
differences, between him and this menagerie of blacks, that separates him from the slaves; differences in the way he stands; differences in the way he carries himself; differences in the way he speaks
and one major difference is that he can read, write and speak French
and English. This advantage he uses to the utmost when he stands

before prospective buyers. Responding to them in French impresses many, amuses even more and one that was most impressed and definitely amused was Samuel Baston, an established stone and marble cutter from New Orleans.

So amused is Samuel Baston, he buys Jean Baptiste. Samuel Baston has two house servants, Nate and Mattie, an older couple, who have been in the employment of Mr. Baston for a number of years. Jean Baptiste does not exclude them from his learning process. There was so much to learn, so much to absorb so much to understand. Jean Baptiste is extremely thirsty to drink the knowledge of this new land. He swallows so much of it he is drunk with the culture he now belongs; but unlike the other wasteful inebriations, he is able to regurgitate it, according to his needs, at will, and when necessary to be used to his advantage.

Nate and Mattie looked at the new addition to Massa Baston's family of slaves and immediately begin to bring young Jean Baptiste up to speed, explaining the duties and life styles of slaves on the plantation.

"Dere are fo' important dates you needs to 'member," said Nate, walking with Jean Baptiste to his new home, the slave quarters.

"And yo' birthday ain't one of dem", said Mattie, welcoming Jean Baptiste inside. Mattie is standing in the doorway. "You will sleep on dat wall," she said, walking away pointing to the southern end of the one room house.

"Dey is", begins Nate again, "Cotton harvests, Christmas, hog killin' and corn shuckin'."

Samuel Baston introduces him to the art of stone cutting and marble preparation for headstones. It is a profession Jean Baptiste learns quickly and he becomes very proficient. He is surprised at the number people who are in a need for granite or stone grave markers. Are that many people dying in New Orleans? But he is impressed even more at the fact that they will pay any amount. Mister Baston, though sympathetic to the need of his customers, used these moments of bereavement to increase his sales. His company is the best stonecutter in New Orleans. He is the most expensive also. Jean Baptiste learns all he can, but not forgetting his roots as a farmer, saves all the money he earns with the intention of buying his freedom, then buying some land. He dreams of owning a piece of the America he sees in Samuel Baston's lifestyle.

It is the winter of 1793 and Jean Baptiste is beginning his new life in this New World. He has become, what constitutes, the inner core of the working class in New Orleans. What goes on within the economy of New Orleans and Louisiana, for that matter, rests on his shoulders and other slaves like him. Even with all this responsibility, he still has no civil rights; he belongs to his master, completely, and if, heaven forbid, Samuel Baston should go into bankruptcy, Jean Baptiste then becomes an asset seized against nonpayment of any outstanding debts. Then it's back to the Maspero Exchange to be part of the other miscellaneous items such as horses, wagons, and plows to be auctioned off again.

During the coming months and years Samuel Baston continues to be impressed with Jean Baptiste. The fact Jean Baptiste is an educated black and shows he understands responsibility, early in his servitude, gives Samuel reason to designate Jean Baptiste to be the one who goes to the piers, by himself, whenever there was a need to pick up supplies. Jean Baptiste takes advantage of these rare opportunities to wander throughout the piers and levees, around the Maspero Exchange, to familiarize himself with his new surroundings. If he is to eventually be a free black of New Orleans, he needs to understand the methods of the people in charge and the city itself.

And Jean Baptiste finds there is so much to learn about the city, the people, and the way business is handled, the way goods are bought and sold.

During the continuing education phase that will last close to ten years, Jean Baptiste also learns, he is free, in the sense of the word, from Saturday night to late Sunday night. It is his greatest extended period of rest and relaxation. Saturday nights are time for dancing to the sounds of banjoes and fiddles and an occasional drink of corn liquor. On Sundays he tends his little plot of land where he grows some vegetables and receives his weekly rations. He is to keep a set of clothes cleaner than his everyday clothes for special occasions, like weddings and funerals. He learns when he enters the big house to come in from the backyard, through the kitchen, then into the rest of the house. Never come in the front door.

From his travels with Nate and Mr. Baston, to other plantations, he learns about the different classes slaves fall into. Nate explains that at the top of the slave ladder are the house servants, the butler, the maids, the nurses, the chambermaids and the cooks. Then come the carriage drivers and the gardeners, and the stable men. If the plantation was of reputable size, next were the wheelwright, the wagoners, the carpenters, the barbers, the blacksmiths and even a slave foreman. Not to be forgotten are the cowmen and those who take care of the dogs. As long as these laboring slaves did their jobs and did them well, they never tasted the whip and most of them had really nice quarters to live in. The lowest classes of slaves are those who work in the fields.

A year on the farm is measured in events instead of months. With the first frost the hog killing begins, then there is corn-shucking season, and then Christmas. Then the planting begins. After planting the tilling, the nurturing, then weeding, then the harvesting and then the frost comes and the killings begins again. In between all of the measured years, there are dances the slaves participate in to celebrate the ending of each successful season. Jean Baptiste sits in this classroom of humanity, like a confused student listening to the teaching of the experienced and knowing he is much better than his teachers. He knows he will do much better than his teacher and their graduating students. He knows what he wants from America and being a slave for the rest of his life is not part of it.

Even though he rides with Mister Baston to town every morning and learns to work the granite and marble and other stones; even though he is sent on errands to the pier to transact business that is vital to the existence of Samuel Baston's business; even though he is permitted to make extra money after working all day; even though he is trusted to do the things no other slave is permitted, to Samuel Baston and the rest of his family, Jean Baptiste St. Claire, freedom fighter, free man in conscience, master of French and English languages, is just a slave, that's all.

He has acquired basic bookkeeping skills, enabling him to figure cost, draw up bills for customers, and keep track of debits and credits. Working in the office and going on the bereavement visits with Mr. Baston, he watches and listens, developing the necessary communication skills needed to work with a demanding audience. Above all he is provided with the valuable experience in how to get along with white folks.

In the year 1812, several events take place in Jean Baptist St. Claire's life. On January 14th, he marries Chloe Johnson, a house servant slave from a neighboring farm. He met her at a soirée given at her master's home. He was standing outside minding the horse and carriage and she came out with some food to give him and he was immediately smitten. They courted for three months and after getting permission from both masters they were married on her master's plantation, and he was given extra space on his master's plantation for them to live.

On April 30th, Louisiana becomes a state and is admitted to the Union and on June 18th opportunity knocks in the form of a war with the British. Volunteers are needed and America itself did not have a real army, in the sense of the word, but it did have a lot of rag-tag volunteers. Mr. Samuel Baston becomes Colonel Samuel Baston and Jean Baptiste is pressed into service with Colonel Baston as a slave fighting for two freedoms, his master's and the country he now lives in.

He spends his first year in service to his master's country helping to widened canals and building defenses along them. He helps fortify the military position and much to the distress of Chloe, he fights in several battles of the Louisiana campaign. Chloe helps to makes clothing, flags and bandages for the troops. She learns how to nurse the wounded at makeshift hospitals and convents.

In September 1813, Colonel Baston, recognizing the good work and commitment Jean Baptiste has shown, makes a deposition in court to grant Jean Baptiste his freedom. An official of the court draws up a certificate of good conduct and the Office of Mortgages, guaranteeing there is no partnership in property with Mister Baston, authorizes another. These papers are posted publicly, informing those who may need to know, of Mister Baston's intention to free Jean Baptiste. The public posting also requests any person having legal objection to this to present themselves before the court within forty days. No one contested and Mister Baston was able to show the court Jean Baptiste would not become a burden of the state because of age, physical or mental impairment or any other cause. Unfortunately, Chloe is not included in the same agreement, so Jean Baptiste St. Claire, now legally a free man, must buy freedom for his wife.

On December 28th, 1814, a slave son is born to Jean Baptiste St. Claire and Chloe and is named after General Andrew Jackson, freedom fighter for New Orleans and Louisiana. Jean Baptiste is now a member of the First Battalion of Free Men of Color, and on December 23rd they fight gallantly against the British on adjacent plantations surrounding New Orleans. In that same battle Colonel Samuel Baston, a member of a rifle company, is seriously wounded and dies before he can receive life saving treatment.

Despite the fact that the Treaty of Ghent had been signed in Belgium, in December, 1814, to end the two and a half year war, it was not until January 1815, when the British made their final failed assault on the city that the British surrendered. General Jackson had high praise for the free people of color and the gallant ways they showed their commitment to New Orleans and Louisiana. Though this was not totally acceptable to most of the white populace, nevertheless, it placed the free black at a higher level of acceptance than what they shared before the war.

Jean Baptiste St. Claire takes his pay for military service in the form of a hundred acres of land. He then borrows money from the bank to buy an additional five hundred and forty acres north of New Orleans. The year is 1815 and since the arrival of the first steamboat in 1812, the traffic for goods in and out of New Orleans seems to be growing out of control. There is money to be made here and Jean Baptiste St. Claire wants to be part of the money producing segment.

It is obvious to Jean Baptiste, New Orleans is quickly becoming the transfer point for American and foreign goods. It becomes more obvious to Jean Baptiste that his farm can be part of the growth in New Orleans. In the first year, he built a cabin for his family, bought two slaves, cleared ten acres of timber and sold the wood for enough profit to contribute to the building of additional slave quarters. He had spent enough time on the piers to see the wheat, corn, lard, pork, furs and hides, whiskey, hemp and lead that lay in neat bundles, containers, and boxes, to know that as a farmer he had an outlet to the world from these piers.

From his vantage point of the Northern suburbs, his land enjoys a high elevation relative to the sea level of New Orleans, Jean Baptiste observes the steamboats, the flatboats and keelboats that bring the cotton, sugar, molasses and tobacco into New Orleans waterways.

When Andrew Jackson St. Claire is ten years old his father is able to finally pay off Chloe's debt. Because of the financial success Jean Baptiste had shown, Andrew, as they now call him, is permitted to stay with his family. To Jean Baptiste it's becomes clear to him what America is all about and that is money.

New Orleans has become the financial center of the Mississippi Valley. The financial worth is being compared to that of New York. Free blacks have expanded with the economy and are exerting their financial muscle, making inroads into the world markets.

It is 1830. Andrew is 16 years old, getting up everyday at dawn, and walking with his father towards New Orleans. He is left at the Johnson Plantation, where he works a full day, then is picked up each evening by his father. Everyday as they walk to and from the plantation, Jean Baptiste talks to Andy about how great opportunities are in New Orleans and how he is going to turn that square mile of land given to him after the war into a big farm, growing cotton, and lumber and corn and all kinds of crops to be shipped out to the rest of the world.

New Orleans is growing and Jean Baptiste is proud to be part of that growth. He wants Andrew to continue growing with New Orleans. Andrew is caught up in what he sees when he travels to the city with his father. There is running water coming from faucets. He's impressed with the street lightings and the fact that the streets are paved with cobblestones. On Sundays, he loves to sit at the piers and watch the steamboats, flatboats and barges, carrying goods dock and unload. The city is alive with excitement and Andrew understands why he needs to be a part of it.

Together with his father he enjoys walking along Canal Street, between the levees and Bourbon Street to look in the windows of the many retail shops. Large open market places dot the levees where small retailers and street vendors hawked their wares. He enjoys walking among the storefronts of the bakers, the butchers, the shoemakers, and furniture makers. His nose is treated to the smelling the woods, the leathers, and the fresh meats. He is intrigued watching the tobacconist, lithographers, and printers, do their crafts. He enjoys listening to his father bargain, converse, trade, and learn from other free African Americans, some of who are the cigar makers, ironworkers, and furniture makers in New Orleans.

When Andrew is seventeen his father tells him he doesn't have to go to the Johnson Plantation everyday, just Thursdays and Fridays. Jean Baptiste has built two slave quarters for a family of slaves he's purchased. Andrew is spending more time with his father in the fields, working side by side with the slaves, learning all he can about farming. His father seems to be on a mission, explaining to Andrew all he knows about farming, the secrets, the methods, and the best ways to get the most out of the ground. He ventures with his father when they go to town to buy supplies and meet his father's friends and business associates. He watches his father and comes to understands how he can manipulate and know when he is being manipulated.

His father has this dream of growing enough cotton, raising enough pigs, cutting enough wood from the surrounding forests on his farm, to become a planter. If he can produce thirty bales of cotton on his twenty-five acres of cleared land his first year, next year he can maybe double his production. The first year of planting he was able to produce twenty-five bales of cotton. It was down because he was clearing more land for future planting. But his reputation for being a farmer and master of the land was becoming known to the neighboring farmers. Andrew is quickly becoming his father's son. He is learning the tricks of the trade in the fields and in the offices downtown and in the slave market. Jean Baptiste is proud of what Andrew has become and what he feels he has yet to be. Andrew's last educational class in his growing and maturing is his need to understand the reason and logic for slavery.

Slavery is a necessary evil, his father has told him. If he is to be successful, he will have to own slaves. They're cheap labor and will reward you if you treat them fairly. It is this understanding and teaching from his father that Andrew carries with him when he visits the Trader Yards. At first he went out of curiosity as a young boy. Then, as a young man, as he is growing into maturity he finds it to be absolutely, positively necessary. The more successful the farm becomes the more slaves his father is able to buy to keep the success of the farm growing.

In the spring of 1833, Jean Baptist St. Claire dies after being treated by a doctor who misdiagnosed him with Yellow fever. Because of the misdiagnosis, the doctor prescribed lethal doses of calomel followed up with herb teas, then laxatives, and bleeding. Actually it was heart failure complicated by pneumonia. Six months later, his mother will die of a broken heart. When Jean Baptist St. Claire died he left in his will to Andrew, besides 640 acres of land, a partially built home, a slave woman named Matilda, who had a two month old child name Jacob, a houngan named Voodoo Man Cato and two middle aged male slaves.

CHAPTER 1
Tuesday, April 16th, 1861

The sale began-young girls were there,
Defenseless in their wretchedness,
Whose stifled sobs of deep despair
Revealed their anguish and distress.
And mothers stood with streaming eyes,
And saw their dearest children sold;
Unheeded rose their bitter cries,
While tyrants bartered them for gold.
And woman, with her love and truth-
For these in sable forms may dwell-
Gaz'd on the husband of her youth,
With anguish none may paint or tell.
And men, whose sole crime was their hue,
The impress of their Maker's hand,
And frail and shrinking children, too,
Were gathered in that mournful band.
Ye who have laid your love to rest,
And wept above their lifeless clay,
Know not the anguish of that breast,
Whose lov'd are rudely torn away.
Ye may not know how desolate
Are bosoms rudely forced to part,
And how a dull and heavy weight
Will press the life-drops from the heart. [i]

It is the smell that lets you know you are near the Trader Yards;
a god-awful smell that emanates from the yards and hangs in the air

25

like a heavy invisible cloud. Most men and women who go into the Trader Yards carry something perfumed to cover their nose; while others find a certain satisfaction from the odor, and suck it in as food for their senses. It is the smell of dirt, feces, urine and unwashed human flesh. There is always mud under foot, even when there is no rain. There are hundreds and hundreds of slave folks, in stalls like the pens they use for livestock. Attached to the front of the stall a curtain hangs.

All or most of them will be sold at auction. Outside the pen, leaning against the fence is the overseer; standing proud and large, with a big blacksnake whip and a pepperbox pistol in his belt. Groups of prospective bidders follow the overseer to each pen. Then, the curtain is pulled up and the bidders crowd in close.

"Come check out these bucks and wenches," yells the overseer, as he herds the penned slaves closer. "Grab a pair of gloves and do your inspection before the real bidding starts. Move up closer you bucks and wenches!"

One of the bidders takes a pair of white gloves and motions to one of the young wenches to come forward. She hesitates, her eyes widen with fear; she shudders into the arms of another male slave, trying to cover her nakedness. The overseer pulls his blacksnake whip back from his belt and lets it unfurl. Then, suddenly there is a quick snap, not much different than that of a pistol discharging. The ankle chains clank; the sting of the overseer's whip has found its mark. There is an agonizing scream from one of the slaves; flesh rises from a shoulder, suddenly gorged with blood, and then bursts.

"Git over here, niggra, I mean you!"

He looks at his driver, a tall, well-built, black man. "Moses, pull that young wench away from that buck." Moses climbs into the pen and wrestles the young wench from the buck and pushes her to the front of the pen. She falls to her knees and is raised by the black handle of the overseer's whip.

"Get up and stand before this Master," demands the overseer.

Except for a tattered loincloth the young wench is naked. The bidder grabs the wench's mouth and forces it open, looking at her teeth. He then checks the hair on her head for lice and ticks. He grabs her breasts, squeezes them enjoying the firmness of them in his hands. Tearing away her loincloth he checks her genitals for disease scars. Satisfied there are no external scars he sticks his finger up inside her. Again he smiles at what he has discovered. She is a virgin.

"A fine young wench she is," smiles the overseer. "Won't find any wenches in better condition anywhere."

The bidder takes off his white gloves, and nods his head in agreement. The group follows the overseer to the next pen, where the process is repeated with another slave; and so it goes, in perpetual motion.

Meanwhile, at the auction block a different display of human bondage is taking place.

"Hey, you buck and wenches, get in your hole. Come out here, all of you," the voice of the auctioneer barks. "What we have here are two full hands, three three-quarter hands and two half hands. Come on, step up here and let the people see you."

The slaves find their position on the platform, with the enthusiastic help of the overseer and the driver. One by one the auctioneer points out the benefits of each by asking them to perform, while he tries to get the best price for them.

"How much for this buck?" he yells, "hey you there buck, let the people see you move. Come on and march back and forth here. He's worth a thousand if not eleven hundred. Hop on one foot; now trot, raise up them legs, boy! Look at that strong young body and check out the size of them loins. A lot of children will come from him. What are your bid? Come on, let me hear from you!"

"One thousand dollars", someone yells.

"Eleven hundred," yells another.

"Show us his teeth," yells another.

Depending on the age of the slave and any craft that was learned determined the value of the slave. A sixteen-year-old male could be worth $1900, but if he knew a craft, like woodworking he could be worth more. Each day this peddling of human flesh continues as if there is a bottomless pit from which these African slaves are brought. Each day the yelling and prodding continues, and each day the sweet and sour pungent odor of human enslavement hangs about the Trader Yards.

* * * * * * * * *

For the free black there was much more to New Orleans than the Trader Yards. There was a section of the Crescent City that was in direct contrast to the Trader Yards. It was in this part of the Crescent City, between North Rampart and North Broad and from Canal Street to St. Bernard Avenue that was known as Faubourg Treme. It is a Parish, north of New Orleans proper, near Lake Pontchartrain, where communities of free blacks live as they have for the last seventy-five years or more. It is not far from the pitiful sounds of people moaning, children crying, and the bellowing voice of the auctioneer. It is those very sounds of agony and pain that have been filtered out of the fresh air by high buildings surrounded by streets with bends and turns. Those ugly sounds of agony cannot circumvent them and travel to the ears of these inhabitants.

It is where the free blacks of New Orleans go about their daily business of living. Most are not from the Trader Yards, though some of their ancestors were; therefore, the problem now is not theirs. They have their own stores and business, their own churches and some have farms where the lifeblood of New Orleans is grown and sold. Inside Burroughs Dry Goods, located at the corner of Broad and Canal, is a dark free person of color. A tall and stout man he is. He is a man with furrowed forehead, bushy eyebrows and darker circles beneath his eyes. Here is a man whose clothes explain his wealth. Here is a man who is known and respected by his peers. Andrew Jackson St. Claire, farmer, father and owner of 640 acres of prime land and the slaves needed to work the land, stands in line looking around as he ponders the sudden rise in price of dry goods and farm equipment.

The cost of everything has been going up almost daily since there is this talk of war with Washington. Seven states have seceded from the Union, South Carolina, Mississippi, Florida, Alabama, Georgia, Louisiana, and Texas. Before the month is over, Arkansas, Tennessee, North Carolina and Virginia will join the other seven, thus forming the Confederate States of America. Andrew is anxious to see the outcome of the secession and what Lincoln will do. He's heard all this talk from the Southern politicians about the need to form a separate country within the Union, but nothing has been confirmed. Through all of this, Andrew just wishes the politicians would make up their minds and decide what to do. Either way he will make money, but he will make more money if there is war. The South will win and he will make even more money.

Andrew owns 640 acres of prime land and has 20 slaves working on it. He is a family man with two sons, Andy Jr., Pierre, a daughter, Margaret and his wife of twenty-five years, Mary. Andrew Jackson St Claire, looking older than his 48 years needed something in his life right now that would make him feel right about what he has done with his life. Living in the South has not been all that easy, but Andrew knows, from his own experiences, it's not much different anywhere else in America, for a person of color whether he is free or not. He has casts his lot with the South and he has had a measure of success as a free person of color, as other free blacks have, while living in New Orleans. But most of the free blacks needed something to show how committed they were to the Confederacy; for those skeptic whites who would doubt they are sincere in their belief in the Confederacy. They wanted to show how thankful they were to the City's Fathers for letting them participate in the economic boom New Orleans is experiencing. There are so many more things Andrew wants to do to show his allegiance to Louisiana. He and others, who think like him, have been unable to find the vehicle that will finally put them on equal footing with the general white population. Part of the problem of getting acceptance by the general white population were the small number of powerful, arrogant, egotistical whites who still believe all blacks should be nothing more than slaves.

Standing in line, waiting for customers in front of him to complete their business, Andrew looks around the interior. He is not looking at anything but seeing everything; the hanging pots and pans, the barrels full of different kinds of nails, the rolls of cloth, the burlap bags of feed, and jars of canned pickles, vegetables, and pickled pig feet. It is quite by accident his eyes stops at the newspaper laying on the counter. At first he didn't see it, even though he was looking directly at it, then, the more he paid attention, the more the headlines of *The Daily Picayune* screamed at him to take notice: THE

CONFEDERATE FLAG WAVING OVER FORT SUMTER. Andrew's eyes widen as he picks up the paper and begins reading. He looks to see if anyone else is as excited as he. He pays two cents for the paper, forgets about why he was in the store, then in a childish inpatient rush, leaves Burroughs Dry Goods and jumps into his waiting wagon.

Filled with enthusiasm from the best news he's heard in quite some time, Andrew charges his horses out of town, north and into the countryside.   He drives the horses with a fever, yelling and whipping at them, trying to make them run faster and faster. There is a great joy in his heart. He knows he has found the missing piece to complete the puzzle he has been struggling with all these years. His heart beats to the rapid sounds of the hoofs clopping on the ground, raising large clouds of dust. He needs to get home. He needs to let everyone know what has happened and how great the news is for them. Andy will agree with him and love the opportunity to fight for the Confederacy; Pierre will disagree, even though he enjoys the spoils; Margaret and Mary will not understand, but they're not suppose to, they're women and what do women know of these manly things?   He doesn't slow the horses until he recognizes the white fence surrounding his farm. Slave children, working in their garden, pause a moment, look at him as he passes, some wave, then return to their work.

Andrew steers his team of horses onto the farm driveway and pushes them toward the two-story wood framed house that's scrapping the morning sky, rising proudly in front of him. An old, shoulder stooping, broken-down looking slave greets him as he halts the horses at the front door.

"Good morning, Massa Andrew," said Charlie Boy, waiting obediently.

And a good morning it is thinks Andrew, giving the reins to Charlie Boy. Finally, he has what he's been looking for, the missing key to the last locked door. Finally he has the key that will unlock the door and allow him and other free blacks to enter into the world of white acceptance. It hasn't always been easy, but the Confederacy has been good to him and his family. So much so he wants to keep their system as it is, regardless of what has been said of it in

Washington DC. Slavery has made him and his farm what it is today and he is not ashamed about it at all. He has heard all the negatives about slavery and he understands in some situations it can be as horrible as some slaves have reported, but he is not that kind of owner. His slaves are his property, yes, and he is responsible for them; they are an investment. He must maintain their well being if he is to maintain his own well being. And he's done that. Slavery is a business and should be look upon as just that.

"Thank-you, Charlie Boy," said Andrew, leaping from the wagon and racing into his house.

Andrew's farm is magnificent. The house stands on the front ten acres of his property. To truly appreciate a view of it you need to be standing in front of the lake, looking back through the cluster of trees. The big house rises proudly, standing straight into the sky. There are three bedroom windows facing the lake, Margaret's, Pierre's and Andy's. Below those windows are two that border the door that leads to the kitchen. Leading from the kitchen door, 50 yards on the right, is the barn, and then across a dirt pathway is the smokehouse and then further to the left are the slave quarters.

There is a path that meanders from the lake past Voodoo Man Cato's hut twisting and turning in and out of the cluster of trees until it ends in the open space in front of the big house. Walking from the kitchen door, there is a well-beaten footpath that ends at a circular driveway in the front of the house. There is a porch, the width of the house, and above the porch roof is the bedroom of Andrew and his wife Mary. Charlie Boy stands by the steps leading onto the porch waiting for Andrew to leap from the wagon. He will take the horses and wagon back to the barn.

Inside the house, Matilda, a one-time childhood playmate to Andrew, but now the house slave, is coming from the kitchen with a tray of breakfast dishes as Andrew bursts into the living room. She sees him and his excitement, but continues her chore of setting the table. Matilda has been with the family for twenty-five years. She and Andrew are about the same age. After placing the dishes and silverware, she returns to the kitchen and back with a pot of steaming water, which she pours into a stainless steel urn. Everyday, except Sunday it's the same for her. Every morning she rises before

Andrew is out of the Big House and prepares breakfast for him before anyone else is up. This morning he left right after eating to go to New Orleans to get some supplies, so he said. She notices there is excitement about him this morning and wonders what it is this time.

"Matilda! Matilda! Have you seen the paper! See, right here! Look! Isn't this wonderful," yells Andrew, frantically moving around Matilda, getting in her way as she tries to finish setting up the table.

Matilda ignores Andrew. She knows he has something important to say, and more than likely it has nothing to do with her. He does the same thing all the time. He comes running to her, excited about something, yelling about something and then calling his family members where he explains what has happened. All this, while she's trying to get her work completed, he's talking to her, practicing on her what he plans to say to the rest of his family. After he appears to be getting angry with her ignoring him she gives him her undivided attention, but for her it is done out of frustration. He has been shoving a newspaper in front of her every move, demanding she read the headlines.

Matilda finally stops what she's doing and addresses Andrew. "Massa Andrew," she whines, "you knows I can't read. I wasn't allowed to learn." She finishes setting up the tea serving. "Now, if you don't mind, I gots lots of work to do."

"I'm sorry Matilda, I forgot," said Andrew, "it's just that I can't hold this inside and I had to tell someone."

Oh, he forgot, thinks Matilda, shaking her head, walking away. How can he forget his father would not let her learn to read while he made sure his son got the education from books he brought home from the city just so Andrew could learn to read and write. How can he forget both of them were raised together as children but under different households? How can he forget while she went to the fields every morning with her parents, he was learning to read and write from his mother? How can he forget his father bought her family and now he owns her?

Andrew races to the bottom of the steps leading upstairs. "Is anyone up, up there? Mother, Mother, come down. Wake up! This is important! Andy, wake up! You gotta see this! Wake up your brother. Mother, knock on Margaret's door on your way down."

Andrew rushes back into the sitting room and waits. Matilda enters from the kitchen with some hot bread.

"Matilda, this is absolutely wonderful! Finally something is being done about those damn Northerners."

"I expect so, Massa Andrew," answers Matilda, going back to the kitchen. She mumbles about how wonderful it is, but to whom? It isn't so wonderful for her. She sees no benefits as a result of what's being done to them damn Northerners. She has heard stories about how up North blacks are free and live in houses just as big as slave owners. She has heard stories that up North, everyone is treated the same. Everything she has heard about how blacks live up North has been a story. Stories she wonders if she can believe.

Mary is first to rush downstairs. Her expression shows concern that something awful has happened to one of the slaves or something terrible has happened in New Orleans. She is anxiously tying her robe around her by the time she is in the living room confronting Andrew.

"Andrew, what is the matter?" inquires Mary St. Claire, drawing her silk robe closed. She enters the room and finds her favorite chair. What can be so important to her she must get up at this time on this particular morning at the beckon call of her husband? This has happened before and each time he does it she responds, feeling miserable about being interrupted from what she is doing, but nevertheless, she continues to respond, being the obedient wife. Even though at times, she complains, she knows he will ignore her and her feelings. "Why do you find it necessary to wake up all of New Orleans this morning," she said, slowly lowering herself into her chair. "Matilda, bring me my morning tea."

"Yes Miss Mary," said Matilda, coming out the kitchen door. She pours the hot tea from the sterling silver urn into a china cup, and then brings the tea to Mary on a tray with the sugar and milk in separate silver serving containers.

Andrew shoves the morning newspaper in Mary's face showing the headlines. "Isn't that wonderful news," boasts Andrew, trying to contain his excitement. "We are finally standing up to Mr. Lincoln and the Republicans." Andrew returns to the bottom of the stairs. "Andy, come down! This is important!"

While reading the paper, Mary adds sugar and milk to her tea. "Oh my Lord Jesus, what have we done?" she sighs. Suddenly her world has changed, again. Suddenly what she thought was over and done with is happening again. Why now, she asks herself. She knows there was talk of this happening, but that was always talk, nothing else. It's those stupid white politician, that's why we are having so many problems, those stupid white politicians.

"I'll tell you what we've done," said Andrew, standing at the bottom of the stairs, "we have taken charge of our own destiny, that's what. And it's about damn time! Sorry Mother."

Andy, the oldest, stumbles into the sitting room then proceeds to the table. He too is dressed in pajamas, and wearing his robe. From what he can remember about last night, getting up this early in the morning was not part of his plan for the day. He has a slight headache and he can still taste gumbo and crawdads from some-place he visited the night before. He feels like hell and looks it, but he doesn't care. To look at Andy, you know somewhere in the blood-line of the St. Claire's there is a broad strain of white. It can be seen clearly when Andy walks in the room. The only blackness showing on Andy is his wavy hair and eyebrows. His color is beyond his mother's corn flake brown. It is obvious his color is more from her side and shades lighter. White folks who don't know him think he's one of them, but black folks know better. They can just look at him and know better. White folks just see color, no other distinctions. "Good morning everybody," he mumbles, running his fingers through his hair. "Papa, there's more to life than getting up at six am every morning." Andrew anxiously takes the newspaper from Mary and thrusts it at Andy to read.

"Here, read this," said Andrew, hardly containing his excite-ment. "Isn't that the best news you can get in the morning? Go on, read it! Read it a couple of times! I did. I couldn't believe my eyes."

Andy stretches his long frame out in a chair and begins reading.

"Matilda, I'll have some of that tea," demands Andy.

"Yes Master Andy," replies Matilda, turning and offering the serving tray.

Andy retrieves a silver plated flask from his robe pocket, removes the cap and pours some of the contents into his tea. It is the only way he drinks what he considers, this *'fucking weak water from Britain'*. He finishes reading the newspaper, turning to his father. "I can't believe this!"

"Believe son, you gotta believe!" shouts Andrew.

"This is too good to be true," continues Andy. "We are finally breaking away from the North."

Breaking away from what, wonders Mary, watching her husband and oldest son talk of these things as if they were discussing the cost of cotton and lumber. She sees her husband thinking that what has been done will somehow settle the dispute between Washington and the South. She hasn't seen this kind of glow in his face in many a year and even though she is happy to see it, the reason it is there saddens her deeply. Mary listens to Andrew's joy but deep inside this was no joy for her. Just when she thought everything was beginning to come together, something stupid like this comes up. They have struggled so long to get this far and now this stupid little incident; this stupid little game men play; this killing and maiming, that turns into badges of courage, to be worn on clothing covering missing limbs. Badges that some will never see, that some will never hold in their hands, that some will never be able to walk around and show off.

"And we are breaking away for good!" Andrew is bragging. "I told you this day was coming; it was just a matter of time before it did. Them Yankees up North ain't got the brains of a catfish, wallowing on the bottom, looking for food, to know what's going on down here. They ain't been doing nothing but meddling in our affairs! Well, now it has stopped! We are at war with the North and we're gonna whup them! This won't take long at all. By the end of summer or even before, this will all be over."

"Matilda, bring me some more tea; I feel a headache coming on," sighs Mary, not willing to raise her head to see anymore of the sparkle in her husband's dark shiny face.

"Yes Miss Mary," said Matilda, rushing to where Mary is sitting, presenting her the tea on a silver serving tray.

Mary retrieves a folded packet of white paper from her robe.

She opens and dumps the contents into the tea, then adds sugar. "Thank-you Matilda," she said, beginning to lift her tea from the tray, but she hesitates. What a good friend Dr. DuBois has been to the family, thinks Mary as she stirs the magic white powder into her cup of tea. It has been with his help she's been able to survive the agonies and stresses of the past, but this time she feels she will need more of Dr. DuBois' help. She decides to empty another packet into the tea.

"Will that be all, Miss Mary?" asks Matilda.

"For the time being," mutters Mary, hearing the overpowering words of what Andrew is saying.

"You know what this means son," Andrew is saying to Andy, strutting about the room like a rooster in a chicken coop, "it completes the circle of acceptance for us a people. This is the missing piece. This will convince the suspicious whites of our allegiance and protect what we have. This is our opportunity to show that we are committed to what the Confederacy stands for. Us helping them win this war guarantees us equal footing. This is what we've been waiting for! We can't pass this up!"

"How many will stand with us?" asks Andy.

"I know hundreds who will," boasts Andrew. "We've moved into the fabric of New Orleans and the state, in every form except the military. This is our chance to show how committed we are. To fight and die for the Confederacy is the ultimate commitment!"

Mary drops her teacup and saucer, spilling its contents onto the carpeted floor, much to Matilda's chagrin. She abruptly rises and charges from the room, crying, stumbling at the foot of the stairs, almost knocking over her daughter Margaret.

Matilda is once again totally irritated with what this family is doing to all her hard work this morning. She just cleaned that rug yesterday; beat all the dirt out of it and then some. Scrubbed it down, hung it up outside in the sun to dry, then dragged it back inside, moved the furniture so she could lay it back on the floor, spotless. And now Miss Mary done gone and spilled some tea on it. What's wrong with these people? Why they always gotta be spilling stuff on the floor? And it's always is some kind of liquid or jelly. She can always tell where Massa Andrew sits because she always finds the most crumbs and food particles around his chair. He will be eating and then starts spitting small particles out of his mouth like there's something wrong with the food. They live like pigs sometimes. If they want to spill something, why not go outside, get upset and spill stuff on the ground. Matilda's mind rambles on as she gets on her knees wiping up the tea from the rug, wrinkling her face at the stain, and shaking her head angrily.

"Mother, Mother!" Margaret questions her obviously disturbed mother as she stumbles up the stairs. "What's the matter?" Margaret hates these early morning wake ups. She needs her beauty rest and that usually requires rising only after 9AM. Papa mostly wakes Andy and Pierre for these occasions. Whatever this is about must be very important to wake her and Mother. Margaret continues watching her mother disappear at the top of the stairs. She is concerned, wondering if her upset behavior is about her headaches. It must be why she is in such a hurry. Lately, they are becoming worst. The medicine from Dr. DuBois only works for a little while, then the pain is back and she has to take more. Lately it seems she is taking more than usual. Her headache must've been really bad for her to rush out like that. Margaret enters the sitting room to see her father and Andy standing together, looking in the direction of the stairs. "Andy, what's wrong with Mother?"

Matilda is finishing the cleaning up of the spilled tea, mumbling under her breath.

Andy looks at his father.

"Papa, what's wrong with Mother?"

Andrew walks to the breakfast table and prepares a couple of biscuits with some marmalade. Looking about the table, Andrew smiles at what Matilda has prepared. She is an amazing slave. Every morning she puts an array of breakfast food like this on the table and does it without complaining. Once again he is happy his father did not sell her off when he had the chance when she was just a child. The opportunity to make some money from her as a young girl appeared many times, because even as young as she was she was still old enough to breed. At a slave auction she would have brought a price close to a thousand dollars, but Andrew cried and hollered and screamed that she was his best playmate and didn't want her to be sold, so she was not. Dr. DuBois has reminded Andrew, on several occasions, he needs to spend less time enjoying Matilda's cooking, but Andrew knows he cannot because he doesn't try. He bites into one of two biscuits, packed with butter and marmalade, before responding to Margaret. "She's got a terrible headache, Margaret," he mumbles, in between chewing.

"Matilda, hurry up with what you're doing and bring me my morning tea," said Margaret, finding a place to sit. "Papa, what is all this hollering about this morning?"

"We're at war Margaret, WAR!" shouts Andy.

"At war with whom?" asks Margaret.

"The Federals, Margaret!" answers Andy. "We're at war with the Republicans in Washington! Here, read this."

Matilda gets up from the floor and looks at what's left of the stain. She will have to come back later and finish it. She slowly walks back to the table, even more upset, where she left the tray with the tea, then maneuvers her way around Andy with Margaret's cup of tea. She wonders if Margaret will get upset and turn something over.

"Thank-you, Matilda," said Margaret, removing the cup and saucer. She stirs her tea and reads the paper. She wonders why she needs to be interested in the dealing of some Captain Stephen D. Lee, or Major Anderson and a General Beauregard. How was the name Beauregard ever created? What kind of person would name someone Beauregard? Men are so silly. She quickly becomes bored and nonchalantly places the paper down. "Why would what has happened at Fort Sumter affect us? That's all the way across the country. Papa, what reasons do we have to be a part of this madness?"

"This is not madness," replies Andrew. "This is a struggle to be free from the Federal government and their meddling into our affairs. What happened at Fort Sumter affects us because what they are fighting for is to maintain our freedom. They are our brothers in uniform. We must support them with everything we have and that includes manpower. My dignity, Andy's, Pierre's, yours and Mother's are all at stake. This is our final link to the white society that keeps us out."

Andrew pauses and rubs his chest. He turns his face to hide the grimace creeping upon it. That strange pain was back again, just below his left collarbone. Every now and then it happens, but mostly when he is extremely excited about something. Once when he was in the fields with the slaves, sitting upon one of the mares, he felt the same pain. He actually fell off the mare, but attributed it to the sun. After drinking some water he felt a lot better. And now it is back. If he is to enjoy the expected victories of the Confederacy he knows he has to take care of himself, according to Dr. DuBois. Life is good and it can only get better.

"If I must show my blood spilled," said Andrew, the words stumbling from his mouth instead of flowing, "so my children and my children's children can walk the streets of New Orleans as equals to the white children, then that's what I'm willing to do!"

Upstairs, Pierre St. Claire hears the rumbling voice of his father and turns over in his bed, covering his head with his pillow; he wants to sleep beyond this 7am hour, but cannot. Pierre does not agree with what his father or his brother Andy believes in. He is a contradiction to their principles and wishes. Why is there this need to be accepted by white folks? Pierre is always amazed at his father's need to be accepted by white folks; as if that acceptance will guarantee a special place here in New Orleans or in heaven. This final link, this missing link that is not the ultimate solution that he thinks it is. What is this need to bond with white folks, and where did he get it? All they really want to do is bound us in chains. It has been clear to Pierre, all his life, that white folks down here want nothing from and for black folks but slavery. Even during his education at the private schools in New Orleans, he was peppered with southern whites letting him know where his place is and that he should never try to leave it. That very school, which today is turning out the black leaders of tomorrow, is doing nothing more than perpetuating the system of slavery. Instead of having dumb ignorant slaves, now they have a few intelligent ignorant slaves. They are teaching it in schools and quoting it in the churches from the Bible. Papa thinks he will be accepted by the white folks if he and other free people of color take up arms with the Confederacy, swear undying allegiance to the Confederacy system, defending this *peculiar institution* to the last dying breath. Andrew and Andy are blinded by the principles of slavery in their approach to treating other black men less than themselves. They do not see how white folks are still treating them like slaves. It is all about money argues Papa, all the time.

"Slavery is a business," he always said.

It's always all about money. This whole damn country is all about money and nothing to do with the human spirit. The Confederacy wants to separate from the North because of money, because the rest of the country is not in agreement with how the Confederate states use the human machine to achieve its goals. How can enslavement be considered a business, considering what it does to the human mind, the spirit and the body? What Papa wants will never happen, but he is willing to spill some of his precious blood to make the scandalous white politicians look good. Unfortunately he thinks there is honor in doing that.

It is not until Pierre hears his mother running to her bedroom and slamming the door, he stumbles from his bed. Either she's run out of Dr. DuBois magic white powder or Papa's said or done something foolish to force her to react so. There is a great deal of misguided and foolish joy downstairs. Not really wanting to go downstairs, but knowing he must, he purposely makes his slow descent to the living room, which gives him time to hear more about the war's beginnings. His father is bubbling with heroic babble as he enters the sitting room. Pierre rejects these perceptions his father has and uses every opportunity he has to show his father how wrong he is.

"Papa, it will never happen," said Pierre, walking to the breakfast table. He prepares a cup of tea, plops in some sugar, then finds a chair and slouches into it. He stirs his tea with his finger.

"Don't you think you ought to use a spoon to do that," said Andy, smirking.

"I know where this finger has been, and it's safe to stir my tea," responds Pierre.

"Good morning Pierre," said Margaret, "have you heard?

"Good morning Master Pierre," say Matilda.

"Matilda, you got to stop calling me Master," demands Pierre. "Now, if you don't I'll put the lash on you, that I promise you."

"Good morning son," said Andrew, "that's no way to talk to a slave, she's giving you respect."

"That's not the kind of respect I need to be getting," said Pierre.

"Another *free the slaves* meeting last night, Pierre," asks Andy, a sarcastic grin showing.

"Yes, and today I'm attending a meeting to *free the minds*, right here in this house," said Pierre.

"I wish you'd show more respect for me and common sense for yourself, by not attending meetings with dreamers," complains Andrew, "who don't want to fit in with this society. It will lead to pain and suffering later on down the road."

Overseeing this plantation is at best a very difficult if not an impossible task and Andrew wishes Pierre would pay more attention to it. He needs to understand what it means to be a manager of people. How to be firm, fair and demanding; but also vigilant, compassionate and knowing how to push to the limits the workers. It requires going to the fields with the slaves, remaining there until the end of each day. It also requires keeping an eye on the livestock, the farm machinery, knowing the contents of the storehouse, and keeping accurate records of how each slave has performed. Improvement is needed in Pierre's library of knowledge in knowing how and when to plant a crop, correct the wrongs of the slaves, organize a strong work force and produce a good crop. Turning in a profitable crop is taking in all the daily activities of running the farm, which includes the slaves, the breeding women, working children, livestock, provisions, good working farming utensils, and land up keep. Andrew has learned that, shouting with rage is not an effective way to manage his property. In the management of slaves, Andrew knows there has to be uniformity of conduct towards them; punishment should be firm, deliberate and consistent with each infraction. Punishment should not be done in anger, but to show the necessity as to why the correction is necessary. And then there are the periodicals that Pierre has yet to read that reinforces these principals. 'De Bow's Review, Southern Cultivator, Farmer's Register', Carolina Planter, and Farmer and Planter' all containing articles similar to "Judicious Management of the Plantation Force," "On the Management of Slaves," The Management of Negroes," Moral Management of Negroes," and "Management of Slaves." Wonderful documents that help farmers understand the task that is at hand in running a farm with slave labor.

Right now this talk of doing away with slavery and freeing them is kept alive by just a few. But Andrew is concern about the impact it has on the free blacks who support the Confederacy. It has been mostly talk on their part, but he knows and understands white folks who protest slavery do so only because they do not see the total picture. When they do, they will come on board and blend in with the other white folks, but for the free blacks it will not be as easy. Free blacks cannot 'just blend in'. They must be on the inside so they can see who the new comers are and also the new comers will see them when they come in. Without slavery, this farm would not function and this family would not have the necessities and more that they enjoy today. He has always believed that what Washington has to offer will take away what he has created.

"You can't fit where you're not wanted," Pierre is saying.

But you are wanted son, Andrew wants to say, but cannot. He is shaking his head in frustration, again for the hundredth time. This conversation is a repeat of previous conversations. How can this son be his? What is it about him that makes him so different from Andy? Andrew has searched and researched his own past to see what he may have done differently that affected Pierre so that he rejects the very life that supports him and his life style.

"It's those abolitionist friends who are not wanted" said Andrew, frustrated. "They can't give anything but words. Words will not make you free; hard work and perseverance makes you free."

"Words begin the process," said Pierre. "Words written in Philadelphia back in '76' began this nation on the road to freedom; but it did not include us as a people."

That written document didn't free a lot of people, Andrew is well aware of that. There's still been a lot of fighting and working against the powers that continue to try and enslave the people who wrote it. Nobody sits on his or her ass depending on a piece of paper for protection, unless you're in the outhouse.

"Frederick Douglas said, we as a people should be a slave to no one", said Pierre.

"That's because Frederick Douglas is out of touch with benefits and progress that gets better and better in developing our system," said Andy. "He's getting old and thinks no blacks are free anywhere in this great land. He doesn't know what's going on down here, and it shows in what he prints in his paper. Slavery has become a business for white and black folks."

"Pierre, we have an opportunity here to complete the Circle of Acceptance," pleads Andrew. "Generations from now will thank us for what we are doing at this moment. This is the piece of the pie we've been looking for."

Pierre walks over to the table and picks up some bacon and a biscuit, spreads some marmalade on it and stuffs it into his mouth. "Like I said before, southern white folks ain't gonna let us into their society as equals. It will never happen."

"You don't know if you don't try!" yells Andrew.

"That's why Mother's upset," interrupts Margaret, "this talk of war."

"This is talk for men folks, Margaret," said Andy.

"Dying is not just men talk," responds Margaret.

"Dying for a cause is men talk," said Andrew, "you women don't understand."

"If I must die for a cause, then let it be for my all of our people's freedom," said Pierre. "We are not free, we are only better off."

You are better off because of what my father did to ensure this freedom, thinks Andrew, holding back his frustration. He's worked hard to maintain this family's freedom and he didn't do it by listening to other men who put dreams of freedom inside the heads of the lazy, confused or feeble minded. Not everybody is a slave; not everybody is waiting to be free. It's just like Pierre not to understand that he is what he is because of what his grandfather was. It all has a direct correlation to what he is today. Andrew feels a heat rising inside his head; he is beginning to push water out and about his forehead. His anger is rising and he knows he shouldn't be getting this excited. These things about his behavior are recognized when he gets like this and even though he may try and hide it, his body language exposes him.

"Papa, it's okay," warns Andy, "calm down, remember what Dr. DuBois said."

Andrew wonders how he can calm down; he has a son who is undermining everything he has spent so many years building. How can a child raised in privilege have so much empathy for the less fortunate? What did he do so wrong with Pierre that he did so right with Andy? Will he ever understand the necessity of this lifestyle? Will he ever understand the importance of maintaining it for the good of mankind regardless of what he may think is wrong with it? With time it can only get better, not worse. It's all about profit and loss. It's all about making money, making your mark, making a contribution to society and eventually getting respect, not because you're black, but because you have learned how the system works and you are using it to your benefit, even if it is at the expense of others.

Margaret is bored with what she hears and gets up. Men are so stupid and silly at times, arguing about something that neither will compromise about and the only way it can be settled is by fighting each other. They are stupid, just plain stupid. Margaret sees Matilda come from the kitchen. She has lost all interest in the conversation of the men folks of her family. If Mother were here she might pay attention more, but since they have upset her there is no need to stay. They won't let her participate anyway. Must be some sort of male thing. Anyway, she has other interests; she has important reasons to speak to Matilda, alone. She touches Matilda on her elbow then motions Matilda to follow her to the other side of the breakfast table, away from everyone else. "Matilda, does Jacob know about this war starting?" whispers Margaret.

"I don't know, Miss Margaret," said Matilda, clearing the dirty dishes from the table. "I ain't seen him all mornin'."

"Not so loud Matilda," said Margaret, pulling Matilda towards herself. Not that Matilda's conversation would over shadow Pierre boisterous voice at the moment.

"I'm not trying to destroy anything," Pierre said to Andrew, "Papa, what I'm trying to get you to see is that, what this Confederacy stands for is not good for us, as a people."

"Look around you son," gestures Andrew, "what do you see

that is not good for us as a people. Look at what we have accomplished under the Confederacy."

Margaret pulls on Matilda's apron. "I must talk to Jacob." Even Matilda had turned to hear what Andrew was talking about. Margaret tugs at Matilda's arm. She has much more important things to discuss than what her father is talking about.

"But Miss Margaret, he so tired when he come home from da fields, sometimes he don't want to talk to anybody, includin' me. Sometimes he stays out in the woods wit Snake Eyes or Big Black. I don't know."

Margaret touches her lips with her finger to quiet Matilda as Pierre is approaching the table for more biscuits and tea. He looks around for a knife to spread the butter and marmalade. He finds one of Matilda's large misshapen biscuits, splits it with his fingers, then with the knife slaps the contents of the butter and marmalade on one side then plops the other side on top.

"What we have here is a lie, Papa, a damn lie," he said, sucking butter and marmalade off his fingers.

"If this is a lie," interrupts Andy, "then I don't want to see the truth, Pierre. Those who don't have the luxuries you have, have blinded you with guilt. You got more than they do and that is why they want you to feel guilty about how you obtained it."

Margaret moves Matilda and herself to another section of the room, near the kitchen door. "Matilda, ask around," she whispers, "find out where he is and tell him I'll meet him in back of Voodoo Man Cato's shanty tonight, after everyone's asleep. He knows what time that will be."

"Voodoo Man don't like people to be sneakin' round his place," warns Matilda.

"You know and I know what Voodoo Man let people do around his place," whispers Margaret, adding her tone of authority.

"Yes Miss Margaret, I'll see what I can do," said Matilda, as Margaret pushes her into the kitchen.

Andy reaches out and yanks Margaret towards him. Margaret is not expecting this and feels embarrassed by Andy's behavior. She snatches her arm out of his grasp and is about to give Andy a piece of her mind, but is interrupted by Andy's boasting.

"Would you want your sister, the pride of the St. Claire's, to be man handled and accosted by some Yankee?" said Andy, hugging Margaret. "Northern men are known not to show respect for their women. You got to protect her honor as well as your dignity, brother."

"This is a white man's war," Pierre sternly tells both of them. "Can't you two see that? Black folks ain't got no business volunteering to be in it. Its bad enough we'll be forced to participate."

"Black folks will be volunteering because they see what they've accomplished since being part of the Confederacy, not because they are forced," said Andrew.

"I can't wait to get a fix on one of them Yankee blue coats," said an enthusiastic Andy, pretending he's holding a gun, "KAPOW! right between the eyes!"

Margaret moves between the excitement of Andrew and Andy. "Papa, I'm going to see how Mother is doing," said Margaret. "Matilda, would you bring some more tea for Mother? I'll meet you upstairs."

Matilda peeks out the kitchen door. "Yes Miss Margaret."

Andrew finds his favorite chair, sits and smiles. He stares at the newspaper, broadening his smile. "There's money to be made here, Andy," he said. "The Armies of the South are going to need lumber, lots of it. We got lots of it to sell them."

"It will be used for coffins and grave markers," said Pierre.

"It doesn't matter what they use it for son," responds Andrew smiling, "just as long as they pay me for it."

"Pierre, my young brother, you got to learn how to appreciate the finer things in life and what it takes to keep them. Now, if the North win this war, we as a people are going to get lost in a wave of Washington Republicans, feeling sorry for us because of a few, who refuse to bring something they can contribute to the system; and as a result, they plan to amount to nothing more than some field niggers. We're better than that! And I intend to stay better than that; and if that means killing somebody, I will!"

As Andy is finishing his boasting, Mary returns to the living room. She moves in between his conversation, walking like she does not hear him. She finds her favorite chair. She briefly stares at Andy, her face stricken with anger, then at Andrew. Pierre sees her face and is ashamed. He cannot look at her. He bows his head. Andrew has seen this look on her face before and knows something serious is about to come from her mouth. He becomes nervous and fidgets, like a little boy, caught doing something terribly wrong, with no excuse that can explain why. And even though he knows she is in distress, he still asks the same question, as if he doesn't recognize the expression. "Mother, is there something wrong?"

Matilda returns from the kitchen with the tea tray and is about to go to the stairs when she sees Mary. "I'm sorry Miss Mary, I thought you was still upstairs." Matilda changes direction and returns to Mary, presenting the tea tray.

Mary prepares herself a cup of tea, dumps another packet white powder into it, then sits, stirring and staring. Andy looks at his father and shrugs his shoulder. Pierre wanders about the room, nervously looking at them, quickly looking away from his mother. Matilda bows and removes herself to the kitchen. Finally, Andrew approaches Mary and nervously sits next to her.

"Mother, are you all right?" he asks, his strong voice shaking some.

Mary takes a sip of her tea, and then deliberately sets it on the small table to her left. "There will be no killing in this house," said Mary, staring straight.

"Pardon me, Mother," said Andrew.

"I said there will be no killing in this house."

"Why mother, where did you get that idea from?"

"I heard Andy down here and you not saying anything to change his mind."

"Mother, you know Andy, he's full of spunk. Why, sometimes he said things without thinking. He really don't mean half the things that come out of his mouth, right Andy?"

Matilda comes from the kitchen and begins gathering the dishes from the table.

"Matilda, I'll have a biscuit and marmalade."

"Yes Miss Mary." Matilda hurries to the kitchen then returns with a tray of biscuit and marmalade on a plate.

"Yeah Mama, I didn't mean nothing by what I said", said Andy.

"If anyone is going to take a life in this house, let God be the one who takes it," said Mary, "not any one of you."

"Its good to see you're feeling better, Miss Mary," said Matilda before she enters the kitchen.

"Mother, we will pray to God to watch over us in these troubled times," begins Andrew. He reaches out to gently hold her hands. "But God has many ways to test our faith. This just may be one of them and if it is necessary to strike down one of our transgressors, then-."

"LET GOD DO IT!" shouts Mary.

Andrew realizes the urgency of his current situation, rises, grabs Andy and Pierre by their arms and begins to walk them toward the stairs. "Andy, Pierre, why don't you two get dressed now. There's a lot that must be done today and I'm going to need both of you to stay close to home." Andrew's eyes follow Andy and Pierre all the way upstairs before returning to Mary. He nervously paces around her chair, trying to put the words together. "Mother, try and understand what's happening here. There is a possibility we could lose everything we have."

"God's not going to let that happen."

"What's God got to do with it?" questions Andrew. All Andrew knows and cares about is there's a war going on a thousand miles from here and who is to say how long it will be before it is at his front door? He's worked too hard to see this destroyed by some meddling Yankees from Washington. Twenty-five years he's struggled to get this far; twenty-five years of toiling for the white man, trying to fit in; trying to be accepted; trying to find out why he can't be looked upon as their equal. He's waited twenty-five years for this opportunity and he can't let it slip away. He and his circle of free Negroes have got to show their support for this war by making a noticeable contribution.

"Andrew, I've been with you twenty-five years", said Mary. "I walked beside you every step of the way and at no time did I say a word against your wishes; but this is different. You don't owe nobody nothin'. You don't have to be accepted by white folks. They ain't that important to our lives as a family. I've toiled along side of you, washing and cleaning laundry of the white folks for years, before you could sustain us. Well, now you can and we live off of what you produce and sell from this land. You built this house for me and told me, whatever I said was law inside the house and whatever you said was law outside the house. We agreed to that, now, didn't we? Okay, now, God blew the breath of life into our three children, inside this house, upstairs in our bedroom. We raised our children to respect human life and not to waste it. Now, we are inside our house and no one has ever killed anyone for anything and we're not about to start now. You don't have to kill a northern Yankee to prove nothin' to anybody! This is my house and in my house, only God can take a life."

CHAPTER 2
Wednesday, April 17th, 1861

On Wednesday morning, April 17th, 1861, for the slaves of Andrew Jackson St. Claire's farm it is just another morning that has come too early after nightfall. Too soon after the aches and pains of working the fields permitted them to sleep. It was much too soon for anybody to want to get out of bed. Every morning, before the sun rises, at or about four thirty, Matilda and 20 other slaves, with their children, begin their day. Their home is a series of four log houses, connected together with a narrow enclosed passageway. Each house is forty feet square with A-lined shaped roofs. Everyone lives in three long houses that look more like the barrel of a shotgun. All the children sleep in one end room and all the adults sleep in the other end rooms. The kitchen is in the middle room. All the beds are made out of pine poles, held together with leather strapping, with hay and straw stuffing for mattresses. The windows are covered with boards and the sills are packed with mud and ash in the winter, to keep the bitter cold out. In the summer, the panes are taken out and an old rag is sometimes hung in their place to let the sweltering Louisiana heat out. A fire is always going in all four rooms in a small wood stove during the winter months. A kettle of something is always cooking in the kitchen. The floors are made of white cypress logs. Most of them have now turned black with age.

Matilda checks how much fire is in the black cast iron stove, then the pot left warming all night, slowly cooking. She adds some water to the pot, and then stirs it. Rising from the bottom of the pot she sees the remains of chicken necks, gizzards and some chicken feet. It will be the morning meal. She adds some seasoning after tasting it. As usual, the first person she sees in the morning is her son Jacob, the slave driver on this farm. He walks up behind her and kisses her on her cheek.

"Mornin', Mama," he said, yawning. Jacob moves to the warming pot, looks in and then looks for some wood.

"Who's on the horn this morning, Jacob?"

"Steely," said Jacob, putting some wood on the fire. "Need to raise dis fire up. Folks gonna be gettin' up and dey gonna be hungry."

"Did anybody ketch anythin' yesterday?"

"Don't know Mama, we was too busy to let anybody go and look at da traps."

"We needs to put somethin' else in dis."

"I'll make sure da children checks da garden and put some 'tatoes and vegetables in it today."

The slave garden is where all kinds of vegetables, like collard greens, snap beans, potatoes, peas, turnips, and okra are grown to supplement the diet. Children too young to work in the fields, work there to keep it clear of weeds and destructive insects.

Matilda inspects the packed cypress wood floor for cleanliness, looking for dirt. The wood is always cool and damp in the morning. Vegetables, dried fruit, herbs and animal skins hang from the ceiling and cover the walls the kitchen. Matilda looks around trying to find something to add substance to the morning meal. She settles for some old potatoes. She can hear the adults making noises in their end of the house. Soon the children are going to get up and want to eat before they start their day. She selects some hot and sweet peppers to add some flavor.

The conch horn is sounded and there is more stirring of tired bodies, moans and groans. Jacob has gone outside and gathered all the tools for the day and baskets that will be needed for the work in the fields. Matilda checks the fires again, greets everyone who passes, then sets up the breakfast bowls with a piece of cornbread for everyone. The children eat at a trough near the fires. She can hear the wheat straw mattresses being shaken down, and the low mumble of morning conversation. She hopes that maybe a possum or raccoon or some squirrels and rabbits are in the traps from yesterday, if someone else hasn't robbed them. Matilda crumbles up some cornbread in the trough and pours some vegetables with pot-liquor over it. Most of the children are under twelve, which was good because it meant a strong labor force was waiting in the wings when the older slaves couldn't work any more. Somewhere between twelve and fourteen years the children begin doing light work around the farm, like setting up the dinner table, or fanning flies away from Mama Sarah. They also learn the fine art of picking up wood chips to start a fire.

"Mornin' Matilda," said an old woman's cracking voice behind her. She is sounding very tired.

"Good mornin' Sarah," replies Matilda, stirring the pot of vegetables and potatoes. "Don't look like much meat in the pot."

"Big Black say he thinks dere may be some possum in one of da trap," said Sarah, looking at what's available to eat. "He say he had a dream last night."

"I found some flour and meal mix, so I'm thinkin' about makin' some kush," said Matilda.

"I'll make sure da children put some taters in the ashes," said Sarah, "so they'll be ready for mid-day eating".

Matilda checks the weekly rations of salt, corn and cornmeal. She knows there will be daily rations of molasses; sometimes there is salt pork, peas or turnips, mainly what ever is left after she finished her days work at the big house.

"Mama 'Tilda," whines a child, tugging on Matilda's dress, "how you cook possum?"

"What's dat you say, child?" asks Matilda.

"Big Black said he dreamed dere is a possum in his trap and he said we gonna have it for dinner."

"You better ask Mama Sarah," replies Matilda.

"Have you washed da sleep off your face, child?" demanded Sarah. "Why you interested in a possum dat ain't been caught yet?"

"Mama Sarah," replies the child, "I done washed all da sleep off my face, see; look real close."

"Okay child," smiles Mama Sarah, "you help me with fixin' dese breakfast bowls and I'll tells you how to cook possum."

The child runs back to get the rest of her friends, yelling, "hey everybody, Mama Sarah's gonna tell us how to cook a possum if we help her fix the breakfast bowls."

Suddenly the kitchen area fills with children, all with smiling faces, all waiting with anticipation. They are directed to the trough where they sit in a line dipping cornbread, waiting for Mama Sarah to tell her story. Matilda stirs in some onions and cabbages into the morning stew.

"You sure you gonna be all right, Mama Sarah," asks Matilda, "I gots to go to Massa Andrews pretty soon."

"I'm gonna be just fine, Matilda; you go on and tonight, don't forget to bring back some butter."

"I need to talk to Jacob before I go," said Matilda, looking around the room for him.

"I seen him walkin' towards Voodoo Man Cato's place," said a voice in the crowd of slaves.

"Tell him to come to the big house at lunch time," said Matilda, throwing a wrap over her shoulders, leaving for the big house.

* * * * * * * *

Before the Europeans started the slave trade, all over Africa the various African cultures and tribes practiced some form of Vodoun. It was a method of their tribal communication between each other internally and externally with neighboring tribes. When the Europeans began the slave trade, colonists believed that by separating the peoples of the tribes and mixing them together with other tribes, they would take away the ability of the slaves to communicate and act as one unit. Instead, this attempted desolation of their families created African syncretism.

Out of the misery of slavery, the Africans found their faith in their individual Gods as their common ground. Because of this common ground, they commingled and made religious adjustments to the rituals known only to them individually. The result of this fusion created a new religion: Voodoo, an Afro-Caribbean religion that mixed practices from the Fon, the Nago, the Ibos, Dahomeans, Congos, Senegalese, Haussar, Caplaous, Mondungues, Mandinge, Angolese, Libyans, Ethiopians and the Malgaches.

From all of this came new generations of houngan, or priests of vodoun. Passed down from generation to generation, which is the usual way one becomes a houngan; vodoun remained a secret society on farms and plantations alike. Training begins at a young age and continues all through their life. By the time a young man is in his early thirties, he is initiated and raised to be a priest. He is given his asson; a ritual rattle made from a hollow calabash filled with stones or small bones and with beads on the handle.

To become a houngan is also to become a bokor. That is someone who understands and knows how to practice black magic. It is necessary for a houngan to know evil in order to be able to combat it. All of the rituals are performed in the hounfort of the houngan. The hounfort is made up of a peristyle, a roofed open space, bordered by a low wall, where rituals take place. A fire burns continuously in the center of the yard with an iron bar in the middle of the fire representing the forge of Ogou.

In the center of the peristyle is the poteau-mitan, or the center post. The post is a symbol of Legba. Legba is saluted at the beginning of every ritual. At the base of the post is a concrete flat-topped piece of material called the socle. This is where offerings are placed. The post is painted in bright rainbow colors in horizontal or spiral bands that are symbolic of Aida-Wedo. The top of the post is the center of the sky and the bottom is the center of Hell. This permits the loa to travel down the post and enter the hounfort. Several altars can be inside the hounfort; each consecrated to a particular loa. In the center of the hounfort is an altar stone called the pe. This platform is the height of a man's chest and is where ritual tools are placed. The pe is covered in offerings like candles, food, amulets, ceremonial rattles and flags, beads, drums and sacred stones. Vodoun rituals are divided into two main types of rites, Rada and Petro. They differ only in the type of loa they address and purpose of the ritual. All rituals open with an invocation to Legba, the loa of the gate and crossroads, entreating him to open the gate. Without Legba's permission, no other loa may cross from the astral plane to the material one. Trees in the yard around the peristyle are sanctuaries, called sacred reposoirs, where certain loa live permanently. Some trees are decorated with white and colored bottles, filled with medicinal waters, dressed to protect the hounfort from any negative intrusions of evil spirits. The glitter of the glass attracts, then captures and removes the evil contained in forces that make up envy, jealousy and dissension. All of this is part of the medicines of the gods, taking on characteristic forms.

* * * * * * * * *

Jacob stands before the hounfort of Voodoo Man Cato, looking for signs he is up and about. He has a desperate need to speak with Voodoo Man Cato. It is about how he is feeling right now and each time he has felt this way before, Voodoo Man Cato has helped. Jacob looks at the stacked collection of objects protecting Voodoo Man Cato. It is a spiritual fence created to keep out the evil that exists in this dimension. All of the items have been carefully laid out for maximum effect. It is an array of broken mirrors, empty buckets, wagon wheels, barrels, bottles filled with different colored water, tattered clothing, chairs, porcelain plates, iron gates, and just about anything not useful to anyone else. All of it is used to protect, entertain, commemorate, filter the good and repel the powers of evil.

Jacob pauses at the door where a twelve-foot T-cross with layers of what use to be white sheeting, suspends from the top. It is one of the many altars that Voodoo Man Cato uses to keep in touch with his Loa. It is an altar dedicated to the ancestors that were and the ancestors to be. He worships here on behalf of the entire slave community. Jacob raises his arm, about to knock, when the door opens and Voodoo Man Cato, dressed in black, with a top hat and long black coat stands, smiling at Jacob.

Jacob bows his head, not looking at the Holy Man. He speaks to the ground. "In the name of Oloddumare," begins Jacob, " Eleggua, Obatala, Oshun, Oya, Yemalla and Shango, I come to you, Voodoo Man Cato; in the spirit of the seven Orishas I come to you Voodoo Man Cato. May dey grant me dis day and all who I see today, may dey grant peace and good tidings."

Voodoo Man Cato stretches out his arms and raises his hands above the head of Jacob. "In the name of Oloddumare, Eleggua, Obatala, Oshun, Oya, Yemalla and Shango, I receive your presence," said Voodoo Man Cato, turning and walking back into his shanty behind drawn black curtains, to his hounfort. A fire burns in the middle of the room. There are objects of every shape and form, everywhere decorating the chamber, protecting the room from evil. "Your soul still rumbles inside," said Voodoo Man Cato, sitting before the fire reading the flames.

"It is because my soul yearns to be free, Voodoo Man Cato," said Jacob, bowing again before the fire and Voodoo Man Cato. "It cannot live another day inside dis mass of flesh, enslaved by da skin and da whip."

"You must learn patience," said Voodoo Man Cato, continuing his reading of the flames. He throws powder into the jumping fire and the flickering orange and red flames suddenly become a puff of purple smoke. "Obatala sends you peace, health and harmony. Eleggua will show the way when the time is right. Be patience, Jacob."

"My patience is as thin as da wind dat passes 'round me," replies Jacob, "soon, very soon I must find a release from dese chains dat hold me and my mama or I will surely die tryin'."

Voodoo Man Cato tosses more powder into the fire and again it erupts but this time into a giant yellow ball that disappears into the ceiling. "You are not in control as to when you shall leave this world and enter into the worlds of the gods. There is reason and purpose for you to be here. Be patience and wait for it to reveal itself to you."

Voodoo Man Cato raises his asson and shakes it three times, to his left then to his right then over the bowed body of Jacob. "Papa Legba, ouvri barrie pou nous passer," said Voodoo Man Cato. He then goes to peristyle and pours water three times before it and then before the poteau-mitan after which he kisses the poteau-mitan twice. He then pours water three times before three drums, each drum a different size from largest to smallest. He then takes some farine from the pe and traces a circle around Jacob. What is left in his hand he blows into the four different compass directions of his hounfort. Then standing in the inside a circle, around the peristyle Voodoo Man chants three times, "In the name of Eleggua, Obatala, Oloddumare, Oshun, Oya, Yemalla and Shango, join with the soul of your servant"

Jacob feels something light, falling onto the nape of his neck. Whatever it was the skin absorbs it. A warm glow suddenly is there.

"Go now and be productive to this earth and to yourself."

"I thank you for passin' their guidance and blessin's upon me," said Jacob. He raises himself and without looking at the face of Voodoo Man, backs out of the hounfort.

Once outside, Jacob turns and leaves the yard of Voodoo Man Cato, feeling somewhat relieved of his anger. He does not know how long he can maintain the patience Voodoo Man Cato said he needs. He knows he is not meant to be a slave. He knows he is meant to be more. He knows he will leave this farm. He knows he will leave his mama. It will break her heart and he will probably die trying, but he knows he must be free.

CHAPTER 3
Monday, April 29th, 1861

Twice a year, all the slaves are given their clothes rations. In the spring each slave was given 6 yards of cotton shirting and 6 yards of cotton cloth, like that used for men's pants, needles, thread and buttons. Each female slave received 6 yards of cotton, 6 yards of cotton drilling, a needle, a skein of thread and ½ dozens buttons. In the fall, each man gets 2 shirts of cotton drilling, a pair of woolen pants and a woolen jacket. Depending on the profits from each planting, it also determines if each year the rations remained the same or were less.

The month of April is when Andrew St. Claire does his parceling of the clothing. He will repeat the same ritual in October. Andrew leaves the sorting of the clothes, that are to be passed out, to his sons, Pierre and Andy. They are in the barn, separating the bundles of shirts, shoes and pants they had purchased in bulk during the winter. It is eight am. Like oil and water, the two brothers are political opposites. It is these political influences passed from the father to the first born that so strongly dwell in Andy Jr. but not passed to or sustained in Pierre. Andy must learn and learn fast what his father has to teach him. Someday he will be the protector, the provider, and the one-in-charge. One day he will be making the decisions that affect the family, the farm, and the slaves; always concerned about the slaves, understanding them to be the all important workforce, the gears that keep the farm running smoothly. These are influences and experiences remembered by Andy, but were shielded from Pierre because he was too young to understand. Pierre was also too young to understand why he enjoyed freedoms and pleasantries, as a free person of color that other blacks did not. Too young to understand slavery and why it was so necessary to the success of the farm he lived on. Too young to understand why all blacks are not free persons of color.

"Well, what do you think?" asks Andy.

"About what?"

"The war man, the war!"

"I think the Confederacy is making a big mistake," said Pierre, counting pairs of pants.

"How can the South be making a mistake about freedom?"

"Freedom for who?"

"You and me and everybody who wants to remain free."

"What about the ones who are not free?"

"You're going to start that shit about slavery again, right?"

"It's not shit, Andy; it's a failure of this Southern society."

"You're not a slave, so what's the problem?"

"We have slaves working for us and that's the problem."

"Do you think Papa and us can run this farm without slaves?"

"If Papa wants to he can."

"Pierre, farming is a business, and in a business people work for you and in this business of farming, the slaves work for Papa, it's all part of the business of running this farm."

"It is wrong, slavery is wrong!"

"You go to New Orleans, into one of them fancy shops, the people who wait on you work for someone. They are just as much a slave to something or someone. What's the difference?"

"They come to work, get paid and go home, that's the difference."

"Pierre, there is only a slight difference. These slaves go to work, get paid, then go to their home. The slight difference being Papa owns the housing. Papa takes care of their clothing, their medical needs. All of it is necessary to the survival of this farm and for the survival of the slaves."

"How can slavery be necessary? This country was born on the concept of freedom from slavery, and now they embrace it. America is showing the world an hypocrisy!"

"Pierre, calm down, you gotta learn to remain calm," said Andy, resting his arm on his brother's shoulder. "For Papa, slavery is a business and not something that is used to suppress human beings."

"That's easy for you to say, you're not the one being suppressed."

* * * * * * * * *

When Andy is in the fields, which is usually three days during the week, everyone else, including Jacob, is bent over working the fields. Andy rides around each acre as it is being worked; looking at each slave making sure everyone is doing his or her job and doing it as quickly and as efficiently as possible. He rides his horse slowly, deliberately, sometimes smiling into the sweaty faces of his workers. Andy loves his position as the man-in-charge. Sometimes he unfurls his whip and lets it hang down off his saddle, dragging in the dirt. Sometimes he will practice his talent with it by snapping off a tree branch.

Jacob is never happy when Andy is in the fields. He constantly uses the whip to taunt the slaves. Even though Massa Andrew pledges he will not whip his slaves, Andy waits for the opportunity to break that pledge. All the slaves, knowing this, do what they must and more so that they do not become victims to Andy's yet-to-be used talents. It seems whenever the quotas are down, or perceived to be low, Andy comes to the fields and soon quotas are back to normal. Jacob will give water breaks and personal breaks every two to three hours, whereas Andy permits one break before lunch and another before dinner.

There is one exception to Andy's strict adherence towards working the slaves and that's when Margaret comes to the fields with water. Andy is never happy when he sees her but doesn't attempt to stop her. When she first started bringing the water Andy chased her away with threats of being the boss and he will determine when water is distributed. Once he actually kicked the ladle out of Jacob's hand and kicked over the water bucket she had brought. Jacob stared at Andy a long time before returning to work. Andy sat on his horse and smiled back at Jacob, while he let loose his whip. Margaret left the fields threatening to tell her father with Andy's sarcastic laughter echoing after her. The rest of the day, Andy paid more attention to what Jacob was doing than what any other slave did, goading Jacob into reacting to him; but Jacob did nothing in return. He did not want to put his mother in danger of coming to the fields for his mistake. The next day Margaret came back with water and this time Andy did nothing to stop her. Like the day before, she started with Jacob, and this time Jacob smiles at Andy.

*   *   *   *   *   *   *   *   *   *

Margaret St. Claire sits on the edge of her bed, nervous, fidgeting, staring at a diamond white moon hanging in the blackness of the sky. From her window she can see the path she will soon be walking. She can see the white light of the moon bouncing off the still waters of the pond, highlighting the surrounding shoreline. Standing, she covers her shoulders with her wrap and slowly opens her bedroom door. Walking quietly and deliberately, she passes her parent's room, then Andrew's, then Pierre's. The stairs muffle her footsteps as she passes over them; soon she is through the kitchen and out the back door.

She walks without hesitation through the trees, listening to the sounds of the night. Remembering what it was like as a child when she ran and played in these woods. Not afraid of the blackness of the night, not afraid of the blackness of the skin of the slaves she played with. This was before her father had as many slaves and the land didn't have places for slave housing. It was a time when all she knew were these woods and the pathways that led to secret places. Margaret, Pierre and Andy played hide n' seek and tag in these very woods; ran away from Matilda when she came looking for them to eat supper. It is also in these woods as children she and Jacob shared their first kiss. Actually, Margaret kissed Jacob and Jacob promptly wiped it from his cheek, upsetting Margaret so, she cried to Matilda the rejection she felt from Jacob. These woods were and still are her friends. She walks with stealth and confidence.

Somewhere in the midnight air, there is the sound of a drum, keeping time with the mild breeze. She pauses at Voodoo Man Cato's shanty, looking for signs of Jacob, but sees nothing. The cotton fields are to her left. The lake is in front of her. She hesitates as she passes

Voodoo Man's shanty, looking more at the shanty than the direction she is walking. Voodoo Man Cato always makes her nervous. Regardless of the times she has walked this path to meet Jacob she shivers slightly from a chill that never matches the temperature of the evening. She can hear his low chanting. More hypnotized by his chanting and the drums she moves towards her anticipated meeting with Jacob. She has left the shanty behind and is standing in the shadow of the trees, looking at the still water of the lake. She wonders if Matilda spoke to Jacob about meeting her tonight. From Voodoo Man Cato's shanty, the beating drums are getting louder.

"Jacob," whispers Margaret into the night, "Jacob, are you here? Jacob, it's me, Margaret." She turns and looks back at Voodoo Man's shanty. "Jacob, come out, please; I need to talk to you." Margaret looks at the lake, notices how the moonlight dances on the ripples of the water and slowly walks towards it. The drums increase their tempo. "Jacob, now is not the time to play hide n' seek. Jacob my love, walk out of this blackness. I want to see you. I'm begging you, Jacob. Jacob, if I don't see you soon, you will not see me at all tonight."

A tall shadowy figure appears behind Margaret. The drums get louder. Suddenly a cape opens and Margaret is surrounded, and then swallowed by blackness.

"JACOB!"

"Ain't nobody gonna hear you out here, dis time of night, gal," said Jacob, throwing his wrap on the ground, then lounging on it.

"Jacob, you scared the life out of me," scolds Margaret "Don't you ever do that again, do you hear me? Why didn't you say something when I first called?"

"I was supposed to meet you in back of Voodoo Man's shanty, not down by da lake."

"Voodoo Man gives me the willies," said Margaret, staring at the shanty. "I was about to leave. I hope you didn't think I was going to hang around here all night?"

"Don't I git a kiss?" teases Jacob.

"For what?"

"Cause I ain't seen ya all day."

"I'm glad you brought up that point," said Margaret, "just where have you been all day?"

"Gimme a kiss and I'll tell ya."

"Jacob, I demand you tell me where you been all day."

"Well now, Miss Margaret," said Jacob, reaching up and grabbing Margaret's hands, "if you makin' demands, I guess I hafta tell you. Well Miss Margaret, I been in the fields all day, working da niggas. Yo' daddy don't like it when da daily quotas ain't met."

"How come your Mama didn't know where you were again this morning," said Margaret, gently pulling away. "How can you not tell your mother where you're going to be?"

"Mama don't never know where I am in da morning, just in da evening. But, like she knows where I am right now; does yo' Mama know where you at, right now?" Jacob gently pulls Margaret down to him, then gathers her in his arms and gently holds her close.

"Don't get smart," said Margaret, enjoying the bulk of his arms around her.

"A slave like me can't never be smart," said Jacob, his hands moving, one finding her breast, the other finding passage between her thighs. He kisses her and she returns the advance, their tongues meeting and dancing together. "You still wants to know where I been?"

"Tell me after you've been there," sighs Margaret, letting him have his way.

Jacob's callus hands opens her blouse until her breasts are exposed and what he has touched with his hand, he now taste with his mouth and tongue. Her skin is soft and smells of flowers and honey. He gently sucks one then the other, feeling her nipples grow hard inside his mouth. He hears a moan slowly crawl from her throat and he enjoys the nipple that has risen inside his mouth. She wants him to take more of her inside his mouth. She holds fast his head against her, enjoying his delight in feasting on her. The drums get louder, the beat more complicated and they appear to be in time with Jacob sensuous assault on her body.

Jacob slowly manipulates his hand down to her skirt, unbuttons it, moves it out of the way. He then finds the place between her opening thighs and feels the delicate moisture of her pubic hairs on his fingertips; her thighs widen and her hips rise to meet his hand. His fingers gently move back and forth over the small bump above her ultimate gift to him. She moans again. Jacob feels Margaret's hands caressing his head, grabbing his hair, guiding his mouth to her other breast. The drums continue to beat, getting louder. He feels his manhood pressing against the insides of his brown homespun pantaloons, demanding release; and then he feels Margaret's hand on his pantaloons, loosening the tie string, reaching inside. Her soft hands are grabbing him, squeezing him, gently sliding him out of his pants, while never letting go of him. She gently rubs and pulls his hardened flesh. She feels him shudder.

"My Jacob," moans Margaret, "my dear Jacob." The woodsy smell of his body, the good earth, the tree sap, seeps into her nose, with all its splendor of feeling him move above and then between her wanting and impatient body. "Come inside, my dear Jacob, come inside, where I wait for you."

Jacob feels his body responding to Margaret and wonders why he, strong in spirit and physical strength is nothing more than soft mud when he is in the hands of Margaret? How is it he can defy her when she makes demands? Then ignore her when they see each other during the day; yet give her his undivided attention when he feels her hands moving about his body? How is it when she is finding his manhood, she is somehow transferring his strength, through her delicate fingers, into her body? She drains his remaining strength from an already love weakened body. This is the only time he knows he is not in control of his being. It scares him to feel this vulnerable with Margaret. But there is nothing he can do about it. His body aches for some kind of release that only Margaret can give.

He is briefly above her, between her opening thighs, his chapped lips moving towards her delicate opening mouth. Jacob's mouth finds Margaret's and they again engage their tongues in a dance of lust.

Margaret tastes Jacob's mouth, inhales deeply as she feels him slides down then up into her. Jacob feels the insides of Margaret's thighs rise squeeze, then press against his member, holding him, momentarily, then releasing him, then holding him, then releasing him, rising to meet him, sliding down to tease him.

On and on they go until Margaret feels the tingling swell of ecstasy, deep inside her loins, spreading down her thighs and legs. It blindly rushes madly and delightfully into her toes, forcing her to curl them. The feelings then retrace its pathway, quickly rushing into her rigid nipples, exploding throughout her breasts. This maddening feeling desperately wants to get out. It pushes against the inside of her excited body, looking somewhere, anywhere, to escape her body. On and on this tantalizing feeling ravages her body, tingling and tickling, sensuously pushing and pulling, looking for a way out.

Jacob sees and feels what was happening to Margaret. It is happening to him also. He owes her this feeling. He is her slave. He feels obligated to satisfy her. He gradually increases his thrusting, moving faster and faster to match her moaning and quickened breathing. He begins to feel that strange but familiar tightening inside his loins, pushing against his insides, rising into his rigid member. It feels so wonderful, forcing him to pump harder, sliding in and out of Margaret with joyous rapture. He pushes himself up from her chest, looks at her, and smiles. He has put joy onto her face. She opens her eyes and smiles back, grabbing his shoulders tightly; she moves her hips against his. She has him. She is in charge of him. He is not in control any longer. And that is when he feels a crowd of good feelings inside his thundering, shuddering member, again, pushing up harder, trying to escape out of his body. Then, he feels Margaret suddenly open up, pulling him deeper inside. He can't stop himself from falling in and she won't let him get out.

She squeezes out of him the beginnings of life, feeling him go rigid while his seeds of life spews forth in jet streams from his quivering member. She accepts all of it from him. She also accepts his gift of immediate joy he has given her. She wants it all inside her and she deliberately drains it all from him, by squeezing and pulling, milking him, feeling slight shudders from him with each pulling movement.

The drums are now at their syncopated peak. Margaret and Jacob can see the moon and stars and the entire universe, in all its glory inside their minds as they moan and growl and claw each other, clasping hands in harmony with each other; their joy of the evening, in synch with the rhythmic drums.

Then, there is nothing but the silence of the night, gently interrupted by the rushed breathing of two spent lovers. Their nocturnal sounds joining the owls hooting, crickets chirping, and frogs croaking. Margaret is feeling his fingers gently slide over her buttocks, down into the crevice then gently up and over the other. Jacob is feeling her mouth sucking his neck, then the nipples of his breast, and then one last gentle squeeze of her hand on his member. Their naked bodies are feeling the breeze passing though the trees, their ears accepting the gentle voice of Voodoo Man Cato's, pas de deux chant.

* * * * * * * * *

Mary St. Claire is restless, quietly tossing and turning in her bed. She looks at her husband, Andrew, his breathing labored, but sleeping nonetheless. She looks at the carriage clock she keeps on her night table, her eyes not sure of the time, presses the top button, and then listens to the chimes. It is two am. Also on the same night table, an envelope with packets of medicine from Dr. DuBois waits for her, when necessary. She reaches out and then hesitates; Dr. DuBois has explained the danger of the packets becoming habit forming. So, she rolls onto her back and stares at the darkness that hovers at the ceiling. Her day has been a disaster, this talk of war. She watches and listens to her husband snoring, labored sleep, then listens to the crackling sounds of activity inside her brain. She is hearing every possible noise the house and her mind can create. She was asleep, but not deeply; instead it was more of the eyes closed and a bobbing and weaving in and out of sleep.

The familiar sounds of her home, and the sounds of anxiety from within her mind are soon joined by a faint sound of drums. Voodoo Man Cato, thinks Mary, must be conjuring up something to be playing drums this hour of the night. It would be nice if he could conjure up some sleep for me, thinks Mary. The drums are beating slowly rhythmically, methodically. Mary finally sits on the edge of her bed, frustrated by her inability to sleep, and reaches for her robe. She decides, she is going downstairs for some tea; but before she leaves, she reaches for one of Dr. DuBois' packet.

Matilda has left some fire in the stove. Mary closes a partially open kitchen window then puts some kindling on top of the smolder embers to make the fire rise. She moves the teakettle holding the hot water over the fire, then sits and waits. Andrew is too old to fight in some war, thinks Mary and her sons are too young to die. The very idea of watching them march off to battle is out of the question. Once again she is in a battle to protect herself. And again it seems all her life has been one personal battle after another.

First, as a child, she battled to remain with her family. The master wanted to separate her from her mother and father, as soon as she was old enough to hold a broom and sweep the floors. She battled with the master, a nine year old, convincing the master, she could sweep the floors cleaner, fan away flies better, than anyone else on the plantation and if he let her go, no one could do it better. She cried. She pleaded. She groveled. She did whatever she had to, to remain with her mother. Her method of pleading with confidence was enough to convince the master to keep her with her family.

When she met Andrew, he was fifteen or sixteen and in his last years of servitude and already showed the promise of being a good man. His father was already a free man of color, with several hundred acres of land and slaves to work the land. On weekends only, they met under the watchful eye of the master's son, while Andrew courted her. Their courtship lasted about three months before Andrew went to the master's son and asked for Mary's hand in marriage, much to the delight of her mother. Mary battled with the master's son to release her from her servitude early. This battle was even more complicated by the fact Andrew's father was a free man of color, which raised the price of Mary's freedom even more. In the end, Andrew's father had to give up 5 young slaves who were capable of breeding and being bred.

After they married, Mary worked along side of Andrew and his father, in the fields, with the slaves, trying to make the land into something they could live off. She left the battle of living on the plantation only to exchange it for the misery of living on a large farm. Her newest adversary now became Mother Nature. She fought back hard as she worked the fields, fighting the enemies of the hot and cold weather. The rains that brought the flooding; the blistering sun that brought drought. She remembers the pain that started in her hands and worked up her arms and into her shoulders and back. It is this type suffering that comes from spending 15 to 20 hours at a time tilling the land, dragging rocks off the planting areas. The pain that is enhanced by clumsily walking behind a mule, fighting the steel knife that always seemed to have a mind of its own. She fought them all and won and now another battle has confronted her; she must go into battle against a war machine; a political war machine that now wants her husband and sons; a political war machine that was built by men, for men, to kill and maim other men.

The water is steaming and beginning to boil. Mary gets a cup and saucer from the cupboard and prepares the tea, wrapping it in a cloth that she places in the cup, and then pours the water into the cup. She finds herself some sugar, and then reaching into her pocket for a kerchief, she discovers one of Dr. DuBois' packets. She had forgotten it was there. Realizing the packet was her reason for coming downstairs, she opens and empties the white powder contents into the cup. Stirring it all together, she sits at the table sipping the tea, feeling the warmth spread down into her lungs, then into her unsettled stomach. She sits at the table, occasionally stirring the tea, staring at the color inside her cup, not understanding what's going on in her life right now. She sits listening to the house, noticing, outside, the drums have stopped.

There must be a place for her to have peace; there has to be an end to this struggle she has endured. There has to be a final day of struggle, a final hour of misery, a final minute of anguish, the worry, and everything that goes with living on this earth. Oh how Mary would welcome death if it came knocking at this moment. She knows she cannot live to see her children die; she knows she cannot live to see Andrew die; she would rather die herself.

Mary rises and places her cup and saucer on the counter by the water pump. Matilda will wash them when she comes in. She looks about her kitchen, the walls, the small table, the stove, the curtains on the windows, the cupboard, the two chairs, the floor, and wonders if all of this will be gone one day because of what was started yesterday. She wonders what will become of the twenty-five years of hard labor put in by her and Andrew. Will it all disappear with the smoke of a rifle's bullet? She passes from the kitchen to her living room touching things that mean so much to her, like she will never see them again. She is about to begin her ascent of the stairs when she hears the kitchen door open. She waits, expecting Matilda. She walks back to the kitchen, to remind Matilda of what she wants for breakfast but instead, she sees her daughter Margaret, rushing in.

"Mother," stutters Margaret, surprised by her mother's presence, "I thought you were in bed."

"Margaret, I thought you were Matilda, where are you coming from?"

"Oh, I couldn't sleep Mother," responds Margaret quickly, covering herself with her wrap. "I went for a walk, hoping the night air would relax me. Why are you still up?"

"I couldn't sleep, thinking about the possibility of Andrew and the boys going off to war."

"Do you really think they will?"

"I pray they do not, but who is to say? This is not like fighting the British. This is more like a family feud. And if it turns out to be just that, it could go on for years."

Margaret hugs her mother, feeling and sharing her pain.

"Maybe it won't last much longer than a season," said Margaret, comforting her mother and herself. "Like Papa said, maybe it won't last that long."

"You better go back to bed and get some sleep," said Mary, releasing Margaret, dabbing her eyes with a kerchief. She moves to the window over the kitchen sink and sees Jacob going into his slave quarters. "I'm just going to straighten up a bit and then I'll be right behind you."

"Good night, mother," said Margaret as she quietly moves upstairs to her room.

Mary puts away her dirty cup and saucer then follows in Margaret's footsteps to the second floor and enters her room to the sound of her husband snoring. Placing her candle lantern next to the bed, she sits and again ponders her life. She wonders what will her life be like a year from now? After getting under the covers, she blows out the candle, and then feeling the effects of the white powder from Dr DuBois, she slowly drifts into an anguished sleep.

CHAPTER 4
Friday, May 3rd, 1861

Andrew St. Claire's father, Jean Baptist St. Claire, called his piece of land Freedom's Acres. The first hundred acres were given to his father as payment, for fighting the British during the Battle of New Orleans in 1815. The property of land is located north of New Orleans, about a half-hour slow ride by horse and buggy. The main house was built first. For many years, all that could be seen was the house and the surrounding forest, except for pockets of cleared land, created for crops. Jean Baptiste St. Claire owned two slaves when he built his house. As his needs grew, more land was cleared and more slaves were purchased to help work the land. Eventually he purchased an additional 540 acres. When Jean Baptist St. Claire died, his son Andrew inherited the farm, keeping the slaves and building his family and his father's family of slaves until he had what he has today.

The main house was built to catch the morning sun and hold it as it passed across the southern portion of the house. In the summer, the top bedrooms were too hot to be in during the day and at night if it weren't for the breeze passing by, sleeping would have been just as unbearable. During the winter months, the sun that baked the occupants now warmed them like muffins in the oven. A lake surrounded by sugar cane to the west, cotton, corn and other vegetables surround the east and southeastern edge and mostly forest is south of the lake. East of the main house are the slave quarters, their garden and the outhouses used by the slaves. A well is located on the western side not far from the main house. The last building was the glorious barn. A building that was more beautiful than the big house. Trees separated the big house from the rest of the farm. Pathways bobbed and weaved through the trees leading to various destinations on the farm.

Andrew Jackson St. Claire was born December 14, 1814, when the house he lives in now was nothing more than four walls and a roof over a dirt floor. His father had been granted his freedom and given a family of slaves to help him clear the land. The slave family had one girl child, Matilda. Andrew and Matilda grew up together, not understanding what they meant to each other until Andrew's father died and he was given control of the farm. His first decision was to make sure Matilda could always come to the big house, first as a friend and later as the family cook. As the years passed, Andrew was able to gain respect from his neighbors by being one of the few free person of color who could read and write and used that knowledge to increase the value of his farm. He and a group of free blacks joined together to form a consortium. Together they were able to establish a free black society within the white society. Eventually they became an economic force to be bargained with in the black and white community. Some free blacks became bricklayers, some teachers, some doctors, some teamsters, while others became pipe fitters. They built their own stores, houses and churches. They put money in white banks and borrowed from the same banks. Their strength in working their way into the economic strata of the New Orleans work force caused many white labors to be excluded from job selections. The free black community of New Orleans had become an economical force to be reckoned with. Andrew is very proud of what he and other free blacks have done for themselves and for the total community of New Orleans.

* * * * * * * *

Andrew Jackson St. Claire stands on his back steps, greedily breathing in the cool morning air. It is seven a.m. and he is thrilled about the morning and what the day will bring. This war can do nothing but help him and the colored folks of New Orleans. He and others like him will do all he can to support the Confederacy and in return the south will grant them the last portion to the 'Circle of

Acceptance'. Finally, their lives will be equal amongst the whites of this town. The Parish of LaPointe is made up of mostly free colored folks and well to do colored folks. Like Andrew, their ancestors received property as payment for their help in fighting against the British, during the Battle of New Orleans.

Andrew steps from his porch and begins his daily routine of checking his farm and the slaves that work it. It is a routine that has expanded from a five-minute walk, twenty-five years ago, to one that now lasts over an hour. He looks forward to these morning walks that are two fold in purpose that he enjoys most. Every morning he takes his walk to the end of his drive, turns around and walks back. Dr. DuBois suggested he begin walking in the morning to strengthen his heart and get the clean fresh air of the morning into his lungs.

Andrew is following the advice of Dr. DuBois. Not that he needs to, but he does to please his family and to please his own needs. Once he has walked to the end of his long driveway he follows his owns advice. He pauses, looks back at all that he owns and lights his pipe, against the advice of Dr. DuBois. Each morning he stands and gazes back at his farm, backing up until he sees all that he has done; his creation; his pride; his joy.

The morning sunlight glows brightly against the white frame house. Smoke gently floats away from the chimney. Andrew admires what he sees and at the same time, makes mental notes of what he must do. He meanders back to the house looking with detail at the fence that needs some whitewash and also needs to be mended; the winter has been harsh. The fruit trees are showing their first blooms. Soon apples, pears and peaches will be ready for harvest. Magnolia and oak trees line the approach to his home, shading him from the morning sun. Behind the magnolias and oak trees, behind the fence, on both sides of the driveway, are the slave's vegetable gardens. Halfway to his house, he turns and enters one the slave's garden, walking to the well house. Charlie Boy is drawing water.

"Good mornin' Massa Andrew," said Charlie Boy, pausing momentarily to bow, before returning to the duty of drawing some water.

"Good morning, Charlie Boy," said Andrew, passing him to inspect the garden.

It is early spring and not much is growing except some left over winter vegetables. Already the children are weeding and digging in the ground looking for worms to use for fishing. His children population numbers seven with three due later this year. The ground moves under his feet. The winter thaw was almost complete. Some of last year's beanpoles still remain upright even though lingering vines attempt to pull them over. Once again the ground is being readied for potatoes, cowpeas, beans and collards. Charlie Boy looks after the children to make sure they keep the garden clear of weeds and yields the maximum vegetables. Because of his age, he and Mama Sarah no longer work the fields. Together, they keep an eye on the children and the garden. "Dem collards still comin' up, Massa," said Charlie Boy, walking by Andrew with two buckets of water. "Dey been comin' up all winter."

Andrew is inspecting the surrounding fruit trees and is startled by Charlie Boy's sudden presence. "What, what'd you say Charlie Boy?"

"Oh nothin' Massa Andrews, I knows you too busy in yo' mind to hear me sometimes. I jus' gonna' go on wit my mornin' chores. Come on you children, lets git da rest of dis gardenin'done."

Andrew watches Charlie Boy walk away, then he checks a few more of the apple trees. He then leaves the fruit orchard and walks towards the hogs pen. The hogs wander throughout a section of the farm that combined the forest as part of the penned up area. There are over a hundred pigs and hogs behind the fenced area, varying in size from a piglet to a couple of old sows, which weigh more than three hundred pounds. All over Andrew's lands are trees. Trees that he cuts for lumber to be sold. Most of the pigs are grown for food and for entertainment during the actual time of the hog killing. The meat supplements the diet for the slave population, and although he will sell some of the meat, most he will keep in the smokehouse. The old sows he keeps to continue the population growth.

"Good mornin' Massa Andrews," said a little boy, tending the pigs.

"Good morning Toome. How are the pigs doing this morning?"

"Oh dey doin' jus' fine, Massa," replies Toome as he finishes dumping the garbage scraps into a trough.

"Did you count how many pigs there are this morning?"

"Yes Massa Andrew I counted one hunert and five pigs dis morning."

"That's good, Toome. You're remembering your numbers."

"Oh yes, Massa Andrew, I practice every night now."

"Has Jacob stopped by to see you this morning?"

"No suh. I ain't seen him.

"Where are they cutting wood this morning, Toome?"

"Dey just on dis side of da lake Massa Andrews."

Andrew watches the pigs eat and listens to their active squeals for a while before walking west, towards the lake. As he gets closer to the lake he can hear the popping and chopping of the axes piercing tree trunks and the vocal conversations of the slave men. One hundred acres and more of timber dot his property and he plans to harvest it all, then sell it. The south is growing and building new things all over; and with the war breaking out, the Confederate Army is going to need lumber, lots of it and he has it to sell. The men are splitting a fallen tree when he comes upon them. He nods at each one who acknowledges his presence. He looks for Jacob but doesn't see him amongst the workers. His stay is short and soon he is meandering southwest around the edge of the lake. He then walks due west, towards the fields where the cotton is being planted.

He can see his home through the trees and there is a crooked line of smoke coming from the chimney. Matilda is probably cooking something good for afternoon meal. He passes behind Voodoo Man Cato's shanty, hearing chants coming from inside. There are colored bottles hanging from trees, cans and all kinds of containers strewn about, surrounding the shanty. Large objects of iron lean against each other as if they are meant to have special meaning. A trickle of smoke breaks into pieces and scratches its way upward, into the sky like clawing fingers. He pauses and looks in at the rear window, then moves on when he sees the figure of Voodoo Man Cato rise inside from beneath the very window and face him.

When he comes out of the woods, fifteen acres of cleared land unfolds before him. Last year's furrows still rise in orderly fashion as he walks into the open field looking and inspecting the dead stems of last year's crop. He hears a horse trotting towards him and he looks up to see Jacob riding in his direction.

"Good mornin' Massa Andrew," said Jacob, climbing down from the horse. "I got dem putting in da seeds dis mornin'."

"That's good, Jacob. The ground is ready. We need to have a good crop this year, Jacob. A really good crop because we need to help the Confederacy in this war."

"Yes, Massa Andrew."

"I don't want no slackers."

"Yes Massa Andrew. I make sure everyone does dere share."

"They've got to do more than their share."

"Yes, Massa Andrew."

"When we win this war, things are gonna' be different. Things are gonna' be better for everyone; just you wait and see."

Jacob watches Andrew walk around him as he speaks; only answering when necessary. It is what Andrew does when he speaks to Jacob. It's like Jacob isn't even there as Andrew charges him with additional daily duties.

"Yes, Massa Andrew."

"I'll be able to fix up everything, including all of the slave's living quarters."

"Yes, Massa Andrew."

"I need you to go back and check on the wood cutters."

"Yes, Massa Andrew."

"I want a wider pathway cut to get more trees out."

Jacob never knew his father. Matilda, his mother, once told him his father was from a neighboring plantation and ran away before he was born. She never heard from or of him after that. Jacob has only known slavery. All of his life has been on Massa Andrew's farm. All his sunrises and sunsets; all his free time as a slave; all his growing up and now growing old; all his childhood memories, all of them, on Massa Andrew's farm.

"I'm looking to have a big harvest, Jacob," Andrew was saying, standing, with his back to Jacob. "Getting the cotton in now will give us maybe two pickings."

"Yes Massa Andrew."

Jacob has been off the farm only once. He thinks he went to New Orleans with his mother, to help her carry some dry goods that Miss Mary purchased. He vaguely remembers seeing tall buildings and lots of people and there was a peculiar smell in the air. Now, he's much older and he remembers what he saw then and now he wants to go back and see what the rest of the country looks like. Something inside of him drives him to want to see what else is out there, away from New Orleans and off this farm. He has resigned himself that the only way he will see what's out there, is to runaway. He is a slave, like his mother, and her mother before that; that's all. He doesn't want to be a slave any more. He's heard about places in this country where he doesn't have to be a slave. That is where he wants to be now. He stands with Massa Andrew, taller than Massa, but still smaller in his eyes. Jacob is not equal to Pierre or Andy. In Massa Andrews' eyes he is their slave also. Jacob cannot continue to live this way. Is this what Mama's God has destined him to be in life, a slave? Maybe the God of this land is stronger than the God of the land Jacob has never seen. Maybe because he is not from the land of his ancestors he is looked upon with less compassion. As good a man Massa Andrews is, and Jacob knows that from his mother saying so, Massa Andrews is still in charge of his life. Massa Andrews still thinks of him as less than a man. And because of this and everything else Jacob knows about himself, about his mother, about this farm, the Massa's family, this life of slavery, he cannot stay on this farm. He knows what it is that he has to do.

"Yes sir Jacob, this is the year when everything will change for the better," Andrew is saying, staring at the workers in the field. "This time next year, I'm looking to have planted more cotton, more cane, cut more lumber, and buy more slaves for you to keep an eye on. That means more responsibility for you, boy, understand?"

"Yes, Massa Andrew."

CHAPTER 5
Thursday, June 27ᵗʰ, 1861

There is a heat that takes up residence in Louisiana in June. Without paying financial compensation to any of the people with whom it stays, it freely languishes like an unwanted relative until late September. Come July, like a spoiled child who has been denied nothing, it is unbearable. The entire state is like hell's kitchen.

No matter how much free time this family has, Matilda is always doing something. She stops, looks at the table and wonders if she has forgotten anything. She dabs a towel across her forehead for the hundredth time, then opens the windows wider and lets more of that rare cool refreshing cross breeze pass through. The comfort is just for a brief moment. The end of the breeze had not come in through the window before Matilda is once again, back and forth, setting out more food, silverware, cups and saucers. It is time for the noonday meal.

Margaret is the first of the family to come in. She is worn out from the heat, panting and fanning herself with her hand, meandering about; trying to get Matilda's attention, but Matilda is too busy to know Margaret is in the room. Margaret clears her throat.

"Good afternoon, Miss Margaret," said Matilda, paying more attention to setting up the table.

Margaret continually moves about the living room, touching things with no intent. She ignores Matilda at first and speaks only when she sees Matilda about to go back to the kitchen.

"Afternoon, Matilda. It's been a beautiful day today, wouldn't you say?

Matilda senses Margaret is playing that childish game with her of hide and seek conversation and as usual, at the wrong time. Matilda, as always, is just too busy to take time out for her. When Margaret was a child she used to play that silly little game. The game meant she wanted Matilda to give her permission to do what her mother had already said she could not. For Matilda, too many years have passed between them for her to stop what she was doing and pay attention to that child. But Matilda also knows, as a slave to this household, she must entertain the thoughts and other mindless dribble that she may be confronted with. She wants to say, "I wouldn't know. I's been in here workin' all mornin'." But she doesn't.

"Yes mam," said Matilda. Matilda pauses at what she is doing and watches Margaret. She is such a pretty young woman, raised in privileged surroundings, but lacking an understanding of human nature. Matilda has an idea as to why Margaret is wandering about, trying to say what she means. However she is not going to help Margaret get to that point, not yet, anyway. She is going to let Margaret stumble along trying to get there all by herself. It will give her time to finish what she has started; mainly having lunch ready by the time everyone else arrives.

"I was just downtown, window shopping and saw the cutest looking dress in the windows of Dubrows. It's the kind of dress you wear for something special."

"Well, dat don't mean nothin' to me, since I ain't got nothin' special to wear somethin' like dat to. 'cuse me Miss Margaret. I forgot somethin'."

Matilda goes to the kitchen and sits in one of the chairs for a moment, waiting to hear Miss Margaret's footsteps on the stairs. She gets up and looks out the window, seeing Charlie Boy and the children playing in their garden. Charlie Boy doesn't move so fast but he can still keep the children on their toes with his sudden jerky movements. She smiles at the children's happiness, impressed by their indifference, as they are oblivious to this misery they are living in. She closes her eyes and suddenly there is water rising out the corners. She quickly dabs them with her apron, then remembering Margaret, she returns to the living room, knowing she has to show respect to Miss Margaret.

"You could wear it to church, Matilda."

"I could wear what, Miss Margaret?"

"The dress I saw today, you know, when you and Jacob go to church.

"God don't be carin' what you wear inside his church, he's mo' interested in what you're wearin' inside your heart."

For what seems to be a long time, no conversation is exchanged between them. The silence was almost unbearable for Margaret. Matilda enjoyed the peace. She also enjoys catching a frustrated Margaret out of the corner of her eye, trying to think of something to say.

"Is there anything I can help you with, Matilda?"

Matilda stops what she is doing and stares at Margaret. Why would she ask something like that? As if Margaret can really help in doing something. And how come she has to ask? She sees all the work that is going on around her, daily. Why not just pick up a broom or a dirty plate or even make up her bed? What is it about the privileged class that they cannot conceive what work is all about? Why do they have to ask if there is anything they can do to help? Problem is there just isn't enough serious worry in her life. What she got to worry about? What her new dress will look like or what time to get out of bed in the morning? What will she wear to the Annual ball? Margaret doesn't want to help; she has other needs right now: needs that require her to be near Matilda. Matilda could ask her to help in doing something, but the task itself would be so menial, that when it doesn't get done, it will not matter. So she wants something else and Matilda thinks she knows exactly what it is. "Miss, Margaret, what you want?"

"What makes you think I want something, Matilda?"

"Because you walkin' around here like a chicken cluckin' for food, scratchin' the ground, hopin' to find somethin', but not carin' if you do or not. So, you must want somethin'." Matilda moves to the kitchen door, pausing before pushing the door open, "Now, I know you're lookin' for Jacob."

Margaret chases Matilda into the kitchen.

"Not so loud, Matilda, I don't want mother to hear."

"Miss Mary not here. She went over to see Miss Sampson. She won't be back 'til after lunch. She told me." Matilda leaves the kitchen with a tray of food for the table. She knows that if the food is not on the table when Massa Andrew arrives he will not be a happy man.

"Matilda, where is Jacob?" asks Margaret, following Matilda. "I haven't seen him in over a month."

"Everyday, he been in da fields, den home, dat's all. Massa Andrews wants the fields kept clean for the cotton and corn to grow good. Dat ain't easy work, you know. He very tired when he gits home."

"What does he talk about before he goes to bed? Does he ask about me?"

"Jacob jus' got one thing on his mind. All he talks 'bout is freedom. All, all us slaves are talkin' 'bout is freedom. The Union Armies up North is gonna free us."

"Where are you hearing that nonsense, Matilda?"

"Dat's what we hearin' from da other farms and plantations. No mo' slave massas. We gonna be free when dis was is over." Matilda straightens her back as she speaks; holds her head high and speaks with a joyful glint in her eyes.

"But Matilda, don't we treat you right?"

Matilda pauses and stares at Margaret again. She wonders, how you treat slaves right? How you enslave someone den treat him or her with dignity and respect? How you look a slave in the eyes and not see how you are treatin' dem? How you just sit and watch a slave doin' the dirty work you should be doin'? How you make demands on a slave, knowin' you hold above dere head their fate in the form of a bullwhip? How you buy another human being like you buy a loaf of bread? How you show such indifference, when you hear da children cryin', beggin', wailing, weepin' and clingin' to the parent dat is about to be sold away from da family unit? Matilda wants to ask Margaret these questions, but realizes she don't have sense enough to under-stand, even with all that high priced private schooling. "Oh yes mam, Miss Margaret, you treats us jus' fine."

"Well, why do you want to be free if Papa treats you right? He provides you a place to stay, sleep and food for you to eat. He doesn't beat you like they do on other plantations.

"Massa Andrew can be very kind to me, but he can be evil

somethin' awful to da rest of the slaves, 'specially da ones dat work da fields."

"Papa's got to be that way because he wants to hold onto what he's got and in order for that to happen, he's gotta sometimes force the workers to produce more. If the slaves don't produce, Papa will lose everything, including you. Then what you gonna do?"

Matilda looks out the window and sees Massa Andrew and his sons coming in from the fields for lunch. She knows for the next hour or so she will have to cater to all their needs. Everyday it's the same. She heads back to the kitchen to get the hot food on the table before they come inside, but pauses at the kitchen door, "What I'm gonna do if I'm free, anything I wants."

* * * * * * * * *

Jacob deliberately urges his black mare around the edge of the cotton field, blowing his whistle. It is hot, damn hot. He holds the reins, wipes his brow and watches the slaves in the fields begin to leave, carrying their hoes, baskets and picks with them. The whistle is his signal to all the slaves; mid-day meal is being served in the shade of the woods. The reddish-orange ball of the morning was now a white ball of fire in the sky hanging stationery over Jacob's head, torturing him. He's uncomfortable. The heat from the leather saddle beneath him boils his thighs and loins. Uncontrollable funky sweat drips from his body. He hates with a strong passion the blistering summer heat of Louisiana. There is a drifting cool breeze somewhere to be appreciated, but it's not upon this black mare. He stays upon his mare recognizing and counting the men and women who stagger into the shady grove designated as the meeting place. They are all accounted for. Some collapse immediately in the shade, others slowly walk to Mama Sarah and weakly create a crooked line, waiting their turn. Mama Sarah stands in the middle of the shaded grove, wooden ladle in hand, waiting for the line to form. A pot of possum stew rests at her feet surrounded by wooden bowls, containing chunks of bread. One by one they slowly come forward, pick up a bowl, nod their head in thanks, and then find a place in the shade to sit, eat, and rest.

Jacob guides the mare to the lake and dismounts at the lake's edge, letting the mare roam free. His friend and confidant, Big Black, is sitting and eating ferociously out of his bowl with his fingers. Jacob was always the last to get something to eat. He knows Mama Sarah will leave him something to dip his bread into. Big Black is the driver in charge when Jacob is not in the fields. He and Big Black were similar yet different in what they wanted out of life. This opposite in mannerism and behavior drew them closer together like magnets. Jacob never knew his father, and Big Black did but for just a short time before he died. He was four or five when he watched him keel over and die while working in the fields. The impact it had on Big Black as a child has stayed with him. The image has taken away any desire to want to be free. On the other hand, Jacob doesn't care who his father was. All he knows is this life of bondage is not for him and everyday the flame is getting hotter with his desire to leave this life of slavery behind. He hopes to show Big Black there is another road to freedom besides dying. From this close friendship, Jacob trusts only Big Black with his inner most thoughts. Big Black is the brother he didn't have. Big Black let Jacob know what is happening at the other plantations from the slave grapevine. Because of his position in the line of authority on the farm, the other slaves do not always trust Jacob. This is just fine with him because of what Jacob intends to do and he doesn't want to take anyone with him.

Jacob pauses and smiles at how quickly Big Black has emptied the wooden bowl, finishing the contents with his fingers. He sits next to him looking at the lake, watching a catfish break the surface of the still water and catch lunch for itself.

"Mama Sarah, sho' knows how to cook up some possum," said Jacob, watching Big Black finish.

"Yes sir, she sho' do," said Big Black. "I knew it was gonna be good when I took it out of da trap. It was big and plump, wit lots of meat."

There is a momentarily, uncanny nervous silence that separates them like a brick wall.

"What does ya hear, Big?" asks Jacob, looking around to see if anyone else is listening.

"You don't wants to do nothin' yet, Jacob," said Big Black, rising and moving towards the lake. "dere's somethin' goin' on somewhere. Too many white folks on da roads at night. Already slaves are runnin' but too many are gittin' caught."

"When I run, I ain't gonna' get caught."

"Dey all sayin' that and dey all gittin' caught."

"When the time is right, I'm leavin' this place."

"What about yo' Mama?"

"I'll tell her jus' befo' I leave, so she don't be worryin' bout it."

"It gonna' break her heart, Jacob."

"If I stays here, it gonna' break mines and hers."

Big Black submerges his gourd into the lake, fills it then drinks from it, letting most of the water spill all over his mouth and down his clothes.

"Dis cool water feel good," he said, dipping the gourd again. "It too hot to work, too hot to sleep, and too hot to run."

"When the weather cools, I'll be ready."

"Didja hear dem hounds last night?" asks Big Black, as the water splashes over his face while he drinks. "Over at da Clanton Plantation, one of dem slave girls did a runner. Dey ain't caught her, yet, but dey gonna look for her 'til dey find her, dead or alive."

"When dey catch her, she's gonna' wish she was dead." Jacob knew what he was saying was so true. It's rough on a man slave who gets caught. The owner usually cut off the toes, or breaks a kneecap or anything that will prevent the runner from ever doing it again. It was not unusual for the runner to experience having the flesh whipped off his back. It's to make an example of him for the other slaves. When they catch a girl slave, she is sometimes gang raped, beaten and then left to die, alone in the woods. It's a sack of woe for both of them.

"She ran 'cause she couldn't take the abuse no more," said Big Black, resting back on his haunches. "You knows how crazy white folks is when it comes to dealin' wit our women. I hear she wants to find out what happened to her brother."

"How she know where he is?" asks Jacob.

"You know dey made Massa Clanton a Colonel in the Confederate Army."

"Dat's what I heard," said Jacob smiling. "Dat man don't know nothin' bout being in the Army let alone being a Colonel."

"Well, when he goes off to war, he takes her brother as a body servant."

"How you gonna' be a servant while the Massa's off fightin?"

"All da massas are doin' it," interrupts Big Black." I think dey make you stand between him and the bullets when dey shootin' at each other."

Jacob looks at Big Black, smiles, and then shakes his head. "You ain't been wearing your hat all da time in this sun, Black. I told you about dat."

Big Black takes off his shoes and submerges his feet into the lake' edge. "Lissen, let me tell you what I heard about Tilda's son. You know he was a runaway too."

"Was?"

"Yup, dey caught him."

* * * * * * * * *

Mama Sarah looks into the kettle, now empty, except for a little pot liquor, rolling around in the black bottom. She pulls a chunk of hard bread from her apron and sops the kettle, then slowly squeezes the liquor from the bread, before she begins to mash the soft texture in her almost toothless mouth, squirting the remaining pot liquor from the bread into her throat. "Dey sure enjoyed it," she said to herself, smiling. That means the kettle will be a lot lighter when she takes it back to the cabin. She carries the kettle to everyone who ate and they drop their bowl into the kettle as she passes. She accepts with pride their compliments and smiles of satisfaction.

She can hear Big Black and Jacob talking about the Clanton girl as she approaches them. What comes to mind is when both of them were born. She can remember when Big Black's father died; he didn't live more than 5 years after he was bought by Massa Andrews. Massa Andrews was real mad because he thought he had bought a healthy slave from the market. She can remember when Matilda had Jacob, alone, because Matilda didn't want to say who the father was. A lot of slave folk think Big Black and Jacob have the same father and neither of them knows it. She can remember when she came to work for Massa Andrew, and her smile becomes larger.

She remembers what life was like for her before she came to Massa Andrews and her heart is broken. Every day she travels down that trail of her past. Trying to find the little good there was and re-evaluate the bad; wanting to chase away the monsters inside her head that constantly come out of their dark caverns to keep her company.

"You sho' do cook good possum, Mama Sarah," she hears Big Black say, as she accepts his clunking bowl into the kettle.

It is the same clunking sound that Mama Sarah heard many, many years ago of an overseer kicking open the door to the slave quarters she shared as a child with her mother, father, brother and another family of four. She and her family were required to be in the cotton field as soon as it was light. There was no such thing as taking a break or a rest in the middle of the day. Most times there was no stopping for dinner. Some nights she ended on the back of her father as he and her mother trudged back to the slave quarters to begin and complete another set of chores. Her chore was to gather kindling so a fire could be started before everyone went to sleep.

Mama Sarah finishes rinsing the bowls in the lake and starts her trek to her slave quarters. There is so much more food to eat now. There was a time when all that was allowed was corn and cold bacon. Weekly allowances for grownups were three and a half pounds of bacon, and a small parcel of corn. For ten years she lived that pattern of life, and in those ten years she saw her best friend, and her first love, sold off the farm to pay debts. This is how she ended up on Massa Andrew's farm. She was final payment for the repair and rebuilding of a barn.

Massa Andrew is a builder. It was his first job by himself after his father died. He looked so young then. He was the first and only free black she had ever seen. She was even more surprised to know he was slave owner; but he's been a good Massa. He's been kind to her. He never beat his slaves. He's been a good Massa.

Mama Sarah pushes open the door to the slave quarters she shares with two other families. Her day is done. Now, she can lay down and let her tired old bones rest awhile; let the moving pain that racks her legs and arms, leave those parts of her body and settle in the small of her back. She closes her eyes and some of that pain rushes to her brain; pain that conjures up images of a child feeding the mules, then the pigs, then over to the corn crib to scavenge for kernels of corn, to be ground later, into corn cakes. Mama Sarah's new pain, wanting more room to roam, pushes water from her eyes in flowing streams. She enjoys the comfort of the bed she rests upon, but suffers the anguish of times past, when all she slept upon was a plank, a tattered cloth for covering and her naked feet reaching for heat before a smoldering fire.

"Oh Lawd, takes me away from here," sings Mama Sarah, "oh Lawd takes me away. Takes me to where da skies are clear, oh Lawd, takes me away. Takes me to where I'll have no fear, oh Lawd, take me away. Takes me to where my Savior is near, oh Lawd, takes me away. Takes me away Lawd, takes me away." Mama Sarah slips into a sleep. Her mind is drifting back into time; back to the pain that never goes away. What is the manor of man, who lives by the laws of God, and still permits man's inhumanity to man? Again she hears the voices of pain, repeating the ordeal; repeating the time, the place and the pain.

* * * * * * * *

"RASHAD! RASHAD!" Mama Sarah hears the screams of her mother, cutting through the heavy blanket of heat in the air, like a serrated knife ripping open flesh. Something was terribly wrong. But Mama Sarah cannot help her; she is too young. "NO MASSA! NO! PLEASE MASSA! RASHAD!" Mama Sarah looks to the other slaves for guidance and help. What should she do? The tobacco plants are too high, the leaves too wide. She cannot see what's going on. All she can do is hear horrifying sounds. She hears her father running through the tobacco fields, the leaves slapping against his body. She can hear his heavy breathing as he runs past her, in a blind rage, to the shrieking sounds of her mother.

"Git yo' black ass back to work, nigger!"

Mama Sarah hears Mister, the overseer yell. She struggles through the fields trying to get to where her parents are, pulling her little brother behind her. She has to see what is going on. The tobacco leafs are so tall and they block every direction she turns. But she keep trying, stopping to pick up her brother who too small to keep up with her. She drags him along, even though he is slowing her down. She remembers what her parents told her about her brother. "Always takes care of him, in case we ain't around to." At this very time in her life when she is torn between her mother and father, she remembers to take care of her brother first.

"HATTIE!"

"I said git back to work, NIGGER!"

Mama Sarah and her brother come out of the field and see her father and Mister, but not her mother. Her father and Mister are yelling at each other. Mister is buttoning his pants. She can hear her mother crying somewhere else, and then she hears her little brother crying near by.

"YOU SONOFABITCH!"

"NIGGER, YOU CAN'T TALK TO A WHITE MAN LIKE THAT!"

"RASHAD! RASHAD!"

"I'LL KILL YOU FOR WHAT YOU DID!"

"RASHAD, NO! IT'S OKAY. RASHAD! RASHAD! DON'T DO IT!"

Mama Sarah is surprised at what she sees next. Her father raises his arm and brings his hardened, tightly balled, black fist down onto Mister, striking him just below his right eye. Before Mister's body hits the ground, there is blood all over his face. By now, all of the other slaves have stopped working to see what has happened. When Mama Sarah's father hit Mister there were gasps of disbelief that echoed, at the same time, from all the slaves.

Mister is on the ground for what seems to be a mighty long time. Mama Sarah sees her mother getting up, pulling her clothes together, and brushing leaves and dirt off of herself. Her father holds her really close and said something into her ear. He then comes to Mama Sarah, gathers her and her brother into his arms kisses their foreheads and after putting them down, takes off running, into the woods.

Mama Sarah didn't see her father again for another two weeks.

She heard other slaves talk about how he had run away and how every white man in the county was looking for him. She heard how the law of the land said, "If a nigger has struck a white man, he shall be given one hundred stripes and his right ear nailed to the whipping post, and then severed from the body." The next time Mama Sarah sees her father, his back is dripping with blood, the right side of his head bloodied from a large knife wound. She hears her mother weeping, her brother crying and her own tears flow like a river gone wild. But before her father is strong enough to walk again, her brother is sold off the plantation, then her mother, and then herself. She is never to see her father, her mother or her brother again. She is never to have a peaceful venture into restful sleep again.

"Mama Sarah, Mama Sarah!" The tiny voice of a slave child comes through the door first, then the child. "Mama Sarah come see how good we done in de garden. Come see, please." The child gently shakes Mama Sarah.

Mama Sarah smiles into face of the child, wiping from her eyes some lingering water. She rises, pulls on a light shoulder wrap and slowly walks behind the child, running excitedly before her. "Hey everybody, here she come! Here she come!"

CHAPTER 6
Saturday, September 14th, 1861

After a night of drinking, gambling and the pleasures of Monique, Andy is always left off at the beginning of the driveway leading to his home. There is a two-fold reason for this. One, he wishes not to disturb anyone in the family with the sounds of the horse and carriage. Two, he enjoys the ultimate pleasure of walking his driveway and seeing all that one day will be his. He knows and understands he will have to share some of it with Pierre, but by the nature of Pierre's own wishes he will not participate in the running of the farm. Not as long as slaves are working the farm and Andy has no intention of doing away with the slaves.

On this night he proudly stands at the end of his driveway, giddy, silly, and gloriously drunk, smiling. It has been another glorious Saturday evening pleasure. Spirits have filled his mind with happiness, the gambling has filled his pockets with dollars and Monique has drained his body and filled his ego at the same time. The lonely walk to his house is shared with all these memories. He staggers and almost falls in one of the wagon wheel ruts and giggles at his clumsiness. He grabs the fence by the slave garden for balance and security. Onward he moves, hand over hand, giggling to himself.

While leaning against the smokehouse, he wonders if his wobbling legs will take him to the kitchen door. Feeling childish he giggles to himself again. Then something coming out of the woods, walking from the direction of the pond catches his eyes. Struggling to remain perfectly still he watches until he can recognize whom the possible intruder is. He reaches for his pistol. It is not there. His eyes follow the figure to the back door of his house. The closer the stranger gets the more identifiable the person becomes. When the kitchen door opens the light exposes the figure and he realizes it's his sister, Margaret. Where is she coming from? Why is she out so late? After she closes the door leading into the kitchen, Andy straightens himself and staggers towards the same door. As he reaches the door, he hears a door closing behind him. Quickly turning, he sees Jacob coming from the outhouse and is on the steps leading to the slave quarters. Is it coincidence? Andy doesn't know but he wants to make sure.

"Jacob!"

Jacob pauses then turns to see who is calling him. It is Master Andy. He watches Master Andy stagger towards him.

"Step down," demands Andy. He gets directly in the face of Jacob. "What the hell are you doing this late at night?"

"I's comin' from da outhouse, Master Andy."

"Is there anything going on between you and Margaret?" demands Andy. Before Jacob can answer, Andy said, "The quickest way for you to feel the tip of my whip is for me to find out you're lying. Jacob, you are just a slave. You is low life. You're not worthy of Margaret. You're ignorant and you smell to high heaven."

"Is dat all Master Andy?"

"If I hear anything different, your mama will find you been sold off this farm. Poppa will make sure of that. Watch your step, boy."

"Dere is nothin' goin' on wit me and Miss Margaret, Master Andy."

"Shut up, boy. I'm sober enough to thrash the hell out of ya. Don't try and take advantage of me, boy. Do you want to wake your mother to the sounds of a whip cutting up the back of her son?"

Jacob lowers his head and nods no.

"I'm gonna be keeping an eye on you, so watch your step Jacob."

Andy staggers back to the kitchen door under the hateful stare of Jacob and an angry stare of Margaret, from her bedroom window.

* * * * * * * * *

Religion as believed and practiced by slaves was paradoxical. On the one hand, Christianity urged resistance to oppression in the Old Testament. Faith provided spiritual solace, participation with emotional release through worship, the surreptitious development of a black intelligentsia (preachers, ministers, and deacons), and the sense of community in a hostile society. On the other hand, whites employed religion as another method of controlling slaves, and the slaves knew it. [ii]

* * * * * * * * *

In the basement of the First Black Freeman's Church of New Orleans, in a parish just outside the city limits of New Orleans, a meeting is being held. Close to two hundred free black men and their sons attend this meeting. The group consists of the most prominent black families of New Orleans. This is an enterprising group of free blacks, who through their own tenacity, have risen above slavery through inheritance or buying their own freedom. Some are two and three generations away from slavery. They are free blacks who now own a part of the New Orleans' economic pie and in some cases are displacing white labor in the process of getting a piece of that pie.

Andrew sits on the first pew, with his sons, Andy and Pierre. Standing perfectly straight, on a podium, in front of the small crowded auditorium is Dr. Aloysius DuBois. He has a distinctly decorated African hand carved walking stick in his left hand. There is a rustle of noises; feet nervously shuffling back and forth, an undertow of voices in muffled tones intermingle with the musty smell of the basement. All this in anticipating something special is going to happen. Dr. DuBois, a towering, dark skinned man, brings his right hand from behind him and signals the anxious crowd to settle down and quiet themselves. He waits until the room is perfectly quiet and still before speaking. It is when the multitudes of black faces has calmed and are looking at him he begins.

"Did everyone bring their Bible?"

There is a show of raised hands with Bibles.

"Those who did not, get near someone who has one. Can we get someone to watch the outside?"

Two volunteers jump up and run upstairs to the outside.

"I'm sure everyone here is aware why this meeting is necessary. As we all know, Washington has seen fit to overstep its authority and has declared war on the Confederate States. The outcome of this war will indeed impact us regardless of who the winner is. Therefore, we should do whatever is necessary for us to continue the lifestyle we have enjoyed and wish to continue to enjoy, regardless of what others may think. Many of us have achieved what we have because of this current government, in spite of the contradictions and hypocrisies that are built into it. Because of this, I think we all agree we must fight to defend the rights of the Confederate States; and to that end, we are here today to form the Native Guards of New Orleans."

Distracting pebbles suddenly bounce down the stairs, then the hurried feet of the volunteers. Those with Bibles open them and in necessary situations, share them. Taking note of this change in situation, Dr. DuBois sits on the first pew with Andrew and Reverend Duchamp immediately stands and begins preaching loudly.

"The Lord God of Heaven, which took me from my father's house, and from the land of my kindred, and which spake unto me, and that sware unto me, saying, Unto thy seed will I give this land; he shall send his angel before thee, and thou shalt take a wife unto my son from thence."

Reverend Duchamp stopped speaking. There are sounds of many feet coming down the stairs, crushing the gravel. Wearing broken down shoes, on some even less than a shoe, the pace of the visitors is slow and deliberate. There's the sound of rustling clothes that combine with their broken down shoes and it all crashes into the dead silence in the auditorium, shattering the stillness into pieces of sounds.

"Good afternoon, boys," interrupts the leader, his voice echoing a heavy, buckra southern accent. "My name is Major Treeman. Some of you may know me from the Clanton Plantation." Major Treeman looks around at the shades of black faces watching him. No one seems to be intimidated by his presence. "Sorry to barge in on yall, but we was just passin' through and we figured we'd stop and check for that missin' niggra. Seems we heard some noise goin' on in here."

Ten armed men follow Major Treeman into the auditorium; two each, walking slowly, down each side, and two walking down the middle, looking carefully at everyone in the audience. Four remain in the back, guns held in preparation to shoot if necessary.

"Just thought we'd stop in and see what the noise was all about," continues Major Treeman.

When Major Treeman turns his searching eyes to Pierre, Pierre stares back at him with just as much hatred and despising as he sees in the face of Major Treeman. Just who the hell does he think he is, Pierre asks himself, his veins pulsating at his temples. He wants to stand and spit into this face; this unshaven, hairy eyebrows, crooked mouth, missing teeth, and mistake of a face.

"Anybody in here seen that runaway Clanton niggra?"

If there be a God in heaven, why doesn't he strike down these transgressors, wonders Pierre. Because there is no God or heaven, Pierre concludes.

"We gonna' find her, no doubt about that," continues Major Treeman, slowly sashaying about in front of everyone. "Yes sir, we definitely gonna' find her."

An uneasy silence is broken as many of the men on the benches begin changing their seating positions.

"We got the best hounds in the world smellin' her out. She can't get far."

Reverend Duchamp finally speaks. "The only folks in here are us men, planning an outing."

"What's behind that door?"

"That's a storage closet," said Reverend Duchamp, "nothing in there but spare hymnals and some Bibles."

"Well then, if that be the case," said Major Treeman, smiling, "then you won't mind if we just checked it out then, would ya."

Major Treeman signals someone to verify what Reverend Duchamp has said. Two armed men come forward and one slowly opens it, while another readies then aims his rifle. The door is badly in need of some paint and oil. It creaks loudly, as it is slowly pulled open. When it is obvious the closet contains no one, Major Treeman signals to everyone to leave.

"Sorry to have disturbed yall. We'll jus' leave now."

Major Treeman is the last one to start up the stairs. Before leaving he slowly turns to show a smirking smile, then tipping his crumpled hat one more time, he marches upstairs. Moments later one of the watchers come downstairs to indicate every thing is all clear.

"Why would I want to associate in a society with scum like that," demands Pierre, rising and pointing his finger in the direction of the door. "They showed no respect for this church and none for us. They are the very reasons we shouldn't be fighting for the Confederacy. We have slept with the devil so long, we are his!"

"Pierre, sit down," pleads Andrew, pulling on Pierre's clothes.

"I won't sit down," argues Pierre. "Somebody has to stand up to those kinds of human beings!"

"God said he that doeth wrong shall receive for the wrong which he hath done," replies Reverend Duchamp rising from his seat. "And from God there is no respect of those persons."

"I don't have time to hear quotations from the Bible," yells Pierre. "Or wait for God to react! Where was he just now? Has he stepped out for a moment?"

"Sit down Pierre," again demands Andrew, "you have no idea what this is all about."

"I will not sit down and I know exactly what this is all about," demands Pierre, "you've slept with the devil and with this war, you will marry him and it's still wrong, even if you do it in the name of God!"

A few of the other younger members of the congregation rise and applaud, supporting Pierre. Several loud discussions, pro versus con, erupt inside the room. Reverend Duchamp realizes he is losing control. He goes back to the front pew, sits and prays silently. Dr. DuBois rises and stands on the front podium, waiting for everyone to get quiet. When it is obvious no one notices him, he raises his walking stick and drives it into the floor, echoing a sound like a loud shot. The sound freezes everyone. They all turn looking from where the noise came from and notices Dr. DuBois' stoic posture. Some immediately sit. Pierre, and those who agree with him, immediately storms out of the auditorium. Andrew reaches out trying to stop Pierre, but Pierre again tears himself away.

"Leave him be, Papa," said Andy, not hiding his anger. "We don't need him or those who are foolish enough to believe as he does."

"But he is my son," said Andrew softly, "he's family."

Dr. DuBois patiently waits until Pierre and his follower's leave then sits next to Andrew. "Andrew, your son and my son are of the same mind set. We can only hope they eventually understand the good we are trying to achieve." Dr. DuBois and Andrew exchange handshakes and comfort each other before Dr. DuBois returns to the podium.

"I want everyone who has remained to pay attention to what I'm about to read. You will be asked to sign it, if you truly believe in what the Confederacy stands for and what it can do for us as free people of color." Dr. DuBois retrieves a document from the inside pocket of his suit coat. "We, the undersigned, free men of color, natives of Louisiana, assemble in committee, have unanimously adopted the following resolution. Be it resolved, that the population to which we belong, as soon as the Governor of this state makes a call for them, will be ready to take arms and form themselves into companies for the defense of their homes, together with the other inhabitants of this city, against any enemy who may come and disturb its tranquility." [iii]

Dr. DuBois places the document on a table in front of him and is the first to sign it. "Now, is there anyone else who is not satisfied with what our intentions are?" Dr. DuBois looks into the face of everyone in the auditorium, seeing what their eyes say. When he finishes, he goes to the closet that did not contain the Clanton runaway and retrieves a wrapped standard. He slides off the covering and exposes a flag. It is the Confederate flag of stars and bars, trimmed in yellow. "Gentlemen, I give you our first National Flag. Soldiers of the Confederacy, this is the flag we will be fighting under. From this day forward we shall call ourselves, The First Native Guards, Protectors of the Confederacy!"

Andrew is the first to stand and enthusiastically applaud. For a brief moment only his hands can be heard. But quickly Andy rises and joins in and then the rest of the members, until there is a loud thundering cheering noise.

*   *   *   *   *   *   *   *

The deserting group, of about 12 or more young men, gathers at the bottom of the steps leading into the church. They huddle around Marcel, only son of Dr. DuBois, until Pierre comes out. When he appears at the top of the steps, there is loud applause and pats on his back as they congratulate and greet him.

"Well," begins Marcel, "now that that's over and done with, what now?"

"We must continue in our efforts to find the Clanton girl," replies Pierre, in hushed tones."

"But where do we look?" asks someone in the crowd.

"She must still be in the swamps," replies Pierre. "We must maintain our vigil until, hopefully, one of us finds her. If and when that happens, follow the usual procedure and contact only the next person in your chain. Agreed?"

There are nodding heads, agreeing with Pierre, and then all disperse in their separate ways.

Standing back into the thicket of the surrounding woods is Major Treeman and a few members of his intruding party. They watch as Pierre and the others talk, standing perfectly still except to swat agitating mosquitoes and flies. A piece of something dangles from the mouth of the Major Treeman, moving erratically from side to side. He watches Pierre and Marcel closer than the others, suspecting they know more than the others do.

"We got to keep them two under watch," said Treeman, turning away. "Yup, one of them two is gonna lead us to that Clanton niggra girl."

Pierre climbs aboard his quarter horse and begins his ride home. He and Marcel fall in behind several others. After about three miles he and Marcel are alone on the dusty dirt road.

"Do you think she's still alive?" asks Marcel, letting his horse find his way home. "Do you really thinks she's still alive?"

"If she was able to get to the swamps and head North, she is," responds Pierre.

"Shame we didn't know about her before she ran. We might have been able to help her."

"It's hard to get enslaved blacks to trust other free blacks since free blacks have chosen to become slave masters."

Pierre's attention is suddenly drawn away from the conversation. He sees something out of the corner of his eye. He raises a finger to his lips and begins looking around.

"What is it?" asks Marcel.

Pierre doesn't say anything, but instead points to their left, about 50 yards through the thicket, a rider moves parallel with them. Pierre recognizes the rider. He is Major Treeman, the leader of the group of men, who entered the church, looking for the Clanton girl. A rifle is resting comfortably in his arms pointing in the direction of Pierre and Marcel. He is not looking directly at Pierre or Marcel, just riding parallel to them, head drooping, as if he is sleeping.

"Now, what do you suppose he wants," comments Pierre.

"Do you think he knows about us," asks Marcel, quietly.

"I don't think so," said Pierre.

They are at a point in the road where to the left will take Pierre home and to the right will take Marcel back to New Orleans, his father's doctor office and home.

"I will be at Congo Square on Sunday at the usual time," said Marcel, as he drifts to the right.

"I will be there," said Pierre, reaching out and shaking Marcel's hand. "Keep your eyes and ears open."

The sun is beginning to drop behind the canopy of bald cypress trees. Pierre is feeling hungry. He knows Andy and his father will be coming home later this evening, probably after dinner. The road twists and turns in front of him, snaking itself along the edge of the bayou. The creatures and critters of the night will soon be waking from their all day slumber; waking to begin their search for food; extending themselves in a life and death struggle in order to have another day of life. Pierre admires the beauty of the Spanish moss hanging delicately on fingered limbs of cypress trees. He can smell the sweetness of wild azaleas; he can hear the sound of water break-

ing. Was that the snapping sounds of alligators or is it catfish breaking the mirror glass of still water? Or maybe it was a black bear just
trying to catch a meal. Pierre watches the last glimpses of the orange sun setting behind the cypress and cottonwood trees, raising a
curtain of eerie shadows. The bayou is dressing itself up before coming out and becoming the dark foreboding place in character that it
does nightly. It is telling all who may want to venture in, come in if
your dare, otherwise, no trespassing.

The horse Pierre is riding turns onto the driveway leading to
his home. The horse has made this journey so many times it moves
deliberately, without assistance from Pierre. By the time they are
approaching the barn, old slave Charlie Boy is waiting.

"Welcome home, Master Pierre."

Pierre climbs down while Charlie Boy holds the reins. "Good
evening Charlie Boy."

"Master Pierre, I's needs to show you somethin'."

"What is it Charlie Boy, I'm hungry and tired."

Charlie Boy slowly walks to the slave garden. Pierre follows.
He stops along the makeshift fence of large tree limbs and dried
bushes.

"See, right chere," said Charlie Boy, pointing at something on
the ground.

Pierre looks but is not sure what he is supposed to see. "What
am I looking at, Charlie Boy?" asks Pierre, still looking. "All I see are
vegetables."

"Yes sir, da vegetibles," said Charlie Boy. "Someone's been
harvestin' the vegetibles early."

"Maybe it's one of the children."

"Dey knows better. See, here, and here and over dere."

Pierre looks and notices there has been a deliberate taking,
without destroying the existing plants. The thief is not an animal.

"How long has this been happening?"

"A couple of days."

Pierre looks at the barn. Up near the loft he thought he saw an
eye peeking out from between the boards. "Have you spoken to anyone else about this, Charlie Boy?"

"No suh Master Pierre," said Charlie Boy.

"Do not talk to anyone else about this, do you understand?"

"Yes suh, I does," replies Charlie Boy.

"Not even my father and especially Andy," said Pierre, looking directly into the face of Charlie Boy.

"Yes suh, I's unnerstand," said Charlie Boy

Pierre has an idea he knows who's been harvesting the vegetables early. He experiences a sudden swell of excitement. His heart begins beating faster. His palms and forehead are feeling damp.

"Charlie Boy, I'll put away my horse. You go and finish your other chores."

Pierre grabs the reins from Charlie Boy and walks back towards the barn. He checks several times to be sure Charlie Boy is walking away from him as he slowly leads his horse into the barn. Walking to one of the three stalls, Pierre listens for sounds other than his feet and that of the horse. It is while he unbridles and removes the saddle Pierre realizes he is being watched. He notices the door to one of the storage bins is ajar. He finishes undressing the horse and after finding a place for the saddle, he closes the door to the cabinet, but not before noticing some of the clothing has been disturbed.

Above his head he hears hay cracking. It has to be the Clanton runaway, but he doesn't want to frighten her any more than she is. He returns to the stall where his horse is and begins brushing him down.

"Listen carefully," begins Pierre, speaking very calmly, "because I can only say this once. Before you go into some sort of panic I want you to know I'm your friend. I have no intention of turning you in or harming you. I can get you out of here, up North, to Canada. You must believe that. It is very important that you believe that. You must be hungry. I will somehow get some food to you. My father and brother will be coming in here later, but do not let them know you are here. I know who you are and where you came from. My father or brother, they will definitely return you to the Clanton place, so wait until I return. Now, do not go into the slave's garden and steal any more food. It will only bring attention to something going on that should not be. My name is Pierre and I'll be back later tonight."

The barn door suddenly opens.

"Who you talkin' to, Master Pierre?" asks Charlie Boy, leading two horses into the barn.

"Nobody, Charlie Boy, nobody," responds Pierre, quickly finishing his brushing down of his horse. "Sometimes you just like to hear what you are thinking and you say things out loud."

"I knows whatcha' mean dere, Master Pierre," said Charlie Boy pulling the horses into their stalls. "Massa Andrew and Master Andy just come home. Dey done went inside."

"Thanks for telling me, Charlie Boy," said Pierre, looking around, trying to see if someone is truly in the barn, and wondering if he, indeed, was just talking to himself.

* * * * * *

Matilda is finishing her setting of the dinner table when Andrew and Andy come in. Mary and Margaret are coming down the stairs.

"Hello Papa, hello Andy," said Margaret.

Andrew goes to Mary and kisses her on her cheek. She smiles and squeezes his hand but said nothing. Andrew opens the newspaper and begins to read.

"Hello Mama, hello Margaret," said Andy, following Andrew to the living room. He is carrying the Confederate flag, sheathed.

"See Andy, it said so right here," begins Andrew. "Free blacks are volunteering all over the south for the opportunity to help the south win this war. In Richmond Virginia, 60 free blacks volunteered their services. Yes sir, we are in this war! Mary, can you believe this?"

Mary looks at Andrew and feigns a half-hearted smile. She sits at one end of the table, quietly waiting for everyone else to come to the table. Margaret finds her place to her mother's right.

"In Charleston, South Carolina, hundreds of free blacks offer their services in any capacity needed by the governor." Andrew can hardly contain his excitement. "Several hundred free blacks in Norfolk, Virginia, volunteer to work on Confederate fortification and gun battery positions. That was a good meeting, Andy. What we did was right."

"How about Pierre," said Andy, sitting at the table. "I was embarrassed when he walked out with the rest of the dissenters."

Mary listens to the conversation and wonders if she should contribute. How should she contribute? She is wondering if she should object to what she is hearing; wondering if she should speak out against the war. She folds her hands in her lap, then unable to contain herself, she rests them on the table, her fingers lightly tapping the tablecloth. She responds to the conversations with her eyes, letting them say all that she cannot, knowing no one is listening to her. Andrew heard her on two occasions when he looked into her face for support, but he chose not to answer her, not now anyway.

"All of them will come around when they see what the rest of the free blacks are doing." Andrew takes his place at the head of the table. "As soon as they see us in uniform, marching the street, he'll come around and so will the rest of them."

"You're going to wear uniforms?" asks Margaret.

"We're in an army, Margaret," said Andy. "Members of armies wear uniforms."

"When will we see them," asks an excited Margaret.

Andrew looks at Mary. "Actually that will depend on mother and how long it takes for you and her to make them."

Mary looks at the sudden childlike features on the face of Andrew. He looks like a little boy caught with his fingers in the cookie jar. He is looking at the tablecloth, playing with the silverware. She didn't say anything, instead, nodding in agreement when Matilda brought her tea. She knew she was going to make the uniforms, even though she hated the very reason they needed them.

"Where have you and Andy been, Papa? And where is Pierre?"

"Matilda, I'll have some sherry," said Andrew, covering his coffee cup with his hand. "We've just come from a meeting with most if not all of the free blacks of New Orleans. We have formed a supporting militia group."

"We, the hommes de couleur libre of Louisiana, have formed the Native Guards," said Andy, toasting the occasion.

"Matilda," interrupts Mary, agitated by the conversation, "we're not going to wait for Pierre."

"Yes, Miss Mary."

"Native Guards," questions Margaret, "why are free men of color calling themselves natives?"

"As free people of color," begins Andrew, "we are native to this land; we are original free blacks of New Orleans. We are not immigrants. You children are the third generation of St. Claire's. This land is ours, and we must guard it to make sure outsiders from within this state or from Washington do not take it away, either.

"You'll see us marching in parades," interrupts Andy, "wearing the Confederate uniform; we'll have a separate unit, but we will all march together as free men."

"Everything is on the table, Miss Mary," said Matilda, placing a plate piled high with biscuits on the table.

"Thank-you Matilda that will be all."

Mary reaches out her hands and holds Margaret's and Andy's. Andy holds Andrew's and Andrew holds Margaret's to complete the circle. They bow their heads and listen to Andrew.

"Oh Lord, we come to you again, thanking you for the blessing bestowed upon us today and ask that you continue blessing us tomorrow. Bless this food we're about to receive for the nourishment of our bodies and bless the hands that have prepared it. We ask these things in your name and for your sake. Amen."

"Why did Pierre walk out of the meeting," asks Margaret.

"Him and his abolitionist friends didn't want to fight for the Confederacy," explains Andy. "Seems they have a conflict fighting for a system that supports slavery. They want to destroy what we free blacks have accomplished and eliminate what has made our style of life possible."

"Son, pass me one of them biscuits," said Andrew, "I'm not about to let go of everything my father fought for when he fought with Andrew Jackson, back in '15'. Pierre doesn't understand what it took to get to this point in my life; maybe he'll understand when this war is over and the Confederacy has won. Margaret put some butter on this for me, thank you. Maybe then he'll come to his senses."

Mary continues to eat silently, smiling politely when she's face to face with someone at the table. She sees the excitement in Andy's eyes and understands the confusion Margaret is experiencing. She hears the determination in Andrew's voice. She feels her home sweet home is about to come to a thundering end, helped along with nothing but heartache. And it's all because of this war, this stupid little men's war.

"Papa, what about the Yankees capturing New Orleans?" asks Margaret.

"They got to get up the Mississippi first," said Andrew, "and that ain't gonna be easy."

"We discussed that at the meeting," interrupted Andy. "New Orleans is too important of a city for the South to lose."

"This is the largest city in the Confederacy," said Andrew. "And the richest. Its seaport exports more of the southern economy than any other seaport in the South. The Confederacy will defend this city to the last man!" Andrew finishes the remainder of his glass. "Too much southern produce is leaving the South through these piers. Matilda, bring me some more sherry!"

"Be careful with the sherry," warns Mary, "you know what Dr. DuBois said."

Matilda comes from the kitchen and hurries to the china closet and removes another bottle of sherry, bringing it quickly to Massa Andrews.

"What Dr. DuBois said," said Andrew defiantly, "is too much sherry will cause me problems, not two glasses. Set it down right here, Matilda."

"Yes Massa Andrew."

"Margaret, before they even get to us," boasts Andy, "they have to pass Fort Jackson, then Fort St. Phillip. Those two forts will sandwich any Union gunboat or steamer that tries to run against the current of the Mississippi."

"And you know something else Andy," said Andrew pouring himself and Andy some sherry, "we got a couple thousand men in each of those forts; sharp shooters everyone. Shoot straighter than the sun settin' due west. No way any blue coat's ship going to get by those forts, no sir." Andrew raises his glass to toast with Andy, they laugh together, and then they both drink. "Ah, but that's good sherry. Yes sir, we're about to win us a war!"

Matilda comes from the kitchen and begins to clear some of the dishes away. Not far behind her comes Pierre.

"Pierre," exclaims Margaret, "where have you been, dinner is almost over?"

With all eyes upon him, Pierre continues through the dining room and walks towards the stairs.

"Where are you going, son?" demands Andrew.

"Upstairs."

"Pierre," said Mary, "come, sit and have some dinner. Matilda don't start clearing just yet."

"Where have you been?" demands Andrew.

"Walking, just walking."

"With your abolitionist friends?" chides Andy.

"That's none of your damn business!" yells Pierre.

"Show some respect for your mother and sister, Pierre," reprimands Andrew.

"Matilda is in the room too. Shouldn't she be included?"

"I make the laws of respect in this house, Pierre," said Andrew, rising from his chair, "and right now you need to show me some respect."

"This must have been a wonderful evening," said Pierre. "Look at all of you. All sitting around the dinner table talking about death and maiming, all for the cause of perpetuating slavery."

"Pierre, when you walked out of that meeting you insulted the family name as well as insulting all the free blacks committed to the state of Louisiana and the Confederacy." Andrew moves away from the table and stands near a chair in the living room. "You and all of your misguided friends are trying to disrupt and set back the progress that our forefathers gained before us. You and your freedom fighters want to have us all free or none of us will be free. What kind of sense is that? If we all can't live in the house, burn the house down? Now none of us have a place to live!"

Mary hated to hear this kind of conversation within the family. Even when Pierre was young, he always use to question why Andrew had slaves. With the private education he received he learned early about slavery and the affect it has on the individual as well as the affect it has on the slave owner. He never understood the need for slave labor to help maintain the farm. He never understood why we as free people of color could enslave our own. Andrew always tried to explain to Pierre it's business, strictly business, but Pierre never could understand its meaning.

"But you're not free!" yells Pierre. "We're not free!"

"You better lower your voice when you speak to Papa!" screams Andy, leaving his chair and charging Pierre. "I'm not going to let you disrespect Papa!"

"Andy! Pierre!" screams Margaret, standing between them. "You two seem to have missed the point of who's fighting who. It should not be brother against brother!"

Andrew leans on the back of the chair for support. It's that strange kind of pain again inside his chest. It comes and goes. Lately when it happens if Andrew stops what he's doing then breathes deeply, like he is doing now, the pain goes away.

Mary sees what is happening to Andrew and immediately goes to him to assist him to a chair. Her bickering children continue their back and forth gibberish of he said, she said conversation, and are blind to what is happening to their father. She gently lifts Andrew's elbow and guides him to the chair. He sits and smiles in appreciation.

Pierre begins explaining how the governor along with the legislature have agreed not to pass any more restrictive legislation on the free blacks of Louisiana as a result of the commitment of the free blacks and some slaves to the Confederate cause. All of this is considered poppycock according to Pierre because, "The governor is doing what is politically necessary, not morally correct," said Pierre. "The Confederacy has no intention of permitting free blacks to fight in this war!"

"You got too much education in your brain, and it is blinding you to the cause of why we free blacks of New Orleans are so successful." Andrew pauses to catch his breath before continuing. "Now, what the governor did would not have been possible if we, as a people, chose to sit on the sidelines, uncommitted. When you have a taste of freedom, in order to keep it, you got to commit yourself to something."

"This freedom stings like salt water in a wound," said Pierre.

"Freedom should be sweet and taste like the nectar of a honeysuckle flower."

"Master Pierre," interrupts Matilda, "are you gonna eat something?"

"Pierre you don't understand what your freedom is because you ain't never been a slave. I was," admonishes Andrew, grabbing his chest. He feels a bit dizzy, and his facial expressions cannot hide it.

"What I understand today is we're half slave and half free!"

"Anything is better than being a total slave!" Andrew pounds his fists on the arms of the chair.

"Papa, don't get excited," said Margaret, "remember what Doctor DuBois said."

"I'm fine Margaret!" reprimands Andrew. "Pierre, I'm not about to go back to the days of slavery with promises from Washington that they can do better for me. I've been North and I've seen their 'promised land' and believe me, from the squalor I saw, seeing how the free blacks are living up there, my slaves live better than they do!"

"But they are free, Papa!"

"Master Pierre," interrupts Matilda again, "I can fix you a plate for later if you want."

"Their freedom is as fleeting as the air they breathe." Andrew struggles out of the chair to his feet. He is somewhat stable leaning on the chair for support. "Their freedom is only on paper, not social acceptance! We now have an opportunity to have both!"

It has jus been within the last year that Andrew began experiencing these pains in his chest, and this worries Mary more and more each day. Dr. DuBois listens to his heart each time he visits, then tells Andrew to cut back on his eating, drinking and smoking. He tells him take long walks for exercise, and keep the excitement down, but Andrew has managed to follow just one suggestion, and that is just a short jaunt to the end of the driveway and back. He gave Andrew a different kind of medicine, one that gives him a false sense of feeling better, while at the same time it does nothing to improve his health.

"Listen to what Papa is saying Pierre," pleads Andy. "Don't be so damn hardheaded."

"Blacks automatically get the promise of freedom, just for com-

ing north," said Andrew. "You would think they are giving away freedom like it was some sort of dry goods. Freedom is not free in the
Confederacy or anywhere up North. There is a price to be paid for
freedom, even up North. The only ones who don't know that are the
ones escaping to the North for a sense of freedom."

"At least their sense of freedom has direction," said Pierre.

"Imagination, that's all them escaping Negroes got, is imagination," said Andrew. "If they worked as hard as their imagination does,
most of them wouldn't be in the position they now occupy. The
South is going through an industrial revolution and I want to be part
of it. Slavery will not last forever, but while its here, we must make
the best of it."

"And it will get better here, for people of color, before up North,"
agrees Andy.

"How about you Miss Mary, would you like some tea," said
Matilda, giving up on serving Pierre.

"Matilda, I need some of my medicine," sighs Mary, rubbing
her forehead.

"Yes mam, I'll go upstairs and get some of your medicine," said
Matilda.

Andrew rises from the chair and moves closer to Pierre, with
Andy close by. He has something to say to Pierre and did not want to
be interrupted. "How Black folks gonna find a place to live when
Northern states including Mr. Lincoln's very own Illinois, are passing "*Black Laws*" to exclude and discourage free blacks from settling
within their state borders. Slaves don't escape to freedom when
they run north. They escape to unemployment, homelessness, lies
and deceptions, separated living, no socialization and poor housing.
They ain't much different than a lazy no count field nigger. White
folks got whole plantations of free blacks living like slaves up north.
In Philadelphia they got social organizations that feel so guilty about
how black folks live they give the free blacks money to live off of
until they can find work. It's a worst form of subjugation and ain't
none of their free blacks figured it out yet! Nowhere in America
does a free black have as much freedom as he does in Louisiana! No
where!"

For a few moments there was a great silence in the room, except for Matilda shuffling about. So great wads the silence, that coming from the outside one could hear the wind lightly blowing, the birds in the trees, the children playing, and the slave quarter's door open and close. From inside, one could hear the clock ticking, the house creaking, nervous feet shuffling, and everyone's eyes turning in the direction of Pierre.

Pierre first looks at his father, then Andy, then Margaret and Mary. He sees in their faces how hopeless it would be to respond. All their expressions say, "Just sit quietly and let your father's word stand, unchallenged. Andrew has spoken. He is law." But there was something inside Pierre, deep down that kept bubbling up. It was pushing out the truth that he saw, even if no one else did. This land of the free is free only for those who are white. It is what he is convinced of and no one can tell him any different. He cannot just sit quietly and let his father's words stand unchallenged. Looking each member of his family in the eyes he said, "And no where in America are the free blacks kept in place by so many hidden chains!"

"Pierre, you are out of place when you contradict Papa," yells Andy. "He's been there, you ain't!"

Pierre is having nothing to do with believing he is out of place with his father. Rather, he is trying to bring his father and brother into the main stream of what tomorrow will be. He is not sure but he knows, in his heart, the Confederacy will not deliver what free blacks expect. They will deliver only what the enslaved already know about. It is a choice between the lesser of two evils; the evil and deceitful whites of the Confederacy or the evil and deceitful free blacks of the South. "We are living a contradiction within this Confederacy!"

Matilda goes about her business, bobbing and weaving in and out and in between the conversations like the wind, invisible to everyone but they always know of her presence. Lately she's wondered why this family argues so much? Since this outbreak of war, everybody is upset about something. Matilda is sure this war is about more than slavery. White folks don't be fighting each other unless it has to do with money or someone has insulted somebody's wife or daughter or sister. And now black folks have risen to that level of logic. She laughs inside each time she hears them going at each other. It's always amazing to her how she can continue to move in between their conversations, in between their behaviors, in between their moving bodies and not be noticed. It's even more amazing how each family member will leave their conversation long enough to take advantage of Matilda then return without so much of an acknowledgement.

"Miss Margaret, would you like some tea also," asks Matilda. "I'll just set it down over here, in case you do. Did you hear me, Miss Margaret?"

"Papa, I cannot fight for a system of government that keeps some of our people in chains."

"My brother, at least you can see the chains down here" said Andy. "And you can see how the chains can be broken. We are in a city of prominent, prosperous free blacks that have generations of freedom. Up North, the chains are invisible to the eyes of them free Negroes. They don't even know they are still fettered; and you can't free yourself from what you can't see."

Andrew listens to Pierre and Andy debate and disagree with each other. He wonders if he is seeing the beginning of the demise of his family. The Confederacy is standing at another 'Y' in the road of its creation. The choice it makes will determine its future and the future of generations of sons and daughters that follow. It has chosen to break from Washington, which can be used to their advantage if the governing bodies of the Confederacy don't make the same mistakes made in Washington under Lincoln and every president before him. This can be a glorious time for free blacks and whites in the Confederacy if we all work together for the common good of the Confederacy. Pierre doesn't understand slavery as to why it is necessary for the success of this farm. He only understands it from the humanity side, which shows it as something ugly. The ugliness is from individuals not from the very system itself. Everyone is a slave to something. There ain't nothing Pierre can get up North that will make him feel any better about what mankind does to mankind. God gave man dominion over all things that live on the earth and sometimes that dominion includes man himself.

"Son, your life stands a better chance of being something more than just a slave to the system in New Orleans, than in Philadelphia." Andrew sits next to Mary, seeing how this conversation has affected her. He looks into her troubled eyes and smiles, gently holding her hands. "Pierre, if Lincoln's Yankees win this war, free blacks, all over America, North and South, will be doomed for the next two hundred years or more. And I'm not about to let that happen to this family."

"Master Pierre, I'm fixin' to clear the table," mumbles Matilda, separating some food and leaving it on the plate. "I'll leave a plate for you with some food on it."

"Andy bring me our flag," said Andrew. He takes off the cover and lets it unfurl. It falls across him. He holds it close, gently clutching it. "Right now, them Stars and Stripes of Washington mean nothing to me. This is now my cloak of freedom. This is now my protector. This is now my benefactor. I fight for the Confederacy so I can remain free to do what I'm doing now; so you, Margaret and Andy can have more than what we have, after we're both gone. I'm not as free as I want to be, but I'm freer than a slave and most northern free Negroes. You may not understand now Pierre, but one day you will. What I do, I do for God, Country and the Confederacy!"

CHAPTER 7
Tuesday, October 1ˢᵗ, 1861

Slave families were understandably unstable because of the nature of the Confederacy's *peculiar institution*. A master could sell members of a family for the slightest of infraction by a slave or if the master found increase value as a result. Somehow despite this hanging above the slave's head, like the sword of Damocles, the family unit remained intact and continued to evolve because of the role played out by the women, primarily the mothers. They were the driving force in maintaining stability in the master's home as well as their own. Masters did not care about the delicate nature of the female slave in the fields, but within the slave community it was recognized and the differentiation was promoted. The men did the trapping and hunting of animals for food while the women did the domestic chores that added more work to the slave women's day. The family unit was important to the slave mother and she did what ever it took to keep them together. It could mean, if she worked in the big house against her will, she would be disruptive enough to be sent to the fields to be with the rest of her family. Or, if she were able, she would get pregnant. The master loved to see his female slaves as baby makers. To be able to increase his ownership of slaves thus increasing his labor force, without additional cost made a master proud of his slaves. The master refrained from trading or selling fertile women.

Women slaves became the ones in charge within their families; even to a point of turning non-aggressive husbands into rebellious slaves against the master. They taught their children to sew or do household chores that were necessary to have in order to be useful to the master. Older women passed on the art of herbal medicine for aches and pains. Women did all of this to keep their families together and healthy and on occasion helped a runaway, even if it were her own, to get started or continue his or her run to freedom.

* * * * * * * * *

Early in the morning, before the sun rises, before the crickets have stopped their mating calls one can hear it. It is the sound that weaves through the swamps before the dew has dropped from the spider webs, before the first leaping fish breaks the high gloss finish of still water gulping their breakfast. It is the alarm that notifies the bullfrogs to say their good byes for the rest of the day. It is a soft deep French horn like sound that floats across the bogs, the swamp, bobbing and weaving between the bald cypress, getting tangled in the Spanish moss. It is the conch horn, waking the slave population.

A wafer thin line of blue smoke twists and turns it way from the slave dwelling's chimney, rising then falling because of the weighty air. The morning air is warm and heavy. It doesn't move; instead it wraps itself around those who move into it. It's four thirty am and Andrew St. Claire's slaves are beginning their day. Matilda is about to go to the big house. Lately, Matilda is concerned about the stories she is hearing about runaway slaves. She knows Jacob is feeling restless and constantly asks him about whether she will see him after spending a day in the field. Again she has asked the same question while they stand in front of their slave quarters, watching the others prepare for the day's work. As always Jacob responds with a big smile on his chocolate face, " Mama, you knows you will. Why you keep askin' me dat?" Jacob checks each slave as they leave to ensure they are prepared to work. "Hey Lonny, where you goin'? Wait 'til everybody's ready and where's yo' brother?"

She again reminds him about what she has been hearing and what happens to them when they get caught. She looks him in the eyes and explains she doesn't want to hear about him running and then being caught. She squeezes his big rough hands, callused with dried blisters. His hands should be softer, she wishes. His clothes should be something other than this drab loose fitting homespun.

"If I run Mama, dey ain't gonna ketch me."

"Dat's what Tilda's son Isaac, over on the McClain's plantation said when he run," begins Matilda. "Told his Mama, "dey ain't gonna' ketch me," but dey did. Dey brought him back in chains, his back so cut up you could see bone. Den dey made him watch while dey put the whip to his Mama. All her children were dere. All her grandchil'en were dere. All her sisters and brothers were dere, watchin' and cryin' and prayin' she would just die so they would stop whippin' on her. Isaac couldn't do nothin' but crawl over to where she was tied and just as he got to her, the overseer would pull him back."

"Mama, dat ain't gonna happen to us 'cause when I run, it will be to the Union lines. Hold on a minute Mama. Samuel, where is dat rake I saw you wit yesterday? Don't give me dat I-don't-know-look, find it!"

Where did he git da idea dere are Northern Armies in da area, ponders Matilda. Matilda ain't heard nothin' of the sort. All she know about dis war is dey is still fightin' up near Washington. He been listenin' to what is going through da slave grapevine, and lately dat ain't been as reliable as befo' da war started. It's somethin' different to be in da big house and hear directly what white folks are sayin', but dey don't know no more den anybody else about da war. News about da war is hard to come by and in most cases it's wrong. Jacob been listenin' to rumors. "Dere ain't no blue coats anywhere near here."

"But dere will be," said Jacob, his eyes suddenly showing a glimmer of hope that will free him from these dismal surroundings. "Dey comin' just as sure as the seasons of the year; and when you hear dat I done run, you'll know da Union armies are not far."

Matilda didn't want to hear that Jacob had run. She wants to know before he leaves. She suddenly grabs Jacob tightly, as if he was drifting from her like a kerchief accidentally dropped in the wind, and holds him close. "Massa Andrew say the Yankees ain't strong enough to win no war 'ginst the Confederacy," said Matilda, her voice trailing off. "I hear him talkin' 'bout a place called Manasas and how the Confederates whupped the Unions armies somethin' awful. Jacob, Massa Andrew say white folks came out and watched the battle from hilltops, like it was a picnic or somethin'. Imagine dat, white folk bringin' picnic baskets, den sittin' to eat just to watch somebody kill somebody. What dis world comin' to?"

"Dis world as we know it is comin' to freedom," said Jacob. "Free blacks up North are beggin' for the chance to fight with the blue coats, just so dey can come down here and free da rest of us. Slaves been runnin' north, joinin' up with da blue coats, who den pay dem to be scouts. Da slaves help da blue coats learn dey way around da woods and swamps."

"Do you think Massa Andrew gonna whup me if you run?" asks Matilda, still holding onto Jacob.

"Miss Mary ain't gonna let Massa Andrew whup nobody. In all my years growing up here, I ain't ever seen Massa Andrew put da whip on nobody. Now, dat Andy, he different. He almost looks white and he startin' to act like it too."

"Dis war is doin' strange things to all da Massas" replies Matilda, pulling her wrap onto her shoulders. "All da neighborin' slaves been sayin' dey seems to be afflicted with somethin'."

"Dat affliction is fear. Everybody down here got dat same affliction." Jacob turns away momentarily. "Hey Moses, make sure everybody has a field tool and make sure all dem children are carryin' baskets," shouts Jacob. "Dey all scared the blue coats gonna' win da war and free all us slaves."

Matilda knew there was much more to their fear than that. All the news from the grapevine is that some Massas are not being as evil as they use to be. They are actually tryin' to show more compassion, 'cause they don't want their slaves to leave, even after the war. This change in behavior is very suspicious to some slaves who have already made up their minds to leave.

"I hear all dem runaways been sendin' messages back home, " continues Jacob, watching the final assembly of slaves, "tellin' families they comin' back to free them and it's scarin' the planters 'cause the planters been tellin' the families of the runaways dey was killed tryin' to escape. Some planters worried da runaways gonna come back and kill dem."

"Slavery ain't never gonna go away in America, Jacob" sighs Matilda. "I bet in a hunert years black folks still gonna be slaves in America. What year of da Lawd is this, Jacob?"

"Eighteen hundred and sixty-one, Mama. Hey Joshua, put a hat on dat baldhead of yours! It's gonna be hot again today!"

"Den dat means our people been in bondage here how long?"

"I hear two hunert years, Mama."

"Two hunert years already; and it will probably take another hunert years or more befo' black folks begin to think we as a people can be free. We been cursed by da Lawd," cries Matilda, looking to the skies. "We been cursed 'cause black folks done learned from white folks how to be Massas and once you enslave your own kind you can nebber be free."

"All slave massas are runnin' out of time 'cause da North will soon be here and we all gonna' be free. You know what I'm gonna' do Mama? Da moment I's free and gettin' paid for da work I do, I's gonna buy you a dress."

"Aw son, you know I don't need much. I's jus'fine wit what I got."

"Yeah I will, Mama. I'm gonna buy you one of dem bell shape dresses, dat spread out at yo' feet and a bonnet dat matches, and ties under your chin, and one of dem para, para, what dey called, Mama?"

"Parasol, Jacob."

"Yeah, dat's it, to keep the sun off yo' pretty face."

"Thank-you Jacob, but right now you better make sure all dem slaves git to the fields on time, and you wear your hat too."

"I love you Mama and I'm gonna' buy you dat dress, I promise, just as soon as dis war is over and we free. Hey Tom, where you think you goin' wit'out me! I'm da one in charge here, not you! Everybody leave when I say so, not you! I gotta' go Mama and don't worry, I'll be back tonight, I promise."

Matilda watches her son leaving for a long time. After she can no longer see him she slowly kneels, folds her hands, and begins to pray.

"Good morning Lawd. I knows you busy. I just wanna' thank you for gittin' me up dis mornin' in yo' darkness, just so I can see yo' light. I wanna' thank you for puttin' the breath of life in Jacob this mornin', blessin' him wit another day. I feel you in my body dis mornin' Lawd, I feel you in my heart and it feels good. But my heart is heavy dis mornin' cause I's worried about Jacob. I's, worried 'cause I know you got somethin' planned for him and I wants you to know, I don't wants you to change dem plans, but I wants you to keep him from harm's way. You knows what in his mind and you knows what's in his heart. Only you can make his feet run. Only you can make his eyes see. Only you can make his mind think. And if you done planned to make his feet run, so his eyes can see you befo' I do, make him think twice about leavin' me here, alone. Spare him my Lawd Jesus, spare him. If you needs to take somebody, take me instead. Now, dat's all I'm gonna' say dis mornin'. I thanks you for givin' me some of yo' time. Now, I gots to go to work."

* * * * * * * * *

Pierre watches Matilda from the front porch, as she walks to the kitchen. He pats his pocket for the wrapped parcel of food he put together from last night meal. As Matilda goes through the kitchen door he quietly leaves the porch and quickly walks to the barn. He has been sneaking food to the visitor of the barn for a couple of weeks now. So far there has been a one-sided conversation between them. He's been trying to convince her he will not turn her in; but she's not confident enough to come out, not trusting enough to believe him.

He puts the food in the usual place then sits and waits for the hand to come from between a crack in the standing wall boards, snatch the parcel then quickly disappear. Then the sound of food, being greedily mouthed is heard. When the sounds are replaced by a series of burps, Pierre would begin, in hushed tones, trying to force an appearance.

"You know, it's been a couple of weeks now and I still don't know what you look like. I need you to show yourself because I need to make the necessary plans to get you safely out of the area and North to freedom."

Pierre moves to where he hears the sounds coming from, hoping to get a glimpse of her; maybe, a face to face so he can try and convince her to show herself. Instead he hears her scamper away. He remembers what he has been told at the meetings he attends.

He needs to gain her trust and he cannot rush her into trusting him. He has heard her quietly humming "Swing Low, Sweet Chariot" or "Go Down Moses" as she eats quietly. He will have to find her some clothes and continue to get food to her until she is ready to leave the farm and move north. There is so much he has to teach her about the trip that she is about to make. Who she can trust and how she can find her way. If he cannot get her aboard a boat or barge or steamboat, going north, then she needs to know how to looks to the night sky and find Polaris. She needs to understand why it is so important to her. She needs to understand why, on clouded nights, when there is no moon or stars above her that she must look for tree moss, which grows on the north side of tree trunks that also will serve as a guide. Slave catchers will patrol the conventional roads and she must rely on the railways of the back roads, or the water-ways. Sometimes she may have to travel as a male. If she is of fair skin, passing as a white man may be necessary. He has stories to tell her about Frederick Douglas and how, posing as a sailor, he escaped to New York. But he hasn't seen her yet and he knows that if he does not gain her confidence soon she will be more trouble to his family than he wants. He moves about the barn as though he is working and is ignoring her, hoping she will gradually show herself.

"There's a forty dollar reward posted all over the parish for your return. Your Master is very interested in getting you back. I tore one of the posters off a tree. I'll read it to you."

Pierre retrieves a folded paper from his pocket, opens it and begins reading.

"*Forty dollars reward*, that's in big letters. Let's see now, the rest said, *Runaway dark niggra girl, from the Subscriber on September 7ᵗʰ a girl named Anna, aged a bout 19 years. She has a pleasing countenance, oval face, brown eyes and curly black hair. She is dark in complexion, medium build and speaks a plausible story not related to her crime. The above reward will be paid on her delivery to me or at any Jail in Louisiana. Alfred J Clanton, Parish of Madison, Louisiana.* Well now, Anna since I now know your name I hope it is obvious to you I have no intention of turning you over to the Clanton plantation or the bounty hunters hired to find you. If you want me to help you you've got to show that you trust me. Anna you've got to come out and let me see you. I'm your friend. You got to believe in me."

There is a rustle of hay above his head. Pieces of straw trail in front of him from above. It is a bare foot that appears first, then a long leg that leads to her torso and finally all of her is looking at him. She clings to the post that support the doorway, head bowed, shy and frightened.

"Don't be afraid," said Pierre, walking slowly towards her. "I won't hurt you, I promise." Just before he is able to gather her into his arms she drops to her knees and grabs his leg, crying and sobbing. "That's not necessary, get up, Anna."

"Are you gonna to turn me over to yo' Massa?"

"No, I don't have a Massa."

"How can dat be, all us coloreds got Massas."

Some of us coloreds got colored massas, thinks Pierre and now Pierre wonders how he will explain to her, he is one of the massas on this farm; poor ignorant thing. It is obvious to Pierre Anna has never been permitted to learn to read or write, which on most farms and plantations was standard. Owners of plantations never like to take time away from working their slaves to let their slaves be educated. To educate them would be contradictory of their principles about the abilities of the Africans. To many, to educate their slaves leads to the slaves teaching others to understand the four points of the compass. Once they learn the direction of north, owners fear they will be heading in that direction. It also reinforces the belief that only white people can be massa and take care of the ignorant class of slaves. Pierre wanted to show her it is not all white massas and black slaves. He also wanted to show her not all massas think or act in the same depriving way in dealing with their slaves. "Except here, the colored are the Masters," said Pierre, trying not to alarm Anna.

"Colored Massas in charge of other slaves?" Anna finds it so hard to believe what she is hearing, but if it is true, she still understands her position and responds to Pierre the only way she knows how, falling and groveling at his feet, clinging to his lower left leg. "Oh Massa, thank you, thank you Lawd, thank you!"

"Anna," said Pierre, lifting her, "you have to get up. I'm not your Massa."

"You my Massa now," confesses Anna, struggling with Pierre to stay down on her knees. "Please don't turn me in suh."

"Anna, keep your voice down, we don't want to wake anybody else." Pierre pulls more biscuits and pieces of ham from his pocket and gives them to her.

Anna, overjoyed, and stunned by what she has been told, sits on a hay bale, shivering, wiping tears of happiness from her face. She begins to frantically stuff food into her mouth, staring at Pierre then paying more attention to the pieces of ham and biscuit, crumbling around her, picking bits and pieces up and stuffing them into her mouth also. She indeed is a good young-breeding woman. The paltry sum of forty dollars is very much under value for what Anna is really worth. She must be worth at least two thousand dollars. Seeing her Pierre understands why the Clanton Plantation wants her back so bad. No doubt plenty of strong healthy children can be guaranteed from her. She is beautiful, even with her hair tattered and filled with straw pieces and forest burrs. She has a long neck and broad shoulders and long limbs. Through the loosely fitted clothing, he sees lash marks on her shoulders, small like they were put there with a switch, and not a whip.

"You worked in the big house, didn't you Anna?"

Anna stops eating and shudders.

"I was da men folk's play thing," she said, holding her head down in shame. "I's so dirty inside. My monthly time has not come and it scares me."

Pierre continues to slowly circle Anna, watching her and she watching him. The clothing she has taken out of the bins are too big, much too big for her frame. "I need to get you some clothes that will fit you, hold on." Pierre opens the clothing storage bin and finds what he needs then returns to a puzzled Anna. "Here, go behind that stall and change into these." Pierre watches her move behind a wall before speaking again. "What happened to the clothes you wore in here?" But before Anna can answer, the barn door opens and Charlie Boy enters holding a lantern high.

"Sorry Master Pierre," said Charlie Boy, "but I thought I heard voices in here and was wondering who it was." Charlie Boy waves the lantern up and down, back and forth to see if anyone else is with

Pierre. Not entirely satisfied there is no one else here, he slowly brings the lantern down, waiting to hear what his eyes did not see.

"It's just me, Charlie Boy," said Pierre, closing the clothes storage bin. "Is there anything else you need?"

"Oh, I just come for da rake and hoe for da garden for the children." Charlie Boy lifts his garden tools hanging from the wall of the barn. "Is everything okay, Master Pierre?"

"Everything is fine, Charlie Boy. Why do you ask?"

Charlie Boy is about to leave when he pauses, turns to Pierre, an apologetic look on his face. "Sometimes, things around me git to be too much, and I be talking to myself and old Sarah, she come up and smack me on my head."

"So."

"Well I just thought if you be having dat same problem old Sarah might have a different kind of medicine for you. If you want, I'll talk to her for you."

"Thank-you, Charlie Boy, but that won't be necessary."

Charlie Boy shrugged. "Okay, Master Pierre just thought I'd mention it." Charlie Boy reluctantly leaves the barn, looking back several times before closing the door.

Pierre then checks to be sure that Charlie Boy is out of earshot before waving Anna from behind the dividing stall.

"What you gonna do about me now, Massa Pierre?"

"Please call me Pierre, Anna."

"But I belongs to you, now Massa, I mean Pierre."

"You belong to no one."

"What you gonna do with me den?"

"You will be put on the Underground Railroad and sent North."

"How you gonna do dat?"

"Let me worry about that. What I need you to do is remain here and be as quiet as you can. I will bring you food when I can and when things are set up, you will be moved. Remember, show your face to no one but me. Not everyone feels the same as I do on this farm." Pierre is about to leave when he suddenly turns. "The clothes you wore here, where are they?"

Anna returns behind the stall and brings forth a tattered cloth that use to be a homespun dress. She drops it on the ground. Pierre finds a burlap sack and stuffs the cloth inside. He hides the sack behind one of the clothes storage cabinets. "I will try and come to see you twice a day, bringing you food with each visit. You've got to trust me, okay? I need to tell you things you need to know for the trip north."

"Yes Massa, I mean Pierre."

"And if you don't hear my voice, don't make a sound, understand?"

"Yes Massa, I mean Pierre."

Pierre leaves the barn and walks back to the front porch, unknown to him, under the watchful eye of Charlie Boy. After Pierre has disappeared inside, Charlie Boy again goes to the barn, opens the door and with his lantern held high; he searches with his eyes and ears inside the barn. Satisfied that no one else is here, he backs out, sadden, wondering just how sick Pierre is and if the rest of his family knows. Anna, upon hearing the barn door latches close, crawls from under a pile of hay. She finishes stuffing the food that remains into her mouth. Collapsing onto her back she stares into the darkness above her, wondering what next will happen to her.

CHAPTER 8
Sunday, October 6ᵗʰ, 1861

The first Africans were bought to Louisiana in 1719, from the Senegambia region by French slavers. Between 1719 and 1731 the French Company of the Indies brought in 7000 slaves. Louisiana became a less oppressive place for blacks to live because of the Code Noir, a set of regulations for the treatment of slaves, developed in 1727 by the French. As word of this spread amongst free blacks, former slaves moved to Louisiana from the Caribbean. In the forty years after 1763, the number of free people of color increased from 99 to 1,355. This is due in part from the immigrants from the Indies and the number of light-skinned mixed Euro-African citizens. By 1860 over 7,500 free people of color lived in Louisiana. By the time the Civil War began, many blacks in Louisiana were 20 generations removed from Africa and 10 or more from slavery.

Add to all of this the numerous Frenchmen who left property to his mixed-race offspring and F.P.O.C., Free Person of Color, came to be used after the name of the person of mixed race. Oppressive as this label was, New Orleans afforded free blacks more rights than any other American city north or south. This included allowing the ownership of property and to seek justice through the judicial system.

* * * * * * * * *

It is Sunday, a day off. A day that God rests and a day the auction houses like the Cabildo, the St. Louis and the St. Charles Hotel and Maspero's Exchange are closed. There is a place, a grassy plain, on the edge of the swamps at the far side of the French Quarter where the gens de couleur libre and slaves will congregate. It is called Congo Square. Under the sycamores, in Congo Square, from early afternoon until light has turned to dark, hundred of slaves and free blacks dance to the rhythms of tom-toms, kalimbas calabashes and crude stringed instruments. The dances are lively and fast paced. They are sensual and erotic. It is where dancers imitate the motions of lovemaking. Some of the dances are joyful, reflecting the influence of European music. There are other dances that are little more than a stamping of feet; but there are ritual dances called the calinda, the carbine, the bamboula and the coujaille. They are the dances the free, the indebted, and the enslaved dance barefoot on the grass in front of hordes of spectators, who have come to town just to see this spectacle. They come to Congo Square for the entertainment; and they come to get an idea of what will be on the market in the morning. Free blacks come to stay in touch with their roots by exchanging conversations with the slaves. This is a place where the African slaves are allowed to meet and dance, speaking in their native Africans tongues and playing their traditional instruments. It is a place where African rituals and ceremonies are kept alive. It is also where the menagerie of people from a variety of tribal groups find a cultural bond. It is a strange exception to the society of Masters and slaves in New Orleans, and only in the African culture, are the free black and the slave socializing together.

Pierre comes to Congo Square to meet with his friends and to discuss the business of getting runaways onto the Underground Railroad. The task requires them to begin the 1000 mile trek by getting the runaway on a steamer going north to Cairo, Missouri, then from there an overland carrier to Chicago, Illinois. In Chicago they meet with other passengers from Chester, or Springfield, Illinois. Others come from Percival, Des Moines and Davenport Iowa. Eventually there is a final stop in Chicago for the boat ride over the great lakes to Collingwood, Canada. This is their final destination, and a beginning experience of freedom.

Everything is done within the boundaries of strictest of secrecy. While they observe the entertainment in Congo Square they speak to each other, smiling at the dancing and clowning by the slaves, but the content of their speech very serious. All around them are spies, black, Creole and white, who would turn them in for a reward.

Pierre worries about the white folks more than the blacks or Creoles. The blacks and Creoles have their roots located somewhere in Congo Square, while the white folks do not. Pierre worries even more about the white buckra slave owners. They treat their slaves much worst than any other group of white slave owners. It is a known fact the buckras don't have much and don't want the free black to have more. They usually are the patrollers that wander the roads at night checking for runaway slaves. They check everyone to be sure all papers are in order even though many cannot read.

As Pierre gazes about the faces in the Sunday crowd he sees all kinds of white faces, black faces, and Creole faces. There are African faces the color of rich dark soil and African faces the shade of a new moon. But the face he sees and pauses on is face of the Major Treeman. The look on Major Treeman's face is one of suspicion. He is looking for the out of the ordinary, the nervous, the sweating face, the eyes that do not look into his cold steely stare. But Pierre is not showing any fear. He stares into the face of Major Treeman, watching him watching everyone else; watching him move about the crowd, bumping into black people, trying to extract an improper emotion, a twitch, a sudden reaction that is not an expected response. Like a predator on the prowl, he circles the dancing, the laughing, the clowning, and the innocent, waiting for the appropriate time to pounce on a victim.

"You see him too," said a voice behind Pierre.

Pierre recognizes the voice of Marcel, smiles, but does not take his eyes off Major Treeman.

"Yeah, I see him. He's looking, but he won't find anything here."

"Have you any news of the runaway?"

"Yup, she's in our barn."

"Congratulations, how did you manage that?"

"She crept into the barn one night last week. I only knew because Charlie Boy noticed food was missing from the slave garden."

"Have you spoken to her?"

"Yes, briefly. She's okay, a bit shaken, but I 'm sure she trusts me. When can she be moved?"

"I have to put some things in place up river. That may take some time. I'll leave tomorrow and start the process."

"Can we still trust everyone?"

"I'll let you know when I get back."

Pierre's nose arches at the scent of some god-awful stench. "What the hell is that stink?"

"He just passed behind us," said Marcel, watching Major Treeman walk away. "Damn, that man really stinks. I don't trust him. He may be trouble."

"Only if we let him," said Pierre, turning his attention back to the frolicking slaves, having a party, enjoying themselves in Congo Square, "only if we let him."

* * * * * * * * *

The city of New Orleans clings to the bends in the Mississippi River like a crescent moon. It hugs the protruding earth like someone desperately hanging on, trying not to be swept away by the mighty Mississippi. It is pressed into the mud and swampland by the spider web of railroad tracks that crisscross the city. The New Orleans and Carrolton Street Railway connects New Orleans with Jefferson City terminating at Canal Street. Then there is the Mexican Gulf Railways that comes from the east and terminates at the levee. Not to be forgotten is the New Orleans and Opelousas railways terminating in Macdonough Parish on the East Side of the Mississippi. If you did not wish to traverse the city by train, an omnibus is always for hire; the driver always ready to satisfy your tastes whatever they are.

New Orleans is a city alive with the good, the bad and the ugly. In 1857 the city passed an ordinance "Concerning Lewd and Abandoned Women," legalized prostitution. It set up a restricted area of operations and a license system for houses and women engaged in the trade, but this was found to be ineffective and was abandoned. In the first part of the nineteenth century the Swamp, a section of Girod Street near the river, was long regarded as the toughest part of town. A succession of barrelhouses, cheap lodgings, and bordellos lined the street. The prostitutes are tough females, many of whom can fight as well as men, as many disgruntled customers find out regularly. Patronized by the rough flatboat men who moor their boats nearby, the Swamp is just one of the many dens of iniquity, ignored by the police, visited by politicians and protected by both. Gallatin Street is a short alley that runs from the French Market to the Mint. It is New Orleans second tenderloin district. Here in saloons and dance houses prostitutes ply their trade on unwary seamen. Against the background of agonizing screams of slaves and their children, the rattle of leg irons, the cracking of cat o nine breaking the funk and stench in the air into pieces, there are also the joys and pleasures of men enjoying the women of the night.

* * * * * * * *

A blanket of darkness has fallen upon the Crescent city and what sleeps during the day now awakens. Those who refuse to sleep during the night return to certain houses for gambling, drinking and ill repute. From the iron lace balconies the near naked ladies stand, laughing drinking, inviting those to enter. Street block upon street block of fine wrought iron work adorns this gallery of buildings in the French Quarter. These are establishments that have double parlors, one to drink in and enjoy the company of their favorite prostitute while the other is to drink in and gamble with the elite gentlemen of the city. The rooms are lavishly furnished in heavy draperies, tapestries and oil paintings. Leopard skins cover furniture; potted palms and curios set off the heavily carved and plush-covered furniture.

It is where the winding Mississippi bends north the furthest; where on land, Canal Street is the west boundary, Burgundy is the north, Esplanade Avenue is the east and the mighty river is the south boundary. It is where, in 1699, Sieur de Bienville and 30 convicted salt smugglers, hacked down razor-sharp palmetto thickets to clear a spot for a few ramshackle houses. From those beginnings was birthed Vieux Carre, the French Quarter. Today the streets are straight and wide, some thirty-six feet wide in most places and bordered by banquettes, or what is known as brick sidewalks. Alongside the sidewalks are gutters that permit the outflow of water from the river to the swamplands. During the rainy season, when the gutters are clogged, the unpaved streets are vast mud puddles.

This is where Andy St. Claire comes to seek his pleasures with the inhabitants of the houses. It is where Andy comes to get away from and forget the life he has at his father's farm. He feels the life of a slave owner has too many down sides. He doesn't like being around slaves all day, smelling them, seeing them as children, therefore the need in keeping an eye on them. This responsibility constantly brings on a stress that only is relieved when he is out of that environment completely. Besides his mother and sister, all the other women on the farm look like rag muffins, what with their hair going every which way, their clothes hanging about them like sacks of loose beans and the general lack of self respect he sees they have of themselves.

From Bourbon Street to Royal Street, he knows where he wants to be for what ever he wants to partake. It is where he comes to visit one or two night during the week. He is well known and his credit is worthy of his name.

"Is there anything else Monsieur St. Claire needs," said Monique, raising her smooth chocolate brown Creole body off Andy. "Have I done all that you've asked?"

Andy reaches for his glass of spirits and slowly drinks. He watches Monique's long body move away from him. She has beautiful round brown buttocks. She reaches for her housecoat of lace and silk, smiling back at him as she puts it on and ties it around her, slowly covering her caramel shaded breasts. She disappears for a moment into the bathroom. He hears her humming a cheerful tune. Then, she is returning to him with a smile and a different housecoat.

"You have done all and more," said Andy, feeling the warmth of the spirits move down his body, passing through his lungs, spreading throughout his shoulders and arms and settling into his loins. Andy finishes the contents of his glass. "You can get me another one of these, please."

Monique takes his glass to the curio that holds the decanter of his favorite spirit and pours another drink for him. This one is always so full of energy, thinks Monique, as she slowly walks back to the bed. She wonders from where he gets it. He pays well and she makes sure he gets his moneys worth. He is not like the others who have one go then fall off to sleep. He enjoys the evening to the fullest. He is the kind of gentleman Monique enjoys entertaining. She too can get total fulfillment from the evening as well as her customer.

"Here you are Monsieur St. Claire," said Monique, bending over, allowing her housecoat to fall away from her. "Does Monsieur St. Claire see anything else?"

Andy motions Monique to come closer, patting the empty space next to him in bed. She smiles, disrobes, and then slowly crawls over him, letting her breasts slowly slide over his face before lying on her side, facing him. With his free hand Andy explores Monique's body, going, not blindly, to her areas of pleasure, watching her face tell him how well his hand is performing. She closes her eyes and smiles, biting her lower lip. It is when he finds the soft rise between her thighs; she quickly inhales, and then slowly exhales. He gently slides across it with his fingers. Back and forth, gently, he rubs, feeling the soft rise become firm. It is then she smiles, relaxes and slowly opens her soft brown thighs. Andy looks into Monique's face and savors her look of submission and joy she is expressing. He relishes the fact he does so much to bring joy to Monique. He is in charge of her pleasure; in charge of her enjoyment. He is master of her. She is his charge. He gently massages her moist inner thighs watching her expression change with each finger probing, each touch of the firm rise at the top of her moist loins.

"Monsieur St. Claire, I feel like a plate-bande, opening her fleur to the warmth of the morning sun, waiting for my honey bee to come and enjoy the gift of my nectar." Monique positions herself against the headboard of the bed, slowly opening her legs. "I offer to you, my petals, my honey bee. I offer to you the nectar of the Gods."

Andy leans forward and gently nibbles at her inner thighs. His loins respond to feeling her tremble beneath his lips. He moistens his finger from the glass of spirits then traces the triangle line of her delicate pubic hair. Next, very slowly, he let's his tongue retrace the same triangle. It is a pleasure for him as he finds the soft opening petals of her body, tasting the mixture of his spirit and her juices. Deeper and deeper he sternly probes her inner secret hiding place with his tongue, and then gently tasting her nectar.

"Draw it all from my very soul, my honey bee," she whispers, raising her hips to meet his probing tongue. "Je jouir, je jouir!

Andy enjoys the true nectar of the Gods, slowly letting the dew from her flower petals roll onto the taste buds of his tongue, mixing with the spirits of mortal man. All of this gives him the strength he will use to conquer this woman of pleasure. He feels like a new man. He feels like someone invincible. He feels like someone who dares to be challenged. He is king of this world and she is his loyal subject. He will torture her with pleasure; weaken her to a point of total submission. Then he will selfishly take some pleasure for himself.

"You have found the soul of my hidden pleasure," moans Monique.

Andy continues to slowly massage Monique's breasts with his hands while savoring the gift of her nectar. The essence of his spirits lingers. He carefully maneuvers her in the bed, continuing his sensuous assault on her body with his mouth and hands.

"Monsieur St. Claire, you should not be the customer," sighs Monique, "If Monsieur St. Claire were the giver of delights, I would demand to be your only customer."

Andy pulls Monique closer and his face feels the soft flesh of her inner thighs, the fragrant of her sex and perfumes fill his nose. Monique collapses into the comforter filled bed and is immediately engulfed by the covers and Andy. He continuously searches her body with his mouth gently biting, sucking enjoying every taste of his flower. At the same time, he enjoys the masterful technique of Monique's hands as they massage his body, knead his flesh, as her mouth begins to devour him. Monique feels her body reacting to him. She feels a growing, trembling, eruption deep down inside her bowels.

"Fuck me hard, my lover" moans Monique, "Fuck me until I'm dry. Fuck me to paradise!"

In between her soft chocolate brown thighs, he maneuvers himself, feeling her gentle hands on his rigid pulsating penis. He almost explodes feeling the moisture from her inner lips as she slowly moves his wanting member up and down the soft opening that is the gateway to the most pleasurable part of her body. She teases him, opening her thighs guiding his trembling member inside her, and then slowly withdrawing it almost out again. Her slippery fluids now cover his rigid curved member like oil, making it easier and smoother for each continuing penetrating motion. Andy suddenly is feeling vulnerable. He is losing control. He is feeling captured. He does not have her. She has him. The tables have turned in her favor, but Andy does not fight this change. He welcomes and surrenders himself to it. He doesn't care anymore. Everything feels too wonderful to care. He is exploding again. The delightful pleasures of his pearl drops are rushing from his body, exploding through the tiny hole in his member driving him to insanity with joyful pleasure and madness.

Together they ravish each other, their bodies in harmony as they moan, shudder, grab, squeeze, suck until finally collapsing into two spent heaps of sweat dripping sated flesh.

By two am, Andy's tired drunken satisfied body is in an omnibus and on his way home. He will generously tip the driver when he is dropped off at the driveway of his father's farm.

* * * * * * * * *

Voodoo Man Cato sits in the center of his hounfort, throwing bones, looking for his future, waiting for the unexpected. It is Wednesday, October 9th, 1861. He has completed his devotion to Damballah, the Great Serpent. His hounfort is decorated with flowers that have perfumed the inside of the hounfort that he has draped in white sheeting. On the floor of his hounfort he has drawn the Ve've' of Damballah, using cornmeal and at the altar he has placed cornmeal, cake, milk and powdered sugar. Two dead white chickens have been placed in the center of the Ve've' of Damballah.

Voodoo Man Cato throws the bones, reads them, gathers them in his hand and throws them again. He continues this until the bones give him a message. He waits to hear from Loco Atisou. Not long after he has thrown the bones there is a knock on his door. Voodoo Man Cato slowly gets to his feet, acknowledges the presence of spirits, and backs out of the hounfort.

He opens his door and Charlie Boy stands before him, head bowed, holding a gift of a chicken for Voodoo Man Cato. Voodoo Man steps aside and lets Charlie Boy enter. Charlie Boy slowly proceeds humbled by years in age and years in slavery. He finds a place to kneel before entering the hounfort, and waits for Voodoo Man Cato. Voodoo Man Cato senses there is trouble in the mind of Charlie Boy. He passes the kneeling body of Charlie Boy and waits at the altar, closing his eyes, asking Loco Atisou for wisdom.

"My houngan who speaks to Zaka and da crops flourish," begins Charlie Boy, "who speaks to Yemanja and da waters flows, who calls upon Ogou Balanjo to keep sickness from da body, who walks wit Erinie above da tallest of trees, you my houngan who sees, hears and knows all, I come to you for guidance."

Voodoo Man Cato has known Charlie Boy for many harvests and knows he would only come to him when he is deeply troubled. Not much has been of concern to Charlie Boy, but lately Voodoo Man Cato has seen a difference in the way Charlie Boy moves about the farm working with the children and especially how he has been relating to Pierre, as if he thinks something is not right with Pierre. Voodoo Man Cato has watched these going on for several weeks now and has waited for Charlie Boy to approach him. Well, the time has come and as he looks at the bent body of Charlie Boy, Voodoo Man Cato knows there is serious trouble somewhere inside his mind.

"It's Massa Andrew's youngest son, Pierre" begins Charlie Boy again. "I seen and caught him, more than a couple of times, talkin' to hisself. And it ain't like he talkin' like he crazy; instead he's talkin' to da animals in da barn or he talkin' to da side wall of da barn. He real mysterious in his behavior. I ain't said nothin' to massa Andrew yet 'cause around him he don't be doin' what I see him doin'."

Voodoo Man Cato listens to Charlie Boy and remembers when Pierre was born. It is the same day he was bought by Massa Andrew. When Massa Andrew came home from New Orleans with Voodoo Man Cato he received word of Pierre being born. As he drove his buckboard wagon up the driveway, Charlie Boy was hollerin' and yellin' about the birth of another son and Massa Andrew was hollerin' and yellin' about how good a price he paid for Voodoo Man Cato and the fact he has a new son and a new slave. Andrew thanked God for delivering a healthy baby boy and Voodoo Man Cato thanked Ayza for delivering him to Massa Andrew.

"I think it's the food," continues Charlie Boy, talking to the ground. "I seen him come out of da kitchen wit food in his hands and pockets, him eating wildly, lookin' to see if anyone is spying. I watch him go inside the barn and then I look through a slit in the barn door and he just sits and talks to the hay. He goes on and on. He be talking in low tones and I can hardly hear him but sometimes I hear him talk about being free. My houngan, Master Pierre is already free. He free as da wind dat blows. I's worried. I thinks maybe he's been eating some left over food, dat maybe da rats done ate some of first and he's eating behind dem and dat's making him go crazy."

Voodoo Man Cato squats next to Charlie Boy and begins to create a ve've' for Sun. He remembers how close he has been to the Massa Andrew. How they worked shoulder to shoulder, clearing the trees, building the big house and how Massa Andrew helped Voodoo Man Cato build his own shanty. In return for all of this kindness, Voodoo Man Cato told Massa Andrew he knew magic and he would ensure his farm would be prosperous and he would keep it from harm. Massa Andrew looked at Voodoo Man Cato and the familiar small corners of his mouth upturned giving Voodoo Man Cato his smile of agreement. He then asked Voodoo Man Cato to finish chopping up the firewood with him. Voodoo Man Cato, from that day has asked the Gods to protect this family from all harm. Massa Andrew has kept his promise and Voodoo Man Cato has kept his promise. Charlie Boy understands the magic of Voodoo Man Cato even though Massa Andrew and his family do not.

To Massa Andrew and his family, especially Miss Mary, when they need help in healing, when they need help in finding the truth, when they need help in securing the safety of a loved one far away, they turn to their God, a white God, manifested by white men, for the belief in white values. They believe their God accepts slavery and bondage. They believe their God rests on the seventh day while slaves do not rest at all. They believe their God calls home his Christian brethren by way of death, whether on the field of battle, the battlefield of life, or on a bed of goose feathers. They believe their God is a mighty God to be feared by everyone. They believe their God is an understanding God who forgives the sins of man, no matter what man has done to other men.

"I done everythin' I could think of, my houngan, tryin' to figure out what wrong wit Master Pierre," said Charlie Boy. "I been in da barn, looking for rat hole to fill, but didn't find any; and I even got down on my knees and prayed to their God to reach down and touch Master Pierre to make him better, but their God takes so long, my houngan. So, I come to you."

For Voodoo Man Cato, it is the magic. It is the magic that makes Voodoo Man Cato believe in a Supreme Being. It is the same magic that makes him believe in the afterlife; magic that makes him believes in the existence of invisible evil spirits and demons. There is the magic that causes him to follow the ceremony of ritual remembering. A self-sacrifice and the need of doing in remembrance, communion through the eating of mock flesh and drinking mock blood. The magic of the Loa in that they were once people who led exceptional lives and are given a single responsibility or special attribute to use when they watch over the living.

Charlie Boy stops speaking.

The chicken he brought with him clucks a few times, then appears to have understood its surroundings. He shows he understands by sitting quietly in a corner. It may have recognized remnants of the two white chickens and realized its pending fate.

Voodoo Man Cato places a black top hat on his head then marches three times around the peristyle. After the third time he stops at the poteau-mitan and places some water on the altar at the base of the pole.

"Ati Bon Legba, ouvri barrie' pou moin, ago ye'!," chants Voodoo Man Cato, "Voudoun Legba, ouvri barrie' pou moin, pou moin ca retre'. L'hei' m'a tounin, m'a remercie' loa-yo." [iv]

Using flour Voodoo Man Cato creates the Ve've' of Danbhalah and Aida We'do.

"Danbhalah We'do, gad'e pitites ou yo, je'! Aida We'do, min

pitites ou yo. He'! Danbhalah We'do, gade' pitites ou yo, oh! A ye' a ye', oh! Danbhalah, min z'enfants ou la'." ᵛ

Charlie Boy squats on his haunches, keeping his eyes close. He knows they are present, in the hounfort at this moment, others besides him and Voodoo Man Cato. He waits until Voodoo Man Cato touches his forehead before speaking.

"Danbhalah We'do, behold your children, Pierre," chants Charlie Boy. "Aida We'do, here are your children, Pierre. Danbhalah We'do, behold your children, Pierre! A yey, a yey, oh! Danbhalah, heal your children, Pierre." After Charlie Boy finishes the chant, he bows again, his forehead touching the floor of the hounfort, waiting for Voodoo Man Cato to speak.

"Rise Charlie Boy. They have heard our requests and will cleanse Pierre of his affliction. Rise Charlie Boy. You have pleased them with your love of your family. Rise Charlie Boy and return to your station in life. You now walk with the spirit of Danbhalah beside you. You are charged with making sure no harm comes to Pierre. They will call you when they need your help. They will call you to help bury the evil that tries to destroy him. Be patient and wait for their call."

Charlie Boy rises and slowly backs out of the hounfort, thanking Voodoo Man Cato for giving him the new responsibility. When he is outside, he quickly walks to the slave quarters. He sits under the shade of a fruit tree, waiting for the children to return and help tend the slave garden.

* * * * * * * * * *

Andrew brought the topic up at the dinner table. It was all part of the dinner conversations, not meant to insult anyone, just conversation. Usually if there is anything to be said, Andrew always said it first. It's more of a ritual. First, everyone stands behind their chairs while Andrew offer thanks and grace to God for another blessed day. Then everyone sits at the table and waits for Andrew to start the table conversation. This usually occurs after portions of everything have been served to him. The bowls and platters are then passed to Mary and then to the children. It is while the children are taking their share of the food that Andrew waits for before he begins the topic of discussion.

"Anybody heard anything about that Clanton runaway?" No one said anything because everyone knows there will be a follow up comment. "The problem with the folks over at the Clanton place is they have no respect for their slaves. I'm surprised they haven't had more runaways" After the follow up comment, it usually means others can join in.

"I feel so sorry for her," sighs Mary, "she must be so frightened, wandering around out there somewhere."

"Why do they want to run away," wonders Margaret, "after all, they are well taken care of, even if they are slaves."

Matilda usually retreats to the kitchen, listening for someone to call out to her for additional food. She sits in the kitchen, half listening to what they have to say, and wondering how they can be so relaxed about enslaving someone, as if the act itself is a necessary tool for survival. She knows there is much more to life than slavery, but she has no desire to fulfill a wish for something she herself has no experience of. She's always been a slave. She's not wishing to be free. At the same time she's not happy being a slave. But seeing the fire in Jacob's eyes and hearing the desire to be free in his voice, she knows she will lose him to freedom. She worries that his freedom may be his death. How can she justify asking him to stay and be part of the St. Claire family? The reality of it all is he is forced to be isolated from this house where this family gathers. Anyway, he has his own family, albeit, just his mother, but that is more than what a lot of other slave children have. And for that she is appreciative to Massa Andrew. He did not want to split up any family on his farm. Now it appears freedom is going to break up the family unit. Freedom should not do that.

"Over at the Clanton plantation", began Pierre, "they treat all their slaves like work animals instead of people."

"They also have the greatest output per acre, per worker on that farm," said Andy. "We need to do the same thing here."

"If we did that here," interrupts Andrew, "we would have a runaway problem like they have at the Clanton plantation. That's the third runaway they've had in as many years. I haven't had any, and don't expect to have any, why, because I treat my slaves like human beings, not animals."

Andrew learned from his father that if you treat a person with respect, they would respond in kind the same way, regardless of where their station is in life. It has not been easy being a free black in Louisiana. It seems every time things seems to be moving in the right direction, something happens that sets the free blacks back a few steps. In 1822 Denmark Vesey raised suspicions of the white man about free blacks. Andrew was just 8 years old, but he remembers his father, being very angry, talking to himself and Andrew at the same time. He spoke with strong distaste about someone named Vesey is creating a rift between free blacks and whites that is erasing the trust we have established in New Orleans' white society. "Vesey is destroying the good will efforts we free blacks have shown in trying to get accepted into this white society", said his father. "There are rules that must be followed in order to be accepted. And I'll tell you something, it's all about money. White folks love money. They love to earn it honestly and they love to steal it honestly. And some just enjoy stealing it no matter who they hurt getting it. It's all part of this system of economics in New Orleans."

It was not until the summer of 1831 that Andrew directly understood how the actions of one black could affect the lives of every black, free and enslaved. He is old enough to help his father run the farm that is getting bigger and more productive every day. The slave count has grown, the cleared land has grown, the housing has grown, and the reputation of the farm has grown. All these positive things demonstrated by free blacks, and slaves, showed how a people can read write and learn the ways of the society they now live in. It was these very human behavioral patterns that showed the white society that free black people have the ability to manage their own affairs without outside interference by white folks; human behavioral patterns that indicate free black people can be self sufficient within the confines of their own communities. It is human behavioral patterns that indicate black people can be needed as well as has needs. Black people are here today and will be here tomorrow, working along side of everyone who cares enough to make the Confederacy as strong as the Union. It has all been done because of what black people believe in. It's all about Andrew and others who think like him. Others who like him, have spent years building relationships with their white counterparts just so the wealth of the South can be shared.

Andrew remembers all the years of working hard to tear down ignorant myths about him and his people. All these achievements by free blacks prove how wrong the minds of the illiterate whites are. All of our hard work and dedication destroyed by one crazy black man. White folks look for excuses not to share their wealth. Not because you're black, but because if you don't learn and play by the rules, you can't participate. The process of trust has to be started all over again. The years, though not as long, are still just as hard. Over and over black people, as the chosen people, must prove again and again that we are a united black people who want desperately to be a part of this system.

"I hear she's still in the area," said Andy.

"Where did you hear that," asks Pierre.

"She can't be that far, don't you notice all the patrollers on the roads," replies Andy. "They know she ain't left the area."

"That means they're back to checking paper," worries Mary. "Make sure you keep your papers on you when you're out."

"Everyone knows the children of Andrew St. Claire," boasts Andy. "I ain't never shown my papers to anyone."

"We shouldn't have to show any papers at all," complains Pierre. "This is more like the land of the free and home of the imprisoned."

"Pierre, pass me some bread," asked Andrew, waving his hand at Pierre. "What she gonna do, wandering around out there in those marshlands. If the dogs don't sniff her out, the gators and snakes will."

"Papa, what would you do if she came tonight, knocking at our door," challenges Pierre, "would you hide her or turn her over."

"She's not our property," answers Andy.

"But she's our people," snaps Pierre.

"Oh Mama," sighs Margaret, "can't they ever talk about anything else?"

"Papa, really, what would you do if she came to our door, asking for help," said Pierre again. "What would you do?"

"There is an unwritten rule among the local farmers and own-

ers and that rule is to return all slaves back to their rightful owners."
Andrew surveys his plate and realizes he is missing something.
"Matilda, bring me some more chicken."

"Andrew," reminds Mary, "you know what Dr. DuBois said about
your food intake."

"Yes I do," said Andrew, while removing several pieces of chicken
from the platter Matilda is holding, "and he said eat when you're
hungry."

Matilda waits until Massa Andrew waves her off. She pauses
near Miss Mary who also waves her away. Margaret doesn't notice
Matilda, continuing to eat, while Andy rakes more chicken onto his
plate. Pierre said, "No thank-you, Matilda." Matilda smiles at Pierre,
then retreats back to her kitchen. Back to where she knows there is
peace of mind. The wealth they have acquired and the people they
enslave have caused the whole family to turn a blind eye to what is
right for humans, except for Pierre. Matilda doesn't remember what
it was like living anywhere else but this farm. She doesn't understand the language she hears from new slaves who arrive on the farm.
She doesn't know she has a past beyond the square mile boundaries
of Massa Andrew's farm. She doesn't know about birthdays and
doesn't remember the day her son Jacob was born, just the year. She
has seen slaves come and go, be born and die on Massa Andrew's
farm. She has seen and heard the voice of Jesus, and been persuaded
to believe in more than one God by Voodoo Man Cato. She doesn't
remember what her Mama or Papa looked like, but she does remember being held, close, by someone, who taught her gentleness, and
kindness. She has been a member of Massa Andrew's family most of
her life. She knows the only time she will be free is when she dies.
But she feels she is freer than Massa Andrew because of what he has
become compared to what she has always been. She doesn't mind
the fact everyone in the family except Pierre feels she is nothing
more than a slave, because that is what she is. When Pierre was old
enough to know the difference between her and him he cried. Sometimes he cried when his mother yelled at her and other times he
cried when Massa Andrew yelled at her. As he grew he stopped
crying and began treating her different than everyone else. She hears
Andy complaining about some secret meetings he attends; and Massa

Andrew is not happy about Pierre attending them, but Massa Andrew does not forbid Pierre from attending. Matilda is convinced she knows where that runaway slave girl is hiding and she thinks Pierre has been smuggling food to her. Matilda has been noticing more portions of leftovers missing each morning.. She is sure the runaway Clanton girl is hiding in the barn. She is sure of this based on conversations she's had with Charlie Boy. But she cannot reveal this information to anyone. She knows what will happen to the runaway and she can't let that girl go through that. She's probably been through enough. And she will not share this with Pierre she knows because she doesn't want him to know she knows. She remembers him as a timid child, easily upset. If what she believes is true, she doesn't want to endanger the entire family also. Crazy white folks will swear everyone on the farm knew about that girl just because everyone on the farm is black. To help Pierre she now leaves food grouped together. The next day it is missing, and that is just fine, but she doesn't say anything to Pierre.

"Matilda."

It is Miss Mary, calling. Matilda slowly rises from her chair, knowing soon a request will come.

"Matilda, we are ready for our coffee now."

Matilda removes from the stove a hot water filled teapot. Inside there are ground coffee beans, wrapped in cheesecloth. She puts the cups and saucers on a large serving tray, large enough to bring back dirty dishes. She knows the coffee means they are finishing dinner and soon she will be washing up the dishes and cleaning the kitchen and making this house look like a home for them again. She's been doing it now for over twenty-five years. Nothing's changed for her in those twenty-five years. She's just a family slave.

Through the kitchen door, she backs into the living room, her arms clutching the tray holding the coffee, cups and saucers. She turns to the expectant faces and feigns a smile. "Yes, Miss Mary, here I come."

CHAPTER 9
Friday, October 25th, 1861

Charlie Boy sits beside the make shift bed, holding the trembling hands of Mama Sarah as she squirms and twists, sleeping through her nightmare. Charlie Boy sees the anguish in her twisted face, feels her strength in her hands squeezing his. He gently dabs her forehead with a damp cloth he keeps near by.

"Don't you worry none now, Mama Sarah, ol' Charlie Boy is right chere."

The two of them are the oldest slaves Andrew St. Claire owns. They have been on the farm almost from the beginning. Charlie Boy knows of Mama Sarah's pain. He knows when she sleeps she only relives her past. Each day is not a day in the present that will become her past. She doesn't look to tomorrow as her future. Charlie Boy knows the sand in the hourglass of Mama Sarah's life is running out and soon the sand will fall no more. Oh to be back in the Motherland again, sighs Charlie Boy, smiling as he dabs more beads of water from Mama Sarah's forehead.

"Don't you try and go home without ol' Charlie Boy, you hear me Mama Sarah?"

Charlie Boy relaxes his grip on Mama Sarah's hands, sits back and thinks about what he use to be and where he use to live. The more he thinks about it the more the water rises in his eyes. There is so much he misses. Once more before he dies he wants the smell of the lion, the elephant and wild dogs to waft into his nose. He yearns for the taste of the wild yams, wild berries and wild animals. He misses the wet that is the water that comes from the rivers flowing from the mountains with white hair. The Gods were kind to

Charlie Boy in the Motherland. Now, he cannot find the mountains with white hair where the Gods live. He is old and he has grown tired of looking. He cannot run like he use to; he cannot laugh like he use to. He looks at the now complacent face of Mama Sarah. She has moved beyond the darkness and pain of her nightmare and now sleeps. Charlie Boy leans back into his chair and drifts into a nightmare of his own.

* * * * * * * * *

Ollatunji is 11 years old when he is kidnapped from the west coast of Africa. Son of a tribal king, three brave bodyguards die trying to prevent this tragedy from happening. He is taken to a holding prison in ankle and hand chains, lock stepped with other captives, to a place of a wide river. Ollatunji is confused that he cannot see the bank on the other side of this river. The air that hangs around him is different. It smells heavier and it hangs about him like a robe soaked in blood. It smells not of the jungle he calls home, instead it smells of pain and misery and rotting human flesh. For three days, he huddles on this wide riverbed with many others like himself. On the morning of the fourth day, he and 400 other captured men, women and children board a ship. He is fed little or nothing and is rarely permitted a release from his laying down position. All the slaves are packed head to toe, very tightly, with the other slaves. Periodically, water is violently splashed on everyone to wash away the feces and urine that has collected beneath and above where he lays.

After many agonizing days across the wide river, the ship docks and Ollatunji is unloaded, having never been unshackled during the entire trip. He follows the slumping body of a man in front of him, down the gangplank, into a large warehouse, into stalls, through the stench of human waste, into the final darkness of slavery.

It is from here, in Annapolis, Maryland he get his first impressions of America, the land of the free and home of the slave. It is from here, he is sold to his first master, a Mr. Alexander James, of Powhatan County, Virginia. He is given to the care of a female slave named Sally Johnson. She already has eight other children of her own. It is under her guidance that he learns how to be a slave. He is no longer a Prince, who one day is to become a King; instead he is considered to be just another dumb ignorant slave who must be taught the ways of this new world. First, he is taught how to understand and speak the natural language; how and when to bow to the master; when to say "No sir," and "Yes sir" and how never to look into the master's face when he speaks to you. He is taught how to pick cotton, carry empty baskets, the hoes, the picks, and the rakes. He is taught how to pick through throw outs from the dinner table of the big house. There is much food that is still edible. It is an education like no other he's had to learn before. He was a boy Prince among men back in his own land. He passed to manhood with his Rite of Passage by stalking and killing a lion alone. But here he is just a slave.

When Ollatunji is seventeen, he is married to a young girl of fourteen from a neighboring plantation. It is an arranged marriage where both plantation owners look to benefit. They agree to share the children borne out of this union equally. In the first year of their marriage, two male twin children are born but die shortly after birth. The next two children survive, and after they are old enough, are divided and sold off the plantation. Ollatunji is never sure if they are alive or dead. The last time he sees either of them they are just ten years old.

His master has the means to travel and does so without regard to the running of the plantation. He leaves that to his sons and the overseer. Rumor amongst the slaves is that when the master married that girl who was young enough to be his kin, he lost all his good sense. The sons and the overseer did enough planting and tilling and harvesting and selling of goods to keep their father traveling and happy. But that is not so for the slaves. The misery and pain, the suffering, the deprivation, the disrespect, and all the horrors that come with being subservient to a cruel white man is bestowed upon Ollatunji and the rest of his slave friends. Ollatunji is sure he will die on this plantation and be buried in some unmarked grave like other slaves. But God's blessing are bestowed upon him in the nature of him going to New Orleans, on a riverboat, as the man servant of one of the reckless sons who is known to be a bad gambler. During the voyage Ollatunji is lost in a poker game to a new master. The value of the money lost and owed is three hundred and fifty dollars.

Ollatunji is thirty-one and his new home is up river from New Orleans, in the city of Natchez, Mississippi. His new master is the overseer of the Johnson plantation and its twenty-five hundred acres of cotton. When Ollatunji and the overseer leave the riverboat, Ollatunji doesn't know what to expect, but he soon finds out. During the short time he's riding to the Johnson Plantation, the overseer, riding in the front of the carriage, yells back at Ollatunji, "Ollatunja, you gonna be my head nigger, my driver. Do you understand, boy?"

Tankerray is the name of the overseer. He is a tall man; a big man with black bushy eyebrows, uncontrollable hair and a acne scared face. His eyes, set deep in his craggy shaped face, are mysterious, blood shot, tired looking. Ollatunji is afraid of Tankerray. He is more afraid now than he was at the James Plantation; here, his fear is much deeper.

Ollatunji discovers his living quarters to be in the same house as Tankerray. Tankerray lived in a large one-room log house and Ollatunji is surprised and very happy he will not be sharing one of the dilapidated shanties dotting the plantation. A middle aged slave woman name Obula waited on Tankerray, hand and foot, but she was given instructions not to wait on Ollatunji for anything. "This here nigger gets no help from you," he growls as he and Ollatunji enter the house. "He's the new driver. Let everyone know so there won't be any trouble in the morning."

"Yes suh, Massa T," said Obula, picking up Tankerray's knapsack and walking stick, then placing them on a table in one corner of the house. She goes to a special floorboard where she applies pressure to one end and the other pops up. She reaches down and pulls out a bottle of whiskey and a glass, which she brings to Tankerray.

Tankerray drinks a lot. Sometime he goes on a binge that lasts up to two or three days, which leaves the running of the plantation to Ollatunji. When Tankerray drinks he loves to talk and he needs someone to talk to so Ollatunji has to stay up all night sometimes just listening. Tankerray always knew when he was going on a binge. He gave tasks to Ollatunji that would take more than a day. In between his incoherence from his drunken stupor, he would ask Ollatunji if those tasks were completed.

Sometimes during his drunken debauchery, he'd brag about how he'd been up and down the Mississippi, won and lost thousands of dollars, cursing and swearing, laughing and retelling old stories of obscenity and blasphemy. There he would sit with his crusty stinking feet pointing to the fire, his hulking body shadows dancing off the wall, everything bathed in orange and yellow hues. He never bathed when he drank. Ollatunji could smell the alcohol and Tankerray's body at the same time. As a result, Ollatunji would leave the door open a few minutes each time he came back to the cabin. He wondered how Obula could stand being around him.

One time Tankerray told a story of how he would order the slave women to pull up their clothes so he could see they ain't hiding food underneath and whip those who did not comply. Then he'd laughed, looking at Ollatunji to join in. When Ollatunji did not Tankerray smacked him across his forehead with the butt of the whip, sending Ollatunji reeling backwards, over a table. "When I tell you a funny story you laugh," said Tankerray, standing over Ollatunji, unrolling his whip. "Do your hear me, nigger boy?"

"Yes sir, Massa T," said Ollatunji, watching the movement of the whip in Tankerray's hand. And what a movement the whip has, slow, sleek, wiggling, gliding oh so lightly above the wooden floor, like it was a big black snake floating on the top of water. And like a swooping nighthawk, rising up from just grabbing its prey, the whip rises, proudly, defiantly. With the strength of the tallest tree in the forest, for a moment it rises straight into the air and Tankerray brings it down in a flash, a whipping, snapping flash, just barely touching Ollatunji. The tip splits the air into tiny shards that sting something awful on Ollatunji's back. Tankerray possesses a master talent with the whip.

Soon after arriving on the plantation, one of the slaves ran away. Ollatunji was demanded to participate in the search. Ollatunji was introduced to two black and brown mongrel dogs, which were kept on the plantations solely for the purpose of catching runaway slaves. These hounds from birth had been taught to chase slaves and are kept penned except for that purpose. Tankerray paid $500 for his two dogs. He seemed to enjoy hunting men as much as that of chasing a fox or a deer. Tankerray let the mongrel dogs go at the first scent of the fugitive and the dogs took off running and barking and growling and howling. Ollatunji took off running after the dogs. He knew the dogs would tear up the fugitive if they got to the slave first. There was no one there to keep them tame.

There was an occasion where Ollatunji was too late in catching up with the dogs. As he made his way around a bend in the trail, he met the dogs returning. Their jaws, heads, feet and body were bloody. The sight of the bloody mongrels froze Ollatunji in his tracks. He began shaking uncontrollably. He could hear the mortally wounded runaway slave in agony, moaning and groaning in the distance, but he was helpless to assist him. He couldn't move his legs. The agonizing, painful moaning lasted for what seemed to be eternity before Tankerray caught up with Ollatunji. After seeing what his dogs looked like, said, "I believe them dogs done killed that nigger." Then Tankerray smiled, turned around and headed back to the plantation. From that day forward Ollatunji and the dogs developed a really close friendship. Tankerray took notice of this and lets Ollatunji continue building that friendship.

Days after that, everywhere Ollatunji went the dogs were with him; in the fields, in the woods, in the slave quarters, even in the outhouse. Even though they were trained to chase runaway slaves, they had a different feeling about Ollatunji. Because of the presence of the dogs, Tankerray didn't have to depend on his whip so much to get things done on the plantation. All Ollatunji had to do was have the big black mongrel with grubby, shaggy hair, glistening eyes and crooked teeth, growl. This was just fine for Ollatunji since he never like putting the whip on the slaves. It was like he was beating himself when he did it, but he knew if he didn't, Tankerray would put the whip on him, twice over the original intent. Tankerray was very fond of his whip and the joy it brought him to inflict pain onto the slaves.

And so, for the next 10 years Ollatunji labored for Tankerray, not seeing the real master of the farm until the fall of 1835. Ollatunji, at this time in his life, as near as he could tell, was thirty years away from his homeland.

The real master was a tall man with thick white hair, neatly combed about his head. He sat in a horse drawn open carriage, his hands pressing the top of an elaborately decorated walking stick. His clothes were of the finest material, and he smoked a long cigar, whose sweet aroma floated gently on the breeze, refreshing the air. A gentleman is what he looked like and what he was, a proper gentleman. At first Ollatunji didn't know who this man was and only realized after he saw the other slaves drop their tools and gather around his carriage, giving him their blessings.

Ollatunji had learned thus far the white man's Lord works in mysterious ways, but he had yet to see any of ways the white man's Lord works. All he had known is the misery of Tankerray and the many Tankerray's that govern this nation to permit such pain and misery to continue. Only the white man's Lord in heaven permits this? Is this man, a gentleman that sits like a king, like his Father use to in the land of his ancestors, God? It amazes Ollatunji to see this man's servants bowing, raising clenched hands, crying out his name, "Massa, Massa, it's so good to see you Massa."

What manner of Lord and what manner of mysterious ways did he have yet to show Ollatunji? This groveling, this crawling, this begging is not how a Lord or a King should be approached; but it is what the Tankerrays of this land have taught slave people to be. Ollatunji remembered how his father's servants approached him and they always gave him the respect he deserved for being their king, but there was never anything like he's seen in this glorious land of white man's freedom.

"Hey Ollatunji," yells Tankerray, waving at him to come to him. "Come over and meet your master."

Ollatunji pauses but for a moment, realizing Tankerray's short temper, then walks towards the carriage, preparing a lie on his face. By the time he is to the carriage, his face glows and his eyes sparkle and with his straw hat in his hand, his head bowed, he purposely lies to his master. "It is good to see you Massa," said Ollatunji.

"This is the driver I told you about I won in that poker game," brags Tankerray.

"He speaks the King's English much better than I would have

imagined, " said Mr. Johnson, admiring the appearance of Ollatunji, standing tall and straight before him.

"He's the finest nigger I've ever come across in a long time," said Tankerray, walking around Ollatunji, looking him up and down. "Yes sir, one of the finest niggers I ever come across."

If I's so fine why don't you treat me like a master treats dem clothes or how much care you show for your horse or your choice in the whiskey you buy, thinks Ollatunji. Why don't you treat me like one of da finest human beings you've ever come across?

"Does he treat you alright, Boy?" inquired Mr. Johnson.

"We has a excellent workin' relationship, suh," again lies Ollatunji, looking at the ground.

"See how he knows how to put them words together," beams Tankerray, "I told you he was a good nigger."

The master didn't spend much more time in the field. Soon he was gone and the slaves were back at their field tools, working. Some worked even harder knowing the time they lost with the master was expected to be made up before any of them could leave the fields for the day. That was the last time that Ollatunji was to see Mr. Johnson. Two years later Tankerray announced to all of the field hands Mr. Johnson had died. He had one son who was in charge of his father's farm in Virginia. As a result the farm had become Tankerray's responsibility until the son, Percy, decided to visit the farm.

Many of the slaves were saddened by this news because many strongly believed the master was going to free them then next time he returned. Some of the slaves were working off a debt and now all of that had become invalid by his death; Tankerray made sure of that. Again Ollatunji wondered about this white man's God and his mysterious ways.

And then just as mysterious as he had been spiritually taught it would happen, two years passed before this white man's Lord revealed himself to Ollatunji. He was in the fields, sitting upon his mare, sweating under a blistering sun that showed no mercy. Suddenly he heard Obula running from the house hollering and screaming that Ollatunji must come quick. Something bad had happened to Tankerray. He had fallen in the barn and was hurt something awful. All the slaves stopped working at the sound of this news, many smiling, hoping the Lord will relieve them of Tankerray at this moment to show them his mercy and grace.

Ollatunji races his mare back to find Tankerray in the barn, impaled on a pitchfork. It looks like he was cleaning one of the stalls and had climbed a ladder to the hayloft then slipped off the ladder and onto the pitchfork. He smelled of whiskey and was too drunk to realize what had happened to him. Ollatunji looks down on this helpless being called Tankerray. His eyes are open but staring into space. His breathing is labored. One of the wooden prongs of the pitchfork showed just below his left collarbone. Another came out of his shoulder. The pitchfork handle had snapped at the base of the pitchfork. Tankerray lay on his back. His left arm shook uncontrollably. As he exhales, bubbles of blood gurgle from his mouth and nose.

Obula stands behind Ollatunji, weeping and whining about what are they going to do to help "Massa T." She keeps pacing back and forth, flapping her apron in the air, crying into the apron each time it hit her face. Ollatunji just stands there looking down at Tankerray, wondering if he should do something, wondering why he should do something. This is the joy that comes from slaving 15 years. Ollatunji was now on the top rail. Tankerray was the bottom rail looking up at the top rail. Now, opportunity is at hand for him to raise his foot and place it on the bottom rail, push hard on it like it was a rotten piece of wood? Maybe he should just stand on the bottom rail and listen to it slowly crack and splinter before it breaks.

"What we gonna' do Ollatunji?" weeps Obula, still pacing.

"I don't know Obula," sighs Ollatunji. "I don't know."

By now more slaves have come from the fields. They stop at the barn door and stare in.

"Is he dade?" someone asked.

"No, not yet", replied Ollatunji.

"Den let him die," said someone else. And then, low mumbles of agreement are heard coming from the rest of the slaves.

Tankerray gurgles louder, blood spilling from his mouth, protesting this discussion of his life. He needs help more than anything else. He can feel life leaving his body. He is dying and all the niggers are staring and laughing at him. He wants to rise and turn his dogs loose on all of them. How dare they be so damn insubordinate? Who do they think they are?

"We gotta do somethin', Ollatunji," cries Obula. "We gotta do somethin'!"

"If the neighboring overseers come by and Tankerray don't greet them, then all of us are in trouble" said Ollatunji. "They'll whip every last one of us because nobody's gonna believe Tankerray did this to himself."

"Ollatunji's right," said a voice in the crowd of slaves. "They'll separate our families and give us all a good lashin' before they sell us off."

"Somebody take my horse and rush to the Bradford farm and bring some help back," said Ollatunji. "The rest of yall git back into the fields."

Ollatunji stares at the broken body of Tankerray. He hears someone get on his mare and gallop off. He wonders if, who ever it was going to get help, they will just keep going and ride off into the woods. There have been enough runaways this year and right now would not be a good time for it to happen again. Then there was the low grumbling of the slaves, some saying they were glad it finally happened; it was the work of the Lord; thank you Jesus; as they all headed back to the fields. Soon all that is left for his ears are the sounds of Obula's whimpering and the overseer, Tankerray, wheezing for breath.

"He don't look so good, Ollatunji," said Obula, standing over Tankerray. "He don't look like he gonna las' til help comes."

"He done lasted long enough, already," said Ollatunji, squatting to get closer to Tankerray. "You really banged yourself up, Massa Tankerray. Yes sir, you really done somethin' awful to yourself this time."

After a while Ollatunji sees the pale color slowly leaving Tankerray's face and the gray shadow of death replacing it. He can smell Tankerray's whiskey escaping from his body. Ollatunji tries to imagine how long it's been since that slave went for help. Maybe he didn't go for help. Maybe he decided to run. Ollatunji sneers at Tankerray, knowing Tankerray can't do anything about it. He looks into Tankerray's eyes and sees no life. Tankerray is staring at the barn's wooden beams in the ceiling. Ollatunji feels no pity for Tankerray right now. He feels nothing inside for this man that lay dying before him. He looks at him as he would observe a fallen log while walking in the forest. Again Ollatunji wonders if help will get here in time and at the same time he doesn't care if it arrives or not.

Tankerray coughs and throws up clots of blood, some of the droplets landing on Ollatunji's shoes. Ollatunji, angry about what just happened, reaches down and uses a handful of dirt to wipe the specs of blood from his shoes. Then speaking in a whisper so low only Tankerray can hear, Ollatunji said, "Bottom rail on top now." He begins wiping dirt from his hands on his clothes. "Yessah, bottom rail on top now." Tankerray gurgles, and wheezes, his right hand clenches the lose dirt beneath it.

"GET AWAY FROM THAT WHITE MAN, NIGGER!"

The words cut into Ollatunji's ears like a cold steel knife piercing his belly. He falls back from Tankerray as if he is physically pushed. He recognizes the voices and knows the speaker does not take kindly to him, as a person of color.

"Tank, did that nigger do this to you!" said another.

Ollatunji feels a cold gun barrel on the back of his neck.

"Ollatunji didn't do nuthin' to Massa T," pleads Obula. "Honest Massa, honest. Massa T did dis' to hisself!"

Ollatunji does not move. He stares at Tankerray's shaking hand. He fears he will feel a jagged piece of hot lead from the barrel that is applying great pressure on the back of his neck. He hears one of the white men try and convict him of a crime he did not commit, while Obula staunchly pleads, defending him.

"Tell me Tank," said the tall lanky white man, "did this nigger do this to you?

"Let me kill him right now," said the short fat white man holding the gun. "He'll be one less nigger we need to question about this."

"Don't shoot Ollatunji, Massa, please don't," cries Obula. "He da driver here and if he die, nobody can run da niggers like he do."

"I don't care if he yo daddy," yells the short fat white man. "If he did this to Tank, he's a dead nigger."

All Tankerray can do is wheeze and gurgle and stink from all the alcohol he has consumed. It is a wonder either of the white men can stand to be near him. Now his bowels have released and the stench from his insides fills the barn and causes Obula to gag and cover her face in her apron.

The man holding Tankerray's head pleads with him to try and tell him what happened. "Tank, can you speak, tell us what happened?" said the tall lanky white man, leaning over Tankerray.

Tankerray wheezes gurgles and struggles for breath. Ollatunji wonders if in his last breath, Tankerray was going to set the record straight. He wonders if Tankerray has any sense of fear of God. He wonders if Tankerray suddenly realizes he has done enough wrong in his life. He wonders if Tankerray wants to do something right for a change before he dies. He wonders if Tankerray will be forgiving. The tall lanky white man leans down again, his ear close to Tankerray. Ollatunji wonders if he will see the rising sun tomorrow.

"Tank is dead," said the tall lanky white man, rising, wiping off his hands.

"Oh no, Lord no!" cries Obula.

"What about the nigger?" asks the short fat white man with the gun.

The tall lanky white man comes over to where Ollatunji is still bent over and using the toe of his shoe, under Ollatunji's chin, he raises his face up. "Tank said the nigger didn't do it."

"Thank you Jesus!" cries Obula.

* * * * * * * * *

The next two months are pure hell for Ollatunji and the slaves. Master Johnson's son, Percy, came back and attempted to run things while borrowing overseers from neighboring farms until he found a replacement for Tankerray. He kept reminding Ollatunji how disappointed he was in him to have let Tankerray accidentally kill himself. He told Ollatunji he didn't know if he could trust him to take care of the farm with the next overseer that he hired. All Percy wanted was to get the crops in. The replacement overseers showed little or no mercy on the slaves or Ollatunji. As soon as all of the fall cotton was in and all the hogs slaughtered, Ollatunji is shackled in heavy chains, sold and put on the next steamboat to New Orleans.

Ollatunji finds his new home to be a stall in a large warehouse he shares with other slaves. Right away he knows he is different from them. They hardly have clothes. His, though dirty, covered all of him. They hardly speak in a uniform language; they squat together, shivering, frightened not knowing or understanding their plight. Ollatunji realizes his situation and decides he is not about to end up a poor ignorant slave like them. He has been a driver of slaves and he needs to show he is better than they to all who come by.

And indeed he tries to impress everyone who comes to see what's for sale. He tries standing when others crouched, he jumps at the voice of the overseer, he smiles at their racial slurs, and he nods his head agreeing with them as they say disparaging things about the other slaves. He does all this to impress the white man who he now knows is his Savior and Satan at the same time. But no white Savior or Satan sees fit to be impressed enough with him to buy him, so Ollatunji serves out a sentence of degradation by assimilation, eventually losing all hope of being sold.

"You there, what's your name? Do you know how to talk?"

Ollatunji remains crouched on the ground, in the corner of the stall, his arms wrapped around his knees, his head resting on his knees. The voice he hears he knows is not for him, so he remains still. The other slaves in the pen stand and move forward.

"Takes me suh!" yells a tall skinny black slave with no bottom teeth.

"Takes me, please, please, please!" yells another, his body scared by the whip.

"I knows how to picks the cotton and shuck the corn!" said another, smiling through gaps in his teeth.

Ollatunji hears the others chanting and singing and dancing, trying to convince the buyers they are his best choice. Regardless of how he felt before, now he feels he is no better than those around him. What have I done Lord, he prays, to deserve this kind of life.

"You there, crouching, stand up and let me see you."

Ollatunji slowly straightens himself, his eyes remain closed, not wanting to see another white face that will reject his being. All he wants to be is a good slave to someone. He wants very badly to leave this wretched hole of broken spirits and stench of dirty bodies. He stands not as proud as he first did, not smiling as he first did, not as straight as he first did, but he just stands there, waiting for the voice to tell him to sit again.

"Open your eyes and come closer."

Ollatunji opens his eyes and sees a short white balding man is standing on the bottom rail of the pen fence, waving him to come closer. Besides him is a taller black man, too well dressed to be a slave. He must be a free black who works for this short white man. He has heard in New Orleans there are more free blacks than any other place in the South. For a fleeting moment it comes to him; to be free; what a thought to have and not hold. But if he works for the short balding white man, he's still a slave. He wonders if the black man is a free black here to buy slaves. He always said he didn't want to work for a free black because he heard they are worst than any white overseer. Working under the whip of a free nigger is worst than working under the whip of a buckra white.

"Turn around and take off your shirt," said the short balding white man.

Ollatunji takes off what remain of his ragged shirt and slowly turns around.

"See, ain't a mark on him. Put your shirt back on, boy."

Ollatunji turns around and looks into the smiling face of the short white man. It is then that he notices the blotches of red showing through his thinning hair and the ruffles of hair above his eyes. Puffs of skin sagged under his eyes and his mouth is crooked when he wasn't speaking. His hands are small. His clothes are much too small. They stretch and gather in bunches around his waist. Pinned inside a belt, pressed tightly around his waist, is a riding crop.

"At six hundred-fifty, this is good money spent for this nigger. He is indeed a fine specimen. What's your name, boy?"

"Ollatunji."

The black man leans over and whispers something into the ear of the short white man.

"Well, Olli whatever your name is,", said the short balding man, "you just been rescued."

After the two of them leave, Ollatunji is lead out of the pen to a waiting buckboard wagon where he is told to sit, while he is chained to the insides of the wagon so he won't escape. Ollatunji waits and watches the people who pass him staring. Some little white boys throw pebbles at him. He is spat on with tobacco juice. About fifteen minutes later tall the black man comes out, gets into the wagon and drives the noisy team of horses out of town.

After riding on a bumpy road for fifteen minutes the wagon stops and the tall black man driver climbs into the back and to Ollatunji's surprise, unlocks the shackles that hold Ollatunji.

"You're not going to need those unless you plan to run away", said the driver, stacking the shackles in a corner of the wagon. "And if you take off now, you'll be stopped by the road patrollers and since you don't have a pass to be on this road, they'll hang you and I'll be out six hundred and fifty dollars."

Ollatunji doesn't speak. He is too shocked to speak. What manner of man is this who frees him? Maybe he died in his sleep and is now just becoming aware of it. He touches his wrists where the heavy chains have rubbed his skin raw. Maybe this black man is a slave also, like he was, an assistant to the overseer. He remains squatting in the back of the wagon.

"Now, what I need you to do is give me your word."

Ollatunji nods his head, agreeing.

"Good. As long as you do what you're told, you will have no need to fear my wrath." Andrew returns his attention to the team of horses and continues his ride home with his new acquisition. "By the way, my name is Andrew Jackson St. Claire and your new name is Charlie Boy. You're in America now and you need a Christian name."

"Thank-you Massa Andrew."

* * * * * * * * *

Charlie Boy is digging up weeds in the slave's garden when he first sees the two white men. Next he sees the dog. It reminded him of Tankerray's dogs. An old mangy black dog that looks like all it needs to satisfy the twisted mouth on its face is to bite somebody black. There is a rope leading from the neck of the dog to a white man who looks like he half dressed himself on purpose. His clothes hang on him like they weren't supposed to fit. And the younger man walking with him is not much better. They are part time bounty hunters, part time patrollers and full time buckras. They have no business coming on Massa Andrew's property, but they come anyway because they know, as white men, they can do whatever they want.

They walk without any fear, not showing any hesitation in their steps. It's as if they are being led onto the farm by the wretched looking black dog, its nose true to the ground that it sniffs, blowing dust balls into the air. Charlie Boy leans on the fence by the slave garden, hushing the children, watching them pass. There is hatred in his eyes. He wants them to look at him. He wants them to know they are not wanted. He has seen that look of disrespect on a white man's face before and knows first hand of the savagery of the dog on the flimsy leash.

Matilda is putting out the evening garbage buckets for the pigs when she sees them passing Charlie Boy and the slave garden. She shakes her head, disgusted at the gall of these two unruly looking white men with a dog that looks like it needs something to eat. They have no business being here but still they continue to approach the back of the house. The way they look, they certainly are not presentable at the front door. The younger one seems to be apprehensive as they get closer to the house, but he is gently pulled along by the old man. They pause just for a moment before they see Matilda and then begin walking in her direction. From what she can see, Matilda does not want to be around for the odor that is sure to precede them. She closes the door leading into the kitchen and walks to the living room where Massa Andrew, his sons and family are resting after their dinner. "Massa Andrew, there are two buckra men, with a dog, walking towards the back door," announces Matilda. "They are either looking for food or looking for somebody."

There is a sudden rush from the living room to the door leading through the kitchen. Andrew is first to leave the kitchen to meet the two white men standing not far from the barn. Andrew looks at them and knows they are not here to rent out any of his slaves, nor are they here for food. The older one is too much in control of his behavior whereas the younger looked nervous. The dog keeps its nose in the air as if it is trying to pick up a scent. Andy and Pierre walk closely behind their father, alternating not taking their eyes from the dog or the older white man. Matilda stands in the doorway with Margaret and Mary, straining to hear.

Andy checks the status of the rifles the men hold. They are broken open. He checks the looks on their faces. The older one shows no fear, while the younger shows confusion. Andy wonders what these two crazy buckra men want. Are they out looking for some food or looking for work? Andrew has hired buckras in the past when he had odd jobs the slaves couldn't do. Andy always found buckras to be amusing; the fact there were whites poorer in America than free blacks, showed true laziness on their part. How is it there are white people that fail in this white-folks-in-charge society? It must have something to do with a lack of will on their part; but even with that lack of will, they have just to ask and they will be given their place in the white society, above the free blacks, except for maybe for these two. It is for this illogical reasoning of white people that Andy feels no pity or even feels it necessary to recognize the buckra when he passed them in his travels.

Pierre recognizes Major Treeman. Along with him, tethered by a flimsy rope, his mangy dog; and from the puncture scars on his master's left hand, no doubt has bitten the hand that feeds him several times. He is not an ordinary hunting dog, but a dog that hunts only runaway slaves. The younger one keeps looking around, nervous about his surroundings. What is he thinking, all the black folks gonna rise up and kill all three of them?

Andrew stares at the two men and wonders why they have a need to be on his property. All the neighboring farmers always send their slaves to the front door to make sure someone is home before entering onto someone's property. These two are not farmers; just two worthless bounty hunters and from their shabbily deprived looks, not very good at doing their job. Andrew suddenly senses a smell of dirty animal carcass and human sweat.

"I trust you two have good reason to be at my door," said Andrew, sternly, looking at them.

The older man steps forward removes then crumbles his hat in his hands. "Begging your pardon, but, my name is Treeman, Major Treeman. I'm from the Clanton plantation. This is my son, JoJo and this here is my dog, Nutmeg. We're lookin' for that runaway niggra named Anna."

"There is no slave on my farm named Anna," said Andrew, "now if you don't mind, I would like both of you to leave my property, now."

Major Treeman reaches into his pocket and brings out a piece tattered cloth, and moves it briskly in front of Nutmeg's nose. The dog begins to yelp, twist and yank at the rope holding him. Major Treeman again rubs the tattered cloth in the nose of the dog, which drives the dog to a feverish pitch of excitement.

"Hold that damn dog!" demands Andrew.

"Hold still Nutmeg!" shouts JoJo. "Hold still, I said! God-damn dog."

Nutmeg yanks and pulls at rope, trying to twist himself out of it. JoJo kneels and tries to calm the mangy animal, but Nutmeg does not respond to him.

"Andy, get my pistol, this dog looks like it's getting ready to bite somebody," said Andrew, looking at the dog.

"Oh no sir, Nutmeg ain't about to bite nobody," said Major Treeman, trying to contain Nutmeg. "He just smells somethin' in the air."

At the same time Andy returns with the pistol, Nutmeg breaks from his rope, much to the surprise of everyone, and runs towards the barn.

"Hey JoJo," yells Major, "go get that damn dog!"

"Yeah, Pa, I will," said the young buckra man, running away, yelling at Nutmeg to stop.

Pierre, seeing the direction Nutmeg is running, grabs the pistol from Andy and runs behind JoJo. By the time he gets to the side of the barn, Nutmeg is anxiously digging in the ground at the bottom of the boards of the barn. JoJo has a hold of Nutmeg by the collar, fighting to keep him from digging up anymore dirt. "Pull that damn dog back," hollers Pierre, "or I will kill him. Do it!" The pistol shakes in the hands of Pierre, making everyone nervous around him.

Mary, Margaret and Matilda have come from the kitchen and are running towards the barn, following in the dust trails of Andrew, Andy and Major. Charlie Boy stops his hoeing in the garden and watches the commotion. Mama Sarah, too upset to watch what is unfolding, goes inside the slave housing and slams the door behind her.

Pierre's hand is shaking uncontrollably. He is afraid his finger will pull the trigger and truly shoot Nutmeg over the yelling objections of JoJo, Major Treeman, Andrew and Andy. Whether he can kill Nutmeg is not clear to him. He's not even sure this old pistol will even fire. He remembers Papa sitting one day in the barn cleaning it up. He had taken the pistol apart and was cleaning and shining each part. Pierre sat across from him watching as he put it back together again. When he was done, he rolled the clicking canister where the bullets are housed, pushed it back in place, pointed it towards the ceiling with one eye open, then smiled and placed it back on the nail barrel. Andrew then got up smiled at what he had done and said, "I wonder if it has enough spring tension to fire a bullet."

Pierre continues to hold the trembling gun's aim at the scratching, clawing dog. Dirt is flying helter-skelter from beneath him. JoJo is pulling and yanking, pleading desperately, trying to coax Nutmeg back from the side of the barn.

Anna saw them when they turned up the driveway. She had prayed she would never have to see either one of them again. She remembers the craggy face of the older man, which always looked like it was wracked in anger. She knows him as 'Mista Major', but his nickname is Nigger Finder, because he is so good at what he does. When a farmer hires him and his son JoJo to find a runaway, part of the understanding between them and the farmer is that he does not guarantee they will bring back the runaway with life still in them. He only guarantees they will bring them back.

Finding small cracks in the boards that covered the frame of the barn, Anna followed the men as they approached the house. She has a sinking feeling in the pit of her stomach. She stops breathing for a moment. She has her eyes wide as she peeks through cracks in the wall of wood. Nutmeg turned his head sharply as they passed the barn. JoJo yanks at the rope holding the dog, forcing him to follow, but Nutmeg's nose remained pointed in the direction of the barn. Anna knows at that moment she had been discovered. She has no place to go. And in the moments that followed she remembered why she feared Mista Major and his son JoJo. She remembered how they brought back her runaway cousin, with his foot half chewed off, his arm mangled from that evil black dog, Nutmeg. She remembered how JoJo found her alone in the slave quarters, laying sick with fever, and he forced her to let him discover his manhood at her expense, leaving the stench of a thousand bath-less nights on her body and the seeds of life for millions of his off-spring. Terrified and weakened by the nasty ordeal Anna still managed to drag her body outside, behind the slave quarters, dig a hole, squat over it and expunge his seeds of life from her body. Then using the cold ashes from a burned out stove fire she vigorously rubbed his stench from her body.

"Pierre, put down the pistol," pleads Andy, speaking in a tone as not to excite. "There is no reason for you to over react. Now, slowly, lower that pistol."

Pierre's arm is getting tired. He didn't know how much longer he could hold the pistol before the weight of it causes him to pull the trigger. He wonders if Anna can see him. Of course she can. He hopes she will remain quiet. He prays to God that she does not give herself away.

The determined black mongrel doesn't care one bit about what's going on around him. He's not aware of the fact there is a pistol aimed at his head. He has no fear of what possibly could happen to him. He smells something and he wants whatever it is that has caught the attention of his nose.

"Just what the hell do you reckon he's digging for," mumbles Major Treeman, staring at Nutmeg. His face is full of questions. "He's gone plum crazy with scent."

Andy reaches out and gently takes the pistol from Pierre and gives it to Andrew, who has finally arrived.

"Must be a muskrat or something," mutters Pierre, trying to remain calm. He begins to kick dirt back into the small hole dug by Nutmeg.

JoJo now has control of Nutmeg and is re-tying the knot in the rope that broke. He pulls Nutmeg away from the barn.

"Yea," said Major Treeman, feigning agreement. "Must be some kind of muskrat or something'." Major Treeman reaches down and makes sure Nutmeg is secured, then begins walking away. "Come on JoJo, let's go. There ain't nothing' here."

Andrew, Andy and Pierre watch the two men and their dog walk down the driveway.

"That was pretty stupid Pierre," said Andrew. "What were you trying to prove?"

"You gonna kill a white man's dog in front of him?" chides Andy. "What sense does that make?"

"If you want to kill something, prepare yourself to kill a Yankee," said Andrew., putting his pistol away in his belt. "Don't waste your time on the likes of that poor white trash."

"The way your hand was shaking, I was afraid you were about to shoot yourself," said Andy. "Now that would have been embarrassing."

Pierre doesn't respond to his father or brother. His heart is still beating at a rapid pace. He is trying to calm down the heaving of his chest. He leans against the wall as he kicks dirt back into the small hole made by Nutmeg.

Andrew leaves Pierre leaning against the wall. He is quickly followed by Andy laughing, as he retells Margaret and Mary about Pierre's behavior. Pierre waits until the buckra visitors are completely out of site before he begins listening to see if Anna is okay. But there is no sound coming from the barn. Looking towards the house, Pierre sees Andy following his sister and mother inside. He slowly walks into the barn and stands in silence, waiting, listening for Anna.

"It's okay Anna, it's me."

There is a rustling of some hay above him, but no response comes from Anna.

"That was close," continues Pierre, going to the side of the barn Nutmeg was digging so furiously. "I better get these old clothes out of here. I should have done it long ago." Pierre reaches behind the storage cabinet and retrieves Anna's original clothes. He bundles them into a small ball then stuffs then into a burlap sack. "As soon as I get a chance I will bring you some food. I better go now before I'm missed."

Pierre leaves the barn with the small burlap sack under his arm and a small can of kerosene. He goes to a place in the yard where a pit is being dug for a fire when the hog killing begins. He drops the sack into the hole, pours some kerosene over it then lights it. It is a small fire, not meant to draw the attention of anyone. He watches the trail of smoke rise straight into the night air. Satisfied it will burn completely he walks towards the house. He knows now he must move Anna as soon as possible. He doesn't trust Major Treeman. He feels in his gut Major Treeman will be back. Pierre pauses at the back door and checks the progress of the small fire. He tells Matilda he's burning a dead rat when she asks about the fire and the same reply to everyone else. He feels confident his secret is safe, for now, but he knows it won't be for long.

Charlie Boy watches Pierre disappear into the house. He walks to the pit where the burning fire is smoldering. He pokes at the ashes with his walking stick. He recognizes what is burning. Charlie Boy looks at the barn. There is no doubt in his old feeble mind who is hiding inside, but he cannot tell anyone. He needs advice. He must talk to Voodoo Man Cato.

CHAPTER 10
Thursday, November 14ᵗʰ, 1861

Dr. DuBois is near the end of his long day. He sits exhausted in his office. He has seen over 100 patients with 100 different ailments and has been paid a hundred different ways. Some ailments and complaints he has never even heard of until today. Dr. DuBois' knowledge of medicine, at this time in America, was mediocre at best. He is doing the best he can with what he has. There are no x-rays, no antibiotics, blood transfusions, and no knowledge of bacteria or viruses and so there were no antiseptics. The good medical schools were at the established colleges up North, and their programs usually lasted 1 year. That important year of medical education consisted of all book instructions, with a few weeks being in residency in a local medical house or small neighborhood hospital. Medical schools were proprietary, had little or no entrance requirements, and provided no clinical training. Most doctors learned their profession through apprenticeships with practicing physicians, who may have learned the same way. Thus many medical procedural mistakes were repeated.

The proprietary nature of medical schools made difficult any improvements in the quality of education. Competition for students, any student, literate or not, resulted in a lowering of standards. Schools were more interested in making a profit because medical schools were separate from the university system and those schools affiliated with universities were only in name. Opening a medical school required only a hall and a group of physicians willing to lecture. Future doctors bought tickets for the lectures, producing outrageous profits for physicians, who lectured very little about patient care.

Occasionally there were lectures that included dissection, but this was rare since most states prohibited dissecting human corpses. New Orleans became a center for medical education because of the large number of unclaimed corpses of poor transients available from the charity hospitals. Poor training of the doctors resulted in poor quality of care and in return, brought little respect to physicians. Patients paid less than five dollars for the most common of procedures and often bartered for other medical services.

Soon, professional people were standing on street corners claiming to have cure- alls for every ailment. Some came to town in buckboard wagons, bragging about how successful their tonic had been in the town they just left. All this contributed to the development of a new medical profession called quackery. One such quack is Dr W. K. F. Fryer. Dr. Fryer said, "by long intercourse with many different tribes of savages and much practice, he can cure scurvy, bilious complaints, fits, fevers, ague, diabetes, ulcers, cancers and bedsores." Dr. Fryer was located at No. 382 Greatmen Street, between Bagatelle and Union in the third district. Not to be out done, Orson S. Fowler claimed a person's character was made up of 37 faculties, which could be 'read' on the cranium at the site where each was located. He called his procedure Phrenology. Mesmerism was promoted by Robert H. Collyer through a procedure that was suppose to correct the invisible magnetic fluids contained in the body that had been disturbed because vital organs had been deprived of said fluid. Doctors used magnets in a skullcap to correct this inbalance. S. R. Wells believed the bodies operated like a magnet with positive and negative charges. He believed if electricity was applied to the areas where charges were out of balance, the patient would be cured. Resourceful entrepreneurs soon began producing electrical garments and products, including corsets, belts, and hairbrushes.

Following right behind the unsubstantiated quackery, came supporting documentation in the form of books that told how the cure was to be administered and showed guaranteed success from formerly ill patients. There were those who believed diseases resulted from a totally clogged body system and could only be cured by purging and sweating. Using distillates of Native American vegetable and combining it with bloodletting, Samuel Thomson received a patent for his system. He promoted his theories in *Thomsonian Materia Medica* and *A New Guide to Health*.

Dr. DuBois' medical training consisted of a few years of following around the previous doctor, then spending a number of years honing his profession as a doctor-in-residence on several small plantations. It was during this time he learned and perfected treatment that included combinations of purges and astringents that also included bloodletting. He learned how to reset bones, repair fractures, pull teeth, drain abscesses and even performed amputations. After writing, collecting and filing notes of patients from the day then putting the petty change box away, he rises from his squeaky chair, stands in the middle of his office and slowly looks around. His library consists of all the latest medical journals, some of which he doesn't even trust or use. Inside some are all the latest cures for every possible known illness. He's committed to his patients and feels what ever he did for his patients, he never could do enough, or know enough about their illness. People come to him with their lives in their hands and when they leave they still carry their fragile lives in their hands. And for all of this he charges one dollar for an initial visit, fifty cents for follow up visits, two dollars for night home visits, twenty-five dollars for birthing a child and somewhere between two and forty dollars for minor operations.

In the city of New Orleans, doctors often charged different rates for blacks and whites. In most cases blacks paid about a third less than whites. Dr. DuBois found middle ground for expected payments received from blacks and whites, rich and not so rich, collecting fees of some kind even from those suffering in poverty. Surrounded by all of the latest and greatest reference manuals pertaining to the healing of the sick, Dr. DuBois also has shelves of ointments. He has salves, calomel, herb teas, laxatives, emetics, quinine, castor oil, morphine white sassafras root, black-eyed peas, horseradish poultice, nutmeg, dried peach leaves, alum, saltpeter, herbs of all kinds, turpentine, honey, onions, cami weed, Jerusalem weeds, a bottle of whiskey and a bottle of brandy. All these make up his arsenal of medical solutions. Dr. DuBois knew everything he needed to know about medicine, but knew little about how to heal and make well his patients. He knew this to be a fact, but his patients didn't. They believed what they wanted, sometimes telling him what to prescribe for them.

Medical science currently thinks it has found a panacea in sulfur baths promised to cure everything from fungus, ringworm, scabies, ulcers, leprosy, attacks of paralysis, rheumatism, fevers, gout, clogged pores, aching bones, yaws, skin ailments of all kinds or weak membranes. Dr. DuBois opens the door leading to his waiting room and sighs. The room is half filled with patients because the rest got tired of waiting and went home to come back tomorrow. There is the normal array of faces he's use to seeing every time he opens the door. It's like a nightmare, always the same faces. This must be what it's like in hell concludes Dr. DuBois, so much misery, everywhere he looks. He's seen them all before, but he sees them again and again. The crooked mouths on the crooked faces, the dark faces with shine, the light faces with blue and green eyes, the brown faces with piercing black eyes; the buckra who can't afford to go anyplace else. The saddened child's face laying in their mother's lap, the sleeping face, with no place else to go, the crying face being washed with tears of pain and all of them staring at him with eyes begging to be next. Surveying his own little hell he wonders, what can I do? He decides to send them all home with a hardy dismissal, telling them to come back tomorrow when he has more time.

"All of you, out of here, now," he yells, "go I tell you. Come back tomorrow after nine am!"

Standing in his office doorway, Dr. DuBois watches and listens to the smothered grumbling as the small crowd of waiting patients saunter from his waiting room. He waits until all have left before closing the door to his office. He returns to his desk and lets his body collapse into the yellow and blue settee by the window with the view of the mighty Mississippi. He closes his eyes and rubs the sides of his head, trying to relieve some of the tension from the day. It seems that since the war has started more poor white folks have more complaints of illnesses. He wonders how long this madness of ill and not-so-ill patients will go on? At first he thought it was because some of the other doctors had left to become officers and medical offices in the Confederacy, but now he knows it's because a lot of poor white men folk don't want to go into the war and only a doctor order can prevent that from happening. He has written seven such orders today, for a reasonable fee, somewhat above what he normally charges and expects for his services.

"Is there any chance a sick man can get some medical treatment in here?"

The words drifted across the room like leaves on a gentle wind. Dr. DuBois, at first didn't recognize the voice and was about to turn and give the intruder a strong piece of his mind, but a familiar face quickly associated with the voice inside his mind.

"If' you've come here for medical treatment, you're going to die waiting for the doctor," said Dr. DuBois. He is always very happy to know his friend and confidant, Andrew Jackson St. Claire is here to see him and be seen by him. "Andrew, my good friend, how are you doing?" Dr. DuBois pumps up his weary body and rises from the settee to shake his friend's hand and hug him. "It is good to see you as the last patient of my day."

"Aloysius, my friend," sighs Andrew, finding a place to sit, "how goes the war?" He reaches into his vest pocket and retrieves two Confederate dollars and gives it to Dr. DuBois.

"The war goes well. We are winning right now and hopefully the winning will continue." Dr. DuBois begins preparing the utensils he'll need to examine Andrew. "Right now though, I'm more interested in how you're feeling?"

Andrew is one of Dr. DuBois' toughest cases. He knows something is going on inside Andrew's body but he cannot tell exactly what it is. Something inside Andrew's body is slowing his heart, slowing his breathing, and is slowly killing him. With all the medical knowledge he has at hand and reference manuals he has read, all that is known to man, he still doesn't know what is killing his friend or how to prevent it from continuing to happen. He looks into the face of his dying friend and wonders if Andrew can see the pain that he hides behind his smile.

"I'm here ain't I," chuckles Andrew, naturally preparing to take off his shirt, knowing Aloysius will be giving him a check up. "I'm walking every morning, just like you asked and I don't eat much heavy food like you said."

Dr. DuBois watches and listens to Andrew as he unbuttons his shirt and is reminded how Andrew and others like him are the reason he hates being a doctor. How can a country that is advanced as America in everything that makes this country move forward, not know more and understand the science of medicine. All the manuals and pamphlets, all the jars of medicine and all the books that lined his shelves, with all of them, none said anything conclusive about the condition his good friend Andrew has.

"You know, folks are still talking about that speech you made at that last meeting. Yup, people are still asking what they can do to help win this war."

Dr. DuBois sits in front of Andrew and checks his eyes then his nostrils, then motions Andrew to stop talking and open his mouth, whereas he checked the insides. He then squeezes both shoulders, raises and stretches the left then right arm of Andrew, noticing there is an increase of loose flesh. The firmness that he remembers from his last visit is now sagging more about his pectoral muscle and his arms. Andrew's exterior body is slowly deteriorating, joining what is happening inside his body. Small, strange unknown white spots were beginning to show on his back and arms.

"How is your wonderful wife, Mary," Dr. DuBois begins tapping on various areas of Andrew's back, then checks for swelling about his neck. "Tell her I miss Matilda's apple pie and I'm waiting for another invite."

Dr. DuBois exhibited a sincere smile when he spoke of Mary St. Claire. He often felt she knew Andrew was dying before he told her about his condition. When he explained how necessary it was for Andrew not get too excited, he did so in order to show how Andrew would cut down on the pain spells he was having about his chest. Because of the anxiety brought on by Andrew's condition, he prescribed a strong powder sedative to calm her. The woman has stood by Andrew and been his sole pillar of support during their union as partners in life. He helped birth all of their children and watched all of them grow to what they are today.

"The woman worries too much about me," complains Andrew,

putting his shirt back on. "You'd think I was dying or something, the way she dolts after me."

"She cares a great deal about you and her family, give her my best."

"So, what's the verdict, Aloysius, am I going to live?'

"You are doing just fine. You will live a long time, my friend," said Dr. DuBois, lying. "You gotta remember to watch what you eat, that's all." Dr. DuBois does not look Andrew in the face when he speaks those words; instead he chooses to turn his back to him as he muttered the words, hoping Andrew does not detect the wavering of his voice as a sign he was not giving him the whole truth. "How are things at that farm of yours?"

"Since the war started, I've been able to sell more lumber than before. So much I think I will need to purchase maybe one or two more slaves."

"Sometimes I wish I had a slave or two to help me out here. Good help is so hard to find. I've had three different aids since the first of the year. And business, if I can use that phrase, has been picking up." Dr. DuBois completes writing notes in the folder belonging to Andrew. "Its amazing how many white folks don't want to go to war."

"Well, once it's over and the Confederacy has won, you won't have to worry about replacing aids, but how to spend the money you'll be making working with the state heading up some clinic or something. You've got a thriving business here, one the Confederacy will appreciate after the war. Then you can buy that big house and hire as many slaves you need to keep it going."

Dr. DuBois listens to Andrew's rambling conversation as he writes another worthless prescription for his medication. A prescription that does nothing more than prolongs what will eventually happen. Dr. DuBois thinks Andrew won't even live to see the end of the war, unless it ends by the early spring of next year. It is times like these when Dr. DuBois wishes he knew more about Black Magic and its properties. Right now he would try anything to save his friend, anything.

"You will be at the parade, after all you are the commanding officer," said Andrew, staring out the window and down onto the streets of New Orleans.

Dr. DuBois knows from what he hears in the back alleys of New Orleans there is something to be said about Black Magic, only he could never understand how those properties are mixed together to achieve what they do. After all he is an educated man, and Black Magic belonged to the ignorant, the poor, the non-believers, and the uneducated. Andrew has a voodoo man on his farm, but he would never ask Andrew to see him mainly because Andrew doesn't believe in that hocus-pocus either. But there must be something going on there unknown to Andrew. Of all the farms in the area, Andrew's farm is the only one he has yet to visit for illnesses of the slaves.

"See you at the parade next week, Aloysius" said Andrew, standing at the door leading out of Dr. DuBois' office. "And don't forget your uniform, Commander."

Dr. DuBois smiles at Andrew, then gives him the okay sign as Andrew closes the door. Then, in silent prayer, he said, "May you walk on the hands of God from this day forward, my friend."

CHAPTER 11
Saturday, November 23rd, 1861

Under pristine blue skies, dotted with white puffs of cotton balls, the Crescent City dressed itself up for a party. The banners were strung across the broadness of Canal Street that stretches from the levees north to the cemeteries. The balconies were draped in magnificent Confederate flags trimmed in yellow; and people standing on them waving smaller flags of the Confederacy cheering the marching men and boys who filled, wall to wall, the dual carriage ways of Canal Street, all singing in loud harmony, I Wish I Was in Dixie's Land.

In all there were more than twenty-five thousand soldiers marching proudly to drums, fifes and horns. Onward the off springs of New Orleans favorite sons strutted through the parent city, some in half uniforms, some in no uniforms, some out of step, some just walking, others stumbling along in a drunken stupor, but still they marched on.

There is a tremendous amount of pride in the air. One can feel it wrap and engulf their bodies as they stand shoulder to shoulder in the cheering crowd. And no one was ever more proud than Mary St. Claire and her daughter Margaret. They are standing on the corner of Basin and Canal Street, singing with the rest of the crowd, watching the marching troops passing, looking with impatient anticipation. Mary, standing on her toes until she cannot anymore, is waiting for her beloved Andrew and her sons Andy and Pierre. She has watched and cheered all the soldiers that have passed until she is almost hoarse and she wants to hold onto what was left of her voice for Andrew. She looks quickly at the passing faces, smiling at friends and loved ones, waiting with her for the opportunity to do the same. Her neck is getting tired from twisting right to left and her feet are getting sore from standing so long. Canal Street is so long and wide. She only hopes they are marching on this side of the street.

"There they are Mother!" Margaret is jumping up and down, grabbing her mother's arm, shaking it frantically. "Oh Mother, there's Papa and there's Andy!"

Mary looks anxiously in the direction Margaret is pointing and sees Andrew marching along side of the Native Guards. He is yelling at them, reminding them about keeping in step and keeping their backs straight. Dr. DuBois is marching in front of them, behind a white officer, looking very much distinguished and in charge. He neither looks right nor left, his eyes looking straight ahead. Mary returns her attention to Andrew, wondering if he's aware she can see him. Margaret is still jumping up and down, trying desperately to get their attention, trying to over shout the noises of the cheering crowds.

Mary's eyes swell with tears. Her Andrew looks so wonderful in his Confederate gray. She has forgotten why he has it on. She had taken special care sewing them for Andrew, Andy and Pierre. The Native Guards' uniforms looked so much better than their white counterparts. Despite the weather, there is still a look of neatness about them. She keeps looking at Andrew, hoping he will show some sign he knows she is near. Mary feels like the teenager she was when she first met Andrew. There is a tingle deep inside her she hadn't felt in a long time.

Mary twists her kerchief after dabbing her eyes, hoping this moment will last just a bit longer, longer than the war itself. The Native Guards are now marching in place, singing and listening to the commands of Andrew. They soon start making a series of left turns, using their rifles to thump the ground as they turn. By the time they are facing the crowd where Mary and Margaret stand cheering, Andrew tips his cap at Mary and smiles. Mary smiles back, wiping the tears from her face. There is one more left turn then Andrew gives a command and the Native Guards march on, enthusiastically to the maddening roar of an approving crowd.

"Oh Mother, didn't they look just wonderful!"

"Yes they did, Margaret," sighs Mary. She watches the Native Guards until she can no longer see Andrew. "Yes they did." Mary waits until Margaret stops trying to see them before she starts mingling with the crowd that is now beginning to breakup.

North on Canal Street, onward and upward, the parade's final members of the twenty-five thousand went, marching and singing. North on Canal Street, past more throngs of cheering supporters, ladies and lads waving from wrought iron balconies, dogs barking and snipping at the ankles of the marchers. At each point where the Native Guards stopped to perform their maneuvers, they received even louder applause from the crowds. Andrew St. Claire is so proud of his Native Guards, and of his son. Andrew knows these free blacks are taking another step in showing the white folks just how much they believe in what the Confederacy has done. It is just a beginning of what white folks will see in the future when the war is over.

Andrew glances around at the smiling faces in the crowd, acknowledging those who salute him and the troops he marches with. It is indeed a glorious day for all the free blacks of New Orleans. He is crossing Claiborne and still the crowds were lining the street. Though not as large as those between the levee and Basin, still they are respectable. Andrew knows the parade will be over soon and this will be nothing but good memories. Now, he needs to find the one smiling face that will set his mind at ease. Even if Pierre doesn't believe in what his father stands for, at least he can come out and cheer for his brother and father for what they believe in. He has been searching for the face of Pierre from the time they lined up at the levees. During the mayhem and madness of getting into position to begin the long march he searched. He and Dr. DuBois looked for their sons and were disappointed not to see them before it was time for them to march.

They are between Johnson and Mirol Street, when Andrew sees Pierre and Dr. DuBois' son, Marcel. They are standing with a group of their friends watching the passing parade. Andrew barks a few commands to straighten the appearance of the troops before they get to Pierre and his friends. He wants to put on a good impression for Pierre. He hopes it would somehow instill some pride in Pierre about what he and Andy are doing. As they approach the corner of

Mirol and Canal Street, Andrew turns his head to nod to Pierre, but instead of seeing Pierre's face he sees the back of Pierre's head and the back of all his friends who are with him.   Andrew's heart is broken. He feels like he's been sucker punched. He gasps for air. He is so hurt he almost loses his concentration. His face is filled with disappointment. It's as if a hot leaded bullet has ripped into him, tearing up his insides. His pain becomes a yolk around his neck, but, he is a soldier first and emotions have no place with a good soldier. In the next marching moment he is beyond Mirol and Canal Street, but not beyond the pain, singing with his men, but not with their enthusiasm, I Wish I Was in Dixie's Land.

*   *   *   *   *   *   *   *   *

Matilda is in a big hurry. She is rushing back and forth from the kitchen to the living room, trying to set the table for Massa Andrew and his family before they come home from the parade. They will be here soon and she is not done setting the food out and she should have been. Somehow she has misplaced a big piece of ham she wants to put in the collards, and can't for the life of her remember how it disappeared. She soon remembers it's Pierre. He is taking much more food than before to the runaway in the barn. In the beginning it was just some biscuits, right after dinner, then it was an extra piece of pie, then some molasses. Before Matilda knew who it was she made small talk with the other slaves about it but no one admitted to sneaking into the kitchen and taking food. Charlie Boy seems to know something then but he wouldn't say and she couldn't get him to admit to anything. Now, with Pierre, it's getting out of hand. She doesn't know how much longer she can cover for Pierre. Her one advantage is nobody in this family really notices when there is food missing; they just eat it.

She was able to make do with a ham bone she threw in the collards. She was going to use that bone in tomorrow morning's soup for the slaves. Right now, she didn't have time to think about what Pierre is doing because she can hear the horse and buggy coming up the driveway. Walking quickly to the dining room and moving the Confederate flag aside to look out the front bay window, she sees

Massa Andrew and Master Andy, laughing and joking as they approach Charlie Boy, waiting to put the horses away.

Her concern about the missing food is quickly replaced with the thought regarding the amount of dirt about to be brought into the house and all over the rug she just swept clean. It has been many years since her last visit to New Orleans, and what she remembers about Canal Street is there was a lot of dirt. A lot of this dirt ended up on the feet of Massa Andrew when he came home. One thing about Massa Andrew and Master Andy is that they do not wipe their feet before they come into the house. They don't even try and knock some dirt off their feet before entering. This afternoon is no different. Matilda stands at the table waiting to greet Massa Andrew as he and Andy come in, but he ignores her and continues his conversation with Master Andy.

"Andy, did you see the look on them white folk's faces when we marched by? If that wasn't a sight to see."

"Couldn't help but see it," laughed Andy, proud of his performance, "some of them running out in the street, just to look at us."

Matilda looks at the shoes of Andrew and Andy. She notices the clumps of dried dirt clinging to the edges of their shoes, waiting for the opportunity to fall off. Matilda goes to the kitchen to get the broom and keep it close at hand. Andy and Andrew continued their laughing and enjoyment from the parade.

"And we was in step too," Andrew is saying, proudly walking around inside the living room. "Yes sir, we looked good. And when we stopped and did that four cornered quickstep and turn, the folks didn't know what to do, except cheer. They went wild!" Andrew stands in front of the Confederate flag admiring it. "Matilda, get the coffee together with water for some tea. Mary and Margaret will be home soon."

Matilda looks at Massa Andrew and can see he was all in his glory, standing in front of that flag, smiling like a little boy right after he finished opening his favorite present on Christmas morning. Matilda knows she will be up half the night cleaning up after this little boy and all the little children who are about to settle down in this house. "Yes, Massa Andrew," she said going to the kitchen.

"Uh, Matilda, before you go," interrupts Andrew, stopping Matilda.

What now, wonders Matilda? This man is great for telling me to do something, then stopping me from doing it. What could possibly be on his mind now, except that stupid parade? He probably wants to tell me something else about the people at the parade, yup, that's probably what it is. "Yes, Massa Andrew."

"Come here, Matilda, closer. Andy you come over here next to me. Come on Matilda, stand over there. I want to ask you something." Andrew straightens his uniform, brushing off some of the dirt from his pants and shirt. He then touches up the appearance of Andy. Both stand smartly, smiling at Matilda. "Well, what do you think?

"About what, Massa Andrew?"

"About what we have on, the uniforms. What do your think about the uniforms?"

Mary worked very hard, sewing those uniforms for her boys. Some nights she sewed almost till dawn, trying to have them ready for the parade. At times, getting the right color gray was an ordeal. Materials are becoming scarce since the beginning of the fall planting. Seems all materials are going towards the war effort. But somehow Mary prevailed and was able to purchase enough material before rationing started. The poor woman missed a couple of stitches, and Matilda offered to help, but Mary wanted to do all of it herself.

"They really look nice for a father and son match set," said Matilda, not sure just what she was suppose to say. When she looked into the face of Massa Andrew, Matilda could tell from his expression that was not the answer he was looking for, but that's all the kind of answer he's going to get. What else was she supposed to say?

"When is lunch gonna be ready, Matilda?"

"When you let me finish doin' what I got to do it'll be on the table, Massa Andrew." Matilda returns to her chores of getting the mid day meal on the table despite Andrew and Andy walking around the table looking and picking at the food, and getting in her way.

"Did you see Mama and Margaret?" asks Andy, looking for some food to snack on. "I was so nervous, I didn't hardly see anybody except the back of the head of the man marching in front of me."

"I saw them both. They were beaming!"

This indeed is a glorious day for Andrew and Andy. Today, they and the rest of the free black community showed to all the white folks how serious they are in maintaining the style of living they and their white counterparts have grown accustomed to; even if it includes slavery as a necessary tool. They will strengthen the South and become a viable contributing player in the economy of the Confederacy. For so long free blacks have not meant that much to the well being of the South. Now, with the advent of the war, just as free blacks have gained a foothold in the economy, they only need to show they are willing to sacrifice limb and body in order to ensure continuing the traditional life style of the South.

Andrew knows and understands just what he is doing and which direction he wants the government of the South to continue. Big accomplishments are based on the building together of small accomplishments. Andrew believes the free black shall be a free voting person of the South. Andrew strongly feels when this war is over and the nation is governed by the likes of Jefferson Davis, the free black will be a participating citizen in every aspect of governing himself. Even to the point of being elected to public office and doing what is right for America and all its citizens.

"Pierre, Papa, did you see Pierre?"

The pain came back for Andrew. It was just as sharp as it was when he first saw Pierre. He felt it again as the words stabbed him again like a knife, cutting his chest open. He knows now Andy didn't see what happened at the corner of Mirol and Canal Street. Andrew loves the dedication of his son Andy, but he doesn't love Pierre any less because his dedication is elsewhere. If only Pierre understood how valuable he could be to the family if he got in line with him and Andy about the war.

Pierre does make a good point about the treatment of slaves, but Andrew is not part of the ruthless slave owners. He has to promote the business of slavery as a positive faction that helps the South gain a financial foothold in the world. He has to show through his efforts that taking care of slaves is the same as taking care of himself, his family, the livestock, and the day-to-day running of the farm. They are hired help, who can earn their freedom by buying it, just like his father did and he himself, through hard work. Andrew's greatest reward for all his hard work is that he can proudly state the fact his children do not have to buy their freedom. Andy, Pierre and Margaret are the first generation of children borne out of slavery and their children will be also, thanks to what his father and he did. It is legacy, a family legacy.

"Pierre and the rest of his friends turned their backs to us as we passed."

The words fell from his mouth like vomit, staining and smelling up the air in the room. Andrew returned to the Confederate flag, wiping it as if the stains of the words had splashed upon it. There is so much to be gained for the alliance of free blacks and the Confederacy, so much to be gained by both.

"Them bastards!" complains Andy, "then the hell with them."

"It hurt me Andy, it really did. I saw Dr. DuBois and his face showed the same pain I felt."

What is happening with the youth of today wonders Andrew? When he was their age, he was working from sun up to way past sundown. It was all about working for the white man, for little or nothing. Somehow out of that little or nothing his father was able to find a way to work for his freedom and he passed that same common sense and energy level to Andrew. Today not all children think like their parents, not all children want to follow in the footsteps of their parents, regardless of how successful their parents are. Life is too easy for the youth of today. They don't have enough to do to keep them busy and out of trouble.

"He is family," Andrew reminds Andy "You never deny family, even if you must deny their beliefs. We don't want this war to pit brother against brother."

"Papa, he shows you no respect," complains Andy, "him and his northern thinking friends. All of them are undermining the whole purpose of our allegiance."

"I can hear Miss Mary and Miss Margaret," said Matilda, walking to the vestibule just in time to meet them as they come in the front door. "Hello Miss Mary, Miss Margaret."

Mary and Margaret drop their wraps on Matilda's outstretched arms, and then proceeds to the living room where Andrew and Andy stand waiting patiently.

"Papa, you looked wonderful marching today," said Margaret, wrapping her arms around Andrew's neck, hugging him close. "I am so proud of you, and you too Andy. Both of you made me very proud today. These uniforms really look good."

"Mother did a great job making them," responds Andrew, turning to Mary. "And may I say thank you again Mother."

Andrew looks at Mary and recognizes the look on her half smiling face. He has seen that look before, many times since the start of the war. He has seen it while she rests her eyes, sitting in her favorite chair, in her face at night just before she sleeps, and at the dinner table as he and Andy speak of the many daily reports about the war. The children never noticed it but he does.

"Mother, you never did really tell me what you think about the uniforms."

Andrew wasn't sure if Mary would respond or run upstairs crying as she has done with him so many times in the past. Hopefully this parade didn't set anything off inside her mind or did it? This was a glorious time for the whole family. Surely she must be willing to share the joy and satisfaction he is experiencing.

"The uniforms looked very nice on everyone," began Mary, try to find a place away from the gaze of Andrew. "I should have taken Andy's in a little bit around the legs, but other than that, they look really nice."

"Nice?" responded Andrew in disbelief. "Mother, I saw your face when we passed. You had a smile that would have lit up New Orleans harbor." Andrew waits for Mary to respond, watching her fidget in the chair she was sitting, twisting and turning the kerchief around her knuckles. Whatever was going on inside her mind, it would not be pretty and it is not something he wanted Andy and Margaret to see. "Andy, Margaret, would you two mind going upstairs while your mother and I talk. Matilda will call you when the meal is ready." Andrew watches Margaret and Andy ascend the stairs until they are out of sight before turning back to Mary. "Okay Mary, my dear, what is it? And this time I want you to tell me everything."

Mary draws in a deep breath. She looks like she doesn't know how to say what's on her mind. She begins then stops. Begins again then stutters to a stop. Finally she looks at her loving husband. "Andrew, when I saw you passing today, I was so proud of you. I saw your face and it glowed with the pride you have in the Confederacy and it made me feel so happy inside for you. Out there, you're a soldier, a warrior, and a defender of the Confederacy. Inside this house you're a husband, a father, and a provider." Mary pauses. She takes in another deep breath. She wants to get this said without breaking down. "Andrew, it breaks my heart to think one day you may not be either because of someone, who you don't know, will shoot a bullet that will find you as its mark." Mary suddenly sobs uncontrollably into her already wet handkerchief.

Andrew goes to Mary and gathers her into his arms, rubbing her shoulders gently. "My dear Mary, nothing will ever come between me and you; not even a stray bullet from a stranger's gun."

"How can you be so confident; I'm speaking as a mother and wife who does not want to become a widower! I don't want to sacrifice any of you for the good of anything!"

"And I'm speaking as a father and husband, who wants to make sure that what we have as a family, we keep as a family. Sometimes there has to be sacrifice. Nobody wants to fight and die, but if it means you and the children will keep this place then it's not in vain."

"Vanity, another word people use when they are doing something stupid and can't explain why." There was new strength in Mary's voice now. " It just seems this country is always at war with itself. First your father, now you and they are trying to include Andy and Pierre; then, there will be no one left. Its not fair men should make all the decisions about life; who should live and should die."

Andrew knows what she is saying is the truth, but he didn't know how to explain the necessity of what he was doing in a way she would agree to. This war has put him in a compromising position. He has to choose between the Confederacy and his family. He knows how important both are to him. Somehow he needs to juggle them both effectively, without dropping either one. In order for him to keep sanity in the family he also has to find a way to juggle everyone's lives. "Mary, this will not last long at all. By next spring all of this will be over and we'll be worrying about getting the planting done on time. You heard and read what happened at Bull Run. I don't believe, we as a people, can advance in America under the current Republican Administration. My successes are the result of state's right; and my continued success will be based on state's rights."

Mary knows she has not gotten through to Andrew enough to have him change his mind. She isn't sure if she can ever get though to him. "I worry so much about all three of you, mostly Pierre. I didn't see him marching in the parade with the rest of you. Was he there?"

"He was there. He was standing about a mile from you and Margaret."

Mary senses sadness in Andrew's voice. The happiness that was there just moments ago, when he spoke of the Confederacy is missing. As much as he loves Pierre, no doubt Pierre must have disappointed him today. She wonders what is it about Pierre to cause him to go against the wishes of father? Why has he rejected what Andrew feels is best for him? Has he not loved him the same as Andy and Margaret? Yes, Pierre, was more sickly than Andy, but that was because he was low in weight at birth. He suckled more than Andy did and longer because of his infant low birth weight, but could that be part of the problem? Maybe it was being the middle child. Mary is confused about Pierre and his erratic behavior and just doesn't know what to do about it.

"You would have been ashamed of him," continues Andrew. "He turned his back on the Native Guards. Him and his abolitionist friends all turned around, ignoring us, pretending they were in conversation. They didn't so much as look up."

"Here comes Pierre", said Matilda, coming from the kitchen with the last of food for the noonday meal. It's about time, thinks Matilda. Matilda has been waiting much too long. She has too much to do to get the house cleaned up for dinner. Adding to her frustration are these folks just taking their good old sweet time. At least they could all come home at the same time, but that would be asking too much. Matilda arrives at the front door just as Pierre was opening it. She was happy to see him even if, according to the pieces of conversation she has heard, Massa Andrew wasn't. She smiles when he takes off his hat and gives it to her. "Good afternoon, Master Pierre."

"We are still struggling with that master, aren't we Matilda?" Pierre walks to the foot of the stairs and is about to go to his room.

Matilda doesn't say anything, bows her head and turns away.

"Wait a minute son," said Andrew, standing in the middle of the living room. "I want a word with you."

Pierre did not want any kind of confrontation at this very moment. He knows his father is upset with him. He hopes he will not have to re-argue his position again. He is not going to change his views and he knows his father is not going to change either, so what's the use of this conversation. "Hello Mama," he said, approaching and hugging her. "Yes Papa, what is it?"

"Your actions today disappointed and hurt me badly, Pierre."

Mary once again is feeling uneasy about what is happening inside her home. Each time in the past that Pierre and his father have argued it has pushed Andrew further along into a direction Dr. DuBois explained would not be good for his health. She worries about him getting so excited that it would affect his heart. Like a mother hen, watching her baby chicks, she hovers about him. "Andrew, show understanding."

"Mother, please, I know what I'm doing."

Pierre grabs his mother's hands and gently squeezes them. "It's okay, Mama. This is a man to man to man thing, right Papa?"

Mary hated it when Pierre would show sarcasm in his conversations with his father. How can he be so insensitive to his father's plight? She had been meaning to talk to him about it, but each time, she let her love for him stand in the way of correcting him.

"I will not tolerate your insolence, Pierre."

"But you are willing to tolerate second class citizenship!"

Enough is enough, thought Mary rising from her chair, walking to where Pierre and Andrew stand. Maybe it finally is time for her to step in and see about keeping this family together. This war is beginning to tear at the very seams of the family, weakening them. With her strong right hand she releases any confusion as to whose side she is on. It is with the same right hand that she defines her position in this house to everyone. It is with this very right hand, like the right hand of God, which comes from above, and strikes Pierre. The sound of the slap travels through the kitchen door, bringing Matilda out, to watch Pierre on his knee before his mother. "Respect Pierre! Your father deserves your respect! You don't know anything about what he's tolerated for you and this family. Don't you dare challenge him on it!"

"I'm sorry Mama," said Pierre.

"Sometimes being sorry is not enough," said Mary retreating back to her chair and sitting. And now Mary is feeling sorry for herself. Suddenly she is feeling sorry for what she did to Pierre and sorry for what she said to him. But there is nothing she can do about it now. Her anger about the war has come out by way of her hand and spoken out of her mouth. She cannot remember the last time she struck Pierre, and she cannot remember a reason for doing it. She always left the discipline up to Andrew, never really challenging him or his methods. Has she over stepped her bounds with Pierre? Should she have been more involved earlier?

"Mama, I cannot accept what Papa believes in," complains Pierre, not trying to get up. "No way will I fight to preserve slavery."

What does he know about slavery, thinks Mary. He's never lived it. Mary's mind went back some twenty plus years remembering again. Pierre, he's only seen it and what he's seen does not give him reason to not want to fight to preserve it. Slavery is not an end all for a people unless they chose it to be. She remembers how she and Andrew were slaves. In spite of the challenges Andrew went through to be a free man, he managed to find a way out. And when he got out he reached back out of love and brought me out. This farm could not be run without slave labor.

"I'm not fighting to preserve slavery," Andrew said to Pierre, "I'm fighting to preserve what we have as a family."

"At the cost of and on the back of our own people," said Pierre, not moving from his convictions or the floor.

Mary sees Andrew becoming more agitated. She doesn't want that to happen and she gently tugs at Andrew's shirt. "Andrew, don't do this to yourself."

"It's okay Mother," said Andrew, pushing her hand away gently.

But it wasn't okay and Mary knew it even if Andrew refused to accept it. Andrew didn't want to think he was sick because he follows Dr. DuBois instructions of exercise every morning, but there was more. She knows Andrew was at a point where he needed to tell Pierre all that he could to convince him why he owned slaves and why they are so necessary for the survival of this farm. Mary is confident with the direction Andrew is moving the family. She knows Andrew feels very strongly and believes strongly that what the Confederacy is doing is for the good of the family. If it is necessary for the Confederacy to create a separate nation, then so be it. She used to enjoy listening to Andrew when he sat around and bragged to his friends about how he and his father started the farm after the War of 1812. Those were the good old days, when you knew if you worked hard, there was a goal to be achieved and for all of Andrews's friends, it was the purchase of their freedom. Not everybody was able to buy their freedom. For those who did, they found it was the result of good honest work that delivered the honest money that freed them. The system worked for them and has continued to work for them all these years. The very benefits this family enjoys are a result of slavery, but the institution of slavery has become a business. A business that shows profit and loss, just like any other business. Mary knows and understands this. She hears it from Andrew every day, the problems of running the farm and taking care of the extended family of slaves who have become his family as much as Mary, Margaret, Andy and Pierre. There are quotas that have to be met by each slave daily. Everyone must work to make this farm successful, including the children. To be a slave is not permanent unless that is all a person wants out of life. Mary thinks about these issues as she continues to watch Andrew and his movements for clues to how he is feeling. The slight grimace that curls his lips up, the sudden blinking of his eyes. All are signs when something is not right inside his aging body. Andrew is so use to his body with its aches and pains that he thinks they are just small kinks in his intestines or a bubble in his veins. She notices a break in his conversations, where he draws in more air, the rubbing of his chest. She has to remind him to remain calm. "Andrew, calm down. You're getting yourself worked up. Remember what Dr. DuBois said."

"I'm fine. It's just something I ate." But it is more than something he ate and Andrew knows it. This time it is a different type of pain that lasts longer than usual. He isn't sure but he feels it in a different place inside his chest this time. It feels closer to his heart. It is like he can feel a clogging inside one of his veins. "I'd rather die believing in something real, than die running after some dream. This is a good life under the Confederacy. Our freedom is real. It is not some dream disguised as freedom, only to turn out to be slavery under another system."

"Freedom should not be dreams for our slaves," pleads Pierre, getting up from the floor. "It is their reality!"

Mary notices Andrew is taking more time to respond to Pierre's rapid fire retorts. He should be paying more attention to his body than to Pierre. When he is able, he goes on to explain the state of all the slaves he owns; what they looked like when they came off the boat, the physical and mental shape; their ignorance of the ways of America, the language barrier and on and on he went. "The reality of freedom means conforming to certain standards and ways of living that will promote self worth," said Andrew, stopping to let out a hardy cough before continuing. "The reality of freedom means respecting and accepting changes, regardless of how it affects you."

Pierre continues to stare at the floor, as if the words from his father's mouth were spilling there, and putting themselves in order for him to read. He doesn't notice what is happening around him.

Mary sees Andrew sway and touch his perspiring forehead, then look for a place to sit. From the expression on his face he is in some kind of pain. Once in the chair he begins rubbing his chest. "Andrew, are you all right," she first said weakly, too frightened to yell any louder. "Pierre, get some water. Matilda! Matilda, come here, hurry! Andy! Margaret! Come down here, now!

Matilda comes from the kitchen, wiping her hands, wondering what all the fuss is about. She barely gets out of Pierre's way as he darts past her.

"Matilda," said a frantic Mary bent over her husband, slumped in a chair, "Matilda, go upstairs and get Mr. St. Claire's medicine from his night table."

"Yes Miss Mary," said Matilda, turning to go upstairs, bumping into Andy coming down. "Excuse me Master Andy." Margaret follows directly behind him.

This family is something, thinks Matilda as she goes to Massa Andrew's room. One thing for sure there is never a dull moment when all of them are home at the same time. Since this war has started there has been more discussion on the well being of Massa's slaves then any time before. Massa Andrew, he does all right for a slave owner. He's not like them buckra white farmers who try and beat the work out of a slave before the slave can get any work done. He does try and give decent living quarters and he don't mind if I take a little something for the morning stew. He does a lot for the slaves, make you wonder why there's such a fuss over us slaves. Why don't they just punish the slave owners who treat their slaves bad and try to hurt them everyday, instead of putting everybody in the pot at one time? When she returns to the living room Matilda rushes over to where Mary still hovers over Andrew and hands her a packet with the medicine in it.

"Thank-you Matilda," said Mary, opening it quickly and emptying the contents into a glass of water from Pierre. "Andrew, drink this, it will make you feel better."

Matilda backs away from the mayhem to wait for further demands. After all that's what she does, wait on these folks. She wonders how long it would be before Andy decides he is in charge of the family.

"Pierre, what happened to Papa?" Andy spoke in a tone that sounded like he was threatening Pierre. "I demand to know what happened, Pierre."

"What you see is what happened," responds Pierre.

Matilda always had a problem liking Andy because he always treated her like she was a slave, even when he was growing up. He use to order her around long before he understood the difference between his lifestyle and hers. It was even worst when he returned from getting his education in France. He seemed to think of himself as royalty or something. For Pierre it was different. He never separated himself from her and her family and often played with Jacob, both of them growing up at the same time. When Pierre came back from his overseas education he brought with him this need to abolish slavery in America and especially on this farm.

"You and Papa were arguing again, right?" Andy pointed his finger at Pierre, his eyes narrowing, his lips tightening.

"I never argue with Papa," said Pierre, staring at his reclined father. "I can never win, so why argue."

Matilda stands in the background of this drama, separated physically, but not emotionally. Her heart goes out for Miss Mary. If anything happened to Massa Andrew, she would be all alone, even with all her children in the house. So, she stands patiently and waits for the next request. Margaret keeps pacing back and forth, rubbing her hands, frowning, pleading, praying, trying to figure out if what is happening is real.

"Mama, is he going to be alright?" asks Margaret, her voice shaking.

Mary said suddenly, "Matilda," her voice is controlled, deliberate, but quivering some, "go upstairs and prepare Mr. St. Claire's bed."

Matilda wants to stay and hear more of the conversation between Andy and Pierre, but she knows she has to do what she is told. She wanted to say, "just a minute, I want to hear this," but she knows she can't do that. So she turns and walks towards the stairs leading up to Massa Andrew's room, hearing Andy's angry voice fade as she ascends the wooden steps.

"I heard you down here hollering at Papa."

"I don't always have to agree with Papa, Andy!"

"Damn it man he's our father, show respect!"

Margaret is surprised Andy and Pierre chose now to have an argument. Papa lies here terribly sick and they are arguing. Men, how insensitive they can be. For a brief moments in her anguish she is distracted by her brothers' behavior. How strange it must be for men to always look to blame someone for something, even when their lives may depend on the outcome of what they are arguing. Finally, she can no longer stand by while these two banter at each other. "Pierre! Andy" shouts Margaret, standing between them, " Papa is in no condition to listen to you two. Both of you need to show respect!"

Matilda, coming down the stairs, is surprised to hear Margaret reprimanding her brothers. It is a side of Margaret she has never seen before. Matilda smiles. This war is turning men into boys and whimpering girls into women. Maybe she is taking her lead from her mother. Maybe she's worried about losing her father, the only strong male image she has in her life.

Mary rises, but not before gently letting Andrew's head rest on a couch pillow. "I need you boys to help get your father upstairs to the bedroom. Be careful."

"Yes, Mama," Andy and Pierre say in unison.

Matilda watches Pierre and Andy remove their father from the couch and gently carry him upstairs. From the bottom of the stairs she watches all of them go into the massa's bedroom. She shakes her head, feeling sorry for this family. She wipes her hands as she heads back to the kitchen to complete her daily chores. Strange, she thinks that she was not deeply sadden by Massa Andrew's attack. But then, he is her massa, and she does work for him, should she feel anything else except that. Matilda is not confused by her feelings and she knows that maybe she should be. While she is completing the clearing of the dinner table, Pierre comes from upstairs and wanders into the living room, finds a chair and flops into it. He stares into space, then is overcome with emotion and breaks down. For Pierre, Matilda does have feelings, and she too has a tear in her eye, not so much for Massa Andrew, but for Pierre.

CHAPTER 12
Sunday, December 1ˢᵗ, 1861

Pierre sits on the edge of his bed listening to the sleeping members of the house. It's what he has been in the habit of doing for weeks now. Each night between the hours of 11PM and midnight after everyone is asleep, he creeps downstairs, and raids the kitchen for food, then he's out to the barn under the watchful eyes of the stars. Anna has begun to relax and shows she trusts and believes in what he said. Once inside he lights the lantern, holds it high and walks to the back of the barn.

He pats his pocket to confirm his promised bounty, then climbs the ladder to the loft and she is there, sitting near an opening, looking out into the night. He hangs the lantern on a nearby nail and approaches her.

Sometimes Anna is asleep and he will stand quietly watching her sleeping. He looks at her chocolate face of beauty, sleeping in the comfort of her dreams. She smiles and turns, curling up, almost into the fetal position. At other times he has seen her chocolate face distorted in anguish, horror, and pain, twisting and turning trying to get away from the pain behind her closed eyelids and hidden deep inside her mind. He feels so much more comfortable when he doesn't see her in the usual place; he knows she is up, waiting for him.

"Do you ever wonder what's up dere?" she asks, without turning around. "It looks like the night sky goes on forever."

"Tonight we start with questions," replies Pierre, "we certainly are in a different spirit tonight."

Pierre takes the bundle of food from his pocket, opens the tied cloth and spreads it on the hay between them as he sits. There are ham chunks, some biscuits with butter, and some string beans. He watches her eat. She does not shove the food into her mouth, the way she did when he first brought her food.

"I wants to show you somethin'," she said, in between bites. "I hope you don't mind, but I wants you to see somethin' after I finish eating."

Pierre wonders what is in this barn that she can show him that he has not already seen? What could be of so much interest to her in this barn that he would object to her seeing?

After Anna finishes the last of the string beans, she rises, bushes herself down, and walks back to the ladder and begins to disappear below.

"Wait for me," said Pierre, quickly scampering to the ladder following her.

To his surprise when she is on the ground level she walks past everything and heads straight for the door leading outside. Pierre darts quickly to get in front of her, blocking her exit.

"Now hold on a minute, Anna," said Pierre, holding his hand in front of her. "Where do you think you're going?"

"Outside," said Anna, plainly. "Why?"

"You can't do that," said Pierre, further blocking her intentions to exit.

"I's already done it," said Anna, moving Pierre's hand out of her way and proceeding stealthily out of the barn with Pierre nervously following.

The night air is crisp, but not cold. There is a full moon and a scattering of clouds that hide some of the twinkling flashes of light. Anna walks likes she knows the farm personally. She is in no hurry, almost playful in her movements. Pierre, constantly looks around as they move away from the barn, towards the lake. He cannot hide his uncomfortable feeling about what she is doing.

"What you nervous 'bout?" whispers Anna, teasing, "You live here." She takes his hand and pulls him with her past the slave quarters, past Voodoo Man Cato's hounfort, into the patch of trees, following the beaten path, to the lake. She stops as they come out of the trees. The lake in all its mirrored majesty sits still before them. The moon is casting long black treetops shadows in front of them. "Look at dis, jus' look at dis! Da hands of God have been here. See what dey have painted."

Pierre looks around this farmland she is talking about and is not seeing the same images she is. He suspects she is suffering from some sort of delirium after spending so much time in the barn loft. There is nothing in front of him but the lake and on the other side the remains of the last harvest of cotton picking. The soil needs to be turned for the next planting. More trees must be cut to fill orders from merchants in the city. What beauty is she talking about?

"You and yo' family have been blessed by God," continues Anna, enjoying her view. "I ain't never seen colored folk wit dis much land and slaves! You colored folks rich 'nough to own slaves?"

Pierre listens to Anna exalt how fortunate he is to live on a farm of this size at this time and be a slaveholder. How can she be envious of this farm as a slave over any other farm? What has this society done to the human spirit where there can be comparisons of human tragedy and suffering? How can one form of human bondage be better than the next? Have the minds of the enslaved been so reduced to the point where all they can do is measure and compare the depth of their misery?

"If yo' daddy was my Massa, I would never run away from dis," said Anna, admiring her surrounding, smiling. "Over at da Clanton farm, all dey got is dirt, dirt and mo' dirt. It's dry, and it crumbles in yo' hand, like it's been cursed. Da only time dere is moisture, is from da blood, sweat and tears of da slaves dat work da land."

Pierre listens to Anna fantasize about being a slave on this farm and all the wonderful things she would have if she lived here instead of the Clanton farm. At times she is almost in a trance carrying the conversation from one topic to another. Every now and then she again reminds Pierre how God has blessed Pierre and his family. She envies the slaves of this farm. She envies their quarters, she envies the clothes they wear, and she envies the abundance of food they eat. She cannot believe that in this time in America, slaves are living in such luxury.

"Misery can disguise itself, even inside a bed of roses," said Pierre. "Believe me inside this bed of roses you see here, are hidden thorns."

"If all I had to worry 'bout were da tiny thorns in rose beds, den I neber would have runned away."

"Anna, you can't stay here."

"Why, can't yo' daddy buy me from da Clantons?"

"Because of certain understandings between the farmers, if he knew you were here, he would be obligated to return you to the Clanton farm."

Anna's composure suddenly changes. The glow in her face darkens; her straightened back suddenly slouches; she drags her feet as she moves back to Pierre. She holds him close for a long time.

Pierre feels her shivering and hears her sobbing. He caresses her, rubbing her shoulders, holding her face in his hands. Tears are slowly sliding over her cheeks. They glisten in the moonlight, reflecting from her dark chocolate face. He bends down and kisses her forehead, then both eyes, tasting her bitter waters, then he moves to her lips. She welcomes his mouth, opening hers as he slides his tongue inside her mouth.

Suddenly, Anna pushes Pierre away, falls to her knees and vomits until all that she has eaten is on the ground. Pierre helps her to her feet and is about to ask what is wrong when she tears herself away from him and runs back through the woods to the barn, with Pierre close behind. Once inside Anna runs to the ladder and charges up to the loft. By the time Pierre is in the loft Anna is sobbing hysterically, balled up like a child, shivering in the chill of the night. Pierre gathers her in his arms and gently rocks her.

"I'm sorry, I shouldn't have," he whispers.

"It's not your fault," said Anna. "It's me." She stops her sobbing. "More den anythin'I wants to make love to you. More den anythin' else I needs to know dat a man wants me. I needs to be touched as a woman needs to be touched; to be able to feel da hands of a black man on my body, rubbing me, probing me, gently raising da fire, that is cold now, down in my loins and touchin' my soul. I needs to feel a gentle black man moving between my thighs, joining me wit him. I needs you Pierre, so badly I needs you." Anna sits up, unbuttons her top and takes it off.

Pierre's eyes behold the beauty of Anna's body from the white light of the moon. He kneels and gently kisses both breasts, gently drawing each into his mouth. He moistens them individually, tasting the salt of her body until he feels the nipples rise inside his mouth. She hold his head in her hands, then pulls his face to hers and softly kisses him.

"I want you, so badly," she cries," but I can't have you, not now, not now."

Anna rolls over onto her stomach and sobs, exposing her back to him. The moonlight that exposed her black beauty now exposes her ugly past from the hands of her white overseer. Now it's Pierre who almost gags and almost vomits. Her back is covered with scars from the results of many lashes. There is not one square centimeter of flesh unscarred by the whip.

Pierre covers her naked scars with her shirt, and then pulls a blanket over her. He leans over to comfort her shaking body, but she pushes him away. After awhile, he quietly retreats to the ladder, her uncontrollable sobbing filling his ears. There is no kind of comfort he can give her now. She needs to be alone. He can never remove the scarred memories from her body or mind.

"I will bring you some more food tomorrow," he said, just before he disappears down the ladder.

* * * * * * * *

Voodoo Man Cato watches, from his pane-less window, Pierre move about the outside of the barn, long after everyone else has gone inside for the night. It's the same pattern every night now for the last two months. Pierre's strange behavior matches what Charlie Boy has told him. It is the same nervous behavior that Voodoo Man Cato first notices about Pierre when those two buckra men came onto the farm. Like the older buckra man, Voodoo Man Cato did not believe there were rats hiding from the dog at the outside wall of the barn or inside the barn. He must go see if what he hears is true. Does Pierre suffer with a troubled mind? It is time for the spirits to take over. His spiritual time is getting shorter every day. Now, he must complete his investigation before he is called to his rightful seat in the next lifetime, next to the Gods.

Voodoo Man Cato has seen too many sunrises and sunsets. He

has seen too many slaves and not enough freedom. He is someone who, as a Captain's boy of a schooner, has traveled around the world more times than he can count. He has met kings and queens, eaten at the most sumptuous of tables. This manner of man has been designated as a gift from God. Three score and ten he has watched the sun rise and set upon these chains on his body; chains that have since moved from his ankles and neck to his heart and soul. His cloudy eyes can no longer see as far and as sharp as they did. His hands are becoming bent and wrinkled like raisins. He has become an old man, a relic, a thing of the past, but also a necessary thing of the present and future. His mind remembers the horrible pain. His body proudly displays the raised welts of resistance. This land of liberty continues to be for the faces that must be painted in colors. This land of freedom continues to be contradictions in human behavior; the good book of their God versus the good book of humanity. Both created by the hand of God, both interpreted by the mind of man. Both gifts misunderstood. This land of prosperity continues to be nothing but window dressing for those blessed by the gods with darkened faces. They are always in the backroom of this country's storefront. It is they who rise before the sun and does not rest until long after the sun has gone to sleep.

It is time to feed the gods; time to replenish what has been taken. It is time to show respect for those who have protected his soul inside this vessel of life. It is the time of the Guede's' loa. It is time for them to come out of the deep beds of their cemeteries. It is time to take possession of their horses and ride them into the hounfort. They do this to amuse themselves, taking on the forms of wandering souls incarnated in the physical or reincarnated in the spirit.

Voodoo Man squats on his earthen floor. Then with deliberate purpose and reason, he places red brick powder, corn meal, powdered charcoal, some ground up bark and roots in piles on a flat rock he uses as a small table. "By the power of the Loa LETE-MAGIE," begins Voodoo Man, now standing in the center of his hounfort, "Negre Danhome, all the ve'ves Negre Bhacoulor Thi-kaka." Voodoo Man begins tracing the ve've he wishes to call. He takes his time as he drips the red brick powder, then the powdered charcoal into two straight lines that turn left then right, then encircle each other. When he finishes using each ingredient, he blows what remains in the palm of his hands towards the four cardinal points. Voodoo Man begins crossing himself by touching his forehead, saying, "Linsah; then his center breast bone, saying "Mawu," then his left shoulder saying "Vovo-Lin-V-Hwe'" and finally his right shoulder saying, "Hevio-Zo." He then makes the sign of the cross over the ground.

It is time to bring forth all the years of pain and suffering; time to bring forth those who can end this pain and suffering. It is time to set free the spirit of his soul and the spirits of the ground; time to save the life of the young so that they may grow old. It is time.

> "Hey! Great saint, great loa
> Guede Nibbho is lost!
> Hey! Great saint, great loa
> Papa Guede is lost." [vi]

Somewhere in the night he hears the voices of the wind whispering to him stories of those who have come before him. Somewhere in the night he smells the odors of blood, sweat and burning flesh. Somewhere in the night there are wailing and cries of sorrow coming from the mouths of the owls, and the wolves. The nocturnal spirits hold court against the white race, which are defended by the royal majesty of progress, and prosecuted by the risen souls of the dead. These nocturnal spirits have been forever trapped between the hereafter and death. He throws a powder into the smoldering chunks of woods and there is a sudden white flame that flies into the ceiling of the hounfort, spreads out then powder falls lightly to the ground. From all of this there is a smoke that rises from the ashes and fills the hounfort. It is this smoke that Voodoo Man Cato begins to slowly take into his lungs. "Rise up from the black earth. Rise into the blackness of night. Rise up from the bowels of the earth. Fly into the life of the living that walks amongst you. Give me the spirit of the strong. Give me the wind to be light of wing. Give me the eyes of the eagle. Give me the claws of the lion who walks at night."

Voodoo Man Cato walks around the ve've inside his hounfort

chanting, listening to the drums of his ancestors, and inhaling the spirit of the night. He throws some animal bones onto the ground and reads them. What he sees is his fate and the fate of the farm and the fate of a stranger who walks on six legs. He knows what he must do. He knows and understands the reason and purpose of his being on this farm. There is reason and purpose in everything the Gods do. All these years he has understood his purpose for being on the farm. Finally he understands the reason. It has been a long wait.

Voodoo Man Cato unfolds his arms and stretches them out at his sides, letting his head tilt backwards, his eyes rolling back into their sockets. He feels his spirit slowly move from this human vessel of flesh and rise into another. When he opens his eyes he is looking down on a sleeping child of the Gods. Then, he is through the window of his hounfort and is on the hands of the wind, being carried to the barn. There is a full moon and it spotlights where he should enter the barn. He finds the opening near the top of the barn and is at once inside, resting on a wooden crossbeam.

She is asleep, covered with some hay and a thin homespun cloth for a blanket. She has fallen asleep cold. Her face is distorted, and she shivers from the bite of the chill in the night air. He walks the beams slowly, carefree of falling off. He watches her breathing waiting for her to waken. He realizes she will not by herself and begins to flap his wings, hoping the fluttering sound will arouse her from the deep sleep. She is a daughter from the good black earth. He sees her long arms and legs. His eyes trace from her narrow waist upward towards her slow rising and falling breasts. Her rumpled top stretches with each inhale and exhale. She is black. She is beautiful. She is woman. She is his beginning. He flutters his wings again and this time she slowly opens her eyes and sees him above her. He spreads his wings and slowly floats to where she is beginning to sit up. He lands at her side and stands before her, head high, wings pressed close to his body.

She is not afraid. She doesn't understand why she's not afraid. She looks at the mighty black bird standing before her as if she knows who he is and why he is here. He is a messenger from God, she thinks. She thinks, she is dreaming. She reaches out to touch the eagle and is surprised when it bows its head, spread its wings and kneel before her, waiting for her touch.

"Thank you Jesus," she said softly, folding her hands in prayer, "I've died and he has sent you to take me to heaven."

The eagle feels the touch of her hand gently caressing his head and immediately feels the pain inside her heart. He senses the anguish inside her soul and the hopelessness inside her mind. She is afraid of the white men who are searching for her and she feels they know she is here. She fears they will come in the still of the night and drag her away and kill her. He looks into her face and sees surrender in her eyes. She has prepared herself for death. He remains under the touch of her hand until she unloads all of her anguish onto him. He spreads his feathers, fluttering them gently.

"Fly away my bird of freedom," she said, placing her hand under his breast lifting him. "Fly away and take my soul to freedom, thank-you Jesus."

He feels her supporting hands and rises, slowly flapping his wings until he is airborne. He circles her twice then flies back to the support beam, where he walks to the place of his entrance. He then launches himself onto the hands of the wind again and is carried back to his hounfort. Once inside he floats into the lingering mist of the smoke that remains hovered above his human vessel of life still slumped on the floor. He opens his wings and floats about himself, then feels his spirit drain from the eagle and slide into his body. What remains in the air are feathers that fall upon Voodoo Man's body, waking him from his suspended sleep.

* * * * * * * * *

It is morning and Voodoo Man hears the slaves going to the fields. There is a light gray mist floating above the lake and the crickets are still calling out to their mates. He sees Charlie Boy and waves at him to come closer.

"Charlie Boy, I needs you to dig a new hole by da outhouse, jus' as wide and jus' as deep. When you finish I needs you to come to me and we will complete da hole adding what is needed to protect da farm."

"Is dere somethin' gonna happen?" asks Charlie Boy. "What we gonna protect da farm from?"

Voodoo Man leans closer to Charlie Boy, "Dere is an evil dat walks on six legs comin' to visit dis farm."

Charlie Boy is confused by what Voodoo Man has said but asks no more questions. He gets the necessary tools and begins digging the new hole, next to he old outhouse. He wonders what walks on six legs that are so evil as to threat the existence of this farm. He knows when he has completed his given task, Voodoo Man will be ready for him.

CHAPTER 13
Sunday, December 15ᵗʰ, 1861

Pierre is not aware that he is being followed until he is standing on the station platform at Commerce Place Basin. He's waiting for the big black and red engine that pulls the passengers train cars belonging to The Pontchartrain Railroad. It was a chilly seven mile ride from his home to the livery stable located in the middle of the block on Hope Street, between Bernard Avenue and St. Anthony Avenue. The few shops he passes, on the way to the station, are decorated for the holidays. By the time he reaches the station he is pretty much chilled to his bones, so he's stamping his feet to keep the blood moving, while slowly turning around. It is while he is doing this warming task that he notices Major Treeman, who is not looking at Pierre, but not hiding his presence. He wants Pierre to know he is there. He tips his crumbled broken down hat in Pierre's direction. Pierre does not respond to him.

The approaching sound of the big black and red engine chugging into the station brings a welcoming smile to the face of Pierre. Soon, he is going to be out of this bitter cold and into unheated train cars, but still warmer than where he is now. The car is crowded, but Pierre manages to find a seat to himself. Major Treeman sits two seats in front of him. The two-mile ride drifts slowly into the next stop. Pierre always rides the train to avoid paying extra for livery stables closer to the river. Pierre realizes Major Treeman is following him and in hindsight, he wishes he had spent the extra money. The train stops once more at St. Claude Avenue, where the Mexican Gulf Railroad runs east, then finally at Washington Square at Levee Street.

When Pierre steps from the train he looks south, along New Levee, then turns and finds Major Treeman has stepped from the train also, but at the opposite end. Pierre begins walking west on Esplanade Street, past Washington Square. Before he gets to Royal Street, he pauses to look into a storefront, and sees the reflection of the bounty hunter stopping also. Pierre turns south onto Royal, then turns east onto Dumaine and follows it to New Levee and the Mississippi River. Walking south, along New Levee, Pierre finally arrives at Public Square.

He finds a bench, sits and waits for Major Treeman. It makes no sense to Pierre to have Major Treeman follow him about the city or take him to Marcel. He needs to confront Major Treeman and find out why he is following him and what he knows if anything. It is a bold move that is a spur of the moment thought that may get him killed. But he can't leave now; he's already committed himself to this moment. He doesn't have his father's gun and normally he doesn't carry one. There is no need. That one time occurrence on the farm was an act of desperation and distraction for Anna's sake. But what if Major Treeman is carrying his pistol? Maybe Major Treeman is and is following Pierre to kill him. Maybe Major Treeman hasn't forgotten about the farm incident. Maybe he's still angry about it, after all black people do not threaten white people with guns, regardless of what the reasons may be. He concluded that incident alone is more than necessary that he meet him in a public place, with lots of people around. Strange that he is without his mangy black dog and his stupid son. Pierre sits, nervous and uncomfortable, waiting for Major Treeman to catch up with him. He doesn't have to wait long.

"Mr. Treeman," said Pierre, showing reluctant respect to him. His father always told him to show respect when in the presence of meeting and greeting white folks. "Please, come sit. It appears you're following me."

Major Treeman finds a seat on a wooden bench across from Pierre. He doesn't say anything. He just sits and stares. His craggy lip on his crooked mouth just hangs loosely on his face, held in place by his jawbone. He still has ugly stubble in pockmarks on his chin and patches of hair in places where there should be clean skin. He reaches into his coat pocket and retrieves a switchblade knife, then picks up some nearby pieces of tree lying on the ground near him. He begins shaving them, one at a time.

"What is it you want?" asks Pierre, staring at the knife and noticing how smoothly and quickly it passes through the wood. "Why are you following me?"

"You're Andrew St. Claire's boy," he said, without looking up, concentrating on the piece of wood and what his knife is doing to it. "Me and my boy were out at your father's farm a few weeks back. We was lookin' for that niggra runaway."

"So what's that got to do with me?" asks Pierre, looking at Major Treeman, trying to see his face. "Have you found her, yet?"

"You know what I do," said the bounty hunter, carefully inspecting his work, then returning to his shaving, "but I didn't know what you did; that is not until recent."

"I'm learning how to run the farm with my brother and father," replies Pierre, "that's pretty plain to see."

Major Treeman stops shaving the piece of wood and inspects it once more. He has fashioned something that is blunt on one end and on the other there is a pointed tip that looks like the blade end of his knife. Without warning he throws this fashioned piece of wood at Pierre and it sticks into the ground between his feet. "Don't lie to me, boy," said Major Treeman, raising his face, his steely coal black eyes staring at Pierre. "I know what you do."

Pierre didn't expect the wooden knife. He jumps in his seat. He looks at Major Treeman to express his anger, but the evil eyes of the bounty hunter pierces his soul like the cold steel blade of the knife he is holding. He jumps again at the sight of Major Treeman's face. Fear grips Pierre and holds him tight. "I'm not sure I know what you mean," stutters Pierre, afraid to take his eyes off of the bounty hunter. Pierre now watches his every move. There is a need to be more careful.

"I think you do," said Major Treeman, returning to shaving another portion of the piece of wood. "And I'll tell you why." Major leans back into his seat, crosses his leg and smiles. He has Pierre's undivided attention. "Ever since Nutmeg went crazy at your daddy's farm I been thinkin'. Why would Nutmeg react that way unless his nose told him somethin'? Nutmeg ain't ever failed me in the past and I'm thinkin' he ain't failin' me now. I'm thinkin' there's somethin' in that barn that only Nutmeg can smell and maybe somebody on that farm may know about. I'm thinkin', why would you grab a gun and threaten to shoot my dog, just for scratchin' at a barn wall. So, I needs to find out what's goin' on at that farm and if Nutmeg's nose is tellin' me the truth."

"Your dog smelled a rat," said Pierre, confidently lying, leaning towards Major Treeman, but before Pierre can confidently lean back, another sharpened stick is thrown by Major Treeman and sticks into the ground, next to the first one.

"Don't play me for a damn fool, boy," demands the bounty hunter, pausing for a moment to stare into the face of Pierre. It's a longer harder colder stare this time; one that chills Pierre even more than before. Major Treeman sees Pierre's lips tremble and he has a problem knowing what to do with his hands. He smiles at his victim, and then returns his attention to shaving the remaining piece of wood. There is an uncomfortable silence between them that is interrupted by the passing sound of people's feet on the pavement. He waits until he hears Pierre shift uncomfortably in his seat before continuing. "I hear you went to a private school and all. I ain't never had no schoolin'. But I want to ask you somethin'. Do you understand the wind, boy? Do you understand what the wind can do? A dog depends on the wind for its lively hood. What you can't see and feel in the wind, Nutmeg sees and feels with his nose. Nutmeg has a great nose for sniffing out slaves. I personally trained him myself. So, guess what we did, Nutmeg, and me, my boy JoJo, that is. Well, at night when everybody was asleep at your daddy's farm, we brought Nutmeg back and stood in the road and waited for the wind to blow into our faces and guess what. When that wind blew into our faces, Nutmeg went crazy each time. My boy and me couldn't feel or see anything, but Nutmeg did. Nutmeg picked up that niggra runaway, Anna."

Pierre stares at Major Treeman, who refuses to pick up his head and look at him. This time there is a fire in Pierre's eyes. He remembers how his hand trembled when he first held his father's pistol, aiming it at Nutmeg. Sitting here now, after hearing what Major

Treeman has said, he knows if given that same opportunity, he would kill the bounty hunter's dog and not feel any remorse for it all. This anger inside is something different than he has ever experienced before. It is not the same anger he feels when arguing with Andy and his father. No, this is something much different. This burning is something coming from deep down inside like a sleeping volcano that suddenly is awakened to eruption. It's all very new to him. Now, it is his composure that is under control, but he's not sure if he's in charge of this anger or this anger is in charge of him. He does know his fear of Major Treeman has gone away, where, he's not sure, but he's glad it's gone. So now Pierre waits for the face of the Major Treeman to turn up and see the face staring back at him. He listens and waits, knowing when this son-of-a-bitch of a man finishes he will see a different face of Pierre's. Again he challenges Major Treeman, this time knowing what to expect. "I said it before and I'll say it again, your dog smelled a rat."

Major Treeman raises his face with its cold stare again, but this time he meets an equally cold stare from Pierre. He puts his knife away, and throws his last piece of wood at Pierre's feet. This time Pierre doesn't budge. "My dog even knows what you smell like," said Major Treeman, rising and standing over Pierre.

Pierre removes the three pieces of wood sticking in the ground, inspects them, breaks them in half then throws them away. He then stares hard at the dirty old funky smelling man, standing in front of him. "You tell your dog Nutmeg, I can smell him too."

Treeman slowly backs away from Pierre staring at him. "Here's hopin' you have a Merry Christmas, where ever you may be." Major Treeman tips his wrinkled, dirty, sweat stained hat.

Pierre watches Major Treeman turn and walk away, wondering just what he meant. He sighs in relief, realizing what has just happened. He is elated that for the time being it is over. He can stop holding his breath and breath normally. He leaves Public Square walking a different path then that of Major Treeman. Twenty minutes later he and Marcel DuBois, are having a good laugh, while enjoying a mid afternoon meal at their favorite gumbo restaurant, Mama Salome's in Treme.

"So, you told Major Treeman his dog stunk," mumbles Marcel,

trying to keep the gumbo in his mouth while he is laughing. "You sure know how to piss somebody off."

"Yeah, he was pretty upset," replies Pierre, stirring his gumbo, still thinking about the last words from Major. "He said he knows what I do and then he wished me a Merry Christmas, where ever I would be."

"You plan on goin' someplace this Christmas," said Marcel. "Wait, don't tell me, you planin' to run away with Anna, right?"

"SHHH, not so loud," cautions Pierre. "The walls have ears."

"You know as well as I," begins Marcel, "when people eat gumbo in Mama Salome's, they don't hear anythin'. They ain't allowed. They got to pay attention to what they're eatin'." All the while Marcel is talking and laughing he is spooning the gumbo into his mouth. Some of it drips down the sides of his mouth. Most of it goes in.

An hour later both men are back at Washington Square, waiting for the train to arrive and take Pierre back to his carriage. Marcel is finishing the instructions to Pierre about how Anna will be put on the Underground Railroad.

"On Christmas Day bring Anna to the docks," Marcel is saying. "Look for a middle aged white man dressed like a priest, with a beautiful walking stick."

"Is he really a man of the cloth," asks Pierre.

"Yes he is," answers Marcel. "He has booked passage to St. Louis on the steamer Baron's Luck for two. Him and his boy servant, so make sure she looks like a boy as close as possible."

"How will I get her out of the barn with everybody at my place hanging around for the holiday?"

"I will convince Papa to invite your family for a dinner. You make an excuse about coming later. You know how much our two parents like to get together. You know and I know Andy will go to his cathouse, leave your mother, father and Margaret to be entertained by my father. He's really been lonely since Mama died."

"Suppose there are two priests, how will I know whose who?"

"When you approach the priest, say, "Marcel would like you to forgive him of his sins." If he is the right one, he will give Anna a hug, then he will bless her and then ask Anna if she is willing to follow the words of Jesus Christ. If he blesses Anna on the spot, find another priest."

"So Anna's name is Marcel for the trip."

"Yes, and make sure she remembers that."

Together they walk back to the station as the mighty red and black engine of The Pontchartrain Railroad chugs into the station. After he said good-bye to his best friend with a hug, amongst the steam and noise and smoke, Pierre gets back on the train. He finds a seat and waves from the window to Marcel. As the train jerks its way away from the station, Pierre sees Major Treeman sitting in a seat in front of him. Major Treeman turns, tips his hat and smiles, then turns around facing the front.

* * * * * * * * *

As Pierre steers his horse up his driveway, he stares at the barn, wondering if Anna is watching. Soon her hiding will be over and she will be away from this place. Matilda is preparing the Sunday evening dinner. A crooked line of smoke drifts from the kitchen chimney. The sun is slowly falling behind him, casting a strangely shaped abstract outline of him on his horse. The slave quarters are quiet. A small trickle of smoke wanders into the cool air. The adults are resting, most likely. Some children are playing outside, running around the well, playing tag. Charlie Boy is still digging a hole for the new slave's outhouse. Pierre sees the top of Charlie Boy's head and then black dirt flying out of the hole and onto a high pile. Even today he works on completing the task. It is as if he has a deadline to meet. One thing about Papa, thinks Pierre, he never objected to slaves who continue to work on Sunday. Normally, it's the slave's day off for everyone.

After breaking down the horse, he walks the mare into the stable. He hears the rustling of hay above his head and he knows she is aware of his presence. He checks his surrounding, particularly outside, then closes the door before speaking.

"I have news," begins Pierre, while brushing the mare down. "You will be moving shortly. It will be Christmas morning, so this is a kind of a early Merry Christmas. In about ten days you'll be on your way to a free state, up North then as far as Canada. I will be delivering you as a servant boy to a Priest. Remember the name Marcel. That will be your name for the trip North."

Anna does not immediately respond to the news from Pierre. Instead, she lay on her back listening to him, staring at the old wooden support beams, holding up the ceiling. They're all she's seen for the last 3 months and now it sounds like she will not see them again, after Christmas. Can it be true? Suddenly the cool air that has surrounded her for so long seems to back away, letting a warm feeling take over. She knows she will miss this place and Pierre. She also knows she will miss her family of slaves. She knows she cannot ever see any of them again without endangering them. Already she has endangered Pierre and his family.

"On Christmas morning," continues Pierre, " I will be taking you to the docks and there we will meet the priest, who will escort you to St. Louis. From there you will be sent to Canada with free papers." Pierre pauses before leaving the barn. Suddenly he is not as happy and enthusiastic as when he came in. He wants to say more, but he now finds it difficult to get the words out of his mouth. A lonesome feeling is taking over inside his mind. After remaining silent for what feels like eternity he blurts out, stuttering, "Anna, I'm going to miss you."

Pierre leaves quickly, not waiting for a response from Anna, closing the barn door behind him.

CHAPTER 14
Friday, December 20ᵗʰ, 1861

It greeted the first light of morning, crawling out of the God made orifices, while other parts of it was slithering out of the man made openings; and there were many more openings made by the evil of man than made by God. It then joins itself, into one entity of something. It creeps along the ground, on a personal mission; careful not to disturb the dirt it passes over. It leaves a trail of itself for anyone who wishes to backtrack it from whence it came. Up the driveway, past the smokehouse, it rolls along the bumpy drive, bobbing and weaving itself over furrows from wagon wheels, horse huffs and around clumps of grass. It is like the cloud of death that beset the people of Egypt, ignoring the homes painted with lamb's blood. It bypasses the slave quarters, the barn and the big house, continuing down into the path that leads into the woods until it finds the home of Voodoo Man Cato. It rises, spreads its wings, raises it horned head and stares at the hounfort. It opens its mouth wide and screams like a banshee. Hot clouds stream from its mouth, carrying a stench of a million souls, dead a million years, erupt and explode from deep inside. It cannot go any further. It must find another way inside.

The moon is still high in the night sky. It shines brightly in the receding blackened sky. The white light shines upon the hounfort. The colored glass bottles, hanging in the trees, broken and gathered in small piles around the hounfort, split the white light into spectrums of colors that act as fences that must be climbed over, not under. The menagerie of things and stuff scattered with purpose stand guard to all who would bring evil onto these premises. It slowly rises, dragging its cloud, looking for a way to the front door; maybe get to an open window, but the hanging colored bottles and piles of broken glass reflect the white light stopping its advance. It collapses on top of itself. It rises again and hangs like a ghostly sheet gently flapping in the morning wind; drifting up and over the menagerie of stuff, falling gently like a feather behind the stuff. It finds a broken window, a crack in the doorjamb, a hole in the wood siding, slips in, and again joins itself then slides down along the dirt packed floor.

Voodoo Man Cato's eyes snap open. His nose tells him immediately what it is that had entered his hounfort, with it putrid smell that scratches his throat like a swallow of bad whiskey. It is the kind of smell that shuts off Voodoo Man Cato's breathing and stops the flow of his blood. It is the kind of smell that reminds Voodoo Man Cato there is darkness behind the eyes, deafness to the ears, and stillness to the senses of someone near. It is the smell of something he vividly remembers from the middle passage. It is the smell of death.

* * * * * * * * * *

The slave children saw it first. They were playing in the slave garden, just behind the fence that protected them from the road that passes by Andrew St. Claire's farm. It was early morning, just after sunrise, about seven am. At first they thought it was just a drunken sleeper and they threw small stones at the body, trying to wake him. When this didn't work they ran to Charlie Boy and told him. Charlie Boy, at first didn't believe them and not until they dragged him to the fence and he saw the clump of flesh did he hurry back to notify Massa Andrew. "It's just laying there like a rumpled pile of rags," said Charlie Boy as he walks with Andrew back to the spot.

Andrew stands on his side of the fence and stares at the crumpled heap of a body, not quite sure just what to do. It has no shoes and its clothes are tattered and torn as if it was dragged to the point where it is now. It is most unusual how one arm is flung behind the body as if it is dislocated and broken in several places.

Andrew notices there is no blood on the ground around the

body, even though he can clearly see open cuts on the exposed back, and legs. There are deep gashes in the hind legs and haunches and the back has all the flesh torn off exposing bone. What ever happened to this man, he suffered a great deal before he died. Only angry white folks kill black people this way, thinks Andrew. There is no kind of wild animal that did this.

"Who do you think it is?" asks Charlie Boy. "He don't look like he human, the way his body is mangled.

"I don't know who it is," said Andrew, turning away from the body. But there was something strangely familiar about the body. Andrew's mind reminded him about certain aspects of the body that identified who it belonged to. Andrew suddenly has an idea of whom the body belongs to, but he didn't want to believe it could be possible. He immediately thinks of his own sons and thanks God neither of them are laying dead, alone, like a pile of wasted rags, on a dirt road. "Charlie Boy, go to the fields and get Andy and Pierre. Tell then to come to the house, immediately."

"Yes sir, Massa Andrew," said Charlie Boy, bowing then scampering off as best he could for man aged as he is.

The walk back to the house is a long, sorrowful, and lonely walk for Andrew. If the body is who he thinks, then he must tell an old friend his prayers and condolences are with him. He must tell an old friend this is unexplainable, not understandable, and a contradiction to what we say we are about as free blacks in New Orleans. What more do they want from us? What more can we do? Regardless, we must stay the course, and realize some of us will fall in the fight. "Matilda, go find Mother and Margaret," said Andrew, walking past her as if in another world. "Tell them to come to the living room. I have some bad news for them." Andrew continues into the living room and waits for his family to gather together. It is not long before he hears the screen door of the kitchen opens and slams shut.

"Papa, Papa," said Pierre, out of breath, rushing in from the kitchen. "Charlie Boy said there is a dead man laying in the road in front of our driveway."

"Yes, its true," said Andrew, not wanting to tell him what he knows. He wishes Pierre had listened to him. He wanted to show

Pierre that what he is doing actually prevents something like this happening. The perception put forward by free blacks is we are all on the same side, working for the same goal. All this talk about freeing the slaves will do more harm to the Confederacy than what others say about the practice. America was built on indebtedness from the beginning, way back from Jamestown to now. How he wishes he can get Pierre to understand that the whole process of indebtedness evolved to what it is today, slavery. It will continue to evolve until the process adapts and integrates itself into the system. "Have a seat son, and wait for your mother and Margaret. Where's Andy?"

"He went with Charlie Boy to look at the body."

"You didn't want to go?"

"I'm not interested in looking at some dead body."

Andrew wants to say so much more. If you knew who it was you would be interested. It was through your secret work in trying to free the oppressed that caused that body to be there. Fact is we're all oppressed in some fashion or another. The struggle to break that oppression is not always what is physically seen or felt. It is also what is in the educated minds of those who are doing the oppression. Pierre needs to understand that by his deeds, he is educating the physically oppressed, as well as the educationally oppressed. Collectively we have the money. We have the property. If we must oppress some of us so that most of us will succeed, then it has to be that way. In the evolving process of life, it has always been that way, even with the white folks. Because black folks are the last in the line, some cannot see what's in front of them, but that is not reason to force your way to the front. It is hard work to move up in the line. If we are willing to work hard we will be in the front of the line, all together, at the same time. The new oppressors will oppress someone else and the evolving saga of life continues. Andrew stares into the eyes of his errant son and again thanks God his son is not laying outside piled up on top of it self.

"Father, Matilda said you have some bad news," said Mary. "What is it? Matilda seemed to be very upset."

Margaret trails behind her mother, unable to speak, her fear more personal. Are we going to lose the farm? Do we have to sell off some land or some slaves? Worst still if we have to sell off some slaves, will Jacob be one of them? Has the price of cotton dropped? Are we losing the War? Every year it has been something.

"There's a body of some black man laying in the road in front of our driveway," said Pierre, getting up from the couch. "He must have fallen asleep drunk and froze to death."

Mary almost faints, grabbing the nearest chair and finding a place to sit. "Matilda, bring me some tea," she said, reaching for a packet from her morning coat.

"Oh my God," shrieks Margaret. "That poor man. Who is it?"

Matilda is somewhat stunned by what Pierre just said. He is so nonchalant about it, like there's always some dead man in the road in front of the house. She doesn't react to Mary's request until she is reminded again. Then, she is off to the kitchen, shaking her head, feeling sorry for the soul of who ever that person on the road may be. As she is setting up the hot water for Miss Mary, Andy rushes in and without acknowledging her presence marches to the living room.

"Papa," screams Andy, more like he couldn't believe what he's just seen, "Papa, it's Marcel, the son of Dr. DuBois, laying in the road. Somebody murdered him!"

"Oh no!" cries Margaret, finding a place to sit and weeping openly.

"OH JESUS NO!" hollers Mary, trembling in her chair, crying.

"I'm coming with your tea," said Matilda, rushing from the kitchen with the tray in hand. "Sorry to take so long."

"I suspected as much," said Andrew, "but I wanted to be sure." Andrew turns to Pierre, "I know how good friends you two were, I'm sorry."

Pierre has a sudden sinking feeling in his stomach. It is as if he's been sucker punched, cold-cocked. He backs away from his father, trying to get out of the way of the comments sent his way, but they hit him again, right in his gut, forcing him to double over, sending more shock waves throughout his body. He reels backwards until he feels a wall, then he slowly begins sliding down, down, down until he is sitting, staring at his feet.

"NO! NO! NO!" screams Pierre. His mind begins racing, remembering, denying the truth. Marcel, dead! Can't be! Must be a mistake! We were just together. We had lunch, we laughed, and we planned Anna's escape. Pierre's mind is trying to make sense of what he's heard and it is not doing it very well. He hears his father speaking to him and Andy too, but he cannot respond back. He sees his shoes and hears their voices. He feels water falling off his face. He hears his mother crying and talking about feeling sorry for the Dr. DuBois and Margaret crying and wondering out loud, why, why, why, but all he can see are his shoes. Backwards in time his mind goes, backwards in time to Pierre and Marcel at age ten, thirteen, seventeen and last Sunday. And now, he has only the memories; there will be no new good times that become good memories.

"Pierre," said Andrew, helping him to his feet and with the help of Andy, he walks Pierre to a chair. "I'm so sorry. I know how much he meant to you."

"Leave me be!" screams Pierre, tearing himself from them both. He wants to be alone. He wants to run away. "I will kill him," thinks Pierre. "I swear I will kill him!"

"Pierre," said Andrew, trying to find the right words. "Were you and Marcel involved in something that might have contributed to him dying the way he did?"

Pierre hears his father and even turns and looks into his concerned face, but he knows he cannot divulge what he and Marcel are involved with. In meetings of the past, both have heard tales of people tempting danger and even heard of people dying, but that was always someone else. Both argued why it would never happen to them; but they both knew that if it did, the survivor is never to divulge what the other was involved with. Well, that time has come.

"No, Papa," said Pierre. "I don't have any idea who would want to kill Marcel." But he did have an idea of who killed Marcel. Marcel's death is a warning to Pierre. It's Major Treeman's way of saying he knows about Anna and it's his way of saying he knows where Anna is hiding. But Pierre can't go and accuse some white man of killing a black and expect justice, even today in New Orleans with it envious justice system. He can't tell his father or Andy the runaway slave Anna is hiding in their barn and has been there for a couple of months. He can't tell his father about the threat from Major Treeman. He can't share any of this information because he's sworn to secrecy by an oath taken by he and Marcel. An oath made in jest because no one ever thought it would ever be tested. Now, more than anything else, Pierre wants to kill Major Treeman, but he knows if he were to do that and get caught, this envious justice system would ignore his logic and reasons for doing such a crime. So, it must be a crime of planning, premeditated, with willful intent to harm, maim and kill. But how is he going to do it? He cannot do it by himself. Who can he ask to help? All this must be done quickly, before Christmas day. How can he do it without raising suspicion with his family?

"Pierre," said Andrew again trying to get the attention of his angry son. "Pierre, I think I know how you feel. You have every right to be angry. But at the same time you need to understand what actions by you and Marcel may have caused this horrible action by some crazed white folks." Andrew felt he was not getting through to his son at all. He didn't know what else to say except, "Listen son, you need to curtail your activities regarding that foolish organization you belong to; at least until things quiet down a bit here. Dr. DuBois is a well respected professional in the black and white community and it would not be in the best interest of anyone, black or white, if rumors began about why Marcel died."

"If you paid attention to Papa," chides Andy, "this never would have happened."

"Marcel lies dead outside our front door," chides Pierre, " and all you are concerned with is public reaction to what he may or may not have been involved with. Suppose it was me out there, instead of Marcel?"

"Pierre, don't say things like that," cries Margaret.

"But it's not you," said Andrew, "and for that, we thank God."

What's God got to do with anything, Pierre wonders. Where was God when Marcel was being murdered? Why hasn't God punished the person who killed Marcel? Why hasn't God punished the people who own slaves? Why does God permit slavery? There is no God. There is no goodness in mankind. There is no righteousness that is the reward for following the word of God. "Somehow," replies Pierre, "the priorities in this family seem to be arranged differently than I expected."

"Pierre," pleads Mary, "you children are our number one priority. All of you know that. And if not for the grace of God, you could be where Marcel is and that is what we're thankful for. That it is not you."

"It is not important that I know your happiness revolves around the fact I'm not dead," said Pierre, rising and walking towards the kitchen door. "Right now there is a depression inside my mind that makes me wish I was the dead body laying in front of our house."

* * * * * * * * *

Matilda is finishing the washing of the morning dishes when Pierre rushes from the living room, through the kitchen, almost knocking her over, then out the back door with a loud slam. She couldn't help but listen through the door to everything that has been said about Marcel DuBois. Everyone was so loud. She is amazed at what she hears from Massa Andrew and his family when the struggles of human life are being discussed. This family, dedicated to God, Country and the Confederacy is not dedicated to the human struggle unless it personally becomes their struggle. Other people's struggle are not of their concern unless it personally requires a sacrifice on their part or one of their slaves is involved. This senseless murder of Marcel DuBois did not require any sacrifice on their part and as a result their concern is respectful and minimal. Young Pierre is the only member of the family who understands what a sacrifice feels like. Even though at first, even he didn't realize how much of an impact Marcel's death would have on him emotionally. And his family, instead of mourning Marcel's death, shows more concern about it not being him. Maybe it's how slave owner's show they appreciate their children. Matilda feels nothing but pain for Marcel and his family. She knows it could have been Jacob lying there and the St. Clair's would be the same about her son. Only God understands why this kind of pain is necessary for people to endure. Only God can claim justice for such crimes. Only God can respond to those who chose not to respect human life. But where is God, now?

Matilda enters the living room again and finds the remaining members of the family absorbed by the luxury of their surroundings. Oh, they still talk about Marcel, but it's mundane history of how long they've known the family. It's as if Andrew and Dr. DuBois' families were never close. This is the same family who has shared many Sunday dinners, hog killing together, Thanksgivings, Christmas dinners, there and here, and now their grief is directed more at what could have happened to their own sons. Their behavior is a contradiction to their Christian beliefs; and those who contradict the laws of God are doomed to his anger and expressed retribution. It always happens when you least expect it, God steps in and makes a decision, understood only by him.

Massa Andrews and Master Andy are still advocating the cause of Marcel's useless death is directly related to his conduct with Pierre and their abolitionist friends. Both conclude Pierre and Marcel and the rest of their deranged group have been discovered and Marcel may be the first of many mysterious deaths. Regardless of how Pierre feels right now, he needs to be aware that he too may be targeted. This conclusion does not sit too well with Mary, who immediately wants to know where he has gone and if he is okay. Margaret has not grasped what is happening to her family and emotionally moves around the fringes of the conversations, reacting emotionally to what she sees and hears.

Dere is a day of reckonin' dis family will face, sadly thinks Matilda, 'cause dey ain't in touch wit da same Lawd she is. Her Lawd is much stronger den dere Lawd. Dey cannot be worshipin' da same God, 'cause God don't be likin' hypocrites, and if dere's somethin' this family is good at being, it's being hypocritical. They may not want to see or even believe dat they are, but God knows better and he sees what deys don't see and even what dey don't want to see. Yes, dere is a day of reckonin' dis family must face. God will visit dem on that day of reckoning, like a thief in the night.

* * * * * * * * *

After the noonday meal, Andrew decides now would be the right time for his family to visit Dr. DuBois' family, and pay their respects. He leaves instructions with Jacob about what needs to be completed while they are away. Pierre balks at the idea of going, saying he could not face them, knowing Marcel would not be there. He wants to remember Marcel as he last saw him. He feels selfish about his grief for Marcel and doesn't want to share it with anyone. Not even with Marcel's family. It would be too painful to sit around listening to other family and friends saying what a wonderful man he was. Then they would speak of how his life was cut so short, and how he never got a chance to grow up. All those flowers they would be giving him, now that he is gone. Flowers they should have given him while he was alive and could smell them. Flowers about how good the work he was doing in helping those who cannot help themselves. No, Pierre decides, he didn't want to be a part of that at all. Pierre asks his father to explain to Dr. DuBois the pain he feels for Marcel's death is too great for him to come and he hopes Dr. DuBois would understand.

Pierre spends the rest of the afternoon sitting in the barn explaining to Anna what has happened. Several times he has to leave to respond to problems in the fields, but he always returns to the barn and talks to Anna, reassuring her nothing has changed and she still will be on her way to freedom despite what has happened to Marcel. For fear of being discovered Anna never shows her self, but Pierre can hear her sadness and can tell by the way she moves above him she is also concerned for his and her safety. This is not how Pierre wants to remember the Christmas holidays, but there is nothing he can do about it now. He spends a lot of time trying not to feel guilty about what has happened to Marcel. He cannot rid himself of feeling responsible for his best friend's death. It will follow him to his dying days.

Now, he must find a way to avenge Marcel's death; one that would be fitting for Major Treeman. It was Major Treeman who did this, Pierre is sure, and he left Marcel's body in front of his home to let Pierre know it was he who did it. Major Treeman is a ruthless man blessed by the devil who knows only ruthlessness in return. Pierre feels a hole in his stomach and senses everything falling out of his body. He shivers, not from the coolness of the air, but it's more like a trembling out of fear. How can he kill this man? He knows he must kill this man, but he wonders if he can and he wonders how? He remembers having problems, holding the pistol steady, when everyone thought he was going to shoot their dog, Nutmeg. Major Treeman is a human being, someone, who, when you look into their face, their eyes tell you what they think about death and dying. They even tell you if they fear or welcome the idea. And where is he going to get the gun necessary to carry out his revenge? He knows he cannot depend on getting Papa's pistol. He knows he must learn how to shoot and learn fast. The gauntlet has been thrown. If Pierre picks it up, he must understand there will be a fight to the death.

Major Treeman is trying to torture his mind and Anna's and right now, he is being very effective. Pierre knows between now and Christmas day, Major Treeman will strike again and he must figure a way to protect his family, himself and Anna without telling Papa and endangering the rest of the family. It is too late to move her and now there's no place to move her to, except on Christmas day, which is three days from now. Can he trust Matilda and the slaves to hide her? Would they forgive him for what he is doing? How would the rest of the slaves react knowing he is not doing the same for them? No, he could not ask them to help.

Pierre loses track of time. He is depressed and only realizes the long hours he's spent in the barn when he leaves and sees Matilda. She is going in the back door to prepare the evening meal. Not long after that, his father and family return from Dr. DuBois, meeting him in the yard. They all have troubled expressions. Pierre sees, understands and chooses not to explore what happened during their visit. Even during the evening meal, there is a different kind of silence at the table. No noise except the scraping of utensils on the plates along with the "yes mams" and "no massa" from Matilda as she dances around the table, responding to demanding requests from everyone. Pierre would not have thought this to be totally out of place, except after dinner. Normally that is when there is conversation about what has transpired from the day; instead Andrew asks Pierre to stay at the table while everyone else removes themselves, passing a glance of despair at Pierre. Even Matilda is asked to remain in the kitchen until she is called for.

Andrew waits until it is just him and Pierre before he rises from the table. He directs Pierre, with a wave of his hand, to follow him to the living room, and points to a couch chair to sit on. He first explains how devastated the family is and how difficult it is for Dr. DuBois to come to grips with Marcel' death. Then he explains how

Dr. DuBois kept asking the question why and always came up with the same answer about Marcel's involvement with you and that group of friends you have. He went on to explain how they agreed that Pierre and Marcel needed to have stopped this foolish talk about freeing slaves and helping them runaway north. Andrew looks at his son who keeps his head in his hands, staring at the floor. "Son, I need you to look at me and listen to what I'm saying." Andrew waits until he sees Pierre's distraught face before he continues. "The more Dr. DuBois talked about his son's death, the angrier he got. While I was there, the coroner arrived with Marcel's clothes and the report about how Marcel died."

"Papa, I don't need to hear any more of this," said Pierre. He is feeling a headache and begins rubbing his forehead.

"Oh yes you do," said Andrew harshly. "Now sit down!" Andrew waits for Pierre to sit before he started reciting from memory what he had read. "Marcel was brutally tortured before he died. Whoever did this is an expert with a knife. The way his body was sliced up, it was done so Marcel would suffer and die slowly. Several of his wounds had salt shaken into them. Near, around and on his genitals there were gashes made by the teeth of a dog or dogs. Both hand knuckles were crushed. Several ribs were broken, and one leg was dislocated at the knee. From the amount of dirt in the wounds, it appears he was finally dragged to his death." Andrew slowly sits back, having finished his recitation.

Pierre continues to hold his head in his hands and is staring at the floor. There are drops of water falling between the fingers of Pierre.

Andrew reaches into the inside pocket of his coat and retrieves an envelope. "Dr. DuBois asked me to give this to you," said Andrew, holding the envelope out for Pierre to take. "He wrote it just before we left to come home." Seeing Pierre is not reaching out for it, Andrew places the envelope on the seat next to Pierre and rises from his chair. "Monday we're all going to Baton Rogue with Dr. DuBois. That is where they plan to bury Marcel. Are you going to accompany us? You need to show your respect to his family."

"I can't do that, Papa," sobs Pierre. "I can't do that." Pierre senses his father standing silently in front of him. It is as if what he is doing is going to force Pierre to change his mind about going. He stands there for maybe another minute then walks away, mumbling something about how Pierre needs to grow up and assume more of his man-like responsibilities. Pierre fingers the envelope containing the letter from Dr. DuBois. Maybe he should have done the same and written a note of condolences instead of not doing anything at all. Maybe he should have gone with his family, making his feelings known instead of letting his father express them for him. Regardless, Pierre and the letter from Dr. DuBois go upstairs together and sleep through the evening, into the early morning. When he awakes he is still dressed from the day before. His mind is a blank and when it reminds him about the incident, he wonders if yesterday was a bad dream? He wonders if it were true? But then the envelope bearing his name, written in the handwriting of Dr. DuBois, convinces him about the reality of yesterday.

CHAPTER 15
Monday December 23rd, 1861

A bitter chill in the air hovers around everyone as they sit in the surrey. The coldness matches the sadness of the journey. Charlie Boy was up early and has hooked the mare to the surrey and was holding the mare when everyone came outside from their early morning breakfast. An eerie silence greeted everyone as they left the kitchen. Even when the back door closed with a bang, it sounded strange to the ear, almost muffled. No one spoke as they boarded the surrey, only acknowledging Charlie Boy's presence. Matilda remained at the kitchen door, watching. Pierre is standing next to the surrey, holding his mother's hand, having already kissed his sister goodbye. Andrew sits facing Mary and Margaret, saying nothing to Pierre. Andy has climbed into the driver's seat and is about to goad the mare forward.

The surrey suddenly lunges forward, catching Pierre by surprise. His mother's hand jerks from his, but he recovers quickly, moving up a step grabbing her hand again. He waits, hoping warm words of support would come from his father and break the icy stare he's getting, but there is no response, only a gentle pat and sympathetic smile from his mother. His father, still angry with him, because of his refusal to go with them Friday and his continued refusal to go to Baton Rogue, has put a canyon of anger between them. Mary, true to her obedience to her husband, does not interfere with Andrew's discipline.

At the insistence of Andrew, Andy lightly snaps the reins against the back of the mare. It lunges forward, pulling the surrey, leaving Pierre standing with Charlie Boy. Mary is slightly thrown back into her seat and against her daughter Margaret. She struggles to turn and see Pierre, as if it would be the last time, but cannot. Again she is reminded why she hates this war. It is the men who play the game of war and she hates the men who make the laws that cause so much family dysfunction.

As Mary straightens herself, she sees him standing at the end of their driveway, looking at her as if he knew something about her she was hiding and didn't want anyone else to know. She nudges Andrew and with her eyes, said something is troubling her and that concern is about the man standing at the end of their driveway. Andrew recognizes him to be the Major Treeman. Not understanding why Major Treeman is standing in front of his driveway and not understanding why Major Treeman has that look of intimidation, Andrew stares just as hard, back at Major Treeman. Andy turns the surrey and points the mare towards the direction of the New Orleans.

Pierre watches Andy drive the mare as it pulls the surrey, with his family sitting so straight, so proper, dressed in the traditional black, away from him, down the driveway to the road where just a few days ago, Marcel's body lay. He waits for his mother, then maybe Margaret, to turn around and wave to him. He is deeply disappointed when they do not. He stands there and stares at the back of the side-to-side rocking of the surrey. Even after Andy has made the right turn out of the driveway and Charlie Boy mumbles something, that Pierre does not hear, Pierre remains, staring at the end of the driveway.

Pierre is not sure what it was that snapped him back to reality, whether it was the door slamming behind Matilda, or the outhouse door slamming behind Charlie Boy, but suddenly he sees Major Treeman. The sight of him hits Pierre like suddenly being slapped in the face. The distance of the long stare seems to have roped him, holding him captive. He doesn't move for what seems to be an eternity. He is not sure how long he is standing there trembling before he is startled again, hearing the door slam and Matilda coming from the kitchen. Relieved that it is her, he watches her walk to the slave quarters.

When he turns to look for Major Treeman again, the bounty

hunter has vanished. Was that really him, or was it not? All of a sudden, Pierre is not sure. All of a sudden he is feeling very afraid inside. If it was him, where is he now? Pierre stands and scrutinizes places around the farm, focusing his eyes where he thinks somebody could be hiding.

He nervously walks down the driveway, past the slave quarters, past the slave garden, and sees no one. He walks back past the slave quarters again, past the outhouse, and stops at the new hole for the slave's outhouse Charlie Boy is finishing. He said nothing to Charlie Boy, but looks deeply into the trees and even deeper into the area of the pigpen and still sees nothing. He does all of this to feel more at ease before he walks to the barn. He is not at all at ease with what he doesn't see, but there's nothing he can do about it now. He decides to go speak to Anna. Major Treeman is not stupid enough to do something in broad daylight, or is he? He pats his coat for the letter from Dr. DuBois. He will read it to Anna. Somehow he hopes it will make her feel better knowing how much Marcel meant to his father and how much his father loved Marcel and how much he believed his son did not die in vain.

Anna is sitting by a narrow crack in the wallboard, looking outside when Pierre reaches the top of the ladder. She is smiling with anticipation, knowing soon that she will be away from this place. She sees the saddened look on the face of Pierre and knows he is missing his friend Marcel. She tries to cheer him. "Pierre I really 'preciate what you and Marcel have done for me. When I's free, I will never forget either of you."

But there is something else in the face of Pierre telling her he has something on his mind, something he needs to speak to her about. Her enthusiasm turns quickly to concern. Pierre is retrieving something from inside his coat; something that looks like a letter. Is it a letter of denial for her freedom? Is it a letter declaring she must be returned to her farm? What ever it is, Pierre is not happy about showing it to her. Anna slowly rises from her bed of hay.

Pierre is slow to explain what the letter said. "I have a letter from Dr. DuBois." Pierre sits with his back against the wall, while Anna sits between his legs looking at words on a piece of paper she cannot understand. "I think it's about how much Dr. DuBois appreciates the friendship between me and Marcel." He begins to read it to her. "Dear Pierre, it is with a saddened and laden heart that I write this letter to you."

What does dis man, Dr. DuBois, know of sadness, thinks Anna. What does he know about havin' a heart? He is a slave owner; regardless of what color he is, he is a kidnapper of livin' souls, holdin' onto dem until dere will to lib dies and leaves jus' a shell of flesh dat holds emotional emptiness. A sadden and laden heart really comes from being forced from your homeland, dragged, drugged and put aboard a foreign vessel and taken to a land known only to the Gods. How dare dese free walkin', free talkin', free thinkin', free blacks 'pect sadness and pity for their brief moments of pain and sorrow. Dey needs dat experience twenty-four hours a day. Dat is real sorrow. Look not to me for pity, look not to me to share in your sorrow, Doctor whatever your name is, I have enough of my own.

Anna holds her head in her hands between her crossed legs. She can smell herself. She longs for a bath. She longs to wash the stench of pain and sorrow from her body. She hates the foul odor wafting up from between her thighs, the caking layer of dirt in her armpits and the clumps of filth in her hair. She wonders what Pierre must think of her, why he would want her.

"Because of the evil some man has done," continues Pierre, quietly, "I have lost a son and you have lost a dear friend. But to put the blame on the person who killed my son and think that he acted alone would be foolish. The contributing blame for his death lies at your feet." Pierre stops reading and lets the letter slowly slide from his hands.

Anna feels Pierre's sorrow as she stares at the letter that now rests in her lap. She tries to make him feel better. She moves closer to him as he drops his head, covers his face and lets the water spill from his eyes. She has witnessed shame being put upon Pierre for the crime of trying to set people free. What is it about this *civilized society* of America, where men find comfort in enslaving other men? This is America, 1861. This is where there are no laws of protection or justice for the indebted servant or slave.

Anna attempts to comfort Pierre as much as she can, feeling

him shake and tremble in her arms. How weak da child of dis master is, thinks Anna.

Pierre has not developed how to control his human spirit. He has not developed the strength not to care. A master of both strengths enslaves, a student of both learns to enslave. Because of what he is, Pierre will be no master and has not begun to understand the teachings to become one.

Anna has seen this before, at the Clanton plantation, before she ran away. There is the strong and there is the weak in every family. For Anna, it is a double edge sword in her life and the life of other slaves. The strong dominate; the weak let the strong dominate. Such are the laws of this society, this family and every other family in the Confederacy.

"You hafta keep readin'", encourages Anna, "no matter what his father has written. You have to read all of it."

Pierre recovers himself, cleans up his face, and begins again. He is embarrassed by his behavior; doing what he did in front of Anna. It is not the manly thing to do, to cry and he is not sure Anna understands. He realizes he must finish reading, regardless of what Dr. DuBois has written. He strongly feels what he and Marcel were doing was right. One day history will vindicate what they and others like them are doing. He can hold his head high even though to do so means pain and heartache because of what his father, Andy and Dr. DuBois feel about what he is doing. Can money be that important to his father? Can he care even less about how he makes his money?

How can his father enslave his own people? His response has always been, "Slavery of one's own people has always been a part of world history. What makes the United States any different? Irish enslave Irish, Italians enslave Italians, what could be so God awful about Negroes enslaving Negroes? All it means is that we free people of color are melding into the current system of our new homeland."

"I have searched my heart for the words to express how I feel about the fate of my son Marcel; but these are all the words that are left inside of me. I do not wish you the same fate, but at the same time I do not wish any fate at all for you." Dr. DuBois did not sign the letter. Pierre folds the letter places it back into the envelope and sits dejected in the hay with Anna.

"Do not worry so much 'bout what the Doctor said," said Anna. "What you are doing is so much more important than what personal feelings that Dr. DuBois may express."

For a long time nothing is said between them. Anna holds Pierre close, feeling his emotions rapidly flowing from his body. He is in so much pain. She gently rocks him in her arms, humming a slave song she learned from the fields. More than an hour passes before they can discuss what is going to happen Christmas morning. Anna understands what is expected of her.

"I will be back about midnight with your last meal and a change of clothing to wear before we leave for New Orleans." Pierre, feeling slightly better about himself, goes to the fields to ensure the day's work gets done. He passes Charlie Boy climbing out of the new hole for the slave's outhouse. Charlie Boy tells Pierre it is all finished and he will roll the old outhouse over it later, but now he needs to rest. In the fields, Jacob is keeping the slaves busy preparing the cotton plants for the last picking of the season.

Pierre stays in the fields well past dinner, returning with them at dusk. Tomorrow is Christmas Eve. Tomorrow he will give them the traditional day off, along with Christmas. It is what his father has always done.

* * * * * * * * *

It is the spirit. It is always the spirit. It is what's inside the shell of the body that really controls everything. It is the Holy Spirit. It is the spirit that never dies. It cannot. It is there because some can feel its presence; some can see its presence; some can call it from the other side; it is spiritual; it is holiness, it is sacred; it is love of life; it is all about the sacrifice of the mind, body and spirit. It is the giving without expecting something in return. "Danbhalah Wedo, Behold your children, hey!" chants Voodoo Man Cato. "Aida Wedo, here are your children, hey! Danbhalah Wedo, Behold your children, oh! A yey, a yey, oh! Danbhalah, here are your children" [vii]

Voodoo Man Cato stands at the center of his hounfort, crosses himself and recites the *priere dior*. With the combination of flour and cornmeal he creates the necessary *ve ves*. Tonight he creates eleven *ve' ves* and with the completion of each he blows the remainder of the mixture from the palm of his hand towards the four cardinal points. He crosses himself saying, "Linsah" when he touches his forehead, considered the East, "Mawu" when he touches his breast considered the West, "Vovo-Lin-V-Hwe", when he touches his left shoulder, considered the North and "Hevio-Z0", when he touches his right shoulder, considered the South. Voodoo Man makes a final sign of the cross over the ground that is now sacred.

Voodoo Man Cato calls upon the loas to protect him from the evil that walks on six legs; to deliver upon him the powers he needs. He needs the strength in speed to move quickly when he has to. He needs the stamina to hold back the pain and suffering. From the center post the ve ves are drawn, spreading out like the rings from a pebble dropped into still water. "Hey! Great saint, great Loa, Guedi Nibbho is lost Hey! Great saint, great loa Papa Guede is lost." [viii]

Voodoo Man Cato places a lighted candle in the center of a circle drawn on a table with the four points of the universe defined. He then calls out the name of each of the loas of the Terrestrial Fluid, "Apolihsahgbadya, Bo Dan Guimin, Ahouengan, Sih-Ye To Menan". Three times he calls the four and at the sound of each name throws three drops of water on the ground in the form of a triangle. He then plants a golden pin within the same circle with a gold chain attached to it, acknowledging the four points of the universe. It is at this time he tells the loas what it is he wishes them to do in helping him to overcome this evil that is about to come into his life. "Mother Brigitte! My mother! Oh! Do you see him? With his six legs, do you see him? We have dug the hole in your womb. We have lain open your soul. Mother Brigitte! My mother. Do you see him? Let him forever sleep in the pit of your bowels."

He calls out the name of Major Treeman to the four corners of the universe then drinks 3 draughts spraying it from his mouth each time to complete the calling. He concludes the ceremony proclaiming, "Ye-ke, mar-ch-allah! ju m bha-lah dya." Voodoo Man Cato sits on the earthen floor, waiting to be mounted again. He is waiting to fly again, and waiting to be called again. He knows this is to be his last time inside his vessel of flesh. Tonight is his flight to freedom.

* * * * * * * * *

The barn on the St. Claire's farm is magnificent. It is second only to their home in its function as a building. It is thirty-three feet wide with two doorways three and a half feet wide at both ends, with stone thresholds. Its length is forty-six feet long with stable doors on the side to store the carriage and a manger on both sides divided by an eight-foot passage, for the two mares. There is a ladder that climbs to the height of twenty-eight feet leading to the hayloft; the loft door opening to the south, catching the morning sun. There is lots of open space at the top, interrupted by beams that hold up the pavilion roof. The eaves of the roof extend more than 10 feet from the walls of the barn on all sides, creating shade that surrounds the building. In the summer, the loft is the last to be cooled after the setting sun and rising moon. In the winter, the heat makes it bearable to sleep with proper covering.

This night, Anna does not feel the chill in the air, nor the roughness of the hay that has been her bed. She does not feel the hopelessness and abandonment that was hers alone just a few months back. There is a fire inside her soul that is warming her body, growing in strength, melting the chains holding her soul as a prisoner. She is about to become a free person of color. She smiles to herself, sitting in the hay, her hands folded in her lap, looking at the morsels of food Pierre has brought. She is too excited to eat. Water continues swelling up in her eyes and slowly sliding down the sides of her face. The loft door is open and a full moon is spotlighting the doorway, shining on Anna, letting her know tonight she is someone special.

Pierre reaches out and gently wipes the tears from her face. She holds onto his hand and presses it closer, squeezing it tenderly, enjoying these last moments together. She knows she must eventually let go of his hand and let go of everything she has experienced in this land of 'white only' opportunity. She thinks about what she will be leaving behind; so many friends, some dead, while others are the walking dead. No more auction block, no more peck of corn, no more pint of salt and no more driver's lash for me.

She will leave everything behind, but her tears. They will follow her wherever she goes. Even though they will lay hidden in the wells of her heart and mind, seeing the pain of others, remembering her own pain, will always find them; and expose them for all to see and not understand. How long has she wished she would be free? How long has she wished she were dead, just to be free? Now, it looks like she will be free and she is living to talk about it. She smiles through sadness, knowing she will continue to have pain and happiness as conflicts of her past life until her dying day. Tomorrow is Christmas and she will be given the greatest gift anyone could give her and that is her freedom. She begins to hum a song of joy, a song of freedom. Pierre hums along with her and soon, together, very softly, they begin to sing, "Free at las', free at las' I thank God, I'm free at las'. Free at las', free at las', I thank God I'm free at las'. Way down yonder in de graveyard walk, I thank God I'm free at las'. Me an' my Jesus gwineter meet an' talk, I thank God I'm free at las.' On my knees when de light pass by, I thank God I'm free at las'. Though my soul would arise and fly, I thank God I'm free at las'. Some o' dese mornin's bright and fair, I thank God I'm free at las'. Gwineter meet my Jesus in de middle of the air, I thank God I'm free at las'." Together they continue to hum the song, letting go of it slowly and quietly. Anna leans forward, embracing Pierre, holding him close. Oh how she wants to share herself with him. She can hear him breathing, feel his arms around her, keeping her warm. She gently kisses him and receives an over powering mouth on hers.

Suddenly, out of the beautiful quiet of the cool night they hear a dog barking. It is much more, much worst than an ordinary barking dog. It's more of a snarling growling sound, shattering the clear still air like glass breaking. The barking is not in the distance, but close, very close.

Pierre quickly brings his fingers to her mouth, preventing the fright on her face from coming out of her open mouth. Uncontrollably, Anna begins trembling like a leaf alone on a tree limb out in the wild wind. She is looking around, panic in her eyes, trying to find a place to hide from that hysterical barking dog. She remembers the sound of that particular barking dog. It takes all of Pierre's strength to restrain Anna and prevent her from leaping from the loft door.

"Quiet" he whispers, now holding his hand snugly over her mouth and holding her struggling body with the other.

Anna wants to getaway from Pierre. She knows all to well the owner of the barking dog. She knows her freedom will be death if she was to be surrendered to the owner of that dog. She would rather kill herself first and the loft door seems to be the quickest method. She struggles with Pierre to release her. Nothing matters now. She will get her freedom. She will get it with God's understanding and blessings. If she cannot be free by the will of the mortal and the immoral white man then she will be free of this body by her own free will. The barking dog is now deafening. It echoes inside her brain. It's echoing inside the barn. It takes her breath away when she realizes where it is coming from. This wild dog, with a banshee growl, was at the bottom of the ladder. There are more hysterical scratching sounds against the wooden steps. He is desperately trying to climb the ladder.

"Easy Nutmeg," said the bounty hunter, pulling back on the rope his collared dog. His voice was sounding confidently sly. There is an evil intention behind the soothing tone to his dog. He rubs the back of his neck vigorously. There is a smile on his ugly face. "I suspected she was up there, now you done told me so." Major Treeman looks up the ladder leading to the loft and smiles. She didn't go far at six cents a mile, but at the charge of two dollars a day, he stands to make a nice piece of change. Add to that, ten dollars for bringing her in, he almost has a hundred dollars. That's more money than he's earned all year. He hears the hay cracking above his head and follows the trail of falling hay between the cracks in the overhead floorboards. "I know you're up there, Anna, don't make me send Nutmeg up to get you." Major Treeman finds a place to rest his weary body.

It has been a long walk from the Clanton Farm and he wants to rest before starting back with his bounty. He releases enough rope so Nutmeg can jump up and down at the ladder, yelping with excitement. Nutmeg is the best nigger chasing dog he's ever had. A mix of rottweiler and something else, maybe bloodhound because his nose trained so quickly for finding runaways. During Nutmeg's training, he was locked up and never allowed to see Negroes, except when he was being trained to catch them. He quickly learned the scent of most of the slaves on the farm. Sometimes in training he was given the scent of a slave man or woman's article of clothing. Then Nutmeg was let loose to find to whom the article of clothing belonged. When he found the slave matching the scented clothing he grabbed onto their clothing, growling, until Major Treeman came and rewarded him with a piece of meat. Nutmeg learned even faster after that first taste of raw meat.

"You got just five more minutes, Anna," said Major Treeman, looking up at the ceiling above his head, "then me and Nutmeg gonna come up there and gitcha."

Pierre and Anna are like two children, feeling lost and alone, shivering in the cold. Pierre is not sure what he can do. He feels empty inside, his brain suddenly going blank, his feelings suddenly emotionless. His heart is trying to get out of his chest. Suddenly he is feeling very cold. The contents of his stomach are moving like water over glass; everything that was in it is now uncontrollably sliding down and through his bowels. He's loosing control of everything about himself. Anna will not look at him. She continues to stare through the floorboards at the source of Major Treeman voice and the growling dog below. Five minutes, that's all the time they have left in the world. Pierre understands how Marcel must've felt. At some point the fear gives way to hopelessness and after hopelessness comes surrender. Pierre's eyes dart around the loft; looking for something he can use to defend himself and Anna. Nothing. All the tools are hanging where they're suppose to be, below them. Pierre can hear his heart beating and little else.

It is Anna who hears the fluttering of wings, pushing the air out of the way above their heads. She looks up and sees the black bird again. She looks directly into the bird's eyes seeing its cold eyes stare back at her. Sitting on a beam, it stretches its wings, unfolding six feet of feathers. Anna cannot take her eyes from the eagle. She sees the bird as some sort of savior, something that has come to save her and Pierre. For the moment she has forgotten about the growling dog and Major Treeman. She stops struggling with Pierre, relaxes, and gently moves away from him.

Pierre looks at her, amazed at her calmness, and then follows the sight of her eyes to the ceiling. He sees what she is looking at but doesn't understand. He hears Major Treeman say three minutes are left. The eagle leaps from the beam and gently floats to Anna. He walks to her, wings still spread out, his head bowed in reverence. Anna kneels and cups the bird's head in her hands and brings it to her face. It's as if she were communicating with it. She gently rubs the bird's feathers, smoothing them. She holds its head for a few moments then gently backs away. They both watch it take wings and fly out from the loft through the open, door into the spotlight of the moon.

"One minute Anna," yells Major Treeman.

"Pull the dog back," demands Pierre, staring at Anna. The fear that was once in her eyes is gone. It was as if she is completely at peace with herself. "We're coming down."

Pierre is the first to descend the ladder, carefully; looking down to be sure Nutmeg is on a short rope. Anna follows and together they stand at the base of the ladder, arm in arm. Pierre stares at Major Treeman. Anna stares at Nutmeg.

"Well, looky here," smiles an almost toothless Major Treeman, putting his knife away. A pile of shaving is between his legs on the ground. "Aiding and abetting a runaway is against the law. Your Pa's gonna lose this farm and everything on it." Major Treeman holds tight the reign on Nutmeg, but lets the dog frantically yank away from him. "This time tomorrow everybody on this farm is going to be a slave, yes sir, everybody. What am I gonna do with you, young Pierre?"

Anna pushes herself away from Pierre and stands alone in front, between Pierre and Major Treeman. Nutmeg reacts to her moving by growling and snapping at her, showing discolored broken teeth. "It is me you want, suh," she pleads. "Let Pierre and his family alone. Dey knew nothing 'bout me."

Anna waits for Major Treeman to answer her and at the same time she waits to hear from her God. She is sure the black bird was a sign from God. Now, she must just wait on the Lord. He will come through. He won't come when she wants him, but he'll be right on time. The black bird was the sign, yes Jesus yes. She lowers herself, kneeling in front of a growling Nutmeg, not afraid of what may happen to her next. There is a wonderful peace inside her, calmness she has never felt before. She has been afraid all the time she hid in the barn; afraid of being found; afraid of having to go back to bondage; afraid of enduring the pain of being whipped for her wrong doing. Now, she wasn't afraid, even in light of kneeling before this viscous drooling dog. What she clearly understands now is she's not afraid to die. How strange the feeling is; it's as if life's yolk of misery and pain has been lifted from her. Anything would be better than what she is being forced to go back to, anything. And right now, she just didn't care about what is happening to her.

Major Treeman, smiling with anticipation, tells Anna to get off her knees. He motions Pierre and Anna to walk towards the door leading outside, under the watchful eyes of him and Nutmeg. One tooth broke through his smile and poked out the side of his mouth, hanging on his unshaven face. His clothes are still dirty, disheveled and tattered about the edges.

An odor emanates about Major Treeman and Nutmeg, like a surrounding invisible boundary, confusing Pierre and Anna so much they cannot tell just which one the odor is coming from. To Anna, the repugnant odor took her mind back to Trader Yards. The odor is bringing back the ugly memories; the ones overflowing with frightened anticipation of what was going to happen to her and her family. To a time that kept her family in continuous suspense due to the nature of the Confederacy's peculiar institution. The continual nagging thought that a master could sell family member, or separate them on the plantation by making them work in different areas. The master could do this without so much as listening to a voice of concern from the family member. Not even listening to the Christian voice of concern that's supposed to be within them. Her family was not her mother or father, but instead was someone she called Sula. When she came from the Trader Yards, the first person she saw was Sula, who pulled the dirty handkerchief from Anna's frightened face. Not since the doomed smile she saw on her mother's face as they were separated, did she see another smile on a black face that comforted her. Sula became her new family.

From Sula she learned the importance of family. Even though they continued their own domestic duties after coming from a full day's work, those extra domestic chores was Sula's way of showing defiance to the master. Regardless of how important the master's work was, maintaining a healthy home environment was more important, even though maintaining a healthy family was an advantage to the master. "This is for me, and my family." Sula always said, when Anna questioned why she did so much work. It was Sula who taught Anna to sew; taught Anna the household chores she needed to be able to do for her family; taught Anna what it is to go from a girl to a woman and taught Anna the secrets of herbal medicine. Anna wondered what ol' Sula was doing now.

To Pierre, this odor most foul, this overpowering funk, this smell of unwashed flesh and clothing, is very familiar. It is a smell that has wrestled with and defeated his sinus membranes, pinning them against the back of his brains, giving him a headache. Like the cold steel of a plow, it cut deep wrinkles into his forehead, turning up his nose. The smell reminded him of fresh dog droppings; plain ordinary dog shit.

* * * * * * * * *

Anna and Pierre stumble through the door, into the still cool night, followed closely by Nutmeg growling and snapping at their heels, then Major Treeman. Perched high on a cypress tree he sits in witness, quickly cocking his head right then left, and rolling his eyes to get a better view. He flutters his broad-feathered wings in the wind, disturbing the silence of the night. He takes flight, soaring above the trees, into the cool night air, floating above the nightwalkers below him. Once he reaches his desired height, he looks down, sees his prey, tucks his head and silently dives. A cool wind passes between and over his feathers as he closes in on his intended victims. Beneath him, in the light of a full white moon, he watches as they slowly walk away from the barn and towards the road leading off the farm. He sets his talons, hanging loosely, below his belly. Like his pointed sharpened beak, his claws are honed to razor sharpness. From what he sees with his sharp eyes, his talons make adjustments to strike the target correctly.

Anna is first to sense something was different shortly after stepping outside. The air feels strange, as if something was pushing it into her face, forcing it on her. The further she and Pierre walk, the stronger the force until something inside her tells her to get down quickly and get out of the way. Anna instantly responds, pulling Pierre with her forward towards the ground. Pierre and Anna are suddenly lying face first into the ground, covering their heads and protecting their ears.

Just before he strikes, the mighty black bird screeches, like a predator screaming his joy of capture, startling everyone. Nutmeg begins to twist and yank madly on the rope that holds him to Major Treeman. In his effort to get away from the strange sound he seeks shelter running between Major Treeman's legs. Major Treeman looks up to see what is making this noise, grabbing his knife with his free hand.

Again the black bird sheiks loudly. Nutmeg gives off a fearful yelp. The black bird strikes his target, digging his talons into human flesh, finding soft underbelly flesh about the face of Major Treeman. With a mighty tearing rip of his talons he extracts some hair and jagged pieces of flesh, dripping with blood, as he swiftly rises into the cool night air. Following him is a painful scream from Major Treeman that eventually overtakes him as the mighty black bird rises into the air. He looks down to see what it is that clings to his talons. A clump of flesh, perhaps a piece of nose or forehead, and in the other, another clump of flesh, this looking more like a piece of an eyeball. He screeches victoriously, rising higher, before turning to strike again.

Anna hears the screeching sound of a bird then the sudden flutter of wings, and then an agonizing scream from Major Treeman. Now, on her hands and knees, Anna is crawling and struggling, to get away as quickly as possible, from Major Treeman and Nutmeg. She is moving but not moving. She can't seem to get far enough away. She must be dreaming, no matter how much she crawls, she can't get away. She turns and sees Major Treeman on his back, holding his face in his hands, crying in agony. Nutmeg is tangled about him, twisting and turning and yelping in a panic.

As the mighty eagle begins his descent again he sees Pierre and Anna, frantically stumbling and crawling away. Major Treeman, moaning in agony, is hysterically twisting and turning on the ground. He is in great pain and is confused about where this surprise attack came from. Even more perplexed is Nutmeg. He is barking while yanking and twisting at the rope, trying to free himself. He senses there is a force much greater than he can overcome and ferociously struggles for his freedom so he can escape and run away.

Major Treeman rolls onto his stomach. He is trying to regain his senses. There is something terribly wrong with his face. It feels so wet and sticky. He is determined to maintain control of Nutmeg and his prisoners. He feels the wetness on his hand and the pain on his face and wonders what has happened. "NUTMEG! NUTMEG!" He screams, trying to reassure his dog of his owner's presence. He untangles himself from Nutmeg, struggles to his feet but is confused that he does not have the same vision he is accustom to. Abruptly he turns his head right then left. He's blind in one eye and through the other eye his bloodied blurred eyesight shows Pierre and Anna crawling towards the slave quarters. He didn't care about himself right now. He needs to re-capture Anna and Pierre. He needs to complete what he has been paid to do. He can't let this injury stop him. He looks at his hand holding Nutmeg. There is an awful lot of blood soaking the rope, sticking to it and dripping through his fingers. In his confusion, he struggles to understand what has happened to him. Out of his one and only eye he sees his two prisoners struggling to flee from him, he hears agony and panic in Nutmeg's bark. The cool air he felt when he went into the barn now has become cooler, no, colder, much colder; so much so that he now trembles and shivers. He rises upright, trying to control his vertigo, feeling Nutmeg untangle himself from between his legs. Nutmeg, responding to his master's voice is now yanking him forward. He's untangling the rope wrapped around Major Treeman's blood soaked hand, growling, showing his crooked and jagged teeth, chasing a crawling stumbling Pierre and Anna.

The black bird adjusts his angle of attack when he sees Major Treeman lurch forward being pulled by Nutmeg. He sets his talons and this time they find their mark on the side of Major Treeman's head, digging into his ear. With his sharpened beak he bites into Major Treeman's head ripping out another clump of flesh. Major

Treeman again collapses to his knees, screaming even more in horrifying agony. Major Treeman reacting to the attack quickly reaches up and grabs whatever it is that is attacking him.

The black bird tries to fly off but cannot because of the heavy rough hand of Major Treeman. He jerks his head, his left eye seeing what has a grasp of him and immediately attacks the Major Treeman's fingers, ripping and yanking flesh with his beak while flapping his wings, desperately trying to escape.

Major Treeman curses and screams, as he violently rips the black bird from his face and throws it away from him.

The black bird feels his body uncontrollably flying through the air. He attempts to take flight, but he cannot right himself. He falls to the ground, hard, just in front of Nutmeg. He has one wing flapping wildly; the other is dislocated, spread open and limp, not functioning at all. As painful as it is, he flutters his wings, trying to get out of the way of Nutmeg's snarling teeth and sharp scratching paws. He leaps into the air above Nutmeg's head, landing on Nutmeg's nose, scratching and clawing at his eyes, blinding him. Nutmeg howls in pain, rising on his hind legs, trying to swipe his nose free of his attacker. Major Treeman, with knife in hand, tries to maintain his balance, takes a swipe at the black bird on Nutmeg's nose. The eagle lunges backward out of harm's way. He senses himself falling to the ground.

On their hands and knees, Pierre and Anna continue to crawl away from the violence happening behind them, towards the slave quarters. Pierre rises, looks at a profusely bleeding Major Treeman and wounded Nutmeg. He reaches down and drags Anna to her feet, staggering together backwards toward the slave quarters.

Major Treeman sees the black bird's wings flutter, its feathers flying as the body of the eagle tumbles out of the air to the ground in front of him and Nutmeg. This bird, this big black bird, this defender of Pierre and Anna, this bastard fowl, has become a barrier between them and their prisoners. Major Treeman can now barely see the black bird. Nutmeg cannot see the bird at all, but he can smell it. The black bird smells familiar, very familiar. It smells like a nigger. It's what he's been trained to smell. His nose becomes the eyes for him and Major Treeman. "Follow what you smell, Nutmeg!

Follow that nigger smell!" Major Treeman's voice is harsh and filled with hate.

The wounded, mighty black bird, again flutters away from the snapping jaws of Nutmeg. Painfully using his dislocated wing, he pushes dirt back into the blind battered eyes of Nutmeg. He cannot get far enough, fast enough to stay out of harm's way, but still he struggles. He screeches in pain as he moves his broken wing. Nutmeg growls, sniffs the ground then growls again, letting what's left of his nose lead the way. Major Treeman struggles to stay on his feet, trying to control Nutmeg and maintain his balance. Nutmeg is now in charge of the direction they are going. They are close to the open pit of the new slave outhouse. The black bird continues his own struggle. With one last effort, at the edge of the pit, the wounded black bird frantically and painfully flaps its wings one last time, and slowly rises into the air. Nutmeg follows the scent above his head and lunges forward, growling and snapping his jaws, pulling Major Treeman with him. When the mighty black bird flutters back to the ground, he lands on the other side of the open pit. When Nutmeg comes back to the ground he falls ten feet further down than where he started. Major Treeman follows him into the black hole. Nutmeg is the first to let out a last gasping painful yelp as cypress shaved spikes, protruding from the bottom of the pit, instantly pierce his body in three places. One enters between his hindquarters, another enters his bowels, and the final spike enters beneath his jaws, coming out the top of his head. Major Treeman screams but for a moment during the fall, then his head, followed by his chest and legs are impaled on a series of the protruding spikes. Then, all is silent.

It seems all creatures great and small, paused in their way of life to see this life and death struggle unfold. It is the owls that are first to realize there is no more to be seen. Theirs is the first sound heard, a mighty hoot, that floats out from the trees and into the yard. The other nocturnal observers, realizing the show is over, slowly drift away. The rodents crawl back into their domains. The birds fly home to their nests. The gators slide back into their swamps. A strong wind suddenly sweeps the air of the foul stench of Major Freeman and his dog, Nutmeg. The wounded black bird lifts itself into the air, and falls. Determined, he tries again with the same result. Again he tries and this time he slowly takes flight, being carried by a new stronger wind. He disappears into the bayou. It is there he will find the herbal medicines that will ease his pain. It is there he will find the herbal medicines that will prepare him for his return to the Gods.

Anna and Pierre sit up and lean against the foundation of the slave quarters they have crawled to. They can hear each other's heart beating. Both are surprised by the sudden sound of silence that surrounds them. They look at each other, checking to see if either of them has been hurt. When it is obvious they are unhurt, they hold each other close, touching, grabbing, kissing and crying, sharing each other's joy. Their hearts still beat at a frightened pace as they struggle to catch their breath. They sit stunned, confused, wondering what has happened to them. Where is the Major Treeman and his dog, Nutmeg? All around them, there is silence and still-ness. Not even the nightlife of nocturnal sounds can be heard. Only the wind has any strength left to move. Only the wind has the energy left to get up and move along, continue its usual routine. Only the wind is strong enough to wash the air of the agonizing screams. Only the wind has the ability to blow away the stench of death. Only the wind has the fortitude to cover the evidence of blood, the evidence of a struggle, the evidence who was the victor and who was the loser. Only the wind has the energy left to get up and move along, continuing its usual routine.

★ ★ ★ ★ ★ ★ ★ ★ ★

The door to the slave quarters suddenly opens and Charlie Boy comes out followed by Jacob, Big Black and two other slaves. He pauses briefly, staring down at Pierre and Anna, shivering like scared orphan children who have been found when they did not want to be. He said nothing to them, but signals to Jacob and everyone to follow him to the barn. They are in a big hurry. They come out shortly with shovels and rope. Once at the pit they begin shoveling dirt into the open hole. At Charlie Boy's signal they stop and lay logs across the beginning of the open pit. They then go to the slave outhouse, lift it from the foundation, place it on the logs and roll it into place over the new open pit. Once the outhouse is secured they fill in the remaining hole from old outhouse, cover it with boards then return the tools back to the barn. Charlie Boy is last to re-enter the slave quarters. He pauses again, looks at Pierre and Anna before going inside, leaving the two of them alone again.

Pierre slowly gets up, brushes himself down, and then helps Anna to her feet and brushes her off. Together they slowly walk to the house, entering through the kitchen door. Once inside, Pierre finds some food for Anna and together they silently eat at the dining room table. After eating Anna has a chance to relax and looks around the home of Pierre. Anna is distracted and impressed by the wealth belonging to this black family and cannot contain her amazement. She walks around the house looking at everything, touching, holding, feeling, and appreciating her new surroundings, even if but only for a few moments. The Christmas tree is up and decorated. She has never been in a big house before. Pierre lets her move about freely, explaining what something is and what it is used for. Anna sits in the middle of the living room floor feeling the rug beneath her feet, laying down on it, letting her arms and legs enjoy the surface.

Leaving Anna to her new simple pleasures, Pierre finds the bathtub and fills it with hot water. In the time it takes him to go to the barn to get some clean clothes and come back, Anna has dozed off. Waking her gently, he explains with urgency the need for her to bathe and dress in the clean clothes. Anna takes a long hot soak, enjoying the comforting, cleansing water and the soap that smells so good. At her request, Pierre fills the tub a second time. Three hours later, at five-twenty am, she is standing at the horse stable, waiting for Pierre to pay the money necessary for him to leave his mare.

CHAPTER 16
Wednesday, December 25th, 1861

Anna is afraid to look up as she quickly walks with Pierre from the stable to the train station at Commerce Place Basin. She is frightened by what she sees about her and of being recognized by someone from the Clanton Farm. She has never been off the farm and what she is seeing is very confusing. She is not sure where she is or where she is going. She looks into the storefront windows and sees pretty dresses on wooden dolls and all kinds of tools for the farms and a barbershop and a store with a wooden Indian standing in front of it. All the buildings look like the big house. She walks on wooden planks that always seem to be under her feet. She marvels at the fact there is mud all about in the street, but she is dry because she's walking on these wooden planks. Pierre calls them sidewalks. When she sees someone approaching her and Pierre, she ducks her head and clings tight to Pierre. There are so many noises, loud noises all about her. She tries to cover her ears but it does not help. She is not use to so much noise she cannot identify. It was up one street and down another; turn left, turn right. Anna is completely lost; but she follows Pierre, just the same, wherever he goes.

It isn't until she's standing on the station platform at Commerce Place Basin and watching the big black and red engine approaching with it choking smoke billowing, that her fear deepens. It's partly from the noise of the engines huffing and puffing, rushing towards them. The front light is surrounded with a weather beaten Christmas wreath. But Anna's fear is also reinforced when she realizes she is truly going someplace different, someplace new, someplace away from here. Pierre helps her aboard, and then pushes her to the left. He opens the door for her and she is astonished to see so many black folks, all dressed up and looking real pretty. Families, men, women and children, all of them dressed up so nicely. She feels so out of place, wearing these clothes that make her look more like a young boy instead of the woman she really is. She wants to ask Pierre if all the black folks riding on this train are as free as he is? Did they own slaves like his family does? They find an empty seat near the front of the car. The train lurches forward, her heart jumps in fright. She grabs Pierre's arm and holds on.

Staring out the window, watching people and things going by, Anna is totally bewildered. This new experience is more than she ever would have expected. There are rows and rows of big houses, connected together as far as her eyes can see. There are horse drawn carriages everywhere. And all these black people; everywhere she looks, bunches of black people. Even more amazing than the number of black people she sees everywhere, is the fact that they look like they were never slaves. She is confused. If there are so many free black people, why then is she still a slave? Why do they not rise up and free her of this misery? How can all these free black people let the human misery of slavery exist?

The train is slowing down. She has more time to see and hear things going on around her. Her face presses more to the glass as the train stops at St. Claude. Many people get off and just as many get on. Then the train is going again, after lurching forward, but this time Anna is not so frightened. She continues to stare at the cornucopia of things she has never seen or heard of before. There is so much to see. Every building she passes has Christmas decorations on it. Everyone is in the Christmas spirit. The train is alive with the joys of Christmas. There is holiday laughter and singing echoing off the ceiling, bouncing around the inside of the coach, bumping into the people, drawing all of them into this party of good feelings.

When the train stops again she sees water, lots of water and all kinds of water vessels. Suddenly the isle of the coach is filled with anxious people trying to get out and continue their bliss outside. Anna and Pierre are the last to leave. Once outside Anna's ears again are assaulted by a loud long hissing, with white and gray steam spilling uncontrollably from all kinds of openings around the engine.

There is still a morning chill that moves briskly with them as they pass the engine, defying the moist clouds of the steam. Anna now feels as if Pierre is dragging her. His gait has increase from what it was when they left the delivery stable. He now moves with more purpose and determination.

"Hold tight to me, Anna," he said to her. "There are people here you cannot trust." He pauses but a moment to give this warning, then squeezing her hand he begins walking again, pulling her along.

Anna wants him to slow down. She wants him to take some time for her to see what New Orleans is like. She wants to see more of what the people look like, and sound like, especially the black folks. There are so many black folks in New Orleans. Where did they all come from? There is so much she wants to learn in so little time. Suddenly her nose perks up. There is the familiar smell of food floating on the air like snowflakes and flowing into her nose with the cool air. It draws her like a magnet closer to Pierre.

"Are you hungry?" asks Pierre, standing before a storefront, grabbing the door.

Before she can answer they are inside finding a table. Inside is so warm. There are not that many people, but there is someone at almost every table. Again she sees nothing but black folks. Working the tables, cooking the food, and one older woman is giving instructions to everyone from the kitchen to the dining area. She escorts her and Pierre to a table. Her name is Mama Salome and this is her restaurant. She reminds Anna of her mother she never had. She could see kindness in Mama Salome's eyes and Anna knew she could not hide, in her own eyes, her desperation. Mama Salome smiles at Anna as she sits. "Child, you look like you ain't ate in days," she said, gently resting her hand on Anna's shoulder. Anna smiles sheepishly feeling embarrassed that she has been exposed. All around are black folks eating without fear. These are proud black folks. She's never seen such calmness in black folks before. She wants to be like them. She wants to be free, like them. She now wants to stand up and shout that she is free, just like they are, but she knows she cannot, not now, anyway.

Pierre orders for both of them. He looks at Anna and smiles at the excitement in her eyes. She is so interested in what is going on around her. Her eyes tell it all. He watches her as she looks around at everything, reacting to every sound, looking at the food that comes from the kitchen, listening to the laughter, the banter and everything that is the life of Mama Salome's. She is like a child, her face full of confusion mixed with fascination. He wishes she could stay. He wishes he could go back to the Clanton farm and buy Anna from them, just so she could stay with him. Pierre is enjoying the happiness that is all aglow on Anna's face. They trade whispered conversations back and forth, laughing and giggling like two people falling in love. But Pierre also masks his own feelings about Mama Salome's. The last time he was here it was with Marcel. When Pierre thinks about their last meeting, it's as if Marcel knew he would not be here today to enjoy getting Anna onto the Railroad. Pierre can still remember Marcel laughing, sitting across from him like Anna is doing right now. He can still remember the way Marcel always slouched back into his chair legs stretched out from under their table, getting in the way of people who passed them. On more than one occasion Mama Salome scolded him about where his feet should be. Pierre didn't let Anna know what he was thinking about inside. He kept on smiling and laughing with her.

Anna leans back into her chair, her eyes wide with anticipation as their breakfast arrives. The plates are filled with potatoes, cornbread, bacon and eggs. Anna attacks her food with enthusiasm. Jabbing at everything, putting some of everything on her fork, as much as it will hold, then pushing it into her mouth. Soon there is nothing but remnants of what was there and her fingers going around the insides, picking up what was left. Pierre looks at his watch. It is six thirty. They have to be at the pier in front of Public Square by six forty-five.

Their walk is brief. The delicious aromas of Mama Salome's still linger in their noses as they walk along the pier looking for the steamer Baron's Luck and the priest that will take her aboard. The steamer is first to be found and while Anna is preoccupied with her surroundings, Pierre searches the crowd for the priest with the walking stick. Strolling casually through the crowd, Pierre is beginning to worry. There are a lot of travelers about him, but most are families, a few sailors, some distinctly dressed blacks, some servants, children, and lots of luggage and cargo. He doesn't see the priest.

It is not until six forty-five, when the last call has been announced, that a priest shows, walking slowly with the assistance of a walking stick; an African walking stick. Pierre meanders towards him, interrupting his path. He bows, introduces himself then requests a blessing for Marcel. The priest collects an apprehensive Anna in his arms and asks if she is willing to follow the teachings of Jesus Christ. When Anna said she is, he blesses her then removes from inside his coat two tickets.

"This is where we must say good-by," said Pierre, holding Anna close. He whispers, "Remember, your name is Marcel." Pierre holds Anna close. He doesn't want to let her go. "I love you Anna."

Anna is crying and trembling. Everything is happening so fast. She clings tightly to Pierre listening to the priest explain that he has a missionary stop in Cairo Illinois, then overland to Chicago, and from there, north to Canada. Suddenly, she didn't want to leave Pierre, resisting his efforts to push her away from him.

"Now is not the time for that," reminds Pierre. "People may get suspicious." He removes a handkerchief from his pocket, dabs her eyes, and then gently pushes her into the waiting arms of the priest. He stands and watches as they walk the gangplank onto the steamer. Anna turns one last time, waves, then she and the priest disappears inside. There is a final letting off of steam through the steamer's whistle, then the removal of the gangplank. Next is the frantic waving of friends and relatives, then the pushing away of the steamer from the pier. Pierre walks away from the pier without turning to see the steamer leave the bay. He cannot bear to look at it. He can hear the toots of the whistle in the distance as he moves across the Public Square and even fainter toots by the time he is at the train station.

* * * * * * * * *

It is eight-thirty when Pierre turns into his driveway, home at last. Smoke trickles from the kitchen chimney. Matilda is preparing the Christmas day meal. Soon the rest of the family will be home from Baton Rogue and there will be the traditional opening of presents, then dinner. Pierre, exhausted, barely able to sit upon his mare, lets the mare find its own way to the barn. He can feel himself collapsing inside, slowly, like a deflating balloon. He slides off the saddle and walks the mare into the barn. When he stumbles outside again, his mind begins showing him how tired it is as well. There are sudden flashes of Major Treeman blocking his way and Nutmeg barking and showing his teeth. Pierre reacts by stumbling backwards, falling into the barn door. And just as suddenly as they are there, they are gone. This brief hallucination leaves him shaken. He begins trembling, uncontrollably. His brow leaks tiny droplets of water. He looks at the slave quarters then the newly standing outhouse next to it. BAM! The door to the outhouse slams as someone leaves it.

He looks at his feet. The ground, except for the impressions left by his mare, show no signs of a struggle. There are no leftover blood droplets or clumps of dirt. Everything looks normal. Even the sun, the moon, the wind, and the trees are acting normal. Surely they were witnesses to what happened. Surely they were disturbed at what happened. Children were playing in the yard. BAM! The door to the outhouse slams again as someone goes inside. Some of the other slaves are sitting on the steps of their houses talking, relaxing, and laughing. Did they know what happened last night? Did anything happen last night? Was it just a dream?

Pierre drags past Matilda, and mutters holiday greetings. She answers, but he doesn't hear her. Matilda continues to prepare for the holiday family meal. Soon he is through the swinging door leading to the dinning room and pulls himself up the stairs to his bedroom. His body is starting to breakdown even more. There is tightness in his leg muscles; his lower back is aching. His mind races in front of his body and is continuing to break down even faster. He can't think straight. He forgets where his room is and momentarily stands at the top of the stairs wondering which way to go. He turns right and pushes open the door. He recognizes his surroundings. He sits on the edge of his bed, holding his head in his hands trying to make sense of everything. Did Marcel really die? Did he really put Anna on a steamer called the Baron's Luck? Maybe it was all a dream. Maybe Anna really didn't exist anywhere but in his mind. Maybe he'll wake up and he'll be twelve years old again. He wants to cry, but cannot figure out why he should. His neck hurts, his head hurts, his body begins to ache. "Oh God," he mutters, calling for help in straightening out what has happened in his life. He's never done this sort of thing before. Will it be easier the next time? Will someone else die? Will he die? He wants to rest, at least until his family comes home. Will he tell them what happened? Will Matilda tell them? Will they believe him? He has no proof. He leans back into the pillow on his bed and lets the overflow of water from his eyes run down his face. He will miss Marcel everyday for the rest of his life. He is so damn tired. He can hardly move the rest of his body onto the bed. He wants to lay down and die, but instead his mind takes over from what he wants to do and forces him into what it wants him to do, sleep.

* * * * * * * * *

Pierre hears Margaret calling him first. Her pleading voice is somewhere in the distance, somewhere in front of him. She calls out his name two, three more times. Pierre starts running toward the sound of her voice, but he is having problems with his legs. He cannot run with them. They seem to be holding him back. Then, he hears his mother calling, but she is more towards his left, still far off, but he hears her voice, calling with concern. He has to make up his mind, does he follow the voice of Margaret or his mother. He turns to follow the direction of his mother's voice. And when he does, he sees Major Treeman and Nutmeg. He hears his mother calling again and this time she sounds like she is standing behind Major Treeman and Nutmeg. The eyeless stare from Major Treeman freezes Pierre. Nutmeg's teeth are larger than he can remember. He hears his mother calling again, then he hears Margaret, and she too sounds like she is standing behind Major Treeman. Major Treeman releases the rope holding Nutmeg and the mad dog lunges at Pierre. Pierre dodges out of the path of Nutmeg's drooling mouth. He runs to the left and Major Treeman blocks him. He runs to the right and Major Treeman blocks him there also. He hears Margaret again and then his mother. They seem to be very excited about seeing him. Major Treeman seems just as determine not to let him see them. Pierre feels something about his ankles and looks down. Nutmeg's jaws have clamped on, but he feels no pain. He struggles to free himself. Major Treeman begins walking towards him, laughing. He pulls a long handled knife from his pocket and shows it to Pierre. The blade is reflecting light from an unknown source. Pierre looks at the knife. Marcel's blood soaked clothes are hanging from the tip of the blade. Major Treeman stands over Pierre looking down at him from empty eye sockets. Pierre feels himself rising with Nutmeg still clamped on his ankle. He hears his mother and Margaret calling again, this time, both seem more anxious about him coming to them. Pierre struggles to free himself from the grasp of Major Treeman and kick loose Nutmeg's mouthy grip. He finally breaks free, but feels himself falling uncontrollably. He can look back and see Major Treeman and Nutmeg above him, watching his descent into nothingness. Major Treeman is laughing and pointing at Pierre as he continues his fall into hell. He hears Margaret and his mother demand he come to them when suddenly he hits the bottom of this endless hole, feeling the rest of his body stack on top of him.

"Massa Pierre," it was Matilda, standing over him, her hands on her hips, "you look like you done had a nightmare and fell out of bed." She helps unwrap him from the entanglement of covers. "Miss Mary, Miss Margaret, Master Andy and Massa Andrew are waiting for you downstairs."

* * * * * * * * *

At the dinner table, while everyone is exchanging gifts, Matilda walks around the table collecting wrapping paper and dirty dishes at the same time. There are lots of thank-yous and how-did-you-knows and it's-what-I've-always-wanted conversations filling the air around the table. Matilda has grown tired of hearing the same phrases over and over. Then there is also exciting talk about how wonderful Baton Rogue is as a city. In between is sandwiched the funeral and how sad the event was. And there were comments about how everyone missed seeing Pierre. After those formalities were completed the conversations meandered to discussing the business opportunities that have opened up. Andrew is thrilled at the prospect of doing business with the free blacks he met in Baton Rogue. Many of them think as he does about the necessity of maintaining status quo, when it comes to the need for slavery. Andrew relishes the new contacts they made for exchanging goods. He feels gratified about the number of additional free blacks willing to take up arms against the North. It all adds up to the promise of free black political muscle after the war is over and the South has won.

There is no questioning to Pierre about what happened while the family was away. There are no questions from Andrew about what the slaves got done. No one asked about how Pierre felt while everyone was away. No one thought of asking what Dr. DuBois put in the letter to Pierre. Everything is in the past, water over the dam and well down stream. The emotional high that may have been there was just as far down stream for everyone, except Pierre. Oh, there is mention of the new outhouse by Andrew and how impressed he is that Charlie Boy finished it by Christmas. Consider it a Christmas present, said Andrew, now feeling lose about the mouth, having had one too many aperitifs, before, during and after the dinner.

Andrew is at the top of his good feelings, strutting around the table. He continues to the dining room and living room like the rooster in a hen house, talking about the success that he will be having in the near future. According to him it will come to be in springtime at the latest. The promise of an improved way of life is destined for this family and Andrew is damn proud he is responsible for it. He looks to Mary for acceptance and she gives him her smile of acceptance. When he looks to Andy he gets a hardy handshake and a loud voice of acceptance. But when he looks at Pierre, Pierre just stares back. Andrew quickly looks back to Andy for additional support and is received with open arms and private conversation.

Matilda has removed all of the food and dishes. Her last task of the day is bringing the silver service tray through the kitchen door, filled with hot water and hot coffee. She wants this day to be over. As she removes the food from the table, she sets some it aside, like she's always has done during the holidays, to take over to her family in the slave quarters. She purposely cooks up extra meats, breads, potatoes, and vegetables knowing there will be leftovers.

All that is not eaten by Massa Andrew's family is shared with the slave family. For the next couple of days, there will be an abundance of food for everyone and then the leftovers from that will be made into soups. It's Massa Andrews's way of rewarding the slaves for all their work for the past year. He thinks he's doing the slaves a favor, offering this extra food at the end of the year; like he can't offer it all during the year. Matilda knows better, since she is in the house at all three meals. She knows better than any of them what's in the icehouse and the smokehouse.

There they sit, enjoying Christmas, exchanging gifts, enjoying the fruits of the slave's labor and then calling it their own. Acting as if they worked the fields, bent over in the hot sun, twelve to sixteen hours a day. Acting if they suffered the aches and pains, the cuts and bruises, the rashes and ticks. How can they be tired from work? With so much wealth in this household, why then are the slaves so poor? After all we are living under his roof. Why can't the homes of the slaves match the intake of the income? Why can't the slaves enjoy the profits from the work they do?

Matilda has created four large bundles of food. One that has meats; one that has breads; one that has vegetables, and one for Voodoo Man Cato containing something from all three. She has accepted holiday greetings from all of her masters. It is now her opportunity to share the remaining holiday spirit with her family of Jacob and extended family of slaves. She is very tired. She has been up since early this morning, cooking and preparing extra food because of the holiday. Her feet hurt, her thighs hurt, her shoulders hurt, her back hurts, and her hair hurts. If Massa Andrew understood what Matilda has done for him and his family, he would be much more appreciative about how important she is to him and his family. He knows what she does, but he doesn't understand. He has forgotten what it is to be a slave. He has forgotten what stress there is in being a slave. He has made sure no one experiences the same stress he did. As a result, this family has no day-to-day serious stress to handle. Day to day living for Massa Andrew is business, strictly business. For Margaret, it is a tease about what she will do with her life. For Andy it is fun and games. For Pierre it is living in a dream of being a savior of enslaved people and for Miss Mary, it is pretending she is having stressful situations so she can enjoy another one of those packets from Dr. DuBois. This family must create stress in their minds in order to survive. Matilda continues to ask herself how can that be?

Matilda stands before Miss Mary and her daughter Margaret, holding the tea tray for their pleasure. She has placed a bottle of sherry on the table for Massa Andrew and Andy. For Pierre she has left the pot with coffee. There still remains some light of day and it will be a joy to be at her own table with her own family, sitting and eating their Christmas meal together. She excuses herself, wishes them a Merry Christmas, then leaves. She sends Jacob back to pick up what she cannot carry, which includes Voodoo Man Cato's bundle. While she and the other slave women set table, Jacob takes Voodoo Man's bundle to his hounfort.

It is right after the blessing of the food by Mama Sarah that Jacob returns and tells everyone Voodoo Man Cato is not in his hounfort. He shows his mother a black feather as all he found inside the hounfort where Voodoo Man Cato usually knelt and prayed. Matilda, Charlie Boy, Big Black, and Jacob sit around their dinner table discussing when they should tell Massa Andrew that Voodoo Man has left the farm. Once that is agreed upon, a decision is then needed to choose who should tell Massa Andrew. Once that is agreed upon, they finish their meal.

Two hours after the slave's dinner has ended, when most of them are just laying about, sleeping off their Christmas meal, Charlie Boy, showing the affects of his age and a full stomach, slowly gets up, and leaves the sated group. Slowly he walks to the kitchen door of the big house and gently knocks on the door.

Pierre greets Charlie Boy and at his request takes him to Massa Andrew. Pierre looks into Charlie Boy's eyes, trying to read what's behind them. Why would he need to speak to his father? Is he about to expose what happened last night? Will he tell how Pierre hid Anna in the barn? Pierre is not quite sure it all happened last night. He wonders why Matilda didn't say anything. It seems to him she was obligated to tell, but for some strange reason she did not. He wonders who's in charge of the farm, the slaves or the masters? Charlie Boy looks Pierre straight in the eyes, waiting to be taken to Massa Andrews.

Massa Andrew, quite tipsy from his over indulgence of sherry, greets Charlie Boy like a long lost friend.

"Charlie Boy, it's good to see you," said a cheerful Andrew. "Merry Christmas to you and yours. You did a fine job with that new outhouse. Yes sir, a fine job. Didn't he, Andy?"

"Yes, Papa, a fine job," said Andy agreeing.

"As a matter of fact, I can't wait until I have the opportunity to use it," continues Andrew. "The other one was about to fall down. I don't know what was holding it up."

"It's Voodoo Man Cato, suh" said Charlie Boy, with his head bowed.

"What's wrong with Voodoo Man," asks Andrew, joking. "Is he sick? He shouldn't be with all those herbs and animal parts he got down there in jars and sacks. I can't get anyone to come out here today, so he's gonna have to heal himself."

"No suh, he ain't sick," said Charlie Boy, playing with the rim of his hat. He still hasn't raised his face to Andrew. "It look like he done left da farm."

"He did what?" asks Andrew. He is suddenly quite serious and sober. He keeps shaking his head trying to sober his mind.

"Why that old fool," chides Andy, "that old damn fool! I never thought he had any good sense, now he's gone and showed I was right. Well, good riddance to him. He never did anything around here except scare the slaves talking about that voodoo mess and spells."

Looking at Charlie Boy, Andrew can see that what Charlie Boy is saying is true.

"I left him pretty much to himself," begins Andrew. "I figured since he was some sort of religious figure, he shouldn't be in the fields. What reason or reasons did he have to run away? He has shown me no respect, no respect at all. Damn him! What is it about how I treat my slaves where what I do is not enough? What did voodoo Man have to do? Nothing, that what; absolutely nothing!

And that was still too much! Damn him! I don't have to do what I do for you slaves, Charlie Boy, but I do. Do you know why?"

"No suh," said Charlie Boy, still looking at the floor.

"Because you're family, that's why!" said Andrew. "I'm concerned about everyone of you. Have I ever treated any of you unfairly? Have I ever put the whip on any of you? What have I done to deserve this kind of disrespect from you?"

"Papa, Papa," interrupts Pierre. "Charlie Boy is not the one who ran away. You don't have to continually berate him."

"It doesn't matter", said Andy, agreeing with his father. "Slaves just don't know how good they have it here."

Not hiding his anger, Andrew said, "I have no feeling for Voodoo Man at all. He's an old man; too old to be running away. But since he's left, he's on his own. I have no pity for him. What he did was stupid and I have no pity for his stupidity."

Andy again loudly agrees.

"Yes suh Massa Andrew," said Charlie Boy, turning to leave. "We sho' do have it good 'round chere."

Pierre thanks Charlie Boy for bringing the timely news and walks him to the back door, leaving his father and Andy still angrily discussing Voodoo Man's departure.

As they are walking through the kitchen Charlie Boy pauses just before opening the back door. "Master Pierre, Jacob found somethin' in Voodoo Man's hounfort."

"And what was that?' ask Pierre, his hand on the door knob.

"He found dis here feather," said Charlie Boy, giving it to Pierre.

Pierre looks at the feather and has another flashback of last night. He stumbles, catching himself against the back door.

"Are you okay, Master Pierre?" asks Charlie Boy.

"I'm fine, Charlie Boy," say Pierre. "I tripped on the floor. I need to pick up my feet."

Opening the door Pierre is once again startled to find someone standing there, just about to knock. It's JoJo, Major Treeman's son. He looks just as dirty and unkempt as he did the first time Pierre made his acquaintance. He just stands there; his hand raised and closed getting ready to knock. Charlie Boy excuses himself and leaves Pierre alone with JoJo.

JoJo, takes off his hat, wrings it in his hands, and bows his head as he speaks to Pierre. "'Scuse me suh, but I was wonderin' if maybe you seen my paw and our dog Nutmeg?

Pierre looks at this sorry mess of a person standing before him. He looks at the feather in his own hands, then looks at the bowed head of JoJo and said, "No, I haven't." Pierre slams the door hard in the face of JoJo. He then returns to the sitting room, ignoring his family and takes the bottle of sherry from the table. He pours a large drink, swallows it in one big gulp, and then said good night to his family.

CHAPTER 17
Friday, January 10th, 1862

Every year at 4am preparations for the slaughter began. A large fire was started and kept burning under a large black cast iron kettle, filled with water. Soon the water was boiling violently for use at daybreak. It is the start of a day that will not be spent in the fields, plowing, tilling, or bent over pulling weeds. There will be no suffering from back pain and blistered hands. The smokehouse has been thoroughly cleaned. Tables and shelves have been set up inside. "S" shaped hooks fashioned from heavy wire hang patiently, waiting to be called for duty. Smoked wood has been gathered and placed in piles near the smoking tubs.

A long wooden table has been set up, with sharp knives placed in different locations. Some of the knives are homemade. Some are from old saws, axes and files. All of them are grindstone sharpened and tempered to the right hardness to hold their edge. The fire beneath the large cast iron kettle, with its three legs resting on brick, attacks the kettle, ripping at its sides like ferocious lions devouring a kill. Inside the kettle the water is churning to a continuous boil. The fire is very hungry and there is a large amount of wood to feed it for several hours nearby.

Several oak whiskey barrels stand empty, waiting to take part in the keeping of the meat; waiting for the end result, to be filled and mixed with the several hundred pounds of salt, lye, bay leaves, sage and cayenne pepper. Large tubs sit around watching and waiting for the their insides to be filled to the brim with what use to be life. Slaked lime and fresh pine bough are thrown into the boiling water to season the water. A clothesline of wooden horses about 5 feet high, stretches across the yard, waiting for the laundry of flesh to be hung from them. The gambols are ready. The strong small straight sticks are ready. The hollow reeds are ready. It is time.

The fenced in pigpen is located east-southeast of the main house. Due west of the pigpen is the slave outhouse, the slave quarters, and then the slave garden. The pigpen catches the first light of the morning sun before anyone else. Sometimes it catches the first wisps of southerly winds and wakes, much to the dismay of those in the main house, everyone from the comfort of their sleep. There are 53 inhabitants of the pigpen. Twenty-two really plump hogs, 8 plump belly-dragging sows, and 23 pigs in various weight classes from piglets to pig. All have spent the last year in the marshes and bayous, fattening themselves, and caring for the new litters. Just before Christmas, Andrew had Big Black, Jacob, and a few of the other slaves call all the pigs, hogs, and sows home. The fat and plump ones were fenced separately, not permitted to return to the marshland and bayous to forage. Instead they are fed a diet of corn only to harden the fat and sweeten the meat.

Matilda has been cooking since early morning. She was up and in the kitchen at 3 AM preparing breakfast for everyone. During this one day of great killing, everyone sits at the same table, slave and slave owner, elbow to elbow. Andrew sits at the head of the long table, with his sons, Andy at his right hand and Pierre at his left. Mary sits at the other end, with Margaret sitting to her right. This one great breakfast feast is the one time there is no counting of the number of eggs used. There is no worry about the amount of bacon cooked. No one cares about the amount of butter that's missing nor do they worry about having enough dough for the biscuits. There is laughing and remembering. There is bragging and daring. Whose hog will weigh the most? Whose hog will bleed the fastest? Who can cut up the most meat? On and on it goes. Plenty of food, plenty of people and for one brief moment in time there is no difference between master and slave.

At 5:30AM, Andrew stands at the head of the table, picks up his cloth napkin and wipes his mouth. He takes his final swallow of coffee, burps and excuses himself amongst the laughter. Charlie Boy pulls his chair away from him as he backs from the table and walks to the barn. Everyone knows what it means. The slave men folk jump from the table with anticipation. The slave women folk begin clearing the dishes, carrying them to the kitchen. They then begin preparing the table for what is about to happen. There isn't much conversation; everyone knows what he or she has to do.

Soon, the barn door is thrown open and a two wheel horse cart, pulled by 4 slaves grasping the shafts comes out. Three more are pushing it while Andrew sits on top preparing the tools needed for the killing. Andy, Jacob, Big Black and Pierre walk behind everyone, holding onto axes, wire, and burlap. There is a high energy level in the slaves, almost too much energy, but they have waited all year for this day. Andrew is well aware of this and does not object to their over zealous behavior. At the pigpen, there is a lot of yelling and bragging about which hog should be killed first and reasons why.

The cart is backed to the fence. Andrew climbs down and walks to the penned area. Jacob and Big Black wait for Andrew's signal. Pierre and Andy hold the wire and burlap. The other men slaves anxiously climb the pigpen fence anticipating the next command.

"That fat black and white one with the crooked ears," said Andrew, pointing his finger.

There is a sudden joyous rush by the other slave men to capture that pig and wrestle it over to the fence. Once at the fence, the head is forced through a slot and held snug. Jacob then stuns it with a mighty blow to the head. Immediately afterward the hog is hung upside down. Big Black immediately stabs the hog in the heart. He then, very quickly, severs the jugular vein. After the bleeding has stopped, the feet of the pig are tied with the wire and dragged, hind legs first, onto the cart. This is repeated until 3 more hogs are killed, and then all are carted to the waiting kettles of boiling water.

The water temperature has to be just right. This prevents the hair on the hog carcass from setting. The only person in charge of knowing when the water has reached the correct temperature is Charlie Boy. By the time the carts have been pushed to the kettles, Charlie Boy is standing there waiting for the right moment. Everyone looks at Charlie Boy, waiting for him to give the okay. Looking at the fires beneath the kettles, and then looking at the bubbling waters, Charlie Boy quickly dips and removes his index finger in the first kettle, smiles and gives the okay. He does the same to the other, smiling again and signaling okay.

The carcasses are then slipped into the boiling water, hind end first and slowly rotated back and forth until the hair slips easily from the carcass. Then, the carcasses are removed and placed on a platform where three to four slave men, with scrapers and knives, quickly begin to remove the hair before the hog cools. They start at the head of the hog and together they work down the hog to its hindquarters. If this is not done quickly, the hair will set and it then requires the carcass to be vigorously cleaned with shaving knives.

After the hair has been completely removed, the hogs are gamboled through the tendons of the hind legs and hung from the wooden clothesline. Again the hogs are cleaned with water and brushes. After this final cleaning, a large tub is placed beneath the carcasses. At this time, Jacob picks out one of the sharpest knives, as does Big Black. Then with the other slaves urging them on, they begin a contest to see who can gut their hog and finish first. Both know they must do this without destroying the large sections of meat. They both have to be precise with their cuts. There is a method they were taught and it is this method they must follow. They begin with opening the belly of the hog, from top to bottom. Then with their left hand they reach inside the opened belly and spread their fingers, using them as a guide they continue to cut open the cavity of the pig until they have slit open the breast of the hanging carcass. They pull their left hand out and the intestines and stomach fall into the tub. Next to fall are the heart, the lungs, the bladder, liver, pancreas and kidneys. Plop, plop, plop, are the sounds heard as the tub catches the organs. Jacob proudly stands back from his carcass and looks at what he has done, then to his left. Big Black is leaning on one of the tables smiling, having finished before Jacob.

Matilda and the other slaves take away the tub with the innards, and transfer the intestines to a different tub. The contents of the intestines are squeezed into a large tub, to be discarded. The intestines are then thrown in a large tub of water and stirred several times. The water is changed often. Eventually, they are all hung and drained, then squeezed, cleaned and washed several more times before they are slid over long reeds, inside out. The exposed insides are washed again then skinned with a very sharp knife. From this final hanging, casings are selected for sausage and put aside in a salt-water solution. A couple of days later, the intestines are boiled outside for several hours, down wind from the house. They become a meal of chitterlings. Because of the abundance, some are given away to neighboring farms and the slave families keep some. Some are sold in market for the slaves and the money kept by Mary for their personal needs.

The gutted hog carcasses are moved to a carving table while Jacob and Big Black wait for the next two to come off the table. On another carving table, one of the slaves cuts loose the legs and feet from the carcass, while another separates the head. The feet are kept in a separate tub to all be pickled together. Before any boiling is done, the toenails and soles are removed. Afterwards, the feet are split and cut to fit into jars for pickling. Half the feet taken today are kept in the slave quarters in jars, pickling. Matilda uses vinegar and salt, plus spices to add flavor while the process takes place.

One of the more experienced women, Mama Sarah, takes the head and cuts it into two halves, top and bottom. From the top half she carefully cuts out the forehead and removes the brains, paying attention to Matilda's playful chiding to be careful. Mama Sarah is smiling with anticipation, knowing there will be brain omelets in the many mornings to come. From the lower half, the jowl is set aside for curing. Because of the number of hog heads, it is necessary to soak them in brine so they can be kept until they are boiled with collards and other garden greens. Some of the heads will be boiled and processed into souse meat; the ears and nose will provide the gelatin necessary to bind the meat into rolls, then, after chilling in the icehouse, they will be ready for eating.

Mary and Margaret work side by side with the women slaves, sharing stories and feelings. They are also in charge of what to do with the fat trimmed from the cuts of meat. It has been cut and cubed for making soap. Using one of the original kettles, that is kept boiling, the cubed pieces are thrown in and cooked until the fat separates from any left over meat texture. This leftover meat is skimmed off and discarded. Lye and other necessary ingredients are added then stirred into the liquid fat. Herbs are added to enhance the fragrances of the finished soap. The liquid fat is poured into troughs six feet long, two inches deep, and allowed to cool overnight. The following day, the cooled soap is sliced into bars then stored for washing clothes, housecleaning and bathing.

Back on the carving table, the thick layers of fat on either side of the backbone was being removed by hand, setting the fat aside for lard processing later in the day. Meanwhile, the carcass is turned over and is split down the backbone with an ax. From here, the loin along the backbone is removed as one piece. Next the hams and shoulders are removed. Both are put in tubs to be prepared for curing. The hocks are kept in a separate container. Most of the belly is carved into bacon slats to be cured. Some portions are cut into smaller pieces for salt pork. Once the sections of the carcass are cut up, it is all stacked in the smokehouse for further processing.

The medium size 'A' frame smoke house has one door and one key. Inside, Charlie Boy has set up old tubs with a couple of inches of dirt in the bottom then using some water soaked cypress wood mixed with some fruit tree wood he begins the smoking process. It is his job to keep the fire and the smoking going each day. His careful attention prevents flare-ups and keeps the smokehouse from burning down. The entire process takes about two weeks and the meat is inspected often to check on the process and to sprinkle pepper, molasses and other combined spices. After the completion of the smoking, the meat can be kept for years without worry of spoilage

From within the smokehouse, the lean meat from the loins and shoulders are mixed with amounts of fat to form sausage. This concoction is hand ground in a meat grinder and then mixed with sage, red pepper, salt, black pepper and other spices. It is then stuffed inside the intestine casings by hand. The casings are twisted off into links to the desired lengths. Some are smoked along with the hams and bacon, but most are eaten since spoilage occurs early in the life of the sausage.

The oak whiskey barrels are ready and waiting. They are filled with the first layer of salt. The whiskey barrels were more acceptable than coke barrels because of the flavor of the barrel passing into the meat. All of the cuts of meats that are to be smoked are rubbed with salt and placed in one of the many barrels between layers of salt. This is where the meat will stay for the next ten days or so. After that time they are removed, brushed off, inspected carefully, to ensure the salt has penetrated the meat completely. 'S' hooks are inserted into each piece and the meat is hung from nails in the rafters of the smokehouse.

By the time the day is done, twenty-nine hogs are slaughtered. What started in the cool of the morning ends in the cold of the night. Andrew and both his families are totally exhausted from the day's work. It was work enjoyed by everyone. It was work done for the good of the farm and it ensured there would be plenty of meat for the coming year.

CHAPTER 18
Thursday, January 16th, 1862

Matilda puts kindling wood in the stove beneath the morning stew pot, stirs it and adds some salt and pepper. She tells Charlie Boy to make sure everyone gets up and is ready for the fields. Without responding to Charlie Boy's inquiries about where she going so early and why in such a hurry, Matilda is out the door and on her way to a rendezvous. Moment's later Matilda is standing by the lake, covered by her shawl to protect her from the morning cold air, while waiting for her Jacob.

She watches the new moon finish painting the canvas still water. Her heart beats fast and heavy with anxiety. Is he going to come? Maybe he's left already. She mumbles a prayer he has not. He is supposed to be here, at this time of the morning. Jacob told her he would be here. He told her last night he was leaving in the morning, but he would wait and say good-bye before he left. He said he didn't want to tell her earlier because she would not have been able to hold it in while working with Massa Andrew and his family.

The air is crisp and clean. It passes into her clothing, to her body, entering her nose, opening up her sinuses, and causing a slight nose drip. She is continuously drawing the nose water back into her head. She remembers what it has been like these last few months on the farm, for Jacob. There is something going on inside his head. It has been showing itself behind his eyes. She's been seeing it each time she talks to him. She sees it when she watches him working. His mind is not here on the farm. His mind is somewhere outside the fence around the farm. More and more he has been coming home later and later from the fields. He staggers home, kicks the mud off his shoes, and changes into some cleaner clothes. He then goes out again, telling her he and Big Black are going back to the fields to finish up, but she knows that is not true. She worries about him; wondering, why does he want to leave? This is the only home he has ever known. It's a safe haven for him. Let just his mind run away.

She stands in the cold, still, morning air waiting, slowly turning looking, shivering, wringing her hands, and pulling the wrap tighter around her. "Jacob, where are you, my son?" she whispers into the cold air, her words falling through the mist coming from her mouth.

"I'm here, Mama." The deep resonating sound of Jacob's voice floats out of the cluster of trees, surrounding Matilda, holding her tight and still. Once she is a secured by his voice he shows himself. He has a bundle tied to a walking stick that he rests over his shoulder. He quietly walks towards his mother. In her face he can see her anguish, but his mind is made up.

"Jacob, my son, come closer. I needs ta hold you."

"I come to say goodbye, Mama."

"Jacob, I don't wants you to go. It's dangerous on da outside of Massa Andrew's property."

"Mama, I can't work here no mo'. I can't stand on my knees any mo'. I ain't gonna be a slave to nobody no mo'."

"Jacob, dere ain't nothin' you can do but be a slave. Where you gonna go and not be a slave?"

"I'm gonna be anythin' but a slave. I told you, like the seasons dat come, so will da blue coats come south and free us. Dey comin', I hear what da other slaves are sayin' on the other plantations and farms. Dey ain't near here yet, but dey will be and when dey get close I wants to be free to go wit dem and I can't do that if I'm still a slave on dis farm. I gotta' leave before Massa Andrew wakes up. I told Big Black to get everybody into the fields this mornin'."

"Massa Andrew gonna be mad and Master Andy is gonna be madder when dey finds out you gone."

"I can't worry 'bout Massa Andrew and his family no more, Mama I gots to worry 'bout me and what da rest of my life is gonna' be 'bout. I don't know how long dis war gonna last, but if da South wins, I'll be a slave for the rest of my life. I don't wanna to be dat. I wants to be free!"

"But you are free Jacob. You ain't workin' in da fields. You's in charge! You's ridin' da horse, whiles everybody else is walkin'.'"

Jacob looks into his mother's face. Her face is begging him to listen to her, begging him not to go, begging him to stay with her. But he knows he can't stay. If he does, he will die a thousand times with each ending day, only to be reborn into this hell known as slavery every morning. "I ain't nothin' but a field nigga Mama. Dat's all Massa Andrew thinks I am, a field nigga. Even though I'm head-nigga-in-charge it don't change my status as a human being to him. I'm just his second class citizen, a slave."

"You can't let Massa Andrew controls what you thinks 'bout yourself, Jacob. Think 'bout what you do as a job. I do. I don't thinks 'bout dat I'm his slave. I jus' works for him. I treats it like it's my job, dat's all."

"Mama, you can't quit your job, or look for 'another job dat pays mo' money. Being free will let me do dat."

"But if you runs away, dey will hunt you down with dogs until dey finds you, no matter how long it takes." Matilda tries to hide her tears. She has been exposed to her greatest fear. Her son is running away to his death, leaving her alone. No child should precede a parent into death. It is the greatest fear of any mother. She was blessed to feel the pleasure of his life inside her body. She had the pleasure of the pain while pushing his life from her body. Finally, she experienced the pleasure of giving nourishment from her body, to her Jacob. "I don't wants to hear 'bout some bounty hunter findin' you or what's left of you somewhere in da swamps."

"Ain't nobody gonna find me Mama," said Jacob, sure of himself. "I'll walks along da river at night and stay in special places. I hears all da way down the river dere are shanty huts, owned by free blacks who don't think like Massa Andrew and other white folks." Jacob unties the wrap on the end of the stick on his shoulder. "See, I gots some bread and ham and some clothes. Dat's all I need. My scent will disappear in da swamps and when I comes out at the river, I will lose my identity. I hears dere are some blue coats at da mouth of the river, and below a place called Baton Rogue. It I gits there, I can joins up wit dem and come back to git you, when dey comes dis way."

Matilda watches her boy folds the wrap again, covering the contents, then tie it to the shoulder stick. He speaks like someone who wants to be in control of his life. He has become someone who doesn't need someone else to take care of him. He can do that all by himself. Matilda has mixed feelings. She feels proud inside, and at the same time, sadden knowing the disappointments he will experience, just because he is what he is. She opens her arms to him. "I needs to hold you jus' one mo' time Jacob. I can't turn your mind around." She holds him tightly and close, pressing his body to her as if she were trying to press him back inside her womb, to protect him from the pending harm he is about to experience. "Jacob, dis is the only life I know. From the time Massa Andrew's Papa bought me, I been with dis family. I been Massa' Andrew's playmate, baby sitter, house servant and anythin' else he wants me to be. When his Papa died, I became his property. It didn't bother me 'cause even den, dis was the only life I knew, being a slave. Jacob, I'm old, too old to even 'preciate freedom. I been workin' for Massa Andrew so long, if I was set free, what would I do? Where would I go? I don't know nothin' bout takin' care of myself, by myself, but I can take care of other folk."

"Mama, I won't let you stay here and die", said Jacob, reassuringly, "You gotta know what it feels like to be a free black woman."

"Jacob, my son", I saw you take your first breath of life and Lawd knows I don't wants to see you takes your last; but if you comes back fo' me, I'm 'fraid I will. Don't you worry 'bout my freedom and me. I got chains on my ankles, but my soul is free Jacob, free! I sees now if I made you stay, I would see you take your last breath, so you better go." Matilda pushes him away, reluctantly, after one final hug. "Don't you worry none 'bout me. I done survived dis long, I sure can survive a little bit longer, believing you's is alive. You gotta get out of here, Jacob. The sun's gonna be up soon and you needs the darkness to travel by. Mama loves you. Don't let nothin' happen to you. Now, turns me loose and go grab you some freedom." Matilda forces Jacob's arms from around her. "Jacob, I'm gonna be all right, now scat! Go on I said and don't turn around."

Matilda watches her son disappear into the cluster of trees. Her tears feel cold against her face. She continues watching long after he has vanished from her sight. She has difficulty understanding what she has permitted to happen, but she knows life has to be better for him than it was for her. Slowly, she begins walking back to the Massa Andrew's house, when suddenly she stops, slowly falls to her knees and folds her hands.

"Well, Lawd, he in yo' hands now. He ain't got nothin' to protect himself with, but yo' hands. He ain't got nothin' to see in da darkness of the night, but yo' eyes. He ain't got nothin' to keep him warm from da cold of da night, but yo' salvation. I needs you to take yo' hands and brush danger out of his way, before he gits to it. I needs you to light his pathway to freedom fo' anyone darkens it again with slavery. I needs you to look down upon him and show him yo' grace and mercy. He's my only son, Lawd and if you askin' me to give him up, I would first ask that you take me first. I'm askin' you dese things in yo' name Lawd, Amen." Matilda gets off her knees and brushes the little bit of dirt from her clothes, hands and dress. "Now, I gots ta go Lawd. Massa Andrew, he gonna be looking for his breakfast, but I sure thank you for takin' time to listen to me." Matilda pulls her wrap about her shoulders and restarts her slow walk to the big house.

* * * * * * * * *

At 6:30 a.m., Matilda is just about finish setting the morning table when she hears Massa Andrew on the stairs. His step is slower than it has been in recent months. He has not been as active as he was a year ago. Sometimes his breathing is labored, sometimes it sounds normal. He is not the man he use to be and it seems he is getting worst every week. Matilda knows there is something wrong with Massa Andrew, the family knows something is wrong with Massa Andrew, but Massa Andrew doesn't think anything is wrong with him.

But it is in his face, the obvious sagging aging factor around the eyes. The new lines in the face that now appear where there were no lines before. His gait is more calculated and constantly self-reassuring. Massa Andrew does not look upon any of this to indicate he is not well, rather he feels it is all part of the aging process not an illness.

Once downstairs he walks to the bay window, where the Confederate flag is draped and peers outside. Because of the elevation of his farm, he can see the piers of New Orleans, a view he cherishes because of how beautiful it is to him, watching the ships come and go. He knows when the ships are moving out, some of his cotton and lumber are on them. He is making money, lots of it since the war started.

"Good morning Massa Andrew," said Matilda, in between setting the last of the dishes on the table. Matilda does not wait for a reply; instead she goes about her business of finishing the table then disappearing back to the kitchen.

Something has captured the attention of Andrew; so much so that he has retrieved the spyglass and is staring intently at the pier below him. He slowly lowers the glass and backs away from the bay window. "Andy", he yells as loud as he possibly can.

Matilda rushes from the kitchen, wiping her hands on her apron. "Are you alright Massa Andrew," she asks. Her voice is filled with concerned about his sudden yelling.

"Andy, get up," continues Andrew, bellowing, "and wake Pierre. I need both of you down here, now!"

"Is somethin' the matter, Massa Andrew?" asks Matilda, noticing the strange expression that has taken over his face.

"Nothing that matters to you," snaps Andrew.

Matilda turns and walks towards the kitchen door, then pauses. "Well, I guess he really doesn't need me," thinks Matilda, feeling insulted. Before going into the kitchen she asks, "Do you want your morning coffee now, Massa Andrew?"

"Bring it and leave it on the table," again snaps Andrew, becoming even more agitated.

Andy hears his father scolding Matilda as he enters the dinning room. "What is it Papa?"

Andrew turns at the sound of Andy's voice and asks, "Where's your brother?"

Andy slowly approaches his father. He can see a disturbance

on his father's face. He has the spyglass at his side, just barely holding onto it. "Pierre is coming. Papa, what's wrong?"

Andrew goes to the table and pours coffee into a cup, spoons in some sugar, all the while his gaze is distant, his movements automatic. He raises the spyglass in the direction of Andy, pointing towards the bay window. "Have a look."

Pierre sits on the edge of his bed, wondering if he should go down stairs. The last time Papa yelled that loud the Confederates had bombed Fort Sumter. What possibly could it be now? Maybe the war is over. Now that would be worth yelling about, unless the South won.

The sun is just starting to show itself through his window. The smokehouse is still curing and smoking. The wonderful aromas from its insides are wafting through the walls and into his room. He knows he must get up and be downstairs before he is called again, so he grabs his robe and quickly moves to the sound of his brother and father conversing. By the time he is in the living room, Andy is at the bay window, staring at something. His father is standing by the breakfast table, sipping his coffee. He is about to speak, but Andy interrupts.

"Papa," said Andy, lowering the spyglass, shocked at what he has seen. "What's going on?"

Matilda coming from the kitchen, setting a plate of food on the table pauses for a moment. "Master Andy, do you want your tea now?"

"I think not Matilda," said Andy, still looking at his father for an answer. "Papa, what's going on down on the pier?"

Pierre is standing in the doorway watching Andy, his father, and Matilda. What ever is going on is happening outside the bay window. Maybe there are Yankees docking in the pier. It must be something awful for Papa to look the way he does, and even more confusing for Andy not to understand what is very obvious to Papa. Pierre has reason to smile as he concludes, that it must be something that will be very pleasing to my eyes.

"Good morning Matilda," sings Pierre. "Good morning Papa, Andy."

"Good mornin', Master Pierre," said Matilda, going towards the kitchen.

"Matilda," asks a frustrated Pierre, "when are you going to stop calling me Master?"

"When I is free and not a day befo'," replies Matilda, pausing at the kitchen door. "Now, do you want yo' tea or don't you?"

"Yes I do," said Pierre, watching his father and Andy.

"Well, it's on de table," said Matilda before disappearing into the kitchen.

"Well now," said Pierre, preparing his tea, "is someone finally going to tell me what is going on?"

Andy gives Pierre the spyglass. "There are several big fires on the pier."

"What?" Pierre sets his tea on the table and proceeds to the bay window. He sees the black smoke rising then follows it down to the point of origin.

"It looks like bales of cotton," said Andy, resigned to the reality of what is happening.

"They've set them on fire," said Andrew, finding a place to sit, then dropping himself into it. Suddenly he is feeling really tired.

"Damn Yankee spies!" charges Andy, standing next to his sitting father.

Pierre continues to survey the pier. There are several large controlled fires burning on the pier. At each fire there are several men making sure the fire does not burn what they don't want it to burn. "Well I'll be damn! Each one of them bales is 500 pounds of packed cotton. They'll burn for days."

"No Yankee spies started them fires," said Andrew, sipping his coffee, maintaining a blank stare across the room.

"If it wasn't them, then it was some of Pierre's abolitionist friends," accuses Andy. "Who did it, Pierre?"

"None of my friends play with matches," said Pierre, returning the spyglass to a table in front of Andy and his father. "Besides, what we want to burn are the laws that protect slavery. Burning cotton bales will not free the slaves."

Andrew fully understands why there are fires on the piers. He just didn't expect it to be happening so soon. There is a lot of money going up in smoke down on the pier; money that could be used to buy the supplies necessary to win this war. The rumors were repeated almost daily since late winter, but no one thought it would come to this.

"Primarily, it's because of Europe", begins Andrew. "The Confederacy needs Europe to recognize our form of Government. The Confederacy needs to be legitimized by governments outside the borders of America and the heads of state in Europe would supply an excellent endorsement."

"If it weren't for this 'peculiar institution' called slavery", interrupts Pierre, "there would be no problem with recognition."

"Slavery is so necessary to the economy of the south," pleads Andrew. "The majority of farmers are not ready to give it up, even though in Europe they have abolished the practice. What do they know? They've been around for over a thousand years and have had more practice than we have. They started just like we are now. This burning of cotton is a revengeful act by the farmer's coalition. They strongly believe when the regular allotment of cotton stops coming over from America, the unemployment in the factories needing this product will be rising all over Europe. I just wished the big planters had waited until late spring before starting this symbolic burning. They're the only ones that are not financially affected as much as the medium size farmers like us."

"Someplace else in the world cotton will be grown, sold and once again become king," said Pierre, "but not here." Pierre raises his cup, toasting, "King Cotton is dead in America, long live the King, somewhere else in the world."

"I don't understand, Papa," said Andy.

"The strategies of war are confusing to the untrained eye," begins Andrew, "Sometimes a soldier will have to walk in darkness of confusion before he will see the light of understanding"

"Andy," said Pierre, "this symbolic act of stupidity is a ploy to create some sort of panic in the streets of America, and maybe create some sort of international headlines. Fact of the matter is, it ain't gonna work. This farm is not losing any money down at that pier."

"Pierre, why can't you show some respect?" demands Andy. "Papa is doing what he feels is best for all of us."

"Papa is looking out for himself," replies Pierre, smirking, "He's making money off of this war, lots of money. All the planters are making money off this war, at the expense of the slaves!"

Andrew listens to Pierre and again wonders why Pierre does not and never has accepted the method of slavery as part of the business side of running this farm. His concern has always been for the slaves, not because they are treated badly, but simply because they are slaves. In the world of today, there will always be slaves and owners of slaves. Being an owner is nothing to be ashamed of, but remaining a slave for your entire life is.

"Yes Pierre, I am making money," responds Andrew, "but that's because I happened to be in a position to do so, not because I planned it that way. I didn't ask for this war, and neither did the rest of the free blacks in this state. But we free blacks have been struggling for years, against the white-powers-to-be, working ourselves into the economy of this state, despite the roadblocks that have been put in front of us, years before this war started. Today we are the carpenters, physicians, merchants, planters, and farmers that are called upon for services for which we are paid. We didn't plan it that way, but we prepared ourselves for whatever came our way. We as a people are now part of this economic society. We have the best skilled and trade jobs in the state. And it is to the envy of poor buckras who think their white color should be their ticket to riches. For them white buckras, having riches is one dollar more than free blacks. The problem for them today is they can't get enough dollars together to have one more dollar than us. It is imperative we participate in this war machine and maintain the status quo of life in this state and this Confederacy!"

"Papa, don't get yourself so excited," interrupts Andy. "Pierre, you better start showing more respect!"

"I'm fine," replies Andrew, shrugging off the assisting arm of Andy. "Our militia's been sanctioned by the state government. We are over a 1000 strong in members. We are finally a political and economical force to be reckoned with. We can no longer be ignored, and making this military service contribution, completes the circle of acceptance."

"This is a white man's war!" protests Pierre.

"Yes it is and it's also about maintaining the free black man's survival," responds Andrew, again raising his voice. "We need to be part of this victory to ensure we get a piece of the spoils!"

Mary sits up in bed when she hears Pierre yell. Then she hears Andy, and now she hears Andrew. She thought she would be able to sleep a little late this morning but now she is awake. It sounds like the Civil War has taken up residence in her living room again. She finds her robe, and begins putting it on. She steps into her slippers and walks to the source of the family's dissension. Matilda sees her coming down the stairs and is about to speak, but Mary motions her not to say anything. By the time she is at the base of the stairs, Pierre is finishing his argument.

"We as a people are being used and abused by this system you so urgently want to become a part of, regardless of what you think you're doing for the Confederacy." Pierre is frantically pacing between the two of them, accenting his conversation with arms flying and fingers pointing in the air. "You're not paid by the Confederacy. You provide your own uniforms, guns, and equipment. You donate your time, effort, and finances to the state. Both of you are paying the state to fight in their stupid war! And to add insult to injury, you can't even have a black officer in charge. That makes the both of you nothing more than free men, fighting as slaves."

"Pierre, that will be enough from you," said Andrew harshly. "I will do what ever it takes to remain a proud free black man!"

"Papa!" pleads Pierre, "Can't you and Andy see? They've turned you both back into just field niggers!"

Andy's right hand crashes into the side of Pierre's face.

"How dare you!" Andy stands over his fallen brother, shaking his balled fist. "Damn you Pierre!"

Andrew pushes Andy back as Andy tries to kick Pierre.

"That's enough," shouts Mary, "from all of you, that's enough! I will not stand for this family destroying itself because of this stupid war!"

"Mother," responds a surprised Andrew, "I didn't know you were up."

"How can I sleep with all this man versus man noise down here!" Mary walks between Andy and the fallen Pierre, past Andrew to her chair. "Get off the floor, Pierre."

"Good morning, Mama," said Pierre, getting up from the floor.

"Morning Mama," said Andy.

"We are family!" scolds Mary, sitting in her chair. "We are one! I will not let this war or difference in principles turn brother against brother, father against son! We are family!"

"Good morning, Miss Mary," said Matilda. "Would you like your morning tea now?"

"Yes I would," yells Mary, then realizing who she is speaking to she calmly said, "thank-you Matilda. This talk of war is splitting this family and I will not permit that to happen. I did not marry you Andrew, birth these two boys, to see them fighting amongst themselves, over a situation they don't know enough about. Manhood is not proven, based on challenges from other men; nor does the number of lifeless bodies left after a battle determine it. Manhood is not some badge of courage to be worn like a ribbon on a shirt in a parade, covering a missing limb." Mary takes a white packet from her robe and empties the contents into her tea.

"Mother," Andrew gently interrupts, "you can't know and understand what this war is doing to the Confederacy, and the impact it will have on us as a people. We are fighting for the stability of every free black in the Confederacy and the future of the Confederacy. If the Confederacy loses this war, free blacks all over America, not just in the Confederacy, will be affected for generations to come."

Mary looks Andrew in the eyes. "If having a stable Confederacy means having a split family, then the Confederacy be damned!"

Andrew realizes he needs to discuss this problem with Mary alone. There should be no distractions such as Pierre and Andy. She does not need to make reference to them as part of her argument. He is sure if just he and her discuss his involvement with the Confederacy she will change her views at least enough to show support in some instances if not all.

"Andy, Pierre," said Andrew, escorting them to the base of the stairs, "both of you need to get cleaned up and then check on Jacob in the fields this morning. I'll be out later, after talking with Mother."

Matilda has been in and out of the kitchen, listening to the arguments and conversations. She hears Andrew's instructions to Pierre and Andy. Jacob now has a 3 hour head start, much of that in the cover of darkness. She knows when they go to the fields they will know what she knows. Then, she too becomes an active family participant of the Civil War inside this house.

Matilda suddenly has a sinking feeling in her stomach. She is very nervous. She wants to go someplace away from everybody, but she knows she cannot. Now would not be a good time for any of them to ask her about Jacob. When Andy and Pierre find out about Jacob she knows she needs to be in her slave quarters and not in this house.

"Is there anything else you want from me this morning, Miss Mary?" asks Matilda, wiping and wringing her hands in her apron. "If you don't mind Mam, I need to go back to my cabin and check on some things."

"No Matilda," replies Mary, obviously frustrated and exhausted already, she stirs the white powder in her tea.

"Make sure you're back in time to clean up this mess for the noon day meal," demands Andrew.

"Yes, Massa Andrew," replies Matilda, attempting to hide her nervousness. She anxiously tears off her apron. She rushes from the room and through the kitchen then out the back door to her cabin to await her fate.

"I don't know if you've noticed, but lately, the slaves have been acting strange," said Andrew. "Seems it takes more talking to them to get things done now days." Andrew finds a place close to Mary and sits next to her, gently holding her hand.

"They are just as affected by this war as we are," said Mary, sipping her tea and enjoying the feeling of the white powder. "Martha Johnson told me they've already had two runaways this winter."

"I'm surprised they haven't had more than that. I've heard her husband and sons do not treat their slaves as human beings. They are always putting the whip on them. They don't understand the value of them as property."

"Is that all they are to you, property?"

"They're just like family to me; you know that Mary. I ain't never put the whip on any of them, because I don't believe in it to get the job done. Matilda's family belonged to my father; she knows that to be true. Matilda's been with us so long, I consider Jacob to be my son. If it weren't for me, where would the rest of the slaves be; in a place a lot worst than this, that's where."

"A lot of them feel they would be free, if they were not here."

"You got to earn your freedom, just like everything else in this country. I earned everything for my freedom; from this house and everything in it. I hear the same thing a thousand times, "Massa Andrew, when you gonna free me?" I ask them right back, what are you gonna do when you free, boy?" And you know something, none of them know what they're gonna do. The only slaves asking to be free are the young ones, who think they have all the answers, but none of the education. They gonna be fields niggas all their life because they don't want to be nothing but free. They don't want to learn a trade or skill or learn to read and write. All they want is to be free. This is 1862 and fields niggas are a dime a dozen. After this war is over, they gonna be worth less than that. Now, if they're smart they will learn to read, then learn a trade. I can give them both, but they have to want to do it. They can be worth up to two thousand dollars once they have achieved that much education. From there, they can buy their freedom and amount to being something."

"Things are not the same as they were when you came along," said Mary, comforting Andrew. "You had nothing, but your father left you something. How many slaves have that kind of opportunity?"

"My good fortune can be shared with them if they are willing to continue to show respect and loyalty to me. If my slaves can just understand that what I do is a business and they are just as important to this business, regardless of what they are. The fact that I house them, provide medical attention, food, and clothing is all part of the business. I share the harvest with them, take their trapped animal skins and sell them and give them the proceeds. I don't treat them like animals as some of the other planters because I want them to be successful. Mary, I plan to leave a legacy with you and the children and that legacy is this. The only way black people will succeed in this land is to have something of value somebody else wants. You've got to be of some value to yourself, your family and your community."

"Andrew, you're not talking about your children, you're talking about your slaves."

"I hope my slaves don't plan to be slaves for the rest of their life. Right now, they're slaves who only know how to be what somebody tells them to be."

"So, after this war, what are you going to tell your slaves to be, free?"

"After this war, I'm hoping they are prepared to be something else but a slave; I have never prevented any of them from learning to read or write. The books are there even if only a bible. All my slaves need to understand if you're free and ignorant, you're still a slave to yourself."

* * * * * * * * *

Pierre notices there is something different in the air before Andy. It's more than the self-imposed silence of Andy's anger between the two of them. It is something definitely different. It began as they started their ride from the stable. Pierre notices the atmosphere in the air this morning is different than yesterday, last week, and even last month. Something has definitely changed, but for the moment Pierre cannot put his finger on it, but he knows something is amiss. There is stillness in the silence that is eerie. The silence is uncanny. It hangs in the air like a net ready to drop on its victims; and once the net drops the noise will return, but for now, only silence. Even when riding past Voodoo Man Cato hounfort, there is silence. It is more than the absence of Voodoo Man Cato's drums. It is also more than not seeing the usual trail of smoke trickling from his chimney. And oddly enough there was no wind playing in the trees, tinkling the hanging glass bottles.

Even in the patch of trees they're passing through, there seems to be stillness. The leaves are not moving, the birds are not singing. There are only the sounds of muffled horse's hoofs pressing into the soft ground. Pierre knows it is not too early for the birds and the wind never sleeps, but this morning it is as if a spell has fallen upon the farm and the silence is hiding something from him and Andy. By the time they are at the lake a thick misty fog is rolling off of it towards them. They turn their horses, following the pathway South around the lake, and then turning west after passing the fence that holds the pigs.

"Andy, don't you sense something?" said Pierre, finally, after passing the pigpen. "Like the sudden quietness. I've never experienced this before."

"It's just the morning," answers Andy, more concerned about checking the progress of the slaves. "The closer we get to the fields, the more noise we'll hear."

They ride slowly. Their horses pass the lumber harvesting, seeing the men busy at their task, but not seeing Jacob or Big Black. Andy pauses and watches the slaves work. They notice him and they pick up their pace. Satisfied with the new energy shown by the slaves, Andy turns his mare towards the fields.

"Why do you do that?" demands Pierre, catching up with Andy.

"They need to know and understand who's in charge," said Andy. "This is a business, Pierre. The more output we produce, the more money we make."

"And what about the slaves, what do we give them in return for their labor?"

""Food, clothing, and a roof over their head," said Andy, "and if they continue to excel in their performance, they won't be traded or sold off this farm."

"If you were a slave, would you think that's fair?" challenges Pierre.

"But I'm not a slave," answers Andy, "So I don't care about what is fair. This is a business."

They come out of the timberland and into the open farmland. There are 150 acres of the remaining cotton to harvest. Soon it will be time to turn the remains over into the soil and begin a new season. The remaining slaves, with their children, are walking the isles of the fields picking and dragging burlap catch bags behind them. Andy keeps riding forward, while Pierre turns right and together they ride the perimeter, observing the progress, and looking for Jacob and his mare.

Pierre notices even here there is an unexpected silence about him even with the slaves working. There is no talking amongst them. There is no singing or humming and the children aren't playing amongst themselves. The sun is on its way up. The morning air is beginning to warm. The gray mist above the lake is evaporating. The black soil is blackening. The green of the foliage is drying and turning greener. The sound of silence continues. He is turning his mare north and ducking beneath a low hanging tree branch, wishing Jacob would show his face. He wants Jacob to give him a progress report of what today's expectations will be. He also has a passing thought, wondering how far Anna has gotten.

"Pierre! Pierre!"

The loud yelling of his name by Andy cuts a jagged hole through the warm still air like a bolt of lightening, streaking from the sky and striking the ground without warning. Pierre is momentarily stunned. He is stunned even more when he hears his name the second time. Something must have happened to Andy. The bent backs of the slaves straightened. They look toward the direction from which Andy is yelling. Andy's voice is excruciating as if in great pain.

"Pierre! It's Jacob!"

The screeching voice of Andy's yelling about Jacob compels Pierre to force his mare into a gallop. Pierre wonders what has happened. Is it Jacob or Andy? Is someone snake bittened? Did one of them fall from his horse? Did Jacob injure himself with one of the tools? Pierre urges his mare up a slight incline to the direction of Andy's agonizing voice. At the top of the knoll, fifty yards in front of him he sees Andy, frantically waving his arms in the air, urging him to come closer as quickly as possible. Big Black is holding Andy's horse's reins as Pierre dismounts. Big Black's head is bowed as if he is ashamed of something. Pierre gives his reins to Big Black, and then looks around for Jacob.

"So what's wrong with Jacob," asks Pierre, looking around, "where is he?"

"The nigger is running," mumbles Andy between clenched

teeth, "after all we've done for him and his Mama, the nigger is running."

Pierre looks at Big Black. "Big Black, where is Jacob?"

"The nigger's running!" yells Andy. He unfurls his whip and with each word, there is a crack of the whip in the air. "RUNNING! RUNNING! RUNNING! THE NIGGER'S RUNNING!"

"Big Black," Pierre again asks, "where is Jacob?"

Big Black continues his silence and stands with his head bowed. He dare not raise his head to look at Pierre for fear of telling the truth. He realizes, right now, Master Andy is crazy with anger and he's libel to do most anything with his whip and Big Black did not want to be the receiver of Master Andy's wrath.

"I've got to tell Papa," said Andy, mounting his mare. Andy cuts a path directly across cotton fields, ranting and raving, "THE NIGGER'S RUNNING, THE STUPID NIGGER IS RUNNING!"

"How long have you known about this, Big Black?" questions Pierre.

"I jus' found out dis mornin' suh", Big Black lies. "He woke me up early dis mornin' and told me to get da slaves out to da fields. I ain't seen him after dat."

Pierre climbs aboard his mare. "Thanks, Big Black," said Pierre. He is disappointed in the behavior of Jacob. He doesn't know if he can believe Big Black, but he has no choice. It was Big Black and Jacob who kept the other slaves in line; kept them moving and kept up the pace to meet the daily quotas. It was also Big Black and Jacob who helped him and Anna. Both shared some influence over the other slaves. Now, there is only Big Black, and Pierre wonders if he too is pondering the idea of running. How many other slaves are pondering the same thing?

"You're in charge now," said Pierre, sternly, before leaving. "Keep them working; push them when necessary. Nothing's changed. Quotas still must be and will be met. Do I make myself clear?"

Big Black nods his head without looking up at Pierre.

Pierre rides his mare back around the perimeter of the cotton field. He sits tall in his saddle. Some of the working slaves, mostly men, pause briefly as he passes. He looks directly into their faces, trying to read their sly smiles, wondering if there's more to what behind their smiles or are they just acknowledging his presence. Is it his imagination or are they all planning something? Some turn their face away others don't even look up. For the first time, while being in the presence of the slaves, Pierre feels uneasy inside, wondering if he will experience their wrath. The same silence he had heard when he and Andy rode out here is once again yelling inside his ears.

* * * * * * * * *

Coming in her window at a rapid pace, Matilda hears the frantic gallop of a horse and rises from her praying knees. She looks out of the window and sees Andy almost fall off his horse as he dismounts. He knows about Jacob, concludes Matilda, he knows. Soon Massa Andrew will know. Soon Massa Andrew and Andy will be coming out of the kitchen door. And shortly after the thought left her mind, the two of them did come out, in a hurry. But instead of coming to the slave quarters, Massa Andrew stares at the quarters. It is a long stare as he sits upon the saddled mare, waiting for Andy to saddle the other horse. Pierre rides up next to his father and they speak briefly. For once they appear to be in agreement about what has happened and what is to happen next. Matilda stands at the window watching Massa Andrew talking to Pierre, and at the same time, continue his staring at the slave quarters. She sees him and she feels he can see her. She didn't care. Her son is now free. She didn't care what happens to her now, as long as Jacob remains free. Andy pulls his horse from the barn, leaps upon it and gallops away, not waiting for Andrew. Matilda waits until Massa Andrew and Pierre have ridden down the driveway and onto the passing road before she leaves and heads back to the big house. They are going to try and find Jacob. Matilda defiantly waits a couple of hours before she decides to go to the big house. Before Matilda leaves for the big house, she said a little prayer asking that God blind the searching eyes of Massa Andrew, Pierre and Andy. She finishes her prayers by confessing to God she will see him first, before she sees her son a slave again.

* * * * * * * * *

At 11AM, Matilda finally comes through the backdoor of the kitchen to the St. Claire's. She has one hour to set up for noonday meal. She moves with deliberate and controlled speed, knowing what she left earlier this morning needs to be cleared before setting the table again. She has much to get done and unlike yesterday, today she is off schedule. She checks the fire in the stove, replacing the low flames with some kindling and a chunk of wood. In the time it takes to clear the dining room table the fire will be up. She places a kettle of water on top of the stove plate. When she comes from the kitchen, she sees Miss Mary and Miss Margaret. They are in their usual places in the living room. She begins to clear the dining room table, trying to be quiet, but not very successful, half way listening to conversations that are not her business. Her mind is elsewhere. She moves automatically as she has for the last twenty some years. Inside she wants to breakdown and cry until there's no water left in her body. She can tell by their body language, Miss Mary and Miss Margaret know about Jacob and they are very upset with her. She has lost their trust, and it depresses her; but then another part of her said she doesn't care what the St. Claire's think. Her son is free and with God's help he will remain free.

"It's just amazing how she can come in here now," said Mary softly, rearranging her position in her chair. "It's as if nothing has happened. You would think an apology would be appropriate, but not so much as a peep from her."

Matilda half way hears their conversations, because Miss Mary and Miss Margaret always talk as if she was never in the room and today is no exception. Matilda knows they are talking about her and Jacob, but her ears are more tuned to hearing a demand for service from them. Everything else is just pieces of conversation.

"Does anyone know when he left?" asks Margaret.

Matilda comes from the kitchen with the tea tray, cups on saucers, teapot, sugar, spoons, and milk. She sets the tray on the dining room table and prepares a cup of tea for Miss Mary, then Miss Margaret. She presents first to Miss Mary, then Miss Margaret. She moves away as indiscriminately as she first appeared. She begins to set the dinning room table for lunch.

"Father thinks it was early this morning," said Mary, stirring her tea. "She certainly hasn't cried, nor has she shown any emotion." Mary sets her tea on an end table then searches for and finds her packet. She dumps the entire contents into her tea and stirs. "You knew Jacob pretty well; did he say anything to you about running away?"

"Why Mama," stutters Margaret, trying to maintain her composure, "what ever do you mean?"

"Well," said Mary, looking over the top of her cup, sipping her tea. "It's just that I used to always see you two talking, that's all."

Matilda comes from the kitchen with more food and dishes.

"So, what's wrong with that," asks Margaret, shrugging, "we're just friends, that's all."

Matilda has set the silverware and is checking to be sure that she has placed enough for everyone. The noonday meal is usually a catch-as-catch-can meal because none of the family really sits down together. It has always been a case of someone coming in, grabbing something from the platter, sitting long enough to create a sandwich or just throwing something into their mouth, then they are gone.

"Well, it's just that your father would be very disappointed in you if he suspected you and him were more than friends. I can only imagine what Andy would do." said Mary.

Matilda comes from the kitchen with her hands filled with two plates and a handful of silverware for the noon day lunch. She pauses for a moment to see if Margaret will reveal to her mother how she really feels about Jacob. Matilda feels so alone right now. She needs to hear something that will make her feel better about herself and Jacob. Margaret can do that and if she does, Matilda will help her explain everything to Miss Mary.

"Mama please," smirks Margaret, "Jacob is just some field nigger."

Suddenly, there is a resounding crash of plates breaking and silverware scattering everywhere on the cypress wood floor. Matilda immediately is on her hands and knees picking up everything.

"Is everything okay, Matilda?" demands Mary.

"Yes Miss Mary," apologizes Matilda, "dey slipped." Why in da world would she ask such a dumb question? Of course everything is not okay. You and yo' daughter sit dere and talk as dough I'm not in dis room. Den talk about my son as if he done somethin' evil, when da evil is right 'chere in da rules in dis house; in da rules of dis society. My son is more den some field nigger, Miss Margaret. He every bit a man, as you well know. I wonder what yo' Papa would say if he knew his precious daughter has fallen in love wit some field nigga. Here I is on my hands and knees, pickin' up bits and pieces of broken plates and all you and yo' precious daughter do is sit dere, waiting for me to finish. One day things will be different and I won't have to answer to either of you. I will answer to my son, Jacob. He gonna' come back and free me. He gonna' come back and bring me dat dress. Jesus is going to protect my son 'til he safe. Jesus will deliver him to da blue coats. Jesus won't fail me. All of dem gonna' show respect when dey talk to me, when my Jacob comes back.

"Well, see that it doesn't happen again," reminds Mary. "Replacements are hard to come by, with this war and everything going on."

Matilda checks the floor to see if she missed any pieces. The large pieces are inside the pockets of her apron. She retrieves a broom from the corner of the dining room and sweeps the remaining pieces into a waiting dustpan. She has managed to set the dining room table despite what she has heard, and how much she had to do, in so little time.

"How long have they been gone now?" wonders Margaret out loud.

"About four hours now," said Mary. "Matilda, I need more hot water for my tea. Father and Andy are riding north, while Pierre is riding south. Father thinks he's headed north to join up with the Union forces in the upper Mississippi. I just hope Pierre finds him first."

"What difference does it make who finds him?"

Matilda brings the teapot with the hot water to Mary and fills her cup, then turns to Margaret, who waves her off. She returns to the dinning room table, folding the napkins and positioning the silverware and plates so everything is just right.

"Andy took his whip with him," begins Mary, "and if he finds him before father, who know what shape he'll be in when father joins them. Yes, I know, father has never put the whip on any of our slaves, but Andy was so angry when he left. I'm sure they'll find him and bring him back. I certainly pray they do. He's a good worker. If one of them white planters find him, they'll kill him and leave his body hanging in a tree, as a warning for other runaways."

"MISS MARY!" interrupts Matilda, crying, "How can you say something like that!" Matilda continues crying and runs to the kitchen sobbing uncontrollably.

Mary places her cup and saucer on the end table. "Matilda, I didn't know you were still there, " she said, turning just as Matilda disappears into the kitchen. "Margaret, go see if she's okay, and tell her how sorry I am. What's she doing listening to our conversation, anyway?"

Before Margaret can get up, the front door is flung open and Andy storms in, throws his whip on a chair in the living room then paces in a circle. Shortly after, Andrew comes in. He is a picture of exhaustion. It clearly shows in his gait.

"Oh, everyone's back," said Mary, rising to greet her husband. "Andrew you look exhausted. Come sit over here."

"We didn't find him, Mother," said Andrew, slowly dropping himself into a chair. "He's somewhere out there, acting like a damn fool."

"He's running hard and fast," said Andy, still pacing in circles. "And if I ever get my hands on him, I'll slow him down a bit."

Andrew is deeply saddened that Jacob has run. After all that he has done for Jacob, he feels betrayed. He feels just as betrayed by Matilda. He wonders if Andy is right. Do the slaves respect him? Has he been too easy? Must he, instead of acting like a human, act like an animal trainer? Must he beat and mutilate his slaves to get the respect he wants and their fear of him? Maybe he should. He can't afford another run away. But whipping has never amounted to anything but hard feelings towards the farmer. If a slave is thinking about running that will convince him to run even more. Andy wants to make examples of runaways like the white planters do. He wants to stop them from running by cutting off the toes of runners. He can't do that. They are his property, valuable property. It is not good business to destroy the means to the success of his farm. Regardless of how Andy feels, he will not succumb to the whims of his anger.

"I will not mutilate my slaves!" cries Andrew.

"It's the only way we'll keep them in line around here now," responds Andy. "We've got to show them who's still in charge!"

Matilda suddenly dashes from the kitchen, crying into her apron, falling at the feet of Andrew, groveling, pulling at Andrew's pants. "Massa Andrew, please don't harm my Jacob," she cries, "when you finds him, please, I'm beggin' you, please don't harm him. He jus' wants to be free, dat's all, free!"

Andy watches Matilda at his father's feet and wishes it were he instead of his father. He has no pity for her, never has. Even as a child he never let her forget who she was and what he was to her. He longs for the day when he will be in charge of the farm. He wishes his father would relinquish that charge to him now. After all, Papa is not in the best of health. He needs to take it easy. He's worked long and hard enough. He needs to stop paying attention to so many details and leave that to him and Pierre. That's what sons are for.

"Well now," begins Andy, " look at this. I guess we're supposed to feel sorry for you, huh Matilda?"

"I've never harmed any of you," pleads Andrew. "I never treated any of you bad; I gave you and Jacob food, clothing and shelter. Why did you do this to me?"

"He say he jus' wants to be free," pleads Matilda again, sobbing into her apron.

More than once he has heard his slaves say they want to be free. But none of them are prepared to be free. All they can do is work in the fields. Most are happy just working the fields. Those who want to be free don't want to do what's necessary to be able to function as a free person of color. They can't read and don't want to learn. He has never denied them books; never denied them the chance to learn a trade. He has always wanted them to be something other than just some common field niggers. Jacob was special to him. He was doing what was expected and more. If he had just been a bit more patient, just a little longer. "Just be patient", Andrew had told him. "You're smart," he told him more than once. "I can prepare you for freedom." But Jacob had no patience.

"But he's' not ready for freedom, Matilda," argues Andrew, tearing himself from Matilda. "He hasn't learned a free trade or skill. He don't know how to read."

Matilda feels so much alone. She cannot understand why Massa Andrew does not care about the human spirit. The same spirit that drives him to remain a free man also drives Jacob to want to become a free man. How can he determine when someone is ready to be free? Who gave him that right? Right now Jacob is walking and talking his way to freedom. Right now Jacob is finally a free man. Matilda can feel it inside her body, inside her very soul.

"He say he'll get a skill when he joins da army," said Matilda, slowly getting up from the floor.

"Jacob wants to join the Native Guards," asks Andy, sarcastically.

"No Master Andy, the Union Army," replies Matilda.

Andy begins to laugh. It starts as a smile that grows across his lips and soon becomes a snickering chuckle, then graduates to full hysterical laughter. "Jacob ran away to join the Union Army?" Andy finds a place to sit and continues laughing. "He's crazier than we thought, Papa."

Andrew's face saddens for a moment. He knows in what Jacob has done may have sealed his own fate. His ignorance of where he is and where he wants to go probably has caused his own death. The swamps and bayous show no mercy to foreigners who dare to venture into them. They take full advantage of those who are not prepared for what they are about to be exposed to.

"It is the middle of winter," said Andrew, speaking softly in tones of pity. "He'll never survive the swamps and cold weather. He's a dead man for sure."

"Oh please don't say dat," Massa Andrew," cries Matilda. "Don't say dat Massa Andrew!"

"He guaranteed his freedom," said Andy, "that's for sure. But only his soul will be free; his body will be dead."

"No one has ever survived the bayous and swamps in the winter," begins Andrew. "There's no food to eat or any place for shelter. The dampness gets into your bones and your joints freeze. It's a painful way to die. I always thought Jacob was smarter than that."

Andrew slowly walks to the table set by Matilda, takes some biscuits, some meat, places them into a kerchief, folds the kerchief and puts it all into one of his pockets. He grabs his coat.

"Well, come on Andy, let's get back to the fields. There's nothing we can do now except wait and see if somebody else finds him, dead or alive. Mother, we'll be late for dinner, so you can eat without us. I'm sorry Matilda, Jacob was a good boy and a good worker."

Andrew leaves through the kitchen door.

"Well, I'm not feeling sorry for him," said Andy, picking up his whip then putting on his coat. He goes to the table and grabs some meat and biscuits and shoves them into his pockets. "I hope he gets what he deserves." Andy follows his father through the kitchen door.

Mary rises from her chair and goes to Matilda. She gently squeezes her hands and looks into her face. She recognizes the sorrow in her eyes. "Oh Matilda," she begins, comforting her with gentle pats, "I'm so sorry." Mary then turns her attention to Margaret. "Margaret, the Debonairs are expecting us for tea this afternoon at three. We better get ready. We should be back around five." Then returning her attention to Matilda, she continues her concern. "Be strong Matilda." Mary pauses, then before she walks away, as an after thought, she adds, "Matilda, things have a way of working themselves out in the end." Mary goes upstairs, leaving Matilda standing in the middle of the living room.

Matilda returns to the table she took so much time to prepare and looks at the mess created by Andy and his father. She begins to remove the clean dishes and put them back into the china closet. Inside she feels hurt and confused. She always thought the St. Claire's cared more about her and Jacob. Now, she's not so sure. She feels so angry with them and wants to do something to strike back at them. She wants to break every glass, every plate and tear up all the linens. Right now she didn't care if Massa Andrew sold her off. It didn't matter, if Jacob were dead. But suppose he ain't dead. Then Jacob would never find her, when he comes back. And she knows he will be coming back. She wants to find a corner and cry, but she knows she must keep busy, not dwell on Jacob so much.

"How could he do this to me?" It is the angry voice of Margaret.

Matilda quickly turns and finds Margaret standing behind her. Her eyes wide open, her nose flaring. She is showing her teeth. She is too close. Matilda backs up and feels the table against her.

"Doesn't he care about me at all?" asks Margaret, her voice hushed. She continues venting her anger at Matilda. "How dare him! He knows how I feel about him!"

Matilda is shamed by Margaret's comments. She was beginning to feel even guiltier about what Jacob has done, when her pride rises from out of her mouth. " I didn't think you really cared, Miss Margaret, him being jus' some field nigga."

Margaret stunned by Matilda's stabbing comment, backs from Matilda. She knows she cannot call out in anger. She cannot do anything but feel the sharp pain of the remark. She quickly turns and runs upstairs.

Matilda sits on the couch, wringing her apron in her hands, sobbing. "Why lord, why?"

Pierre rushes into the living room, looking for his family. He sees Matilda sitting on the couch. He looks at her and he knows she can read the expression on his face. It clearly tells her he has not found Jacob. Pierre tries to speak, but cannot get any words to come out. He slowly backs away. He stops at the table and picks up some food then runs out the door through the kitchen, leaving Matilda.

Matilda slides off the couch to her knees, folds her hands in prayer, saying, "Thy kingdom come; thy will be done."

CHAPTER 19
Friday, February 20th, 1862

Jacob is very cold, starving for food, scared and lost. He is somewhere between New Orleans and Baton Rogue or New Orleans and the Gulf. The warmth of the comforting sun deserted the sky a long time ago. A blanket of blackness sprinkled with flecks of light has replaced it. He has lost sight of the North Star and he sees moss growing all around the trunk of the trees. Even the moon has deserted the night sky. Jacob is not sure where he went wrong in his escape. His greatest fear is upon him. He's walking in circles. He's sure he's seeing the same trees and shrubs from different sides. A couple days ago he finished the last of his food. He really believes that by now he should have reached his destination.

He remembers the image of his mother's face when he left her. He wishes now he was at home. At home he would be warm, and fed and around people he loved. Here he is cold and hungry and surrounded by strangers whose language he does not understand. He is frightened by the strange new sounds of the night. He hears things that move silently in the night. Getting closer to him are the screeching and yelping sounds of death that constantly remind him he is a stranger who has become their prey. He is beginning to think that what he did was a mistake. Is his freedom more important than his life? He was willing to die for his freedom, but he didn't want to suffer this much for it. Maybe he should've waited. He's not willing to die out here alone. He doesn't want his lifeless body devoured and torn apart by some of the non-caring residents of this hellhole. In between the fear and the hunger he wonders what will become of his soul?

For a number of days now, Jacob has been wandering around, inside one of the many bald cypress swamps that are part of the Mississippi Gulf. Exhausted, he has found a resting place on what is considered to be the Noble tree, the Cypress Tree, taxodium distichum. Like a sentinel it stands guard over an empire of trees, water and all creatures, big and small. It is the tree that never dies, even when it is harvested. It is a tree that decides what is good for itself and determines where to take root in the mud flats bordering rivers. Then growing out of the water, sometimes over 100 feet into the air, it penetrates the canopy of smaller trees and they become its subjects. In the spring its foliage is vivid green, contrasting the pale almost gray color of its enormous trunk and branches. On cloudy days, with Spanish moss hanging from its limbs, the mighty cypress contributes to the dark, spooky, pest-ridden, disease causing, and nasty atmosphere of the swamp. The tree stands proudly with it swollen buttressed base, called knees, sometimes rising to heights of twelve feet and swelling up to 10 feet in diameter.

Jacob has found such a tree. It is his resting-place, his sanctuary, while trying to stay alive, hiding out from the water basin, wandering cottonmouth snakes and the expert tree climbing rat snake. But that is not enough. He is constantly smacking himself to free his body from the mosquitoes that attack him in great numbers. They are attracted to his rich dark skin. When he brushes away what he has killed from a mighty smack, he sees his blood dripping. Unlike Jacob, vultures, hawks, and falcons do not struggle in their attempts to stay alive in the swamp. Jacob has observed them watching him and he wonders if they are not waiting for him to die. On more than one occasion he has awakened from his sleep crying out for his mother, disturbing all that is about him. He does not hear her caring voice returning his cry, but instead hears a rustling in the trees, disruptions in the waters and distinctive horrifying responses from creatures he is not sure are of this earth.

It takes him too long to go to sleep at night. The morning light comes too soon, much to soon. His ears have grown accustomed to the non-caring rapid drumming woodpecker's rat-at-tat-tat-tat, drilling a nest hole, looking for bark beetles, or termites. It is not as pleasant as the conch horns that use to whisper a light melody three times during his working day. The sound of the morning dove is close, but there is sorrow in its drawn out call. Jacob has grown oblivious to the beauty of the red clusters of berries surrounded by green leaves of the Winterberry holy, or the Spider lily with its white spider legs coming from beneath the flower petals. He does not admire the Yellow Jessamine, Cardinal Flower, and Southern Magnolia that greet Jacob each morning with sparkling colors. What he thought was his new found land of freedom and beauty has become his new found decorated land of incarceration. His ears do not recognize the friendliness in the chirp of the Yellow-Billed Cuckoo, or the friendly conversation from the common cackle of the Blue Jay. Good morning, they are saying, but to Jacob the sounds are irritating, and filled with mockery. They are laughing at him, whispering to each other what a fool he must be to walk into this beautiful garden of evil.

Jacob has accepted the fact he is about to die, alone, out here in this vast jungle of swampland. He will die and his body, before it has decayed, will be devoured a piece at a time by everything that lives here. Someone, many days, weeks, or months from this night will stumble across his scattered bones and wonder just who was this fool. They will laugh at his bones and not care that they do not know to whom they belong. He wonders if there is a God. And if there is, where is he now? How come he has not shown him the light out of this darkness? Where is God and why does he not hear his cry? If there's a hell in this world then he has surely found it.

Jacob is destined to spend his final dying moments in this earthly hell because the only sin he has committed is being born a slave with the uncontrollable urge to be a free man, burning deep inside. No one taught him to want to be free. He has always felt the need to be free, to do what he wants, when he wants. In his delirium he hears his mother calling him back from the road, but he didn't stop walking. He hears her calling him back from the woods, but he didn't stop walking. He hears her calling him back from the edge of the swamp. He turns completely around looking, but he can't figure out where she is. He screams out for her in frustration. She cannot hear him. Is she in front of him, just a few steps away or is she behind him trying to catch up to him?

He could have stayed on Massa Andrew's farm. But there was always more outside the wooden fences of the farm he needed to discover. He didn't understand why, he just knew he had to find out what was out there. If Massa Andrew was a free man, why not him? How can Massa Andrew be born of a free class and not himself? Is this a decision made by God or man? At the roughest times of his childhood, he can remember his mama saying, "turn it over to the Lawd. He'll fix it." Now, he thinks, "if dat be da case, how come God ain't fixed it yet?" Is his only chance of freedom the freedom given to his soul when it leaves his body? How can he thank God for this kind of love? How can he thank God for waking him up to this misery every morning? How can he thank God for this kind of grace and mercy?

He remembers his mama telling him the word 'slave' is mentioned only twice in the Bible; in Jeremiah and Revelations. She didn't read it, but she heard it from the revern'd, during one of his sermons. From what his mama said about Jeremiah, Jacob wondered why this is the land God led slave people to, from the motherland? How did the slaves forsake God to be punished so? Again the word is mentioned in Revelation, at the end of the world, but is that how long it will take for slaves to get their freedom? What gives these God fearing Christians the authority to be master over another? Nowhere in the Bible is slavery accepted. Why then does it exist in this free Christian society?

* * * * * * * * *

Three sounds over shadowed the crack of dawn on Monday, February 23rd, 1862. The first was the roar of alligators. Many confuse their sound with that of woodpeckers, tapping upon a hollow cypress tree. Like a chorus of a hundred gators waking at the same time, their sound reverberates throughout the swamp. The second was the continuous painful screams of Jacob responding to two large blood sucking yellow female horseflies, one, delighting in sucking blood from an exposed thigh, the other drawing sufficient fluid from the side of his forehead. Smacking his forehead he manages to splatter one yellow horsefly, containing his own blood, over his insect bitten scared face. Blindly swatting at his leg with his other hand, only forces the other families of horseflies to lift away to seek their meal someplace else on Jacob's exposed body. The third was that of yelping dogs, their ears following the painful cries of Jacob. His agonizing screams compete with the alligator's sounds of rapid knocking, echoing off the hardwood of the bald cypress trees.

Jacob, sitting on folded legs, cries out again and again, raising his folded hands in prayer, begging his God to end his life and end it quickly. He moans and cries and whimpers, reacting to each new bite of the insect. Pock marks that look like moon craters now cover all of his exposed flesh. He cannot wipe them quickly enough from his face and body. His face now drips in blood. Welts and scratches prominently display themselves before bursting exposing open flesh. He cries in extended agony, finally struggling to his feet, smacking and swatting and wiping and screaming. "Where are you Lawd? Why have you left me to suffer so at da hand of my massa? You must be a white God to treat black folks da way you do. I hate you Lawd I hate you! I can't take dis pain much longer. If you're what my mama said den strike me down. I dare you Lawd, strike me down!" Jacob opens his arms wide, waiting.

God answers Jacob. Jacob hears the voices of God below him. Looking down from his cypress sanctuary he sees six yelping dogs, surrounding him, jumping up against the knees of the cypress, clawing and scratching, trying to mount them and get to Jacob.

Jacob sees through his blood stained eyes blurred images of the mad dogs jumping at him. He recognizes them as the sign from God he's been waiting for. He thinks, what more pain can he suffer from the ripping bites of mad dogs that can bring a pain any more bitterly than what he has endured already? Again he challenges God. He screams at Him. This kind of death God has planned is nothing that he fears. "I've already suffered pain from yo' insects. I've suffered pain from my hunger. Do you think dere pain is greater den dat of mad dogs?" he yells. Jacob begins laughing uncontrollably, feeling madness over taking his mind and body. He graciously accepts his fate, without fear, and looks forward to releasing his scarred soul. Jacob stretches his arms wide, refusing to swat away the mosquitoes, insects and horseflies that are feasting on his flesh. He is feeling the pain and sensing the blood draining from him. Jacob falls forward, his body dropping into the muddy waters, infested with snakes, alligators, and now, mad dogs.

"Here da fuck I come, Lawd," he cries, feeling cool air pass over his body before he hears a splash. He then feels the cool waters engulf his insect bite riddled body. The water is very comforting to him. Jacob is not afraid anymore. The water is beginning to seep into his mouth, his nose and into his body. He is beginning to feel at peace.

* * * * * * * * *

The soldiers on horseback hurriedly ride in the direction of the hysterical barking dogs. They charge forward with even more urgency when they hear a big splash. The first soldier there is the dogs' trainer. Seeing the dogs nipping at what appears to be a body, he instantly yells at them to back away, calling each dog by name. He yells louder, even smacking and kicking them, when some of them do not respond to his demanding voice of authority. He is the first to find out what the dogs are all excited about. He calls out to his comrades to hurry along as he turns the body over. By the time they catch up to him, he is dragging the body to higher ground. He begins pressing repeatedly on the stomach forcing water out through the mouth.

"What do ya have dere soldier?"

"Smells like shit suh, but looks like contraband."

"Is he alive?"

At that moment, out of Jacob's mouth, comes a long stream of muddy water, bile and chunks of what little else is left in his stomach. Jacob slowly opens his eyes and sees the many strange, shaggy bearded black faces staring at him. They are talking to him and laughing at him, all at the same time, but he cannot hear or understand what they are saying. He's convinced he's died and gone to Hell. This welcoming committee must be disciples of the devil.

CHAPTER 20
Saturday, March 22nd, 1862

In New Orleans, during the spring of 1862, manufacturing has been greatly reduced. The war is now taking its toll on commerce even though the city appears to be a strong center of business. It continues to essentially be a trading and shipping center, and there are still a considerable number of merchants making money. Now, it is a year later and there are changes going on daily in the city. The blockade of the gulf is proving to be more effective than first thought. The Crescent City is beginning to show frayed edges. Rumors cause panic buying in the streets daily. No one is sure what is going on, but they hear rumors about Union gunboats steaming up the Mississippi to capture New Orleans. As much as they try to show otherwise, the citizens of New Orleans are concerned, especially the merchants of the city. Products that flowed freely and were stocked regularly are now beginning to be in short supply.

* * * * * * * * *

Mary notices things are not right with the city as she walks about it. She senses it in the way people hurry around her, like she is moving too slow in what she is doing. It is clear to her the city is on edge. There's something going on down river. Mary knows this even though Andrew is not saying anything about it. All the merchants appear extra nervous today. Even the bank tellers act strange when she withdraws some money, like they didn't want her to take it out. It's my money, why they acting like it's theirs? It would be great if we had a black owned bank to deal with. Mary remembers

Andrew telling her when the Confederacy wins the war he's going to have enough money to open his own bank. She smiles to herself thinking, this war is creating nightmares and pipe dreams at the same time.

Mary and Margaret St. Claire are coming in from a frustrating day of adventure shopping in New Orleans. All day they have been shopping and all they have to show for it are two packages of sewing cloth, wrapped in twine, being carried by Margaret. Mary is extremely tired from walking up and down Canal Street, trying to find new and different items for her home and buy other things for her slave family. Margaret is just tired of walking all day.

"It's a shame nothing is available in the shops anymore," complains Mary. She noticed the difference in the store windows and in speaking to the owners. No one knows when there will be new stock coming in. What he or she has to sell they have inflated the price based on the scarcity of the item. She didn't find anything she wanted and all the money she paid for the sewing cloth amounts to nothing. What can she do with the little bit of cloth she brought home? Nothing.

Mary is depressed. She couldn't buy what she wanted and she was even more disappointed that the pretty things she use to seeing in the storefronts were no longer there. A year ago, this would not have been a problem; but then a year ago she and her family were at peace with themselves, with their slave family and with the rest of the world. Today, Jacob and Voodoo Man Cato have run away; the men in her family are split about who's right regarding this stupid little war; Pierre's best friend has been murdered and the entire Confederacy is at war with the rest of the world. She needs one of Dr. DuBois' packets.

Margaret collapses into one of the chairs. It's times like these, thinks Margaret, when Matilda can really be appreciated. All her life Matilda has been there, doing things for her and the family. She really cannot understand why any slave would want to leave her family farm. At a lot of the neighboring farms and plantations she hears stories of brutal beatings of slaves by their owners. She hears about slaves rising up against the brutality of the owners and fighting back, sometimes seriously maiming, or killing their masters. All the time she hears about slaves running away, but on those farms they have good reason. But not on her father's farm. That was until Voodoo Man Cato ran away, but he's old and won't really be missed, concludes Margaret. Jacob is another story. Jacob had no right running away. Jacob's running away deeply hurt her. He was treated more than fairly, much better than the rest of the slaves. If he'd stayed he would have been more than just a slave to this family. He just needed to show a bit more patience. "Matilda, come help get my shoes off. I'm just too tired to move right now."

Matilda is about to return to the kitchen, when the request from Margaret's demanding voice stops her. I didn't help you put dem on, Matilda wants to say, but doesn't. Instead, it is her mind that speaks silently to Margaret. I been workin' here all day gettin' exhausted, while you been jus' walkin' around, lookin' in pretty store windows, and gettin' exhausted. What makes you think yo' day has been harder? If yo' feet are tired, that means yo' feet also stink right 'bout now.

Matilda slowly walks to where Margaret has found a resting place and kneels at her feet. Even though her hands do what is expected, her mind is elsewhere. Everything about Margaret, her attitude, her prissiness, her spoiled behavior, all reminds her of another reason why Jacob left. He was a slave to more than one master.

Matilda is missing Jacob much more than she first thought. She thought her son's running away would be a good thing for her. Knowing her son was no longer a slave made her feel so completely happy and wonderful inside. "My son is free," she keeps telling herself. She carries these feelings inside that he is going to be all right. But she is also troubled. In her heart she also knows that by now she should have heard something. Usually, through the slave grapevine, word letting her know he was all right would have filtered down to her. Instead, she has heard nothing. Every day since he's been gone, she mentions her worries to Big Black, as he comes from the fields, but he just shakes his head no. It's been over a month and according to the Runaway Laws of Slavery, if you haven't heard anything about a runaway within a month, then they're dead. She doesn't want to believe her son is dead, but it is becoming more difficult to hold back that belief.

"Thank-you so much," said Margaret as Matilda pulls off one shoe then the other. "You just don't know how good that feels."

I may not know how good dat feels, thinks Matilda, slowly walking back to the kitchen, but I do knows how bad dem feet stink.

Mary has found her favorite chair and is sitting, fanning herself. "Matilda, I will have my tea over here while I wait for Mr. St. Claire to come home."

"Yes Miss Mary," said Matilda.

"So will I Matilda," echoes Margaret.

Mary watches Matilda as she enters the kitchen. There is sadness on Matilda's face that has found permanent residence since Jacob ran away.

"She hasn't been the same since Jacob ran away," said Mary, speaking low, staring at the kitchen door. "It's a shame. She doesn't move about like she use to. Oh she gets her chores done like she use to but she takes longer. She hasn't neglected any one in the family, but she is neglecting herself. Her eyes are always red; she is always blowing her nose into some old rag she keeps dangling from her apron. She is slowly dying inside and there's nothing we can do about it."

"Oh, Mama, must we talk about that again?"

"Haven't you noticed how much she's changed over the last few months? Right after he ran away, she kept up hope he would return or be found alive. Oh, my feet are tired. I feel like I've walked to Baton Rogue and back. They really need a rest. Anyway, after a while she began to realize he wasn't coming back."

"Mama, please, we shouldn't be talking like this, with her still in the house." Margaret pauses for a few moments, twisting her hands, trying to find something to do with them. "I don't know about you, but I really miss him."

"I miss him too," sighs Mary, "but it's Matilda I'm concerned about. She really thought she would hear something through the slave grapevine, but nothing has come through. She told me she had Mama Sarah roll some bones for her, but they didn't say anything about whether he was dead or alive. Mama Sarah said he was somewhere in between."

"You don't believe in that voodoo stuff, do you Mama?"

"Matilda does and that's all that matters."

Margaret rises and begins to pace, trying to hide her feeling from her Mother. She constantly moves around, keeping her back to her Mother.

"Margaret, what's wrong?"

"Mother, why haven't we heard something by now? We should have heard something by now."

"Margaret, something is going on inside you? You want to talk about it?"

"Nothing to talk about; he's gone and that's the end of that." Margaret retrieves a kerchief from the sleeve of her dress and begins sobbing.

Mary hears in her daughter's voice what she herself has felt and still feels in her heart about Andrew. That ache, that pain that only a woman knows; that frustration that can only reveal itself in tears, she hears in her daughter's voice.

"Come here my daughter."

"Mama, I'm so confused. I don't know what to do."

"You're not confused, you're in love."

What does she know 'bout love, thinks Matilda, bringing the tea from the kitchen. All she knows is da fact her heart is broken 'cause of a secret love she hides from her father. She doesn't know 'bout true love dat comes wit heartache and pain. I'm da one who knows da pain and da heartache; I'm da one who birthed him out of love and pain. I'm da one who worked wit him on my back in da fields out of love and pain. I cared for him out of love and pain; hid my daily life's pain from him 'cause of love. What do you know of love and de pain dat comes with it? Yo' pain is like a fast moving wind, little girl. Yo' pain is wit dout the foundation of true love and devotion. Yo' pain is imaginary.

"Where shall I put the tea, Miss Mary?"

"Set it on the end table, Matilda. We'll serve ourselves, thank you."

Mary waits for Matilda to leave the room before continuing her conversation. She even makes a cup of tea for Margaret while waiting to hear the sounds indicating Matilda is in the kitchen working.

"You know, your father wasn't much more than a slave when we got married. Even though his freedom had been guaranteed, it had not been granted. Your grandfather, Jean Baptist had to work and save until the following spring before he secured your father's freedom."

"You mean Papa was a field hand when you two got married?"

"Most free blacks at that time started as slaves and secured their freedom by buying it or having a family member buy it. Your father was a very determined field hand, at that. After we got married, he promised, if we had a little girl, no one else in his family would marry a field hand as long as he lived. He knew he was going to make life better for the both of us and so far, he has."

"But what am I going to do?" ask Margaret, pacing about the room. "Suppose Jacob comes back or they find him alive. I have to tell Papa so nothing happens to him. I can't hold this inside much longer. I love Jacob."

"I know how you feel daughter. I know Father will be difficult to talk to and explain, but I've got an idea. If Jacob never comes home, Papa doesn't have to know. I know that's a thought you dread bringing to mind, but we must be realistic about what he's done. Now, if they find Jacob alive let me talk to your father first. I know from where your father started. I can use that to remind him why Jacob must be repurchased or gotten out of jail, if that is where he is, and brought back here, alive. After he's back we'll work on your father. "

CHAPTER 21
Thursday, April 24th, 1862

On the morning of the 24th no one in New Orleans dreamed the city was in imminent danger. Reports from 75 miles down river the evening before gave the impression the magnificent Fort St. Philip and Fort Jackson, had survived the heavy bombing through the night. The newspaper reports boasted no further casualties except two men slightly wounded. They were holding the Union Navy down river. This is what the morning paper reported.

Andrew has one of the newspapers as he races home to give the good news to his family. By the time he storms into his living room, Andy is dressed in uniform. Pierre is not. The Native Guards have been dressing daily in uniform then reporting to their headquarters along the river. They are under the control of Major General Mansfield Lovell and report to him every morning their readiness for whenever and wherever they may be needed. Andrew and Andy ride out together to their headquarters to share the news with their Confederate comrades. Pierre waits ten minutes, wasting time, doing everything he can, not to go, but at last leaving.

A year ago New Orleans was brimming with gaiety and optimism. The city, being the largest in the South with a population of 168,800, enjoyed the strongest of economies in the South. But that was not to last as 1861 wore on. Serious problems have developed at several of the mouths of the Mississippi just below New Orleans. Rumors have turned out to be true. The dock and levees that used to be lined with tall masted ships, crowded with stevedores loading cotton, sugar and rice are now deserted. There is strong Union activity in the Gulf, south of Biloxi, Mississippi. The Union army has been building up for months; from the North there are Union troop moving south, in a river flotilla commanded by Flag Officer Andrew Foote.

The burning of the cotton bales has become more intense. Now, the clouds of black smoke stretch for miles into the air and down the Mississippi. All available carts, wagons, and anything with wheels have been impressed to haul the remaining cotton from the storehouses to the levees for burning. Panic is setting in. The protectors of the city, Confederate soldiers, are observed pushing people from their carts and driving off with them to empty the storehouses.

On this morning, something else happened. If you read the morning paper you did not expect to hear anything else but the cheer of the crowds running through the city. But it was not to be. The newspaper's account of what was happening down river was not totally true.

It happens while the 1ˢᵗ Native Guards are completing their morning roll call, after breakfast that the sound is heard. It reverberated over the levees, and through the cane and cotton fields, rolling over the bayous, in and out of the swamps, floating gently on wind that carried it. It is the alarm bell, ringing out a sequence of strokes from the tower in New Orleans. What the people hear are twelve strokes, four times repeated, summoning all able-bodied armed soldiers to their headquarters. It happens at half past nine. Andrew and Dr. DuBois realizing the importance of the moment tell their soldiers to prepare themselves for battle. Moments later one of the soldiers on watch comes running towards them, yelling franticly and joyously. General Mansfield Lovell, their commander, is riding towards them in a rush. Andrew and Dr. DuBois smile at each other. They both realize this is the moment they've been waiting for. Finally the 1ˢᵗ Native Guards will be asked to participate in the defense of the Confederacy. Their task will be the participation in the saving of New Orleans. It will be a glorious and victorious morning for the Native Guards and the city of New Orleans. Andrew and Dr. DuBois give each other a big handshake, patting each other on the their shoulders and hugging each other. Andrew can hardly contain his excitement. He becomes confused looking for his hat and rifle. Dr. DuBois and Andrew collide many times as they rush around, like children on Christmas morning, preparing themselves for General Lovell. They rush outside just in time.

In a clear sharp voice, Andrew demands the troops fall in. He can see General Lovell approaching.

Dr. DuBois calls his men to attention, and the stomping feet of 275 men echo around Dr. DuBois. He draws his saber and then sharply turns one hundred and eighty degrees, facing the charging, oncoming General Lovell. Holding his saber at attention, looking military smart, Dr. DuBois stares straight ahead. He hears the galloping General Lovell, standing tall in his saddle, rushing his stallion towards the proud black Confederate troops.

"Present, arms," screams Dr. DuBois, waiting for the General to stop, dismount, and leave orders.

But General Lovell does not stop. He doesn't so much as acknowledge the existence of the respectfully standing 1st Native Guards. To see his face is to see much fear and panic. What he has seen down river, from where he is coming, is the whole Union fleet. They have successfully passed the forts, destroyed the Confederate flotilla, and are approaching New Orleans.

Members of the 1st Native Guards are confused by the behavior they just witnessed. Dr. DuBois and Andrew don't know what to say, but they know they have to maintain order within their troops.

"What was that all about suh?" someone yells.

The rest of the troops begin mumbling angry words amongst themselves. Neither Andrew nor Dr. DuBois knows how to answer that question. Andrew decides it is probably best he release the squad to go home and take care of their families. There are anxious expressions on the faces of the troops, as Andrew dismisses them, suggesting they all return home to protect their families. Some jump immediately on their horses, while others break out in a sprint. Andrew tells Andy they have important things to do at home immediately. They need to take care of some personnel business. Everyone leaves Dr. DuBois standing alone, saluting the rising dust, with tears rolling down his deep chocolate colored cheeks.

* * * * * * * * *

By midday, Rear Admiral Farragut's ships are steaming upriver unchallenged, having run the gauntlet between Fort Jackson and Fort St. Philip before dawn. By the afternoon of April 24th, in New Orleans, despair has set in. The city's remaining defenses are distressed by what is going on and woefully insufficient. Major General Mansfield Lovell had only 3,000 militiamen. Some of them so green that he refuses to put ammunition in their hands for fear they would shoot themselves in the foot before sighting the enemy. Because of these and many other deficiencies within the ranks of his troops, General Mansfield Lovell is troubled with his command. He does have a few hundred loyal men. But because of these problems within the ranks, he was quick to tell the mayor of New Orleans, "Let me get back to you," when asked to help defend the city. He then chose the most direct route to the wooded swamps and bayous that surrounded New Orleans, leaving the city totally defenseless.

* * * * * * * * *

Mary and Margaret are enjoying their normal mid-day tea. Mary is darning socks and Margaret is reading a book. The front door is suddenly flung open, Andrew and Andy rush in. Andy runs upstairs, leaping them two at a time while Andrew goes to the cabinet and begins opening and closing drawers, looking for papers. He reads some quickly, discards them, and then reads others. Those he needs he places in a leather satchel. He has no time for Mary and her wish to have conversation with him. Now is not a good time and he's not sure if there will ever be a good time. The foreign consulates are crowded with frantic businessmen trying to deposit their valuables under foreign flags. Andrew knows the importance of such a move and is trying to do the same.

"I've got the papers," yells Andy, running down the stairs.

Andrew tells Andy to saddle another fresh horse and get to the bank and withdraw all their money. He explains to Mary why it is so important for them to deposit their valuable in a foreign consulate. "It's like moving their money out of the country," he said as he shoves the last of his papers into the satchel then gives it to Andy. After Andy is gone, Andrew sits and explains to Mary what happened at the Native Guards' headquarters. He tells her the Union fleet has passed forts and a galley of war ships are moving up the Mississippi. Right now all that is left for the Native Guards to defend is their own property until reinforcements come.

"Andrew, I told you there will be no killing in this house," reminds Mary sternly, "and I still mean it."

Andrew doesn't respond. He knows this is one of those conversations where it's best he kept his mouth shut. Even though he was not about to let anybody, especially a Union soldier, come into his home and take charge of everything in it. He's worked too hard to get all of this and he intends on keeping all of it. His family will not be made homeless by likes of some Union soldier. He gently looks into the stern eyes of Mary. She is not moving from her position. He still remains closed mouthed.

There is an uneasy silence in the room as Pierre enters. From the drawn looks on everyone's face he concludes they know what he knows. "I see everyone has finally gotten the news." Pierre finds a place to sit. "I've been walking among the slave shanties along the river. The slave grapevine said Union ships are moving up river and New Orleans will probably fall tomorrow." Pierre smiles." You should have seen how many slaves were on the levees watching the ships pass. There were so many there you couldn't see the sugar cane fields." Pierre looks at his father and Andy. "For us, the war is over," concludes Pierre. "Tomorrow there will be a fleet of Yankee warships in New Orleans Bay."

Andrew is not about to give up. "You should be ashamed of yourself for frightening your mother and sister. What can we believe coming from ignorant slaves? Most of them can't read or write. What do they know about what's going on down river? Instead of talking about defeat you should instead be preparing to stand shoulder to shoulder with the Native Guards to protect this family and New Orleans. Outsiders are trying to change our successful way of life. No one can tell you how to live. I'm not about to let somebody else tell me how I should run my life; especially some blue coated Lincoln Republican from Washington."

"All the white planters are saying things like that," said Pierre.

"I guess since you think like them, you find those words very appropriate."

Mary has listened long enough to Andrew and Pierre going back and forth. She cannot sit any longer listening to Pierre insulting his father. As much as she loves Pierre, she loves Andrew even more and knows without him she would have nothing and be nothing. Children do not always understand how they happen to have what they have, only that it's always been there for them. It is the duty of the parents to remind children of this fact when they are wrong even when they think they are so right. So, when she got up from her seat, she did so to remind Pierre that what he has was earned. How it was earned is not clear to Pierre. It never is to children. So when Mary slaps Pierre to the floor she hopes she is making it clearer to him. She feels no regrets, only anger. She hears Margaret cry out in protest, but Andrew agrees with Mary's decision.

"Margaret," demands Andrew, "leave him alone!"

Mary stands defiantly over her fallen Pierre with Margaret kneeling over him. "Your father was a slave first before he became a free man! He's worked the fields with his slaves even though he didn't have to. He's bowed his head many times before the white man just to get to where he is today. He and your grandfather pulled themselves up from slavery by working until they earned enough to buy their freedom. Then your father bought my freedom. Don't you ever associate your father with the white planter's principles again! Unlike your father's, theirs are deceitful and show no compassion."

Andrew is so proud of Mary. He gathers her into his arms and gently holds her close. He feels her trembling and sobbing. He comforts her with words of encouragement. He sees her growing stronger in her belief that what he is doing is right. For so long he was not sure just where she stood. She supports him much more than he ever thought. He knows now he must succeed. He can't let Mary down. He loves her even more. He holds her while she beats her fists on his chest, sobbing uncontrollably saying, "Look what this war has done to us! Look at what this war has done to us!"

* * * * * * * * *

Matilda continues walking in and out of the kitchen listening and not listening to Massa Andrew and his family. They seem to be getting stranger day after day. Regardless of what goes on in the house, at any given time, she still knows she has her work to do; even if this house is burning down, if it does not interfere with her daily chores, she has to finish her work. While she is setting the table, Andrew and Andy may rush in and before she can complete setting the table Andrew and Andy grab something from the table and both then rush out. While standing at the chest, pulling out papers and stuffing them in a satchel, Andrew tries to explain what was going on in the war. Understanding this conversation has nothing to do with her, Matilda continues getting together some of the leftover food from last night and getting it into the oven to warm up. She has also prepared some fresh biscuits.

By the time Pierre comes home she is putting the meal on the table and almost burns the biscuits listening to Massa Andrew as he dresses down Pierre. By the time she finishes setting the table, Pierre is commenting on something about white folks and Massa Andrew. So Matilda goes to the kitchen, sits in her favorite chair, and waits to hear from one of the family members too lazy to get up and get something themselves. She would have stayed in that position except she heard a slap, a scream, and then a thud. Not caring if she appears nosey, Matilda slowly pokes her head out of the door to see what has happened. She sees Pierre lying on the floor with Margaret tending to him, crying. Miss Mary is crying on Massa Andrew's shoulder and Andy is nowhere to be seen. Realizing how much work she has to do after dinner, and knowing she does not want to be in this house any longer than necessary, she asks, "Is yall ready to eat dinner yet?"

* * * * * * * * *

For the citizens of New Orleans, there is reason to desert the city. A lot of the citizens feel the city is being surrendered. General Mansfield Lovell has abandoned the city, literally running off into the swamps, bayous and hills surrounding the Crescent City. Several hundred of his troops follow him, while others removed their uniforms with the intention of remaining behind, blending in with the maddening crowds. Governor Moore finds the swiftest of steamer he can secure and flees up river scattering proclamations, ordering the burning of every bale of cotton and destroying every barrel of sugar so the enemy could not benefit from them. The police are powerless and the mayor realizing this fact turns to the European brigade to take charge of the city. 15,000 bales of cotton, piled on the riverbank are put to the torch. A score of cotton filled ships and steamboats, are set ablaze, and then set loose to float down river. The heads of thousand of barrels of sugar and hogsheads of molasses are caved in then spilled on the ground. Men, women, and children pause in their efforts to escape to do their best to scoop up all they can in pails, baskets, tubs, and aprons before leaving New Orleans.

* * * * * * * *

An hour after the family is seated for a very nervous and quiet dinner the front door opens and Andy staggers in disheveled and angry. "Papa, the whole city has gone mad! You can't believe what is going on out there! The city has been deserted by the Confederacy! We are defenseless! "

"If I cannot defend the city I will defend this farm," demands Andrew, rising from his chair. "Andy, break out the guns from the closet."

"Andrew, I will not stand for any violence," warns Mary. She grabs Andrew by his arm. "There will be no killing!"

"The forts didn't stop them," begins Pierre, "the river didn't stop them. The blockades didn't stop them. Poppa, the Yankees are here!"

"Pierre," reminds Andrew, "this is the opportunity we as a people have been waiting for. The rest of the world is watching us. The Confederacy is watching us, regardless of General Lovell. We need to give them a good representation. Now, Pierre you need to put on your uniform. You must be dressed to show your allegiance."

"No Papa, I will not put on that uniform."

"Do what Papa said," demands Andy.

"No, Andy, and don't ask me again!"

Margaret pleads with him.

Mary asks him, just to please his father.

Pierre remains obstinate. "Poppa, this is a white man's war!" You're making a big mistake, Papa. If what Andy has seen is true, then it's every man for himself!"

Andrew will have nothing to do with what Pierre has to say. He is so pumped up with anger. He wants to tell his wayward son where he has gone wrong in his thinking, but suddenly realizes he cannot hear any of the hectic conversation going on around him or even his own voice. Suddenly, without warning he is paralyzed and cannot say anything. He begins heaving his chest, trying to suck in more air. There is something terribly wrong. A pain shoots down his left arm then back. It feels like a bullet has entered his shoulder and left a big hole. He grabs his chest, trying to rip the pain from his chest with his hand so he can throw it away, but instead stumbles forward. "Andrew!" He hears Mary scream his name. "Papa!" now that's Margaret, remembers Andrew. "Andy, Pierre, help get him on the couch." That's Mary giving orders but why is Pierre helping, wonders Andrew, he should be getting his uniform on. "I'm alright, my dear," Andrew thinks he hears himself say.

"Matilda," yells Mary. When Matilda rushes from the kitchen, Mary sternly tells her, "Go upstairs and get Master Andrew's medicine. Do not waste time, Matilda." While Matilda is gone, a throw pillow is placed under Andrew's head. After his shoes are removed, his feet are raised by another throw pillow. Pierre asks if there is anything else to be done and Mary reminds him to put on his uniform. Pierre does not move, but Mary looks at him and there is something on her face that comes out of her eyes that changes his mind. Pierre passes Matilda with a tray holding the medicine and a glass of water. Mary takes a packet of medicine and dumps it into the water, stirs it, and then with Margaret's help, holds Andrew's head while they try to get him to drink it. "Matilda, go get Big Black. We need to get Master Andrew upstairs." Mary holds Andrew close to her, gently rocking back and forth. She hums his favorite hymn, while praying for Andrew. Margaret holds her father's hands, quietly sobbing.

Mary worries if she is about to lose her Andrew for good. She feels so helpless. Why didn't he listen to Dr. DuBois? Sometimes he can be so stubborn. Pierre gets his stubbornness honestly from Andrew. Andrew can't even recognize it when he's arguing with himself. Time has passed so quickly for the both of them. It seems like only yesterday they both were just starting their lives together. Life was so less complicated then. New Orleans seemed much kinder then. The world was at his feet. Andrew was a young man full of energy and dreams. Now, he just has dreams, and not enough energy to see them through to completion. How cruel life is to keep the dream alive but not supply the energy needed to complete the dream.

"Mary," said Andrew very weak.

"Be still Andrew," said Mary whispering. "You must remain quiet and rest. You need to let the medicine take affect."

Pierre returns, wearing the uniform she's made, but he has not buttoned all the buttons nor tucked in his shirt.

"Margaret, fix Pierre's clothing," demands Mary.

"Mama," objects Pierre. "I'm fine."

"No you're not," scolds Mary. "Margaret, finish tucking in his shirt. Either she does it or you do it yourself."

"Mary, where is Pierre?" Andrew's voice is even weaker.

Mary tells Andrew he is close by, and then beckons Pierre to come closer.

Pierre reluctantly approaches. Even though his father lay ill, possible dying he still finds this Judas clothing repulsive. As important as it is for his father, it is just as unimportant for him. This dull gray cloth that shines so brightly in his eyes has blinded him to the truth about the future for black folks. He stands before his father, his head bowed, eyes closed, not wanting to see him, not wanting to stare into his father's eyes for fear of saying something he shouldn't. He stands before his father wondering if respect of his father means he must follow him blindly down a pathway of destruction. He wonders if, because he is his father, he is always right and he himself is always wrong. When will he be ready to decide his own fate? Must he wait until his father dies? Is that what's about to occur now? If it is, why doesn't he feel anxious with anticipation of freedom?

"Hold your head up, son," Andrew said weakly. "Be proud about the uniform. It stands for something. You may not agree with it, but do not spite it."

Pierre does not proudly hold his head high, but instead looks at the ceiling while his father speaks. He hears the sharp words cutting into his ears and tries to prevent them from piercing his heart. Because even though the words are all wrong, the sound of his father's weakened voice demands and get his respect.

"Miss Mary," said Matilda, quietly, "Big Black is here as you axed."

"Big Black, I need you to carry Massa Andrew upstairs," say Mary. "Matilda, go to the kitchen for some fresh water and damp towels. Margaret, go upstairs and prepare you father's bed. Andy, make sure all the remaining important papers have been taken care of properly. If you have to go back to town, take something to protect yourself. Pierre, I will not tolerate any more disrespect to your father from you."

Mary watches Big Black lift Andrew's sickly body, then walks in front like she is clearing a path for Big Black to follow. She holds her head high as she climbs the stairs followed by Big Black, a sobbing Margaret then Matilda. Pierre remains in the living room, standing, staring at the ceiling until he is alone, trying to hold back the water that has overfilled the wells of his eyes. He hears the door close as Andy leaves and is about to sit when he hears Matilda and Big Black on the stairs. They walk past Pierre without acknowledging his presence.

"We have to depend on God," Matilda is saying to Big Black. "He knows what's best right now."

Then, there is nothing but the sound of silence. Pierre is alone. He finds the couch where his father lay just a few moments ago and collapses on it, burying his face in one of the throw pillows shaking and crying, wondering what has he done. Are freeing slaves worth enslaving his family? He now questions himself, what's more important, his family values or his own?

CHAPTER 22
Friday, April 25th, 1862

TO THE PEOPLE OF NEW ORLEANS
Mayoralty of New Orleans
CITY HALL, April 25TH, 1862

After an obstinate and heroic defense by our troops on the river, there appears to be imminent danger that the insolent enemy will succeed in capturing your city. The forts have not fallen; they have not succumbed even beneath the terrors of a bombardment unparalleled in the history of warfare. Their defenders have done all that becomes men fighting for their homes, their country and their liberty; but in spite of their efforts, the ships of the enemy have been able to avoid them, and threaten the city. In view of this contingency, I call on you to be calm, to meet the enemy, not with submissiveness nor with indecent alacrity; but if the military authorities are no longer able to defend you, to wait with hope and confidence, the inevitable moment when the valor of your sons and of your fellow-countrymen will achieve your deliverance. I shall remain among you, to protect you and your property, so far as my power or authority as Chief Magistrate can avail.

JOHN T. MONROE,
MAYOR

When the fading morning sun rays finish splashing upon Captain David G. Farragut, he's standing proudly on the deck of the U.S.S Hartford moving cautiously up the Mississippi river just minutes away from entering the port of New Orleans. He has followed a trail of black smoke up river from Fort St. Philips. Finally, he is near the mouth of the port. What he and his men see are evidence of a city hell bent on self-destruction. Burning cotton ships and all kinds of shipyard apparatus are still burning or smoldering as they come floating by. The closer he gets to the city the more fires he sees along the shore. Burning vessels are erratically parked in streams, waiting to burn down to the water line to go out. The levees are lined with angry mobs taunting Farragut's fleet as they approach the bay. At noon the fleet rounds the bend and comes into the view of a still smoldering New Orleans. The enemy has arrived in the appearance of Captain Farragut and his Union fleet of 20 ships. They drop anchor in the river during a driving rain. The driving rain is hard enough to put everything that was ablaze out. The clumps of molasses and sugar softened and ran wild into the drains. Where there was solid ground, now there is deep, boot clinging, and shoe sticking mud.

* * * * * * * * *

The slaves stopped working when the rains began. The farm became one big mud hole. It was a strange rain. The water fell straight down with a quiet rolling thunder. Usually there was loud crashing thunder with lightening strikes and loud rumbling of water crashing down from the heavens demanding attention. Even the animals of the swamp found places for refuge when these kinds of cloud bursting storms visited. Horses and other livestock returned to the barn without being summoned. This rain was unusually quiet as if it knew the outcome of the day and it was sharing with the citizens the sadness and misery that had fallen upon the city of New Orleans.

Mary St. Claire stands at her bedroom window looking out at the quiet driving rain. Andrew has been delirious, in and out of consciousness, all night. Between her, Margaret and Matilda, they've been taking turns watching him. There is something comforting in the rain for Mary. It takes her mind away from what is happening and places it somewhere else. She is away from this nightmare for the moment. She keeps hoping she will awaken from this agony. What has she done to deserve this kind of treatment from God? She and Andrew are supposed to grow old together, gracefully. He's not supposed to be dying right now. God is supposed to be taking care of her and her family. Has she not been a faithful servant? Is God not the giver of life? Can God not, at this time, spare her Andrew and give her the hope, joy, and peace she so desperately needs right now? Somewhere out her window, through the torrents of falling rain, up into the heavy gray clouds she hopes her prayers and wishes are being received. If it is true that God is always there, then she needs to hear from him right now. Mary turns and looks at Andrew. She sits facing him, holding his hand, and rubbing it gently. "Andrew," she calls softly, holding his hand to her mouth, kissing it then rubbing her cheek with it, "I love you so much."

"Keep that line straight men," stutters Andrew, his voice breaking and trailing off.

A sudden ray of hope brings a smile to Mary's face. It is a sign from God. "Don't say anything Andrew, you need to save your strength."

"Hold your fire until you hear my word," said Andrew, deliriously. His mind is wandering in and out of his body.

"Stay with me Andrew," pleads Mary. "I'm right here beside you Andrew. You're not on the battlefield." Mary begins to cry. "Stay with me Andrew, please stay with me."

"Remember, we do this for God, country and the Confederacy!"

Andrew attempts to raise himself from his bed but is gently restrained by Mary.

"Lord God in heaven, please bring back my Andrew." Mary kneels at Andrew's bedside. "He's not much in the eyes of others, but he's all I've got. You have blessed my family a hundred fold and me. Now I ask for one more blessing. Hear my prayer, Jesus, hear my prayer."

Andrew stays alert for a few moments more, mumbling orders to phantom troops, then drifts back into his nightmarish sleep. Mary rises from her prayers and looks at her Andrew. His face is twisted with anxiety. She wipes his forehead with a damp towel then reluctantly decides to leave him for a few moments and goes downstairs to wait for Andy. She is close to total exhaustion.

* * * * * * * * *

Pierre stomps and scrapes his feet outside the kitchen door trying to get as much Louisiana mud off his boots as possible. He does not want to soil Matilda's floors. When he opens the door, he removes his boots and starts across the kitchen. Matilda is at the stove preparing the mid-day meal. Pierre notices she looks down at his feet. He is sure she was checking to see if he was tracking mud. In the dinning room Matilda has prepared the table like she always does. The events happening in New Orleans have not changed her routine in the least. It was the same for the slaves in the fields. They did what they have always done without any mention about the invasion from the North. Do they understand what this means for them? Is it the beginning of the end of their enslavement?

The rain has become very symbolic to Pierre. It is washing away the shackles and cleaning the wounds created by the metal anklets. Why can't the slaves see and understand that? It is so obvious to Pierre. He wants to stand upon a soapbox and shout it to all of New Orleans. And so it has come to this. Anna is free. Soon all of the slaves will be free. This is indeed a wondrous victory, for everyone, except Marcel. But Marcel is also free. When Pierre thinks about what lies ahead for him, he envies Marcel because Marcel does not have to worry about tomorrow. Now that everyone is free or going to be free, Pierre senses he's becoming a prisoner. Maybe he's been a prisoner all along and didn't realize it, until now. He needs to escape. He needs to add something else to his life. He knows he can't stay here, but he doesn't know where he can go. He cannot continue to be in this partnership with slavery.

Margaret greets him as he enters the dinning room. Pierre forces a smile in response. There is so much confusion going on inside his mind.

Mary enters the dinning room from the stairs. Worry and exhaustion paints her face. "Your father is doing fine," she tells Pierre and Margaret. "He is still weak, but he doing just fine." She accepts a hug from Pierre before she finds her favorite place on the couch and sits.

Margaret gently squeezes her mother's hand reassuringly. So much has happen to her family in this last year. She wonders what will become of her family now that New Orleans has fallen? She wonders what will become of her family's farm? Will the Union soldiers take it over? Union soldiers can't run a farm. They don't know the first thing about bringing in the crops, when and how to do it. They're going to need us to help them run this farm and they're going to need our slaves. Our slaves will not run away from us because we've treated them so well, even if Jacob thought differently. Margaret wonders if Jacob wishes he were back home with his family now. She wishes he were back home. She still wonders if he's alive. She hopes and prays he is. She still remembers the last time they were together. From deep down inside her loins she shudders.

Andy returns home just after the sun has disappeared. He rests his gun against the closet door and casually walks into the dining room. He kisses his mother, said hello to Pierre and Margaret, and then asks about his father. He falls into a chair and calls out to Matilda for some tea while he retrieves his flask. While he drinks his tea, he tells the sad story about the continuing confusion that is going on in the city. He was at the levee when two Union officers stepped ashore and he stayed with the crowd as they followed and jeered the officer as they walked to City Hall. Andy was sure he was about to see a lynching of the Union officers with all the abuse they were subjected to. Some of the white folks held back those who were most angry in the mob so no harm would come to them. "But the real anger should be directed at Mayor Monroe," said Andy.

"Here we are, the entire city, abandoned by the Confederacy, and when order is needed, instead of calling on the Native Guard, he calls on foreigners. It was like we weren't even considered as being part of the available resources to defend the city." Andy's voice is getting louder and louder as his anger gets stronger and stronger.

"Andy, not so loud," reminds Margaret. "Papa is resting upstairs."

Andy falls quiet for a moment, and then said, "We were all

sitting in Mamma Salome's watching the madness of the city pass by. Dr. DuBois was there. One thing we all agreed upon, Papa and Dr. DuBois may have been wrong about the Confederacy. If he were to go to New Orleans now, he would find the Union Army in charge of everything. There are a lot of angry members of the Native Guards out there. They are angry because they feel the Johnny Rebs deserted them. Some wanted to go into the streets and start killing white folks." Andy turns his flask up and takes a large final swallow of the contents, then looks inside to see if any liquid remain. "Yes sir," said Andy, sadly, "tonight, nobody would have even listened to Papa. In the end those who were there agreed since the Confederacy wouldn't let us fight with them, then with Dr. DuBois blessings, they agreed to fight against them."

Mary's heart sinks. Just when she thought she was getting her boys back with the surrender of New Orleans, it seems she is loosing them again. What stupid things men do, just to be men. Margaret didn't quite know what to say. Pierre is happy Andy has finally seen the light. Maybe now they can both fight on the same side for the same cause.

* * * * * * * * *

Matilda is putting the finishing touches on the cleared dining room table when she tells Miss Mary she will be checking on Massa Andrews before she leaves for the night. She goes to the kitchen and returns with some hot water on a tray. After checking with everyone about the status of his or her tea she leaves Andy and his captive audience downstairs and retreats to Massa Andrews. Andy has raided the china closet and refilled his flask. Already Andy is beginning to act like he is head of the family.

Standing over Andrew, Matilda wonders what's going through his mind right now. She wonders if his life is passing in review. Ever since her Jacob left he has treated her differently, like she was responsible for his leaving. But what was she supposed to do? She cannot hold back the dreams of her son anymore than he would with his sons. What makes his sons better than her Jacob? In the eyes of God they are both the same. And the reward in heaven will be the

same. How come Massa Andrew and his Miss Mary don't understand that? Are they not afraid of the wrath of God, or do they know
something about God she doesn't?

Massa Andrew mutters something Matilda doesn't understand.
He continues to do so. It is not that unusual since he's been going
in and out of consciousness since the attack yesterday. She takes a
towel, dampens it, and dabs his brow. The cool water appears to be
calming him. Suddenly Andrew tries to get out of bed, but Matilda
gently restrains him and adds words of encouragement and understanding. He's dying, thinks Matilda. She wonders if he knows it.
Inside she feels sympathy for the family, but with his death, how
much change can she expect from the remaining members. From
what she has heard, the farm may not be theirs anymore anyway.
What does that mean for her and the rest of the slaves? Suppose
Jacob is alive and comes to the farm looking for her and she's not
here? Suppose the farm is not here? Maybe being set free is not as
good as it seems. What else can she and the slaves do if they are
free? We can't read, we can't write, we don't know anything but
being a slave. Who's gonna take care of us?

Matilda holds Massa Andrew's head while she tries to get him
to drink more of his medicine. She lies and tells him he needs to get
well because Matilda is gonna' miss him. "You needs to git well
'cause I needs your guidance," she lies again. "You needs to git better 'cause the slaves needs you to keep them here." More lies. She
steadies his head until he finishes what's in the glass. She then dabs
the corners of his mouth before gently positioning his head back on
the pillows. She pulls the bed covering snugly about him. She must
go to the kitchen and finish washing the dishes. She has no time for
him now. She leaves him mumbling incoherently.

Andrew and his mind are someplace between life and death,
standing on the edge of insanity. He is fighting the final battle of
this war inside his mind. He is standing in his front yard, his gun in
his hand, walking guard on his property. He is marching back and
forth, back and forth, looking, and listening for the enemy. He has
secured his family and slaves behind him. He alone stands between
them and certain death at the hands of the Union forces. The sounds
of those bastard Yankee cannons echo around him. But he is not

frightened. He will defend his home, his family, his human property and all surrounding land that belongs to him. They have no right being down here trying to change his way of life to fit their lifestyles. Again he hears gunfire on his right and turns quickly to see where it's coming from. Now, it's coming from his left. He raises his rifle and fires in the direction of the repeating sounds, cursing the bullets that leave his gun, hoping they will strike many a Yankee dead. He screams his vengeance into the night air. He challenges those who chose to fight from behind the security of trees or hide in the dark confines of the swamps, to come out and face him, one on one. He stands ready to charge anything that dares to come into his site. With fixed bayonet, he jabs and thrusts, parries and blocks, fighting off his mind's demons. Then suddenly Andrew hears something frightening; something he did not expect to hear coming from his home. It is a horrible scream that makes him shudder with fear. It is a scream that could only mean the Yankees are attacking from his rear and have entered his home. It is a scream that tells him Mary is in danger. Andrew turns and tries to run back to his house. There is something wrong with his legs. They won't work. He struggles, trying to force his legs to move. He can't get them to respond. Andrew is getting desperate. He drops his weapon then yanks and pulls his legs until they are free. He is loose and begins staggering to the source of the screaming sound, vowing to kill any Yankee who has dared to invade his home.

* * * * * * * *

Matilda pauses just a few moments to clear the table as Mary finishes explaining her distress about how delirious Andrew is.

"He doesn't seem to be getting any better," Mary was saying. "It is good he doesn't know what has happened in New Orleans."

Andy and Pierre agree it's probably best he doesn't find out. After all, this have not been one of the Confederacy's greatest hours.

"Pierre, Andy," said Margaret, "I thought the war was over for you two. New Orleans is lost to the Union armies. Why do you two need to continue fighting?"

"We can still lose everything we have," answers Andy. "We don't want Union soldiers using this house as headquarters. This farm must remain in the hands of the St. Claire's. Pierre and I will do anything necessary to make sure that happens."

Pierre," pleads Margaret, "you didn't want to fight for the Confederacy. Why fight for the Union?"

"Because they're fighting for what I'm fighting for," answers Pierre confidently.

"Of all things for you two to agree on, why this?

"I won't let either of you go," said Mary, finally making her last stand. "This is not our war. You said so yourself Pierre. It's the white man's war!"

Again Matilda listens to this mundane bickering back and forth by everyone. She is wishing they all would just shut up since no one in this family cares about anything but their own well being right now. She stacks the remaining dishes and cups on the tray and slowly backs into the kitchen. When she turns to place them on the small table, in the dim light she sees an image of a man standing at the door leading outside. He is dressed in Union blue. Matilda freezes, unable to say anything. She stares intently into the face of the intruder. She feels her hand begin to tremble, and hears the rattling of the cups, saucers, and dishes. Then, she recognizes the face. But who she sees cannot be alive. He's dead. She's being punished and teased by God with this aberration. This thing standing in front of her is a ghost. It cannot be true flesh and blood. Finally, the tray of cups and dishes falls from her hands. Her screaming competes with the crashing noise of breaking glass and loose silverware. God's grace and mercy has passed her by and he is punishing her for her thoughts of vengeance upon this family. She has sinned and is now being cursed with this hallucination.

Matilda slowly backs out of the kitchen, bumping into Pierre. She cannot stop staring at the face of the soldier, now slowly walking towards her. When she is in the living room she drops to her knees and begins mumbling, very quickly, "Our father, who art in heaben, hal-led be dye name, dye kingdom come, dye will be done, on earth as in heaben. Gib us dis day, our daily bread and forgib us our sins as we forgib dose who sinned aginst us. Lead us not into 'tation, but delivers us from ebel, for dine is dey kingdoms, de powers, and de glorys foreber and eber, AMEN! AMEN! AMEN!" Matilda has her crumpled apron in her hands, covering her face, peeking over it, and then hiding her face like a frightened child. "Forgib me Lawd, please forgib me. Takes me into yo' bosom Lawd, takes me home." Matilda begins pounding on the floor hysterically. "We made a bargain Lawd! You promised to take me first! It was I who sinned, not him! Take me Lawd!"

Pierre and the rest of his family are stunned and do not know what to make of Matilda's behavior. They stand around watching her, wondering what it is that has frightened her so. No one tries to assist her. No one tries to comfort her. Whatever has upset her is still in the kitchen. All eyes are on the swinging kitchen door, waiting to see who comes out. Pierre walks around a sobbing Matilda, and quietly walks towards the swinging door.

Andy signals him to wait until he gets his gun and quietly moves towards the closet by the stairs where he left it. Before he can get there the door swings wide and stays open with the towering figure of a Union soldier, a rough looking, unkempt figure of a man. He needs a haircut and a shave. His face is pitted from the insect's bites, but it is obvious who the stranger is, Jacob.

Pierre recognizes him first and speaks his name quietly, "Jacob."

"Jacob!" Margaret screams his name, freezing Andy before he can raise his gun. Mary collapses back into her seat and is tended to immediately by Margaret.

"Thank you Jesus," cries Matilda. "You delivered my boy home. Thank you Jesus!"

"I'm no ghost, Mama," said Jacob, his deep voice of confidence filling the room. "It's me. I've come back for you, just like I said. Git up Mama. Git off the floor." Jacob reaches down and lifts his mother and helps her to the couch next to Mary.

Pierre extends his hand and welcomes Jacob. "It's good to see you again, Jacob. We all thought you were dead."

"I thought so too a couple of times," replies Jacob.

"You was walkin' under da watchful eyes of God," said Matilda. "Thank God you home, Jacob."

"When did you join he Union forces," asks an embarrassed Andy.

Jacob tells how he was found in the swamp just when he had

given up on living. Now he is a scout teamster, part of General Butler's advance troops. He and some of the other colored troops, who know this area really well, are leading the infantry through the swamps and bayous.

"You must be starvin'," said Matilda, rising. "Let me fix somethin' for ya."

"Don't move, Mama!" Jacob tells his mother. "One thing da Union army has done is to make sho' I ain't hungry. I done come back to buy my mama's freedom." Jacob looks at Mary St. Claire. "I'm prepared to give a fair price."

A sudden silence overtakes the room, leaving everyone uncomfortable. Matilda, sobbing, begins rocking back and forth, then side to side, in her seat, raising her hands in the air, thanking Jesus. Mary wants to say that decision is up to Andrew, but the words cannot come out.

"Jacob, you don't know how happy I am to see you," stutters Margaret, breaking up the uneasy silence. "Buying Matilda's freedom is okay, with us. Right Pierre, right Andy? As a matter of fact she can stay here until this silly war is over, okay?"

All of a sudden the room is filled with a lot of loud talking. Confusion has entered as everyone tries to explain that what has just happened is okay with them. They agree that Matilda's new status is okay too. No one notices Andrew staggering down the stairs where he sees Andy's gun leaning against the closet wall in a corner. No one hears him mumble about saving his house and family from the Yankees as he retrieves the gun, then leaning against the wall, checks it for ammunition. No one even knows he's downstairs until he stands in the wide doorway between the living room and dining room and points his gun at the invading Union soldier and announces his intention to rescue his family.

"How dare you," challenges a wavering Andrew, "Damnation to your soul Yankee! Now die!"

Mary screams, "Don't shoot Andrew! Put down the gun!"

But it is to no avail. Andrew is determined to rid his home of this Yankee intruder.

"Poppa, this is not some Yankee, it's Jacob!" shouts Margaret joining her mother's pleading.

Pierre is shocked his father is out of bed and even more shocked at his father's deranged behavior. He's seen that look on his father's face before and it's a look of deliberate determination. He is unable to move beyond the hate he sees in his father's face. It holds him fast. He is too scared to try stopping his father's madness. No words can come out of his mouth. Inside his mind he hears himself saying, "Poppa, please don't do this. This can't be happening."

Andy attempts to reason with his father, "Papa, it's me Andy! Remember me? I'm your oldest son. Papa, you're jumping to conclusions!" Andy realizes none of his pleas are working. "PAPA! Put down the damn gun!"

Matilda sees her son is in the direct line of fire and rushes to get between Jacob and Massa Andrew. She has never challenged Massa Andrew before, but now she has no other choice. There is nothing that will come between her and her son, but God; and God has seen fit to bring him home to her. She is sure God has no intention of letting his life be taken from him at this time. Maybe this is why he brought him home so she can give him the gift of life again. She charges into the line of fire with no concern for her own safety.

Andrew staggers back being forced to change his unsteady aim. He wants to know why Matilda trying to stand in his way? Has she gone mad? Why is everyone else yelling and screaming? He hears them shouting his name. Don't they see him? He is here to save them. Don't they see him standing here? He wants to speak to them. He wants to tell them not to worry. He now has his gun aimed directly at this Union intruder. He can't miss. He feels blessed. God is good to give him this opportunity to show his love of family, love of country and love of the Confederacy. It's a shame that blood will be spilled, but what is good about it is, it won't be his. He is sure Mary, his dear Mary, will understand once he's had a chance to speak to her. She must know she is in danger. She must know the necessity of his actions and will be able to forgive him.

Mary struggles out of her chair, continuing her pleading with her husband. She is following the direction of the wavering barrel, standing between it and its victim for a brief moment. She moves in front of Margaret, then Andy, then Pierre, and at the same time hers is one of the many voices bombarding Andrew with pleas to stop this insanity. Mary sees Matilda rushing Andrew and pleads, "Matilda, please, do not to hurt him, he doesn't know what he's doing!"

"Your soul will find final rest in Hell, Yankee, " shouts Andrew, trying to steady his aim.

Matilda uses Andrew's confusion as her opportunity to try and wrestle the gun from him. She charges him before he can set his sights again. She doesn't hear Miss Mary yelling to be gentle. All she can see is Massa Andrew is trying to kill her son and she can't let that happen. She grabs the gun not caring where it is aimed, as long as it is not at Jacob. The last thing she hears is the pop as it fires and then her ears begin to ring. She can't see Master Pierre and Andy trying to get to Massa Andrew before he pulls the trigger. She doesn't hear Miss Margaret scream, nor hear Miss Mary moan after being hit by the errant bullet. She smells the powder from the shot and struggles with Massa Andrew telling him, "I can't let you do this to my Jacob!"

Andrew has fire in his eyes as he looks at Matilda. He is upset with her. She has caused him to miss. Then suddenly the fire goes out in Andrew's eyes. His mind sees only blackness.

Andrew goes limp and Matilda finds herself holding his gun in her hands as Andrew collapses, sliding down the front of her, into a pile of flesh at her feet.

Mary feels a stinging pain that throws her backwards. She remembers falling back, hitting the end table, knocking over the cups and saucers. She could hear Margaret screaming hysterically, calling out to her.

Jacob rushes his shaken and stunned mother, taking the smoking gun from her. Matilda is in shock. She doesn't hear him telling her, "Mama it's okay." She doesn't feel his arm on hers as he leads her to a nearby chair. The ringing in her ears have taken over her mind. She doesn't know Miss Mary's been shot. She doesn't hear Miss Margaret crying, holding her mother in her arms. She doesn't know Master Pierre and Master Andy are now hovering over their father trying to lift him to the couch. She just sits in the chair, staring into nothingness, listening to the overpowering ringing inside her head wondering, what has happened?

Once he has settled his mother, Jacob rips some tattered cloth from her apron and tends to Mary's wound. He struggles with Margaret, trying to separate her from Miss Mary. Pierre helps Jacob separate Margaret from her mother. It is an ugly flesh wound on her shoulder. She is in a great deal of pain.

"Damn you all!" screams Margaret. She sits in the middle of the floor sobbing and crying. "Damn all of you and your guns and your stupid little war! Look what the Confederacy has cost us! Andy, you and Pierre can go to hell!" Margaret is striking the hardwood floor with balled fists. She has broken the skin on her knuckles and they begin to bleed. "Stay the hell away from me!" She resists Pierre and Andy's efforts to calm her.

Mary struggles with Jacob, trying to get up. Through her pain and agony she has just one concern and that is to find out about her Andrew. She only wants to see how Andrew is doing. His well-being is more important than hers. "Andrew, where is my Andrew," she asks. She needs to know where he is. She struggles to her feet, desperately looking for her Andrew. She feels the trickle of blood sliding down her arm. She finally sees his still body on the couch.

"No, my Lord, not now, please God, NO! Andy, Pierre, somebody, where's his medicine?" screams Mary. She struggles to the couch, kneeling, praying to God.

Jacob feels Andrew for a pulse, starting with Andrew's wrist, then his neck. Jacob finally bends over listening to Andrew's heart. "I'm sorry, Miss Mary, he's with God now."

Mary screams, then collapses across Andrew weeping.

Jacob returns to his mother and gently helps her from her seat. He adjusts her shoulder wrap, fixes her hair, and then wipes the water from her face. With his hands he raises her face and looks into her tear filled eyes, then softly kisses her forehead. He reaches into his coat and retrieves a large wad of Union money. He leaves it on a nearby end table. Jacob then whispers in his mother's ear, "Come on Mama, you free now." Jacob leads his mother through the kitchen. Matilda stops and takes off her apron and neatly hangs it on the same nail hook where she has always hung it after finishing her chores. She and Jacob then walk out the back door of the St. Claire's for the last time.

Margaret watches Jacob and Matilda leave and begins screaming louder, demanding that he come back. She then begins to moan, rocking back and forth. Her hands are a mass of black and blue bruised flesh, dripping blood. She looks around the room. Her mothers' been shot, her father has died and Jacob is leaving her. The most important men in her life have left her. She curses the two remaining men left in her life.

Pierre grabs Margaret and pulls her to her feet, crying with her, holding her close, letting her pound his face and body hysterically. He cannot say enough to her to comfort and calm her, though he tries. He deeply feels, he is the reason his father lies dead before him. He submits himself to Margaret's pounding as punishment for his sins against his father.

Andy stands alone, above his stricken father, gulping carelessly, from his flask, spilling more than what's going into his mouth. He can only stare at the ceiling while he fights back the watery pain trying to escape through his eyes. What he has always wanted is now his, but this is not how he wanted to acquire it. Suddenly he feels the contents of his stomach rise into the back of his mouth. He covers his mouth to prevent it from spilling, trying to swallow it. Some of it juts from his nose before he can force it back down.

Mary gently kisses Andrew's face while wiping away her falling tears. She forces a small smile on her face. She looks at Andrew's face. Finally, he looks so calm and so much at peace. She gently squeezes his lifeless hands, waiting for him to respond by squeezing hers. She knows he will not. "Andrew, my Andrew, God has called you home." Mary touches Andrew on his face, patting his hair neat. She begins wiping away specs of dust from his face and fixing his clothes, while reminding him, "Our God is a mighty God, my Andrew. Even now, he has not failed me. In my house, my Andrew, only God can take a life and he has seen fit to take you away from me."

THE END

NOTES

i.   Frances E. W. Harper, (1825-1911), *The Black Poets*, Dudley Randall, Bantam Poetry

ii.   *Black confederates and Afro-Yankees in Civil War Virginia*, Ervin L. Jordan, Jr.

iii.   *The Louisiana Native Guards*, James G. Hollandsworth, Jr, Page 2

iv.   *Secrets of Voodoo*, Milo Rigaud, City Lights Books, San Francisco, Page 92

v.   ibid., page 129

vi.   ibid. page 131

vii.   *Secrets of Voodoo*, Milo Riguad, City Lights Books, San Francisco

viii. ibid.

BIBLIOGRAPHY

HARPER'S PICTORIAL OF THE CIVIL WAR, Alfred H. Guernsey & Henry M. Alden, The Fairfax Press (OS 937.7 G)

BLACK CONFEDERATES & AFRO-YANKEES IN CIVIL WAR VIRGINIA, Ervin L. Jordan, Jr. University Press of Virginia (973.7475 J)

NEW ORLEANS – Bethany Ewald Bultman, Fodor's Travel Publications

CIVIL WAR FRONT PAGES – Edited by John Wagman - A collection of 157 front pages from the North and South (OS 973.7 C)

NEW ORLEANS A Pictorial History– Leonard V Huber, Crown Publishers, (917.63 H)

DOCUMENTING THE AMERICAN SOUTH: THE SOUTHERN EXPERIENCE IN 19TH CENTURY AMERICA - Academic Affairs Library at UNC at Chapel Hill

BLACK MASTERS, A Free Family of Color in the Old South – Michael P. Johnson & James L. Roark, W. W. Norton & Company (975.7 J)

THE UNDERGROUND RAILROAD, First person Narratives of Escapes to Freedom in the North, Charles L. Blockson – Prentice Hall Press (973.7115 B)

SINGING THE MASTER, The Emergence of African American Culture in the Plantation South – Roger D. Abrahams, Pantheon Books, New York (975.0049 A)

DAILY LIFE in LOUISIANA, 1815-1830, LILIANE CRETE, Translated by Patrick Gregory – Louisiana State University Press (976.305 C)

BEFORE FREEDOM CAME, African-American Life in the Antebellum South, The Museum of the Confederacy and the University Press of Virginia (975 B)

NEW ORLEANS, The Battle of the Bayous, Harry Albright (973.5239 A)

THE BAYOUS, The American Wilderness/Time-Life Books, Peter S. Feibleman, and the Editors of Time-Life Books (917.63 F)

SECRETS OF VOODOO, MILO RIGAUD, City Light Books, San Francisco

JOAN G. CALDWELL, Head, Louisiana Collection, Tulane University Libraries, New Orleans LA. (map of the city, 1860)

THE LOUISIANA NATIVE GUARDS, James G. Hollandsworth, Jr. Louisiana State University Press

THE BLACK POETS, A New Anthology, Edited By Dudley Randall, Bantam Books.

THE GREAT CYPRESS SWAMPS, John V. Dennis, Louisiana State University Press/Baton Rouge (508.73D)

RUNAWAY SLAVES, Rebels on the Plantation, John Hope Franklin, Loren Schweninger, Oxford University Press.

THE COASTAL WAR, Chesapeake Bay to Rio Grande, Peter M. Chaitin and The Editors of Time-Life Books(973.75 C)

BULLWHIP DAYS – The Slaves Remember, James Mellon, Avon Books

THE CONFEDERATE NATION 1861 – 1865, EMORY M. THOMAS

Printed in the United States
69387LVS00001B/85-168

9 780971 941489